APPOINTMENT ON THE EDGE OF FOREVER

The Ryo Myths
Book One

Perrin Pring

First Published in Great Britain 2013 by Glastonbury Publishing

First edition: 2011
Second edition: 2013

Any reference to real names and places are purely fictional and are constructs of the author. Any offence the references produce is unintentional and in no way reflects the reality of any locations or people involved.

A copy of this work is available through the British Library.

ISBN: 978-1-909224-71-1

Glastonbury Publishing
Mirador
Wearne Lane
Langport
Somerset
TA10 9HB

For the most awesome man to ever brave the cross country journey in a Kia Sephia
Daniel Hobbs

Chapter 1

The girl ran, her white dress catching on a low branch. She didn't stop as the dress tore and red blossomed beneath the rip.

Technicolor branches and leaves converged in on her. The forest was thick, and she was slowed because of it. Every step was a battle. She knocked into a reedy tree. A spray of aqua leaves and yellow fruit erupted into the air. The fruit bounced beneath her feet and she fell. Her knees hit the dirt then her palms. Exhaling, she looked over her shoulder. She wasn't moving fast enough. A stocky man crashed after her. If things continued as they were, he would catch her within moments. She pushed herself from the ground and stumbled forward. Her feet were heavy and her pace was uneven. A log lay across her path. She jumped over it and then over a small creek.

Her foot snagged on a root. She tripped, hit the ground and rolled.

What... Where am I? Ryo stood up, breathing hard. Her right leg hurt. She looked down. Blood pulsed from her thigh. *What happened?*

Something hit her from the left, and she slammed into the ground. Coughing, she struggled to stand, but a man was on top of her. He snarled.

"Ya though' ya could git away did ya? Well, yer wroong!" Dirt streaked and scarred, the man thrust his face towards her. One of his eyes didn't open entirely, and his breath reeked of fish. He grabbed her by the scruff and pulled her to her feet.

"We don' take kindly ta yer kind here," he hissed.

She struggled in his hold, but he only tightened his grip.

"Yer an abomination. I don' care if ya say that ya ain't one. Ya are. You know it. I know it, an' mos' importan'ly Yalki knows it. You'll be punished. You'll be kilt. An' I'm gonna be tha one who gives you ta her." He began to walk, dragging her behind him.

What?

"I'm gonna be a hero. Better yet I'll git promoted. No more catchin' low lifes. Na, wid a real witch, I'm gonna move up. Maybe Yalki's personal guard. Maybe even my own bunk! Yup, yer gonna make my life real sweet."

Where am I?

Ryo looked around. She was in a forest. Tall trees masked the sky, but shafts of sunlight broke their ceiling. The golden streaks permeated the foliage and illuminated the world below. This was no ordinary forest though. Its trees were brightly colored, some with purple trunks and green leaves, and others with blue trunks and red leaves. Long yellow vines spanned between the trees. Dangling from those vines hung smaller vines. Bushes and flowers crowded the ground. Purple, black, and electric green leaves crunched under

Ryo's feet. A sharp chattering echoed around her. She watched a flock of long feathered birds take flight. They hovered for a moment, calling shrilly, and then sped away, twisting through the trees. The forest was warm and alive. Ryo could feel it pulse with life – a creature caught a vine and swung to another and another – a deep grunt sounded behind her. Then there was the air – soft and almost comforting– and its smell, it reminded her of something. Something from a long time ago…

Ryo snapped from the memory as a thorn caught her ankle. What was this place? And who was this ogre who had a hold of her? She spun again. He only tightened his grip.

"Who are you, and where are you taking me?" She demanded, doing her best to dig her heels into the ground.

"Ya know wheres yer goin'. As fer me," he stopped walking and forced his face inches from her own. "I'm Kalib. Jus' know, fer tha short time ya got left, I'm tha one that brought ya to yer death." His lips curled, and he spat.

His mucus stung her eyes.

It was then that she felt the bubbling. It started deep inside of her as a dull warmth, but then that warmth grew and became all encompassing. Soon, it was all she could focus on. It spread from her toes to her legs, to her torso and then to her arms and finally to her head. Her body was on fire! The forest faded. The sound of her breathing, the stench of the man's breath, all of it blew away, leaving her engulfed in a tornado of hot anger. Then the anger was gone – and in its place – something far more dangerous.

Kalib released her. "What tha? Don' ya be tryin' no witch magic on me." He backed up, his hands trembling. "I'll… you'll be sorry…" He continued to back away from her.

Ryo ignored the man. Power, confidence and control coursed through her veins. She was detached from the world around her and from the man in front of her, her mind on a higher plane, but that didn't mean she couldn't feel. With this distance came a deeper connection. She could feel his fear. She could feel her strength. She could feel the forest buzzing, and she could feel the planet spinning. She could feel *everything*.

Something stirred in her right forearm, and she turned it so her palm faced the sky. Her arm seemed to blur, as if a thick cloud surrounded it. She watched with a vague curiosity. The cloud grew. It shifted from translucent grey to blue and back to grey again. Then suddenly she knew what to do. She extended her arm and pointed her right fingers at Kalib. He shook.

"Please, no. No. I'll not tell anyone of ya'. Please. Jus' le' me live. I promise, you'll git no more trouble from me. Ple…"

She wasn't listening, nor did she wait for him to finish his plea. She let go.

Kalib's eyes widened as the force hit him. It threw him backwards, smashing him into a wide tree. Bits of orange bark showered down on him, but he did not move. Ryo approached him.

6

"You will not pursue me. The townspeople will not pursue me. This *Yalki* will not pursue me. *No one* will pursue me."

"I would ask for your word, but I know that it means nothing. As a result, you will wait here until someone finds you, and when they do, you will remember nothing other than you are a wretched fish monger who deserves nothing more than a solitary life on a wet, cold boat. You will go to sea, and you will die at sea. You chose this. This is your doing."

His eyes widened even more. Ryo could feel his frantic wish to move and run, but he didn't. He barely even breathed. She turned and walked away, his eyes heavy on her back.

Ryo walked until she knew Kalib could no longer see her. Then she stopped.

What is going on? Where am I? Who am I? What did I do back there?

Suddenly, she was terrified.

She barreled blindly through the forest, not knowing where she was going, only that she had to go. She had to get away, away from whom she didn't know, but she had to move. They were watching her.

Memories flooded through her. She was on a ship, she was in a car, she was healing the sick, she was giving orders, she was lost. These memories weren't hers, yet they felt so natural. They felt so real. It was her, Ryo, in those memories, but she couldn't recall any of them any more than one could truly recall a dream.

She stopped running. Her side ached from the exertion, and her right leg still bled painfully. She peeled back the dark, sticky dress. The cut was deep. It wasn't going to heal on its own. Then the bubbling came back.

Her hands moved over her leg, and she gasped. The bubbling grew, the hotness, the confidence, the power; all of it came back. She closed her eyes and the pain peaked, then it was gone. She waited several breaths, and then finally opened her eyes. Other than the dried blood and torn dress, one would never have known her leg had been injured. The skin was flawless without even a hint of a scar. She looked at her hands. She had known exactly where to put them. It was as if she had done this every day of her life...

She stood up and quickly sat back down. Her legs shook, and her breathing was ragged. What was happening to her?

Who was she?

Chapter 2

Thog was a planet of intellectuals. With a top Federation research university and several high grossing Federation funded R & D corporations, Thog was the place to be for anyone with political aspirations. The best and the brightest came to Thog, and only the brightest of the best stayed. On Thog, secrecy and cover-ups were part of everyday life, and it was a point of contention, among even the best of friends, of who knew the most secrets and who had the highest clearance. Outsiders to Thog believed that the Thogians were no different than the actors and actresses of Galaxy Studios – the top entertainment planet in the system. Shallow, showy, and conceited, it was easy for an outsider to confuse a Thog elite and a top system actor. Such accusations did not faze the Thogians though. They knew what separated them from the dimwits of Galaxy Studios, and everyone else for that matter – their brains. Their brains were what got them to Thog, and their brains were what allowed them to stay on Thog. Those with the most well developed brains had the most clandestine of jobs and hence the most money and power on Thog.

There was, however, a subculture on Thog, one that the aesthetically conscious members of the planet wished did not exist. There were members of the Thog elite that did not care to engage in the normal banter of the planet. These people did not care who had a higher clearance, nor did they care to have the latest fashions. These were the true elite of Thog – the idiot savants. They could solve the mysteries of the universe but fail to wear shoes to a dinner with the president. They were the shame and pride of Thog, and Filion Ker III was one of them. Brilliant and dense, Filion Ker III had just become, in a matter of mere seconds, the most important person on Thog.

Filion awoke with a start. It was time. She had awakened! He could feel it.

"Grawlix! I'm not ready! There's not enough time!" He struggled in his blankets. Thrashing wildly, he kicked and clawed, seeming to only entangle himself even more. His silken night hat slid over his eyes. He yelled again.

Awake! So suddenly! He had thought there would have been more warning, some kind of sign, anything. Not that they had said there would be... he had just assumed... but there had been nothing! He had been peacefully asleep, dreaming of all sorts of nice things – cool grapes, girls with pretty smiles, warm sun and pleasant music – when it dropped on him like a bomb. The girls, the grapes, all of it, disappeared, and in their place remained only a heavy, urgent feeling. He knew what it meant. He didn't have to be a top graduate of the best Dream Searcher Academy in the universe to know what it meant. She was conscious. This was the most important moment of his life, and here he was, *still* stuck in his blankets!

With a final kick Filion launched the last blanket from his body. He stood. At ten feet tall, Filion was short for a lossal, but he made up for his small stature in other ways. Sure, he had exceptionally fine fur, but what really set Filion apart was that he was the youngest Graftin graduate in history. This was quite a feat considering Graftin was the best Dream Searcher Academy in the universe (well, what they *knew* of the universe). There were other Searcher Academies – For, Var, and C-ton – but none of them came close to Graftin. Graftin was the best, which is why most Graftin graduates were at least in their 200's, if not their 300's, when they *started*. Graftin demanded a certain degree of maturity from its students, and Filion had graduated at the top of his class when he was only 106! Not only that, but he had graduated in only 10 years, a mere blink of a lossal's eye. He had been told he would do great things, and he had. Recruited by Thog fresh out of the academy, his job was to influence the outcomes of politically sensitive situations. He had stopped wars, prevented famine, and saved entire planets, but none of it compared to what he now faced.

Filion stood motionless, temporarily unsure of how to proceed. His thick snout quivered, and he could feel his tall ears burning, a result of nerves no doubt. He gnawed on his lower lip causing his sharp teeth to prick his skin. His silver fur bristled restlessly and his legs shook. Taking a ragged breath, Filion ran his hand over his face. He closed his green eyes, and then opened them. They fell on his Searcher's badge. Normally he felt intense pride and strength when he looked at his badge but not this time. This time he felt inadequate. He had no idea what he was supposed to do. A typical Summoning didn't work this way. A typical Summoning would have required him to go back to sleep. But not this one, this one was different.

Filion looked past the badge to a framed paper on the wall. The paper was a page from an old textbook. The ink was faded, but the words were clear. He often read the page before meditating. It helped him center himself. It helped him remember how simple his job was, when he really broke it down. He read it again, even though he knew it by heart.

Dream Searching Defined

Dream Searchers are a rare breed. To be a Searcher, one must be able to access the Tierameng [Dream World], and such a requirement is not for the faint of heart. The Tierameng is a dimension separate from ours, foreign, dangerous, and even beautiful; the Tierameng is full of potential. No one knows all or even most, of what goes on in the Tierameng, but we have discovered enough to understand how to Search and Summon.

Searchers are granted access to the Tierameng through intense, focused meditation. Once inside of the Tierameng, Searchers continue to meditate, but that meditation must become less focused and more open. Such meditation primes a Searcher's mind to receive a *Summoning*.

Summoners send Summonings, but even the most novice of Searchers knows that anyone can Summon. Only the exceptional can Search.

After a Searcher has made contact with a potential Summoning, the Searcher must then prove her or himself. The Searcher must show the Summoning that s/he is worthy of that Summoning. Proving oneself worthy can mean anything from answering a question correctly to having been arbitrarily born on the right planet.

Once a Searcher proves his or her worthiness, the Searcher then must determine whose dream to enter. Most often the Searcher enters the dream of the person who has the power to directly fulfill the Summoning in the physical world.

With the correct person chosen and their dream located, the Searcher may then *link*. A link can be established between a Searcher and any dream whose dreamer's physical body is in the same dimension as the Searcher's physical body. Once linked, the Searcher can then enter and influence the dreamer's dream.

Such actions, while seemingly immoral and illegal, are not. Because of the Searcher's Code and the Summoner's Pact, a summoned Dream Searcher may legally and morally enter anyone's dream in the universe. The Searcher is also granted the legal right to influence that person's dream, as long as that influence, either directly or indirectly, leads to the fulfillment of the Summoning.

This particular Summoning had started like any other. Filion had been in the Tierameng, floating in a cloud of energy (known to Searchers as an Orku), somewhere between here and there and somewhere between us and them. Where *there* was, or who *us* were, were of no importance. When he was summoned, he was *always* between us and them, and here and there, and he was *always* in an Orku. In order to be summoned, one had to exist in a small space in an infinite place, and Tierameng energy clouds were ideal for this. Floating in an Orku was something any Graftin grad could do but staying in one was not. Most grads could maintain meditation only long enough to catch the first Summoning they encountered. Filion could remain in an Orku for hours, which is why he was one of the best. It was also why he had received this particular Summoning.

The Orku had been yellow that night, something that, while not normal, was not a reason to worry. He had meditated, as he usually did, for several hours but had received no Summonings. He was about to leave when he felt a distant tug. He let it take him. His ability to follow, as well as lead, was also what made him great. To be a Searcher, a good Searcher, one couldn't be overly headstrong. To say meekness was better wasn't quite right either. No, one needed courage, but one couldn't have a thirst for personal glory. Following leaders, persuading leaders, letting the right suggestion drop at the right time, and knowing that he would get no public credit for the events that he prevented or caused, was why Filion was the best. He was not afraid to go where he was taken nor did he need his name up in lights. These traits allowed him to prove himself worthy of the most difficult Summonings. Most Searchers were either too afraid to follow, or once they caught a Summoning, they wanted to prove themselves. His flaws were neither, which is why the Summoning had tugged at Filion and allowed him to follow it.

Or at least he had started to follow, but it quickly turned into a pursuit. The Summoning was running from him, daring him to chase it. Such a dangerous game it played, skirting in and out of other's dreams, treading on empty space and plowing through waves of energy. He had never worked as hard to catch a Summoning as he had her, not that he knew then that it was for her. At the time it was merely curiosity and the thrill of a true challenge that had led him to give chase.

The pursuit lasted for what seemed like days, not that he could be sure. Time flowed differently in the Tierameng. The curves and twists of dreams had a tendency to shorten or lengthen time as the Searcher knew it. He watched three sunsets and four sunrises during his chase. On the fourth day he found himself outside of a crashed ship, a Redhawk, used for interplanetary travel. He entered and the world shifted. Everything slid sideways. The colors of his body blurred into the colors of the burned ship. The blues and blacks exploded into yellow, and he was back in the Orku.

You are quite a Dream Searcher
More like a Dream Runner
Is that humor I detect
Perhaps We all change sometime
Hmmmm

The voices filled his ears and his body. It seemed they came from nowhere and everywhere. He could feel them in every cell of his being. The Orku pulsed with life. He had felt it do this only a few times before. The energy moved like this when he was about to receive a very important Summoning.

Filion you are the best Dream Searcher in the universe
Filion do you know who we are
No.
We are Eoan
Filion's heart skipped a beat.

We are not just of stories We exist We created you We created your world your planets your universe
We also unleashed the plague that threatens to destroy your universe
You must help save your universe
We have information that you need
Should you choose to accept this Summoning You will be responsible for the last hope of your universe
Do you Filion Ker III accept

Chapter 3

They told him that he was to speak of his Summoning to no one, not even the Board of Summonings. Technically that was illegal, but they told him he would not live beyond a few days if he reported it. Besides, until she awoke, he would not be required to do any work. He could devote his time to his other Summonings. It could be years before he had to find her, or days, but when it was time, that was when his life would change.

The Eoans told him that he would be required to leave everything he knew behind. His position as a senior Dream Searcher III on Thog would have to be abandoned, as well as most of his physical possessions. He could not tell anyone, not even his mother, of where he was going or what he was going to do. Once he got the sign, he was to go directly to the Right Town Ship Terminus and access locker 234. He knew the combination. Everything he would need to start his journey would be inside the locker.

*****

Time was of the essence. Every minute she spent conscious but without context was another minute she was vulnerable. He threw on his red vest and brown pants without thought and then stopped. He was leaving, potentially forever. Perhaps he had better prepare himself for the occasion. He took a deep breath, the kind they taught to the first years to help them better open themselves to the Tierameng. Such a breath was calming, relaxing, and head gathering. He took another and looked around. His reflection stared at him from a polished shield. His green eyes shone with worry, and the silver fur and black skin around his snout and ears were bunched in concern. He took another breath. As he exhaled, the creases in his face fell away. His eyes softened. Here he was, standing in his favorite clothes, getting ready for the most important job of his life. He flashed a brief smile. His straight white teeth glinted back at him.

He could do this.

They had said he could take a small bag of his most required possessions. Tokens of appreciation from Queens, Primes, Captains, Generals, Presidents and the like cluttered his room. He had objects that were worth more than most people made in a lifetime. The polished shield, an antique from the Great War, inlaid with precious metal and hand carved, had been a gift from a grateful General. Then there was the woolen Ika hat. Interwoven with liquid silver, it had been a gift from the people of the high planes of Yulip. What about the Indicore figurines, and the dancing Tamin plants, and... He was just supposed to abandon all of this? For a brief instant he was sad, then the importance of what he was about to do resurfaced. Calmly, he took another breath and began to pack, first taking the battered textbook page from its frame and folding it into his Searcher's Codebook.

*****

Within the hour he was at the ship terminus. For 3:00am, the terminus was relatively busy. Most of the people in the building were miners heading to other planets for their day's work. These were the people whose families inhabited Thog before the University and the R and D corporations. These were the people who now had to go off planet to survive. They would be back later that night, giving them only a few precious hours to sleep, eat, and be with their families. Filion tried to ignore them. While he was a Dream Searcher, he had another talent, one that very few people knew of. He could sense living creature's auras. One of the miners who passed him emitted a brown aura. Like a wafting cloud, the aura followed the man with every step he took. It seemed to suffocate him and press down on him. The man was sick. He wouldn't make it through the week. Another miner passed. Her green aura sparkled and danced as she moved. The woman was hopeful.

He couldn't read everyone, but he could read most people. There were those who shrouded their auras, or worse, those who had none. People who hid their auras were up to something, but people who didn't have an aura at all… such were most definitely dangerous people.

He shuffled to the locker section, doing his best to ignore the auras he sensed. He didn't often go out in public because he had a hard time seeing past the colors. He liked the Tierameng because he could sense when he wanted to and turn it off when he didn't. It was a valuable tool. He had recently persuaded a king to not attack a neighboring country solely because Filion had been able to read the king's aura. He wouldn't trade the skill for anything; he just wished he had more control of it in the real world.

The locker bank stood in a distant wing of the terminus. Few people populated the wing, and he sensed most who did were tired and only vaguely aware of him. He walked, scanning the numbers. There it was, locker 234. He stopped. It was near the top, over 8 feet from the floor.

Filion gasped, and took a step back. An orange aura came from the locker. Something alive was inside the locker.

Chapter 4

Filion took a deep breath, dialed the combination, and threw open the door.

His first glance of the locker's inside was deceiving. It was large, with several cubic feet of space, and initially he saw nothing. Then his eyes adjusted to the dim light, and he saw three objects near the right back corner. The aura was much stronger now that the door was open. He sensed excitement. Slowly, he put his hand inside, and one by one, withdrew the objects.

The first item was a small leather bag. He opened it. Inside were several gold pieces, all stamped with the Federation's logo. He frowned. This wasn't much gold. He didn't know how much money he would need, but if the Summoning went at all how he thought it would, he would be gone a while, and that meant he would need more money than what was in this bag. He put his hand into the bag. He grabbed a handful of gold and let it slip through his fingers. He could use his personal money, but that wasn't how Summonings were supposed to work. Then again, most Summonings took place in the Tierameng, so normally real money was of no use. He put the bag in his pocket, and temporarily pushed the matter from his mind.

The next thing in the locker was a small blue orb made of what appeared to be glass. He picked it up. Light and cool to the touch, he sensed energy, but it wasn't the energy responsible for the aura. What was he supposed to do with this? He shook it and rolled it in his fingers. Nothing happened. He dropped it into his pocket and reached for the third object.

As soon as he touched it, he knew. This object was alive. Cautiously, he picked it up and pulled it into the light.

He held a leather bound book, and it pulsed with life. He turned the book over gingerly. Both the front and back covers were devoid of any sort of script, but someone had taken great care to etch complex patterns into both covers. Filion had never seen such patterns, and was unsure what to make of them. He opened the book. The first page was blank. He flipped to the second page, then to the third. They were all blank. Perhaps he had mistakenly opened the book from the back. He flipped the book over and opened the other cover. The result was the same. Annoyed, Filion let out a huff.

Don't huff at me!

Filion nearly dropped the book. The words had appeared on the page out of nothing. The book had spoken to him! He couldn't believe it. In his studies he had read of 'Living Documents,' but like most of his instructors and all of his peers, Filion had *known* such objects to be matters of myth.

Filion didn't know what to do. Should he talk to it? Should he write in it?

14

Should he think at it? He had been to a lecture on Living Documents once, a *long* time ago. He tried to remember what the instructor had said.

The class, which had been a first year elective, had sounded much better on paper than it had been in person. He rarely went, and when he did, he often regretted going. Professor Donavit III (he had been a level III! The class should have been good!) was always lecturing on 'what you could encounter in the Tierameng, if you opened your mind to it'. Donavit was well known among the students as a light grader, as well as, unbeknownst to Filion at the time of registration, a complete nut. No one took anything he said seriously, both students and faculty alike, but for some reason he kept teaching. Filion racked his brain but came up empty.

What... who are you? Filion thought.

Nothing happened. Filion looked around. The few people who had been in the wing were gone. As surreptitiously as he could manage, he brought the book close to his mouth.

"Who are you?" He asked softly.

Don't put me so close to your mouth! Do you have any idea what sorts of germs live there?

Filion jerked the book away from him. It hadn't answered his question, but it had responded. He looked around again.

"Where did you come from?"

Does it matter? I've been waiting for you for weeks! We need to get moving.

"I didn't get the sign until an hour ago. How could I have known you were here?" Filion whispered.

The book said nothing.

"Where should we go?" Filion asked.

Where you need to go.

"Where is that?"

Really?

"What does that mean? Do you know where we should go?"

I can't believe you're the best they could find. Maybe the universe deserves what's coming.

Filion snapped the book shut and stuffed it into his pocket. He hoped he had hurt the book, well, only enough to startle it. He didn't want to think about what was happening to the universe, and he certainly didn't like an *inanimate* object, no matter how alive it seemed, ridiculing him.

He grabbed the locker door, and with a final glance inside, he began to swing the door shut. He stopped right before it latched and jerked the door open again. There was something else, something he hadn't noticed. Two ID cards sat where the Living Document had been. They must have been under it. Snatching them from the locker, he eyed them hopefully. Both cards had a black and gold line rimming their edges. He gasped. The black and gold lines granted their owners unlimited access throughout *all* Federation planets. He had only seen such a card once, during a very intricate summoning. His smiling face winked at him from the first card. He held his breath and looked at the next card. There was no name on it, and its picture was blurry, as if it had been taken at dusk. Filion couldn't quite make out the face, but he could tell she had blue eyes. They burned through the fuzzy picture with electrifying clarity. Then the eyes disappeared.

He had to hurry.

Chapter 5

Night had come, and with it Ryo had made a small fire. The fire afforded enough light to see a few feet in every direction, but that was it. Beyond the flame's glow was nothing but black. If there were any stars or moons visible tonight, the trees prevented their light from reaching her. The forest was different without sunlight. It was still alive but in a more sinister way. Unseen rustling and grunting, along with uneven cries and the occasional sound of breathing filled her ears. She sat without moving, strangely unafraid of the surrounding noises. Instead, she concentrated on the two piles of fruit in front of her. She had gathered them before dark had fallen, but she had yet to eat anything from them. The pile to her right was poisonous. The pile to her left was not. She did not know how she knew this, but she did.

She sighed. The afternoon had gone by in a blur, and she couldn't remember much of it. There was that man, her leg, and now, here she sat, in the dark, staring at two piles of fruit. She wondered why she had even bothered to gather the poisonous fruits, but she didn't dwell on it. She reached out and grabbed a clump of green berries from the left pile. She popped some into her mouth. They were delicious. To say she had never tasted them before would have been a lie. She knew them, but she just couldn't place how she knew them.

She went over what she knew of her life, again, which was pretty much nothing. She had a vague recollection of being some sort of healer. She had been respected, revered even, but somehow that had gotten her into trouble. The fact that she had been able to heal her leg and shoot unseen forces from her hands shouldn't have come as a surprise to her. According to her freshest memories, such actions were commonplace. No matter how many ways she worked it though, the fact that she had been able to do such things was amazing – impossible even.

But they obviously weren't impossible, which is why she had a problem. She had foggy memories of other places, other lives. She could hazily remember when she didn't live on this planet. She could remember when "magic" didn't exist, when space travel was impossible, and yet, when space travel was her whole life. The memories were distant and scratchy but true. She would have bet her life that they were, not that that made it any easier. It seemed that with every new memory she came across, she found another one that directly countered it. The harder she tried to remember who she was, and what she stood for, the more confused she became.

Her existential crisis was exhausting. She ate another berry and looked at the fire. She had memories of a time when building a fire from nothing meant using two sticks and creating a coal from friction. Tonight, however, she had

17

started this fire with her mind, and she had done it as if she had done it every day of her life.

It was almost comical that she could do so much with her mind yet still have no idea of who, or what, she was. After she started the fire, she had tried to 'think' herself out of the forest, but what resulted from that was simply a splitting headache. Luckily, she had 'thought' that away as well. Through several hours of trial and error she learned that there was a limit to what she could 'think' into existence. Starting the fire had required her to think in a unique way, and she knew the only reason she could do it was because she had done it many times before. When she started the fire, she had issued no command, nor had she desired anything. The idea of telling the fire to start, or asking it to, was not how it worked. Instead, she thought about what physically happened when a fire was started. She thought about how she would feel if a fire was started and how the ground would feel if a fire was started. She thought about what a fire would mean for her and the surrounding area, and she thought about the consequences of a fire. She thought about how a fire would aid her and how it would hinder her. Then she took all of these thoughts and spliced and mashed and organized them into a format that resulted in the ever more familiar bubbling feeling. From that the fire started. From her first thoughts, to the actual fire itself, creating it had taken no more than a few seconds.

The trick was the organization of her thoughts. It was easy enough to think the right questions, but putting them into the right order seemed to be what caught her up the most. Clearly everything she 'thought' into existence she had thought into existence before. Lighting the fire came very naturally. Stopping to examine how she did it was unnatural. The sequences and patterns that she found made little to no sense, and she knew that she could not do anything new. Not now at least. Not until she figured out how it worked.

She thought more berries into her hands and instantly the green berries left the ground. She broke down the process of lifting the berries. It didn't make any sense either. As far as she could tell, there weren't any similarities between the organization of the fire thoughts and the berry thoughts.

She sighed and angrily stuffed the berries into her mouth. As she chewed, a pervasive tiredness spread through her body. She lay down, shut her eyes, and within moments she was asleep.

Chapter 6

Filion shut the locker, unsure what to do. He had expected instructions, but all he'd been given was a strange assortment of objects. He pulled the Living Document out of his pocket. Opening it he said, "What do I do now?"

The book didn't respond. Harrumphing into his facial furs, Filion shut the book but gently this time. He put it back into his pocket. Well, at least he knew it had feelings.

He pulled the glass orb from his pocket. It was no longer blue but now a pale pulsing grey. To Filion's surprise, the orb was also quite warm. Actually it was hot, so hot in fact, he nearly dropped it. He juggled it from hand to hand, and as he did, the orb seemed to roll to the tips of his fingers. He inched forward to prevent the orb from falling, but it kept rolling forward. He continued walking, afraid it would fall if he didn't. After several steps the orb seemed to cool. It also slowed and ceased to move.

"Huh," Filion said.

Keeping his hand flat and outstretched, Filion turned around to retrieve his bag, which he had left at the locker. The orb heated up and rolled to the heel of his hand. He hurriedly grabbed his bag and turned around. The orb rolled back towards his fingertips. After a few steps it cooled. He kept his hand flat and walked in the direction the orb indicated.

Filion left the locker wing and reached an intersection. The orb rolled to the left. Filion followed. He wound his way through the terminus. Signs blinked at him and mechanical voices called to him, cajoling him to buy the latest communicator, the newest ship, or the best shoes on all of Thog. Filion ignored the ads, but he couldn't ignore the stares. People watched him as he walked, his hand outstretched and his face tense. He tried to ignore them and their auras, but he couldn't block them completely. He was self-conscious, and there was too much going on around him. *How long had it been since he had been in such a public place?*

Finally, he reached a line of ticket booths. They stood against a towering wall of glass windows. A sign showing at least 80 different available flights flashed above the booths.

Great, Filion thought. *Now what?*

The orb was a warm yellow, and Filion could sense its energy had changed. He placed it back into his pocket and withdrew the Living Document. Moving to an empty corner, Filion opened the book.

"I'm sorry," he started. "But you had no right to mock me so."

Nothing appeared on the book's pages.

"Could you please help me? I think I need to buy a ticket, but I don't know which ticket to buy. Do you have any idea?"

Ink swirled on the page. Filion waited, but no words appeared.

"I'm sorry," Filion repeated.

Bok

Filion looked at the screen. Only one ticket to Bok remained. The ship departed in twenty minutes.

"Thanks!" Filion said, closing the book and stuffing it into his pocket. He ran to one of the windows.

"One ticket to Bok please."

The teller looked at him with disinterest. She chomped heavily on a piece of yellow gum, and she gave off the aura that she would rather be doing anything other than helping Filion. "That'll be 75 gold," she said in a flat, bored voice.

"75 gold! That's robbery!" Filion exclaimed.

"You want the ticket or not? Bok's a difficult planet to reach, especially this time of year, monsoons and all. Take it or leave it," she said as she snapped a bubble at him. Her tone didn't change.

Irritated, he dug in his pocket for the bag of gold. Then a thought occurred to him. He withdrew his new ID card.

"Can you charge it?"

"Whatever."

"So, is that a yes?" Filion asked.

The teller moved her head in an exaggerated nod.

"Ok! That's what I want!"

"By imprinting your card you agree to follow the rules and regulations of Thog Transportation Authorities. If you break…" the teller started.

"Yeah, sure, fine," Filion said, placing his thumb on the imprint area of the card. He thrust the card back at her. She took it and carefully placed it under the scanner. The scanner's light turned green. She hesitated, as if she didn't believe the light, then she slowly picked up the card.

"Please, I need to go, the ship's about to leave!" Filion cried.

With an eye roll, she passed the card back to him. "Have a nice flight and thank you for choosing the Right Town Ship Terminus for all your interstellar needs."

Filion took the card and ran.

20

Chapter 7

Filion knew little about Bok other than it supposedly had terrible weather. According to the flight papers, it would take the ship approximately ten hours to reach the planet. It would then take another hour or so to land, if everything went well. As the ticket cashier mentioned, it was monsoon season on Bok, and that didn't bode well for landing. Filion was confused as to why they were going to Bok at all. It seemed like an odd place for her to be, not that anywhere seemed like the right place, but something in his gut told him that she wasn't there, and his gut had a good track record.

Filion glanced around the ship. Its interior was clean, and its furniture was well kept. The carpet was springy and freshly laundered. Its walls shined, and every light he passed was bright. The ship even smelled good. Despite all this, Filion guessed the ship, a Model H, was at least twenty years old. Seam welded from a continuous piece of metal, the ship would last another twenty years, barring any catastrophe.

Filion found his seat. It turned out he had his own pod. In his pod was a seat that turned into a bed and a desk. Embedded in the wall above the desk was a monitor. Filion arranged himself in his chair and emptied his pockets, placing the bag of gold, the orb, and the Living Document onto the desk. He kept the ID cards in his pocket. Idly, he turned on the screen. A newscaster sat behind a desk.

"In other news," the green newscaster said. "Tioris have attacked Handu. It is advised that no one, for any reason, attempt to land on Handu. To do so would most definitely lead to immediate enslavement or death. As of now, Handu is considered a Black Planet. Federation leaders met today to discuss possible options for the release of Handu's inhabitants. There has been no word on any decisions."

Filion shut off the screen, disturbed. This was odd. *Usually* Tioris were more subtle which meant the Federation *usually* didn't find out a planet had been taken over until it was too late. Tioris were smart and persuasive, very persuasive. In order for a Tiori to enslave anyone, a person had to truly believe the Tiori was a worthy leader, which spoke to the Tioris' charisma. When enslaving a planet, Tioris started small and ended big. They usually started in tiny rural villages, gaining the trust of the villagers by performing so called 'miracles'. Tioris would cure the sick, punish the bad, and guarantee a good harvest with return. The villagers would see the Tiori's power and come to respect and fear them. After the Tiori decided that she (or he) had gained enough of the villager's trust, she would announce that she was a god, sent down from the Heavens to reclaim what was rightfully hers.

21

The villagers would be her first disciples. The Tiori would then throw a feast in the village's honor. The feast was the moment of truth.

It wasn't until a few years ago that any of this was even known. How the Tioris enslaved people, and why people went along with it had been a mystery. Planets of all types had been enslaved – technologically advanced planets, rural planets, planets with dominant religions, and planets without any religion. How and why Tioris were able to convince such different groups that they were gods was unknown.

At least it was unknown, until a student researcher by the name of Raheta Foglith from Catilla University (at the time a no name school, now *the* hot bed of Tiori warfare research) set up a remote video feed and a pathogen net in a no name village (now known as Tryx Tiori) on the planet of Tryx. Originally, Foglith was trying to determine if there were any visible indicators of unseen pathogens in farming populations throughout Tryx. During a weeklong trip, Foglith set up her equipment in seven different farming communities throughout the planet. When the week was over, she went back to Catilla to monitor the data.

A Tiori by the name of Willika appeared in Tryx Tiori not long after Foglith set up her research equipment. Foglith, unknowingly, recorded the rise of Willika in the small village. After the fact, researchers were able to go through the recorded feed and see Willika revive a dead infant, correctly forecast the weather, and catch and kill a man who was found to be hoarding more than his share of food. The villagers came to revere her. She announced who she really was and set the date for the feast.

The night of the feast, Foglith's pathogen net spiked. A new virus appeared in Tryx Tiori. This virus had no known similarities to any other virus on Tryx Tiori or anywhere else for that matter. The pathogen net sent the virus's biological and chemical data back to Foglith's lab, allowing her to analyze it from the comfort of Catilla, three planets away.

*****

Willika sat at the head of a long table. Her chair had been elevated so she could look down on all of her future disciples. She peered at the teeming mass of people seated before her. Dressed in their finest rags, these people were the bottom of the barrel, but she had to start somewhere. She raised her goblet.

"This is a moment to be remembered. For after this toast, there is no going back. Those of you who are loyal to me will be rewarded justly. Those of you who are not, those of you who doubt me… you will be found, and you will be punished. I am your all-knowing, all-seeing God. I will not tolerate treachery. I will reward loyalty. Let us drink!"

With that, she lowered her glass and drank. The village followed. At first nothing happened. Then there was a scream, followed by another, and another. People fell to the ground, withering and crying. Boils formed on their faces, their skin broke, blood poured from their bodies. Some people simply seemed to exsanguinate and die. They were the lucky ones. Others exploded, their bodies bloating, their eyes and hands spinning in panic, until they finally burst, ending their screaming.

That didn't end all of the screaming though. Those who were alive, unharmed other than by what they had just seen, continued to scream, their mouths seemingly stuck open. After the last non-believer died, convulsing on the ground until Willika struck him with her heel, Willika smiled and put her hand in the air.

Several minutes passed as the villagers attempted to quiet themselves. Once their screaming stopped, Willika spoke again.

"You, my faithful, have been rewarded. Rewarded with life. May you remember this moment until you pass from here to there. I have demonstrated my power. You need not test me. I am your God. Now kneel."

And the villagers did so, sobbing and gasping.

*****

By the time researchers realized what they were dealing with, it was too late. Willika had control of most of the planet, using the original villagers as a sort of make shift army as she moved from town to town, converting or killing everyone in her path.

From this event, it was discovered that the Tioris fought by psychological and chemical warfare. The virus that they used, dubbed T. Tryx, only enslaved a person if their brain was open to it. T. Tryx did not kill those who believed that Willika was a God. It merely sealed the deal, essentially re-writing the believers' brains in a way that could not be undone. Not only that, but the virus was passed from mother to child, the fetus apparently malleable enough to accept the virus without a fight.

If a person did not believe Willika was a god, however, their brain could not support nor fight the virus. The virus needed a foothold in the brain before it could reproduce. If a person's brain was unwilling to grant that foothold (believe Willika was a god) the body of the virus would break and spill toxins into the brain. These toxins would move from the brain to the rest of the body, overwhelming the non-believer's systems and then killing them.

The Federation, by policy, did not interfere in inner-planetary domestic squabbles. Civil wars, riots, and rebellions, all were untouchable by the Federation's laissez faire policy. Such a policy had allowed the Tioris to capture hundreds of planets before the Federation realized that they had been duped, and by then it was too late for those planet's denizens. Normally, by the time it was known a Tiori had invaded a planet, most of the planet, if not all of it, was theirs. To try and fight the Tioris, especially now that it was known that they fought with an incurable and deadly virus, was suicide. Not that the Federation hadn't tried though, at least in the beginning.

Initially, the Federation had sent soldiers, and then machines, to fight the Tioris, but it was a losing battle. Obviously, sending people to fight a Tiori was a death sentence, and sending machines had so far only proved to be wasteful. Millions in gold had been spent on trying to create Tiori worthy troops, but so far nothing had worked. While places like Catilla University still worked to research and develop Tiori worthy weapons (anti-virus bombs, interplanetary stealth rockets, etc.), the Federation just didn't have the resources to fight back. When a planet was declared Black, it was considered lost. No one went in, no one came out. Those who lived there were either dead, or worse, enslaved. The Federation erected a statue in memoriam of the planet and its occupants on Moneta, the Federation's capital planet, but otherwise, no one did anything.

Which was why Filion was so surprised to hear that the Federation was attempting to negotiate.

Without warning the Living Document flipped open.

They grow stronger.

The book startled Filion, but he did his best to conceal it. At least the book was talking to him again. Filion opened his mouth to say something but looked around instead. All of the pods around him were occupied. He could clearly hear the conversation from the pod next to him. A man and a woman were in a heated discussion about the best way to cook shredded opalfish.

He had an idea. Filion found a pencil in his bag and hesitantly touched it to the Living Document's first page.

Who grows stronger? He wrote, lightly, just in case. His words stayed on the page for a few seconds, and then faded into nothing.

Who do you think? The book replied. *The Afortiori.*

Filion frowned. The Afortiori? Did the book mean the Tioris? Had the book heard the news?

Are you talking about the Tioris? Filion wrote. *Did you hear the news report? They don't usually attack like that.*

They are not a subtle race. I find it surprising it took them this long to be so ostentatious.

You know of the Tioris? Filion scratched.

The book did not answer. Finally words appeared.

Do you know what you are getting into?

Filion frowned again. The Eoans had said that the girl was the key to saving the universe and that Filion was to help her. He was to keep her safe and run interference for her while she did what she needed to do. They had said that they would tell him what he needed to know, when he needed to know it.

Filion thought about what he knew. He knew this Summoning had to do with the Tioris, or at least he thought it did. They were the plague that was threatening the universe, at least according to the Eoans. Was she supposed to fight the Tioris by herself? That sounded extreme. She was supposed to do *something*, but what hadn't been explained to him.

What do you mean? Filion wrote.

24

The book paused for so long that Filion didn't think it was going to respond. Finally ink appeared.

She is one of the last.

Last what? Filion scribed.

Chozen. They didn't explain anything to you, did they?

Filion didn't say anything.

I'll start at the beginning, as I would for her.

Chapter 8

The universe, as we know it, was created as a result of an exercise of thought. In another dimension, far away from here, there is a race of beings known as the Eoan. The Eoans, unlike us, do not have bodies. In fact, they are unable to interact in a physical world just as we could not exist in an ethereal one. Their world is nothing more than clouds of raw elements, those elements constantly crashing into one another. The Eoan are the energy that propels these clouds, the book said.

Like an Orku? Filion wrote.

Where do you think the Orku came from? The Living Document replied. The book ruffled his pages, clearly annoyed, and then continued as if Filion had not interrupted him.

Do not assume, however, that the Eoan are a primitive race. It was the Eoans that created our universe. They sought a challenge. They sought to create something merely because they willed it to be so, and from their will our universe was born, but this was only the first step.

Filion took a breath. The Eoans created the universe? If so, that would mean... that would mean they were gods...

A universe without life is barren, the Living Document proceeded. *Each Eoan took it upon itself to create a world within the universe. There were no set parameters as to what each Eoan could or could not will into existence. The only limits were each Eoan's imagination. Planets, bacteria, plants and animals followed. This took time, but time is an inconsistent force to an Eoan. What may have taken billions of years in our universe could have been mere seconds to an Eoan, or vice versa.*

Filion took another breath. They could *think* things into existence? He had been *thought* into existence? No, he had been born, but lossals... lossals had been imagined and then created?

It is important to note, that the Eoans are not like us in an emotional sense either. In addition to existing only as energy, they do not feel as we do. Love, hate, compassion – these emotions are dulled. While it can be said that the Eoans are able to feel, relative to us, they are cold. They seem only motivated to push the limits of what is possible by thought. To put the creation of our universe in terms we can understand, the Eoans went about creating us as a nation goes about creating technology during an arms race. The Eoans were motivated to out do their peers but not as a means of gaining fame or wealth, the Living Document paused. *You see, their motivation comes from their desire to be the first to discover what is beyond the frontier of their perceived limit of creation. This is what drives an Eoan.*

They don't feel? Filion wrote. *Then why do we feel?*

They feel. Are you not listening? Just not like we do. Our emotions are just unrefined versions of their own. We are... less advanced.

Filion frowned. Dream Searchers were considered to be very advanced.

It was then a particular Eoan discovered how to create self-consciousness and free will. Within a blink of an eye, our universe was populated by freethinking beings. This is the foundation for the war we now wage.

Free will was created? Filion wrote.

Yes. Now, let me continue.

Filion huffed. This Living Document was very rude.

With the creation of free will, the Eoans were faced with a dilemma. We would call it a 'moral' dilemma, but the Eoans wouldn't go so far. Did they want to continue to craft and manipulate a universe whose inhabitants were able to think, create, and destroy on their own? Some Eoans fervently believed that our universe was theirs – that the Eoans could do what they wanted because they had made us. But a growing number of Eoans were developing a sort of conscience themselves, which was a surprise. To suddenly feel responsibility and guilt, as muted as it was, was a violent shift for some of the Eoans.

Not so advanced after all... Filion thought.

Consequently, the Eoans split. A small faction, the self proclaimed Afortiori, believed that they had the right to continue to manipulate our universe as they pleased. The majority did not believe this. The Eoans and Afortiori went to war.

The Tioris... Filion wrote.

Yes. The Living Document said. *Unfortunately,* it continued. *That war spilled into our universe. Two sides without the physical ability to battle, but the ability to create physical battles merely by thinking of them, proved dangerous to us. Wars ravaged our universe. Entire races died, planets were destroyed, but in the end the Eoans won. Our universe was granted autonomy.*

"The Dark Ages," Filion breathed. Everyone knew about the Dark Ages, but no one knew what had caused them. Filion swallowed. This was a lot to take in.

The vanquished Afortiori were punished, something that had never before occurred in Eoan society. The Eoans took away the Afortiori's ability to create. Unknown to the Eoan at the time, this also made the Afortiori mortal. The Afortiori became second-class citizens, no better than slaves. Hate bubbled under the veneer of Eoan society. The Eoans chose to ignore the new emotion. The Afortiori fed on it.

Filion was beginning to feel sick.

As in all societies, however, the Eoans were not free from spies. The Afortiori had agents among the Eoans. A particular Afortiori spy was formerly one of the Eoan's brightest minds. This Afortiori, whose energy signature is known as J-10, was the same Eoan who discovered the ability to create consciousness in our universe. J-10 was not going to watch its

27

Afortiori family wither and die under the ruling Eoans. J-10 willed a gateway between our dimension and the Eoan's. The gateway allowed the Afortiori to escape their reality and enter ours. J-10 unleashed the Afortiori upon us, and they have plagued us ever since.

So, the Tioris are Afortiori, who used to be Eoans, who actually helped create our universe, but now are trying to subjugate it? Filion wrote.

Yes, the Living Document replied, and without pausing he said, *Once the Eoans realized the Afortiori had passed through the gateway and into our universe, it was only a matter of time before they understood what had happened, and what was happening. Our universe was being enslaved. Beings previously excluded from the boons of the physical world wanted all they could get. Entire planets were enslaved to cater to the Afortioris' every desire. Wars raged, people died.*

Wars still rage and people still die, Filion wrote.

The Living Document ignored him.

With our universe in chaos, the Eoans captured the remaining Afortiori, at least those who had not passed through the portal, including J-10. This subdued the violence, but it did not undo what had already been done. The Afortiori were still in our universe.

And still are... Filion wrote.

J-10's abilities were no secret, the Living Document went on. *J-10 had made it public, long before the war, that it wanted to create a portal between the Eoan dimension and ours. It had just been assumed that J-10 had never done it. Now that the possibility of portals had been realized, the Eoans faced yet another juncture. Should they retrieve the escaped Afortiori? Or should they abandon our universe as they had agreed?*

They were going to abandon us?! Even after they found out about the Tioris?! Filion scribbled.

Let me finish! Once again, emotion entered an equation that should have been emotionless. The Eoans concluded they would not hunt the escaped Afortiori, but they would aid us. They created one being per inhabited planet in our universe. Such beings, called Chozen, were to be our last hope. Each Chozen was given the ability to always keep their consciousness. If a Chozen's body were to be damaged beyond repair, another body would generate, and that Chozen's consciousness would transfer to the new body, at least in theory. The Eoans also gave the Chozen the power to will what they wanted into existence. They were to have all of the powers of an Eoan, along with a physical body. It could be said that the Chozen were designed to be more powerful than either the Eoans or Afortiori.

So, the Eoans created immortal super beings who can do anything with their brains? Filion wrote, secretly terrified.

Yes, the book said.

And she... Filion started.

She is a Chozen.

Chapter 9

Filion didn't say anything for some time. He sat, breathing deeply and trying to stay calm. The idea of a Chozen petrified him, even more so than the idea of Tioris, and the Tioris made him want to crawl into a hole and never leave. What if these omnipotent Chozens decided being evil was more fun than being good? What if they turned against the universe as the Tioris had? They could do more damage than the Tioris, and that… that would be the end of the universe. Then again, if the Tioris enslaved everyone first… He took a breath. *Think about something else… something happy…*

His mind settled on the Eoans, which wasn't necessarily a happy topic but certainly a less terrifying one than Tioris and Chozen. The Eoans said they created the universe, but they hadn't really explained it, and Filion hadn't really understood. Now, within a matter of minutes, this Living Document had challenged his entire perception of reality, truth and fact. What he had believed, what he had known – all of it was wrong. If he had been a religious man, he might have cried. The Eoans were their Gods, yet Filion had never even heard of them. He had Gods, tangible Gods, who had spoken to him, who had chosen him, and he had been too dumb to realize it.

"They're Gods…" Filion whispered.

There was a pause.

Who? The Living Document asked.

"The Eoans…" Filion said, picking up his pencil.

I guess they are, technically. Though they don't really act like gods.

What do you mean? Filion wrote.

Well, according to most religions, a god, or gods, have a stake in what's going on in the universe. The Eoans don't. They essentially abandoned us, with the exception of the Chozen. One thing that makes an Eoan an Eoan, and not an Afortiori, is the fact that Eoans have never wanted to be worshiped. Once we became self-aware, the Eoans wanted out. The Afortiori, on the other hand, have always wanted control. If the Eoans are gods, so are the Afortiori, and the Afortiori act like gods. Vengeful gods, but gods nonetheless.

"Tioris are gods. They're actually gods…" Filion whispered again. "I always just assumed they were a band of anti-Federation rebels."

Well, that's what everyone who doesn't know the truth thinks.

Filion didn't respond. Finally the Living Document said.

Forget what you think you know about 'gods'. Yes, the Eoans and the Afortiori created you, but the Eoans fought for your autonomy, and they won. Your gods, the stronger of your gods, want the universe to be free. Just because the Afortiori helped create you means nothing. They lost, and what they are doing is wrong. It needs to be stopped, or we all die, or worse.

Which is why the Eoans created the Chozen? Filion wrote.

Yes. The Chozen were the Eoans' hands off answer to saving our universe.

So, Chozen aren't just more powerful Tioris? Filion wrote slowly.

No, The Living Document said. *They are here to help us, not enslave us. Have you not been listening? They are our last hope.*

Filion took a deep breath. *So, the Chozen can't turn against us, like the Tioris did?*

The Living Document bristled. *No,* it finally wrote. *If you only listen to one thing I say, hear this: They were created to save us. They are our last and only hope.*

Filion was embarrassed. Finally he wrote,

So, why haven't they saved us?

Chozen are imperfect.

What do you mean, imperfect?

Chozen, in theory, are stronger than the Eoan and Afortiori, but the amount of time it takes a Chozen to mature is much longer than the Eoans originally expected. A Chozen can die and be reborn for centuries without ever knowing it is a Chozen. This immature phase gives the Afortiori plenty of time to hunt and kill, permanently kill, the Chozen. You don't think that their attacks are random do you? All Chozen give off a specific energy signature that is impossible to detect unless you are an Afortiori, an Eoan, or a Chozen yourself. As an immature Chozen begins to metamorphose into its mature state, its energy signature becomes stronger. The Afortiori target planets they believe harbor Chozen. Once they find a Chozen...

Filion waited for the Living Document to finish his thought. When the Living Document didn't Filion wrote,

If Chozen are immortal, how can the Tioris kill them?

Immortal is an imperfect word, as is kill. When a mature Chozen dies, its consciousness is preserved in the used body until a new body is generated. In theory, this should occur within a short time, as in a few hours after death. When a Chozen's body is killed, the Afortiori have no way of stopping this cycle. When an Afortiori permanently kills a Chozen, it is not its immortality that they kill, but its consciousness – its Eoan knowledge. The Afortiori Erase that knowledge. They essentially reprogram the Chozen so that each time it dies, the knowledge of its life is erased. Without the knowledge of its previous lives, and more importantly, without its Eoan knowledge, a Chozen is just like anyone else, powerless against the Afortiori. Not only that, but when an Erased Chozen dies, it cannot generate a new body. Instead, it is reborn as an infant, as it would have been before it matured, or, as any normal person would be. There are thousands of former Chozen, dying and being reborn across the universe, all of whom mature into the same sentient being they had been in their previous lives, and all of whom have no idea they've been

*reincarnated for generations. They will never know that they are 'immortal',
so they might as well not be.*

How do they do it? Erase the knowledge?

Again, the Living Document paused. Finally it wrote,

*I don't wish to speak of it. I will tell you that it is painful. After the process
is done, the Chozen is made a slave to whatever Afortiori led the Erasing.
The Chozen will know for the rest of its life that something very important
was taken from it, but it will never know what. Most go mad.*

Filion wanted to change the subject.

*You said that a Chozen should, in theory, regenerate a body after they're
killed. What do you mean in theory? Shouldn't you know?* Filion asked.

If a book could sigh, the Living Document did.

*I say in theory because no mature Chozen has ever been killed and
regenerated. We don't know if the regeneration even works. If it does, we
don't know if the Chozen's last body is replicated, or an entirely new body is
created. She is one of the last. We know of no other Chozen who have yet to,
or who have, successfully matured.*

*The Tioris have killed all of the Chozen but her? I thought you said there
were thousands of Chozen?* Filion wrote.

There were. Which is why what we are doing is so important.

Filion took a breath. The more he learned the more stressed he became.

*Why did the Eoans wait until now to act? The Tioris must have been at
this a long time. The Eoans had to have known that the Chozen were being
wiped out. Why wait so long?* Filion penciled.

They were conflicted as to whether or not they should intervene, the
Living Document wrote.

So why don't they just make more Chozen?

*Because that is not how they work. They gave us our chance. We aren't
going to get a second one.*

Filion let out a huff. That was the worst excuse he had ever heard. He took
a few deep breaths then wrote,

You said 'we' didn't know of any others, who is we?

The Eoans.

Are you an Eoan?!

*No, no. I am not, but I hold the knowledge of the Eoans. I am one of the
last of my kind as well. There is a reason why the first thing the Afortiori do
to a newly conquered planet is burn all of its books. My kind, we were the
keepers of the truth. We were to accompany each Chozen, to give them the
knowledge they needed as they metamorphosed from normal to
extraordinary. A Chozen's metamorphosis leaves it very fragile. Its mind is
under intense pressure. Without the guidance of a Living Document, the
Chozen is left to uncover its purpose on its own. Such an endeavor can drive
the Chozen to madness. We need to find her soon. It is believed that the few
Chozen who did escape the wrath of the Afortiori went mad during their*

31

transformation without the guidance of their Living Document. Some of the universe's most powerful beings are probably locked away in hospital cells right now. What's worse is that we have no evidence that once a mad Chozen dies it is reborn with its Eoan knowledge. Once it dies, we fear it's lost. Whether a Chozen is Erased or goes mad, the Afortiori win.

Filion took another breath. *I don't understand. How did the Living Documents get separated from the Chozen? Didn't the Eoans realize that would happen when a Chozen died for the first time?* Filion wrote.

Originally, the Eoans expected the Chozen to realize their full potential in their first life. There was no contingency plan to keep a Living Document with a Chozen if it was reborn before it matured.

Well, what about after they mature? What if they died and are reborn on a different planet without their Living Document?

Again, in theory, that isn't supposed to happen. Once a Chozen dies its new body should be generated on the same planet, near where it was killed.

Can't that be dangerous? I mean what if a Chozen dies on a battlefield? Regenerating there might just kill it again.

Which is why, the Living Document wrote, *the Chozen may be regenerated near where it was killed.*

How?

I don't know. I didn't create them. Again, this is all theoretical.

Filion let out another huff.

We need to find her.

The Living Document gave off an aura of sadness. Muted blues and grays clouded its pages.

Neither said anything for some time. Finally Filion asked,

Do you have a name?

LD 10988x

Do you have a nickname?

Didrik

Didrik, I'm Filion.

Hi Filion

Do you know why we are going to Bok? I don't think she's there.

No, she isn't, but Bok can get us to her.

Where is she?

Handu.

Chapter 10

Yalki paced the palace corridor, if one could really call this a palace. A shambled two-story building with broken wooden floors, this had been the nicest edifice she had been able to find on such short notice, not that that was an excuse.

She reached the end of the corridor and stopped. To her right was a large double window. It offered her a view of Timum, the largest city on Handu, and unfortunately for her, her current home. The city, built of faded and cracked wooden buildings, sprawled over miles of barren dirt. Devoid of plant life, everything in the city was colored some shade of yellow or brown and nothing was new or in good condition. She let out a huff. What a wretched city, what a wretched planet. Backwards and hot, this miserable speck of rock wasn't worth conquering, other than for the obvious reason.

Yalki put her hands on the windowsill and took a deep breath. The yellow air was dry and dusty, no doubt compounded by the grime rising from the unsprayed streets below her. She watched a cart full of withered vegetables pulled by a sickly ungulate move towards the trading district. The cart owner mirrored his mule, his skin wrinkled and loose, and his head down in the hot suns. Suns! Why did this planet have to have two suns? It wasn't even mid morning and she was sweating. No wonder this city and these people were so far behind.

Yalki knew that Timum hadn't always been this way. In fact, Timum hadn't always *been* at all. The city had been built on land that had once been a forest, which meant the Timumians had once been forest people. The forest had provided everything they had needed, *including*, she thought, *shade*, but the Timumians had been discovered. Over a century ago, a Federation business team had landed on Handu and uncovered its unique wood. Bright and multicolored, the wood was the perfect material to build luxury furniture. A naturally magenta wooden armoire? A forest green dining table? Yes please, the demand was there. The business team had convinced the Timumians to build Timum, a mill town, and mill the planet's wood for interstellar trade.

Stupid people.

They let foreign business people negotiate their trade terms, and now look at them – sunburned, poor and unhappy. Their once grand and brightly colored city was now sun bleached and dying, as were they. Their cutting had been unsustainable. The mills had poisoned the soil and the nearby sea. Timumian's crops and the surrounding forest died. The sea became brackish and dead. The Timumian people cut the forest further and further from town until Unifree stepped in and preserved ninety percent of Handu's forests, protecting them from the unsustainable harvesting. Unifree's conservation halted all economic growth in Timum. Timum would have no industry until the forest grew back, and that couldn't happen until the soil was remediated, but the soil couldn't be cleaned until the sea was purified. None of this would happen though, until some outside financial source took an interest in Timum's plight. Unfortunately, no one would because another 'Handu' had been discovered, another planet with beautiful technicolored wood. Buyers didn't care if Timum had no industry. They could get their psychedelic wood elsewhere, and with Yalki on Handu, buyers had the perfect excuse not to help Timum – it wasn't safe.

The Timumians were stuck. Their city and people were dying, and they couldn't go back to the forest because they had forgotten how to live there. It never ceased to amaze Yalki how people of this universe could fail to see the big picture. There was a reason these people shouldn't be free. The Timumians had done this to themselves, and they knew it. Their lack of morale had made it easy to conquer the city. She hoped the rest of the planet was as downtrodden and exploited. From her readings though, she didn't have much to worry about. The planet seemed to be sparsely populated outside of Timum. She knew most of the planet's population had flocked to the city during its glory days. Still, she didn't hold the entire planet, which is why she only had one ally. Very unusual battle techniques indeed, but this was a unique situation.

Scrape.

Yalki heard the noise and turned. The ex-mayor of Timum stood behind her, holding a tray. This so called palace had belonged to her and her husband. Both were now Yalki's personal slaves.

"Would you like some more tea, my Goddess Yalki?" The once proud woman kneeled, holding up the battered tray laden with mismatched porcelain.

Yalki sneered, and lifted her fist to knock the tray from the idiot woman's hands. She stopped herself before bringing her arm down. The woman *was* doing what Yalki wanted. Perhaps more importantly than that, the porcelain was the nicest this horrible rock had to offer. Yalki certainly didn't want to drink from anything worse.

"No. Leave me. Tell the rest of the servants I am not to be disturbed until supper."

The former mayor looked hurt. She continued to kneel, the tray suspended in air, a dumb look on her pretty face.

"Go!" Yalki roared.

Startled, the woman leapt to her feet and scampered down the hallway.

Yalki resumed pacing. She was sure that the Chozen was here. It had to be. She had felt its energy in her bones. It had been some time since she had felt such energy, but she knew it when she felt it. There was a Chozen on this planet.

The other Afortiori hadn't believed her. "We've destroyed all of the remaining Chozen." "The universe is as good as conquered," and blah, blah, blah. But none of this stopped the stories. Her fellow Afortiori denied the existence of another Chozen, yet they would recount occurrences that could only happen if a Chozen were involved. She listened to stories of battles fought, storms weathered, and the mundane turned extraordinary, and always the Afortiori telling the story would miss a breath. Their eyes would dart, they would fiddle with their hands, pull at their clothes or mess with their hair. Something was not right, and they didn't want to admit it. They all knew what it was, but only Yalki would say it. There was still one out there. What scared them though wasn't that there was a Chozen somewhere out there, but rather, the *kind* of Chozen that was out there.

When the Eoans had created the Chozen, J-10, despite its capture, had been able to implant a few wrong thoughts into the creation process. What resulted was a delay in the Chozen's development, and an obvious energy spike during their maturation. The Eoans had believed these errors to be their own, never suspecting J-10 or the Afortiori. These two 'errors' had allowed the Afortiori to easily and systematically wipe out the Chozen, planet by planet.

No new invention is without flaws, however. The Eoans *and* the Afortiori made mistakes when creating the Chozen. While J-10 had managed to poison the majority of the Chozen, an unexpected mutation had occurred. While it was difficult to pinpoint the exact nature and location of the mutation, it was thought that at least one, if not more, of the Chozen had been given superpowers. Supposedly, these powers were beyond those of a normal Chozen, Eoan, or Afortiori. Known only in myths as Etulosba, such Chozen were feared by Afortiori above anything else, which is why the Afortiori would not admit their existence. The Afortiori knew that if anything could destroy them, it was an Etulosba. What such an Etulosba could do exactly was unknown, since theoretically a regular Chozen could do anything. Campfire stories suggested an Etulosba would be a quick and powerful learner. The time it took an Etulosba to learn the most difficult tasks would be only a fraction of the time it took the most gifted Afortiori or Eoan. The Etulosba would be able to create and destroy in a way neither the Eoans nor Afortiori could. In theory, the Etulosba would be able to rewrite the universe's code.

Yalki feared she was dealing with an Etulosba now.

Her proof was limited, tenuous at best, but that didn't make her feel any better. This Chozen's energy signature was not the same as the others she had dealt with. Its energy, rather than appearing weak, seemed masked. As a result, it was very difficult to pinpoint where it was. Yalki had been lucky to be flying near Handu when the energy signature had flashed. Perhaps the Chozen was coming into its own, or perhaps it had been a fluke, maybe a moment of extreme emotion in an otherwise normal life. Whatever had happened, Yalki had taken the planet by storm. Not the usual Afortiori approach, but Yalki knew that such an opportunity might never come again. Such pure luck and coincidence was not to be ignored. She couldn't waste time by slowly capturing the planet. That could take generations. She and the rest of the Afortiori didn't have that kind of time, not that her fellow Afortiori would admit it. Yalki knew that they just didn't want to face the truth. They would rather live in ignorance and hope, than take action and face the Etulosba that they had created by their own hand. As a result, only one Afortiori now rendered aid in her attempt to subjugate the planet, the rest claiming they didn't like the obvious way in which she waged war. Her one ally was as scared as she.

She looked out of the battered glass window. She had only sensed its energy once in four days. Such a big planet, and she had so little support. She had sent slaves in every direction in hopes they would find something, but she knew they would come back with nothing, if they came back at all. Even the biggest, dumbest, and meanest of goons was no match for what might be out there. A feeble attempt, but she had to do something, anything.

It was out there, somewhere, but she might as well be blind.

Chapter 11

Handu!? She's on Handu?! How are we supposed to get to her?

That's why we are going to Bok. Didrik responded.

Tioris have invaded Handu. The news says we can't get there.

No, they say we shouldn't *go there, which is why we are going to Bok first.*

What's on Bok?

You'll see.

Filion sat back. He wanted to ask more, but Didrik's aura suggested that he wasn't going to be helpful. He looked out of the window. They had left Thog's atmosphere. Stars speckled the inky sky. According to Filion's pocket watch, they still had over ten hours to travel. He was tired. He normally slept until at least 9:00 am, the early morning being one of the best times to dream. Filion grabbed the bag of gold and the orb and stuffed them into his pocket. He thought about adding Didrik, but didn't know if Didrik would prefer to stay on the desk. Not wanting to ask him, Filion left him and clicked the conversion button on his chair. The chair banged and flattened. He lay down, barely closing his eyes before he fell asleep.

*****

Filion awoke as his head smashed into the wall. A tinny voice came from overhead.

We are about to begin our descent into Bok's atmosphere. Please return your seats to their upright position. It appears two storms have converged on our alpha landing pad, so we will be rerouting to our beta pad. It will be at least an hour, if not more, before we land.

Filion's fellow passengers let out a loud collective groan, and another sharp bump rocked the ship. The tinny voice continued to speak in a dialect with which Filion was unfamiliar. He wondered why they entered Bok's atmosphere at all if they were just going to cruise further around the planet. He shook his head as he hit the conversion button.

Filion glanced at Didrik. He still lay open on the desk. His aura suggested he was sleeping. Filion gently picked him up, a jolt of yellow shot through the aura.

"It's okay, it's me," Filion said quietly.

Oh, Didrik responded.

The alpha landing site is blocked by storms. It looks like we're going to be here for a while, Filion wrote.

Hmmmm.

What do we do when we land? Filion asked.

We find her.

I thought she wasn't on Bok.
Not her, Amalia. Didrik responded as if he was talking to a child.
Amalia? Who's that?
The Portal Keeper.

*****

Four hours later the ship touched down. Filion gathered his bag and Didrik, and waited with the rest of the passengers to exit the ship. He stared out of the windows. Thick, horizontal rain streaked their glass. He could barely make out the floating bubbles that carried the first class passengers to the beta terminus. It looked miserable out there. He hoped that wherever this Amalia was, she was indoors.

As it neared his turn to exit, he was able to see through the open door. He had heard that Bok was a rainy planet, and that was confirmed now that he was here, but that was all he knew. He peered into the cold outside and saw a high metal fence surrounding the concrete landing pads. Beyond the fence were thick, huge plants – a jungle.

Cra-Ra!

Filion took a step back. *What was that?* He squinted at the plants beyond the fence. The tops of the several story high trees swayed and kicked. Then a head appeared. Thick and shaggy with orange eyes, the creature was as tall as the trees, if not taller.

"Mom! Look! A gatilion!"

Filion looked towards the voice. A young girl stood holding her mom's hand, smiling, and pointing at the creature.

"So it is honey, let's go. It's our turn."

Filion watched as they stepped up to the exit, then he re-focused on the creature – the gatilion – but it was gone. He shivered. The girl and her mother stepped from the ship. He moved to the open door.

The rain whipped at his face and clothes. The door scanned him and then told him to proceed. He took a deep breath. This part always scared him. What if the bubble didn't form and he crashed straight into the ground? Without thinking, he glanced at the ground. It was at least thirty feet below him. The passenger behind him said something and another chimed in.

"Let's go buddy! I ain't got all day!"

Filion took another breath and stepped into the open air.

As it was designed to, the bubble formed and floated him without any problem. He did not plummet to the cold ground but instead drifted, warm and dry, through the monsoon and towards the ship terminus.

Filion reached the terminus three minutes later. As the bubble slid into the landing area, the bubble attendant approached him. Small, blue and strong, the woman had no trouble pushing him and his bubble into the deactivation area. Once the bubble was scanned, it popped, leaving Filion feeling heavy. The attendant stood, looking expectantly at Filion, and he dug into his pocket. Reluctantly, he pulled out the bag of gold. He opened it knowing that

38

a single piece was worth 100 times more than what he should tip her, but he pulled out a coin anyway.

In his hand sat a small copper mark, the perfect amount for a proper tip. He looked at it, confused, and opened the bag further. Inside were only copper pieces. He stood dumbfounded.

"Kali shha. Gitia!" The woman said.

Filion looked up. She waved at the next incoming bubble. He blinked and handed her the mark, and she smiled and nodded. Filion scurried from the landing area.

From his bubble, Filion had been able to make out the terminus as a one story sprawling building. The design had appeared old, but the rain had prevented him from making a conclusive judgment. As Filion walked down the hallway to the terminus, he was able to conclude that the building had indeed been built several decades ago. The walls, thin and cheap, were made from polyhurdin, a material that broke down in UV light. The floor, made mostly of cracking tiles, was dirt in some spots, and the lights were dim, some flickering or dead all together. To top it all off, the entire building seemed to flex with the wind.

As Filion rounded the final corner of the hallway, a wave of roaring voices washed over him. He resisted the urge to clamp his hands over his ears. The babble of voices and announcements were a mixture of Fedlang and whatever other languages were native to Bok. Filion understood several languages, but none of those seemed to be spoken here, other than Fedlang of course.

After the Federation formed, they began to standardize everything they could on all Fed planets, including time measurement and language. Fed time was a time and calendar system based off of the natural cycles of Moneta. Most Federation planets had adopted Fed time without much dispute. The Federation required all Fed planets to conduct all interplanetary business via Fed time, but the Federation permitted their planets to continue to celebrate their native holidays and religious ceremonies according to their native calendars.

Fedlang, however, the standard language that was to be used on all Federation planets, didn't go over as well as Fed time. Some planets rejected Fedlang on the basis that losing their native languages would distance younger generations from their heritage and ancestors. Perhaps the biggest problem with Fedlang though, was the amount of time and resources it took to introduce Fedlang effectively. Each planet was responsible for teaching Fedlang to its inhabitants. This was expensive, no matter how it was taught or downloaded.

Some of the wealthier planets were able to use Brain Bridge technology to download the language directly into their inhabitant's brains. Most planets, however, could not afford Brain Bridge technology, so a majority of Fed planets taught Fedlang in their schools. This presented another problem though, as on some Fed planets, education was only available to the upper class. As a result, those who were poor, or dropped out of school, usually had a weak understanding of Fedlang. A good indicator of the state of a planet's education system was its spoken rate of Fedlang. From that number, other conclusions about a planet could be extrapolated. Things like a planet's economic state to its civil liberties were directly tied to its inhabitant's use of Fedlang. From what Filion had observed, after being on Bok for an entire five minutes, Bok was not one of the Federation's most productive or advanced planets.

Filion reached the entryway to the terminus. Hundreds of people and hundreds of auras flooded his view. There was a reason Filion never really left his quarters on Thog! He stumbled through the crowd of people, bombarded by colors and feelings. A man hawking shoes in a make shift booth screamed over the crowd, but it wasn't his voice that upset Filion, it was his aura. He was a bad man, and his dark aura was so strong it seemed to swallow out everything around him. Filion shut his eyes and bumped into something. Raising one eyebrow, Filion found himself face to face with a male sticker. The lanky grey creature was dressed in enforcement clothing.

"Watch where you're going, lossal!" the sticker said, flexing his long, gaunt arms, and tapping his badge.

"Sorry," Filion said, spinning away from the guard.

He pushed his way through the mass of people. A bubbling group of racs suddenly filled the space in front of him. The two feet tall, green fuzzy creatures were all dressed in some sort of ceremonial outfit. They sang as they wound their way around Filion, some of them reaching out and touching his legs. Their auras flashed and bounced, oscillating between bright yellows and pinks, but they weren't dangerous. He stood immobilized until they passed. Once the racs were gone, he side skirted two arguing humans, both of whom were dressed in robes and in black face paint. He was becoming overwhelmed, and fast. Breathing hard, Filion stopped near an advertisement wall where a beautiful ringer seemed to be extolling the benefits of cosmetic wing surgery. He couldn't be sure of what she was saying. She spoke the same dialect as the bubble attendant, but he had seen such advertisements before. Filion stared at the digital ringer. He had always wondered what it would be like to be a ringer – a human with wings. Sometimes he wondered what it would be like to be just a human but being a ringer seemed like a much better deal.

"Functional and beautiful wings, an oxymoron, right? Wrong!"

Filion jumped. The advertisement had switched to Fedlang. The ringer smiled at him with perfect teeth. He stared at her for a moment longer, then picked up his bag and continued walking.

Nonchalantly, Filion pulled Didrik from his pocket and opened him, but didn't look at him. Casually, as if Filion were talking into an embedded communication chip, Filion said, "So what now?"

We need to find Amalia.

"I know that, how?"

We need to get to a town called Hifora.

"And?"

And what? That is what we need to do.

Filion groaned. "Okay," he said.

He put Didrik back into his coat pocket. They wound their way through the crowded terminus until Filion found an information booth. A tall skinny youth sat behind the counter.

"Excuse me," Filion said. "Um, could you please tell me how to get to Hifora?"

"Why would you want to go there?" The pimple faced attendant asked, his hat sliding over his eyes.

Filion hesitated. He had to lie. He was terrible at lying. Well, he was terrible at lying outside of the Tierameng. "Uh, *want* is the wrong word. I have a drunkard brother-in-law out there who needs his stars realigned. He beats my sister, and it's about to stop. The sooner you tell me how to get there, the sooner I can leave."

The attendant shifted uncomfortably. He pushed the hat out of his eyes and adjusted his badly sheered hair. His uniform was too big, and it exaggerated his awkwardness. "A lossal? In Hifora? You sure she's still alive?"

Filion looked at him sharply. "As far as I know she is. Why wouldn't she be?"

The attendant looked away quickly, his hat sliding over his eyes again. "Ahh, no reason other than her husband, you know?" He pushed the hat back into place and spun around and opened a drawer. "Do you mind paper? We haven't really gotten around to updating our systems. Can you read paper?" He spoke quickly.

"Sure, give me what you've got."

The attendant fumbled with something for a moment then turned to reface Filion. Filion noticed his nametag. Salin.

"Now, don't worry, the paper's waterproof and rip proof. I've highlighted the route to Hifora for you. There are two ways to get there, other than walking, and that would take days, and you probably wouldn't make it." Salin stopped as if he'd swallowed a bug. He preemptively pushed his hat to the top of this head. "Ahhh, you know, the gatilions are mating, it's dangerous to be out there... Anyway, you can catch the local shuttle to Diana," he recovered, pointing to a dot labeled Diana. "And then take the bus to Hifora, or you can hire a private ship to take you straight to Hifora."

Filion looked at the map trying to gauge distances. Salin continued talking.

"I know, I know, busses went out of style on most Federation planets centuries ago, but we still use them here." Salin brightened. "You know though, according to research they're technically safer than a shuttle. Unfortunately, the bus that goes to Hifora from Diana only runs once a week. It left this morning at 8:00, so you'll have to wait until next week to get there."

Filion harrumphed into his mustaches. He couldn't wait that long.

"How much does a private ship cost?"

"Uh, let's see, a ship to Hifora will cost…" Salin punched numbers into his keyboard.

"100 silver, 75 if the silver is Federation marked."

Filion's eyes widened. He looked at the map again. Hifora was half way across the planet.

"I know. It's expensive right? The shuttle to Diana would cost…" Salin started, entering more numbers into his computer.

Filion cut him off. "And the ship would be private?"

"Yeah that's the price for your own ship."

"How long would it take?"

"Ahh, not more than half a day, if the weather holds." Salin looked towards the rain-streaked window. "Yeah, with weather this good it shouldn't take more than half a day."

Filion couldn't believe his luck. Chartering a private ship to fly half way around the planet would have cost a fortune on Thog. 100 silver was nothing. He pulled the bag from his pocket and glanced inside. The pieces had changed from copper to silver, and they were Federation marked. He smiled.

"Where do I go to hire a private ship?"

Salin studied him.

"Ahhhhhh," Salin paused. Finally he said, "Go down that hallway to your left, and you'll see the private for hire booth. There should be some pilots there."

"Thanks," Filion said, picking up his bag.

"Uh, sir?"

"Yes?" Filion said.

"Be careful, some of those pilots are less than, well, honest, you know? Make sure you don't pay full upfront."

Filion smiled. "Thank you Salin."

Salin nodded but didn't say anything.

Chapter 12

Ryo awoke. Her fire had gone out, but she wasn't cold. She didn't know how long she had slept, but it seemed to be mid morning. The air was warm and bright, and if it hadn't been for the trees Ryo guessed that the air would have been hot – stifling in fact – but it wasn't. Through the kaleidoscopic canopy she could see two suns, one a far dot, and the other much closer.

She sat up, once again hearing the sounds of the forest – chattering birds, swaying leaves – it was peaceful. She stretched, expecting to feel sore. The hard ground hadn't exactly been comfortable, but she felt fine, not fine, but good, great even. Her knees didn't ache, her legs felt strong and refreshed – her back, her hips, everything – everything felt great.

She did a final stretch and stood, and then sat back down, not knowing what she was doing or where she was going. She thought, and it all came back to her. Not that she had forgotten the events of the previous day, but they had been pushed into a far alcove of her mind – the man, her 'powers', and the memories... She wanted to vomit.

With the nausea came a sudden panic, and the forest seemed too still. Someone was watching her, someone very bad, evil even. She had memories of similar feelings. This was not a feeling to ignore. She sprang to her feet and scanned the area, simultaneously moving away from the cold fire. She moved with surprising speed and stealth. Satisfied with her distance from the fire, Ryo temporarily dropped behind a dead tree. She had seen no one. The feeling was less severe now but still there. Whoever they were, she had temporarily confused them.

Chapter 13

Yalki sat at the rickety table in the dining room, annoyed she was in this dump. The room was pitiful, though astonishingly, not by Timum standards. With no adornment other than the wretched table and hard chairs, the room reminded Yalki of a prison cell. Its wooden floors and walls had faded, and there was nothing, other than Yalki herself, worth looking at in the room, especially not the meal before her.

The ex-mayor and her husband stood before Yalki. They had just finished serving Yalki breakfast, and their faces betrayed their need for praise. All of the food was inferior compared to even the lowest of Yalki's standards, and this only added to her sour mood. Yalki picked through the limp vegetables and soggy breakfast cakes. She didn't care if Timum was starving. She was their God, she deserved better. Shoving the food away, she stood up, the ex-mayor and her husband scrambling to their knees. They were like dogs.

"Your food disgusts me. I will not eat until you prepare me proper food."

The woman looked as if she were going to cry. "Goddess Yalki, we are sorry we have failed. Please give us another chance to prove ourselves," the ex-mayor stammered.

Yalki was about to respond when it flashed in her brain, like a volcanic explosion, the Chozen's energy signature was visible. Yalki stood, frozen. Her brain reeled. Where was it? It was definitely on this planet; the signal was so powerful. Yalki couldn't be sure if the signal's strength was because the Chozen was either very close or very strong. She swallowed as the third possibility hit her, but right now it didn't matter. She had to find it.

Chapter 14

Ryo knew that running blindly could easily kill her. A less trained person might have kept moving away from the fire without taking the necessary time to center herself, but Ryo knew better. She took a moment to breathe and think.

A less trained person... trained in what?

A memory surfaced.

She was some sort of cadet. Dressed in a shapeless tan uniform, she was training, training to fight, to kill, and to win. She had to pass a breath control test. The test was simple. She had to inhale for 8 seconds, hold her breath for 8 seconds, exhale for 8 seconds, and then hold her breath again for 8 seconds. She had to repeat this for at least 8 cycles, and for every cycle over 8 her score improved.

Breath control...

"Breath control calms a warrior and forces him or her to act out of logic and reason, rather than emotion."

The clarity of the memory startled her. Major Teller. She had been Ryo's instructor at one point. When, or where, or why Ryo didn't know, but Major Teller had been one of the best.

Ryo inhaled 1... 2... 3... 4... 5... 6... 7... 8. Hold 1... 2... 3... 4... The world seemed to melt away, her fears melting with it. She completed the first cycle, and started a second, then a third, and a fourth.

Chapter 15

Springing into motion, Yalki pushed past the slaves and into the hall. *Harick!* She had to find Harick. He was staying in a makeshift palace, even more dilapidated than hers, closer to the center of town. Silently she cursed her body. The Afortiori had made vast improvements since their falling, but they still were weaker than they had once been. They could no longer create just by willing. They had to play by the rules of the universe. Luckily, since they had helped create the universe, they knew the rules, all of the rules, and they knew them very well. What most people thought was impossible or magical, was not. Those people simply did not know the rules.

She burst through the palace's front door, coughing on the dust from the street. The suns' heat hit her and she knew it wouldn't be long before she was drenched in sweat. Cursing, she shielded her eyes and scanned the dry, cracked road. No one was around. She didn't know what she expected to find. The Chozen certainly wouldn't be standing in front of her palace.

No! The energy signature was fading! Where was Harick?! Panicking, she searched for his signature. She felt it, faint, but readable, in the center of town. She had to get there.

NO! NO! NO! It was gone. The Chozen's signature had faded completely. She cursed again. If they had just lost their only chance, she would kill him. She had killed for less.

Chapter 16

Ryo opened her eyes. The sunlight was more direct now, and the air was growing hot. She glanced around. She sat behind some sort of dead tree, its dry bark purple and split. Why had she moved here? She thought back. The feeling, the feeling had made her move. Lazily, she looked around. She sensed no one watching her. A small thought tugged at the back of her brain. *Fear*. It seemed so far away, yet she considered it.

The moment she opened her mind to the fear, the panic returned. Ryo sat up, as if electrocuted. The transition had been so sudden. She had been so calm and then that calm was gone, shattered like a broken glass. Not only that, but the feeling that she was being watched was back. She jumped up and moved further from the fire. Again, the feeling dissipated, but only slightly.

Inhale 1… 2… 3… 4… 5… 6… 7… 8. Hold 1… 2… 3… 4… 5… 6… 7… 8. She dove back into her breathing exercises, and continued them for eight cycles.

Chapter 17

Fuming, Yalki visualized the spot she always used when she went to town – a small empty fruit stand that no one dared enter. When she and Harick had first come to town, they had made clear to the town's people that the fruit stand was cursed. To enter it was to damn oneself. It was clear that, initially, some of the town's people were a bit skeptical of the veracity of such a claim. After they watched the fruit stand's owner seemingly spontaneously combust, they were more convinced. No one went near the fruit stand.

Yalki gathered her silken robes and thought. The most important thing about Jumping was making sure that *all* of you made it there. If only a single molecule was left behind, you could be killed. She had known Afortiori who had been distracted (or lazy) when attempting to Jump. Those who survived were never the same again. She closed her eyes and emptied her mind. The anger slid from her body. She took a deep breath and focused.

As she reached the apex of the breath, she began to spin. Slowly at first, then faster and faster until she could feel her body tearing apart. Bit by bit her molecules broke free of each other, and were swept into the whirlwind that was the Jump. Parts of her arms whipped by her eyes, she could feel a toe nail crash into a fragment of her shin. She kept focused though. *Keep the pain out. Keep the destination in mind. Don't lose a single molecule.* Her life depended on it. She strengthened her focus and the flash of energy came. She opened her eyes.

She was in the fruit stand. She smiled. Not only had she made it, but the fruit stand was also in the shade. How she hated the heat! Taking a breath she looked into the street. It was packed with peddlers, although the adjacent stands been abandoned. Men and women, mostly dark skinned humans, called out their wares. Nothing they sold was worth anything and there seemed to be more peddlers than shoppers, but that didn't discourage any of the hawkers. A woman cried that she had bolts of colored foreign silk. The man next to her claimed he had fresh cloudplums. Yalki knew both were lying.

She stepped from the fruit stand and stopped, her heart missing a beat. The Chozen's energy signature was back, and it was stronger this time. She probed it, attempting to determine its location. She had to reach Harick.

No one seemed to be watching her, but she didn't doubt that every person on the street knew she was there. She had to look Godly, despite the intense concentration required to locate the Chozen and Harick.

She strode from the fruit stand with a feigned grace that could have fooled a king. While she hated to walk, preferring to float, she couldn't float and locate the Chozen and Harick at the same time. This was Harick's fault. If she hadn't needed him so much, she would have killed him when she found him. Oh, how she hated walking!

She moved through the street. The sea of people parting around her, leaving her way unmarred, if she didn't count the sickening feeling she got when she came so close to slaves. She resisted the urge to run. The Chozen's signature was fading, again.

The signature disappeared as she reached the end of the street. A festering anger took its place. She was no closer to finding its location! Angrily, she concentrated on Harick's signature. Maybe she would kill him. She didn't need him *that* much. His signature drew her to a dingy shack off of the main road. His energy was vibrant. Yalki shook her head. Harick was a good general, but that was all. He was weak, too drawn to the excesses of a physical life. He often put his own physical gratification before the achievement of his mission goals. His indiscretions were normally tolerable, but this was unacceptable. The Chozen was alive and on the planet, and here he was wasting his time with some pretty slave. Yalki blew the door from its hinges. Inside a man screamed.

Yalki waited a moment before speaking.

"Harick! We have business to attend to. Dismiss your whore and get out here, NOW!" she growled.

For a moment Yalki heard nothing but sobbing and quick, panicked movement from inside the excuse for a structure. Then a tall dark skinned human stepped from the sagging building. Holding his shirt over his privates, the terrified man took one look at Yalki and ran down the street.

"Get out here!" Yalki yelled. She certainly wasn't going in there.

After an unacceptably long time, Harick emerged. Harick could be considered a handsome man, if you could get over his short, bowlegged stature. At 4'11" Harick was one of the smallest human Afortiori, male or female, in the universe. When the Afortiori had escaped through J-10's portal, they had had very little time to find a suitable body to subsist in. The Afortiori who had been unable to take a host within the first several minutes of entering this universe had died. Apparently, in this universe, they could not exist in their natural form. Harick had taken the only body he could find, an incredibly short human man who had a good jawline but was so bowlegged you could set him on a horse and he still would have appeared bowlegged.

"Yalki, you're a real bitch, you know that?" Harick stepped onto the street, still dressing.

"While you were busy dicking your time away, the Chozen showed itself. Twice," she barked, resisting the urge to injure him.

Harick looked up from his belt. "What?"

"That's right, this morning I felt it. Once in my palace, and the other as I tried to locate you." She struggled to keep her anger under control. Her

49

voice wavered with heat, and her fingers twitched. Harick did not look at her.

"It's here and either very close or very strong, maybe both. I can't believe you didn't feel it," she added, knowing he had been too engrossed in other things to do his job. "The second signature disappeared just a moment ago, but I have never been more sure of anything in my life."

Harick didn't say anything. He finished with his belt and bent down to tie his boots. After a few moments he stood.

"Then we had better get started," he said.

Chapter 18

When Ryo opened her eyes for the second time, the feeling of being watched was once again gone. Carefully, she considered what was happening. She could neither see nor hear anyone. The only indication that someone was watching her was that feeling, that internal fear. Nothing about her physical surroundings suggested someone watching her. It was as if it was all in her head. What if it was?

She closed her eyes, turned inward, and considered her mind.

She saw herself sitting in the forest, its brightly colored trees swaying in the breeze. Then, suddenly, the forest blurred as if it were being sucked away. Its reds, blues, purples, and yellows smeared into a roaring streak of color and then BAM! The forest was gone. She now floated, suspended in space. Infinite nothingness surrounded her. She had made it. She was inside her mind. With a single thought she could be anywhere her brain had ever been. She thought about the fire she had made. Instantly it was there, burning hot and flickering orange. The thought process that she had used to create it was suspended beside it, visually as if she were reading a book.

She pushed that away. She needed to find the fear. She felt it, instantly, tugging at her, but it was distant. She was afraid of the fear. She didn't want to think about it, and something told her she shouldn't.

Maybe she could get at it indirectly. If this was her brain, there had to be some system of organization. The fear was somewhere, and more importantly, it was next to something. She concentrated on what was next to the fear.

Memories – hundreds of them.

At first Ryo thought they just bordered the fear, then she understood – they imprisoned it. Snapshots of idyllic beaches, sun drenched mountains, and pristine lakes surrounded the fear. The fear's creeping, cold tentacles sucked at the memories' edges, but went no further. The memories formed a barricade, a weak and loose barricade, but a temporarily effective one nonetheless. Ryo poked at the memories. They shifted precariously, some even winking in and out of sight. What happened if these guarding thoughts weren't so calming? She browsed through them, stopping at one of her atop a tall mountain. What if it were to storm?

The mountain was easily the tallest thing she had ever stood upon. It towered over the surrounding peaks, and those peaks all stood well above tree line. She could see for miles in every direction. It seemed she could see to the end of the world. The cerulean sky was cloudless, the air – motionless, and the sun – warm. If she stood on her tiptoes, she might reach Heaven. She smiled. She had worked very hard to come here, but to stay too long would be wrong. This was a sacred place. Her time was up, but a few more seconds couldn't hurt.

She closed her eyes and took another long breath. The sun was so inviting, and the mountain so calming. She took another breath, and another. Finally, she opened her eyes and turned to descend, but something in the distance caught her attention.

Small fluffy white clouds appeared in the sky at the edges of her vision. She squinted. The clouds grew bigger. They multiplied. Goosebumps prickled her skin, and the air began to stir. A slight wind blew from the north, or was it the east? The clouds continued to expand. They moved towards her, no, they *raced* towards her. She spun. The graying clouds now engulfed her peak. The sun disappeared. The air grew cold. A distant crash of thunder sounded. Then the wind swelled, catching small rocks and throwing them at her. She looked up. Black clouds pressed in on her. The wind howled, and lightning struck a neighboring peak. It began to rain.

The fear poured from the clouds in fat, spiky droplets, drenching her in seconds. It stung every time a drop hit her. She writhed in pain, trying to avoid the cold beads. There was no shelter on the high mountaintop – nowhere to hide from the torrential downpour, the thunder, or the lightning. The fear soaked through her clothes and into her skin. She wanted to scream, but was too afraid. Lightning continued to crash. Her hair stood on end. She couldn't see. She sunk to the ground. She was going to die, here, on this remote summit on an unknown planet, *in her own mind.*

She was going to die in her own mind.

Chapter 19

Yalki stared at Harick. He believed her, and his sudden acceptance of the truth was virtually an apology. For a moment the anger dulled, then it resurfaced. Two chances to locate it wasted! What if they didn't get a third? She watched him finish straightening his clothes when... BAM! It was like being struck with lightning. Harick stumbled forward and Yalki swayed. This time they both felt it, the Chozen's energy signature. Neither said anything for several seconds, then finally Harick breathed, "You're right. It is either very strong or very close, maybe both. We need to get to the troops."

Yalki nodded, paralyzed by the intensity of the signature. This signature was stronger than the last, and much stronger than the first. She was afraid.

They hurried down the street, the pain making it impossible to travel by anything other than foot. Harick's troops were in the barren fields outside of town. Walking, it would take nearly half an hour to reach them.

Rat Eoans. Yalki thought as they dodged the carts and slaves that cluttered the streets. Here she was, her head pounding, and having to run (as best she could), not float, not Jump, but run, and so close to slaves. She hated them – the slaves, the Chozen, but most of all – the Eoans. If they ever figured out how to get back...

They reached the dead crop fields. Panting, Harick located one of his primes. "Rally the troops! Our objective is here!" He wheezed.

The prime's eyes widened. He made a short bow and then left hurriedly, his underlings scurrying to their stations.

Yalki and Harick staggered into his war tent. Yalki sat down unsteadily. The signature was so brilliant now. She felt as if her brain were being electrocuted from the inside out. It was all she could do not to scream. Harick seemed to be having no better of a time. His breathing was ragged, and he stumbled as he walked. He jerkily pulled a map from a shelf. Pausing for a moment, he stood, his face contorted and sweating.

"It is strong, not just close," Yalki stammered.

"Yes," Harick said as he shuffled to his map table. He put one foot on his stepping stool and tried to step up. He stopped, map halfway over the table. His eyes were on the map, but he did not see it. Yalki did not move. The pain was so great. She wanted to vomit.

She wanted to die.

Chapter 20

Crying, Ryo tried to take a deep breath. She choked on her snot and on the smoke from the surrounding lightning strikes. Sniffling, she tried again. This time she got a lungful of air. She inhaled again, and again, faster, and faster. The storm grew worse. The air sparked with cold, and her soaked body shivered desperately. She took another breath. This time she held it. She exhaled and held it again. She inhaled 1… 2… 3… 4… 5… 6… 7… 8.

The storm diminished. The rain thinned, and the clouds lightened. She kept counting and breathing. She didn't stop until the sun had dried her clothes. When she opened her eyes she was back in the forest, crouched behind a tree, completely dry and unharmed.

She relaxed and fell against the tree. The fear was distant but not gone, just like her watchers. She shut her eyes and continued her breathing cycles. She didn't think about the fear or what had just happened. Instead she thought about her lungs expanding, the air entering her mouth, and her blood filling with oxygen. She thought only of the physical implications of her own breathing.

Chapter 21

Yalki squeezed her eyes tight. The pain... it was incapacitating... then... then the signature began to fade. Yalki jumped from her chair. She had to locate it before the energy was gone, or worse, before it came back. Harick opened the map, his movements flustered and rushed.

Yalki concentrated, but the signature was disappearing so quickly and her brain was moving so slowly. She fought to do anything. She attempted the most basic of location techniques – to simply identify the direction of the Chozen – but her brain was numb. She couldn't even do that.

Chapter 22

After an undeterminably long time, Ryo opened her eyes. The fear and the feeling of being watched were gone, but with a quick probe, she knew those feelings would come back the moment she considered the fear. She focused on the barricade between her and her fear. It was like an old wire fence – wobbly and holey – effective but barely. She concentrated. Closing her eyes, she attempted to recall any calming thought that she could wrap her mind around. Ryo didn't care if the memories seemed like hers or someone else's. She wanted any calming moment she could remember.

A smiling woman with green skin handed her a silver necklace... She was on a boat with a woman, Ryo's head on the woman's chest. Ryo could hear her heart beat... Ryo stood with a young girl. The girl laughed... A man held Ryo's hand and squeezed... Ryo lay in green grass. Two women and three men lay near her, all of them quiet in the warm sun... A shaggy animal jumped on Ryo. It licked her face.

Ryo compiled all of the memories. She needed them to help her isolate the fear. She thought about the young girl, dressed in a yellow and pink sundress, and then she thought of the pre-storm mountain. The girl appeared on top of the mountain, still laughing. The girl took a step and was on a white beach, the sun dropping behind the sapphire water. Ryo turned from the girl and the man who had held her hand now stood in the sand. He smiled and took a step towards her. She stepped towards him and onto a dock. The two women and three men swam in the water below her. They motioned for her to join them. She jumped from the dock and landed on a soft bed. The furry animal lay curled up beside her.

She integrated the new memories into the barricade. She tested the newly fortified wall. It was stronger. The fear was there, but barely. She briefly considered the fear. It didn't come as quickly. The feeling of being watched came back, but slowly, as if it were wading through mud. She let the fear go, and it rocketed away. There was no one watching her. She stood up and walked back to the fire.

Reaching the spot where she had slept, she sat. What should she do now? Clearly someone or something wanted to find her, but she had no idea who or what they were. Then again, she had no idea who or what she was. Maybe she was the bad one in the equation. Maybe she should turn herself in but to whom?

She dismissed the idea. If whoever or whatever found her, she would suffer immeasurable pain, of that much she was sure. That fear had been unlike anything she could recall, even from all of her memories.

She sighed, what should she do?

She considered staying in the forest. *What was she going to do, spend the rest of her life in this forest? Lost on some unknown planet, living off the land, and hiding from her fear?* That sounded lonely. She kicked the fire apart, scattered the poisonous fruits, and then started walking.

Chapter 23

The energy disappeared completely. Harick slumped to the floor.

"It's gone," Yalki whispered, clutching a bookshelf.

"It's not gone. It's still here but hidden. Far worse," Harick said, his eyes shut. "You know what we're dealing with."

Yalki nodded but couldn't bring herself to speak the word. They were no longer dealing with theories and ghost stories. Their worst fears had just been realized. She looked out of the tent and past the troops.

An Etulosba was out there.

Chapter 24

Captain Eri looked at the figures for the fifth time. There was no denying it. They were in trouble. Their last job hadn't paid nearly as much as it should have. She couldn't believe that on the day she and her crew were to deliver a shipload of Bromils to the hospitals on Bok, the market had collapsed. They had gone through so much trouble to get them too, the prickly little plants. Until today, Bromils were thought to only grow on Cofky, something that should have worked in her favor. Supposedly used in heart surgeries, the light green plant's thorns were ground into some sort of paste, which helped keep the blood oxygenated despite a temporarily incapacitated heart. Who would have thought, that after all their planning and their mostly legal transport process, a wild Bromil garden would have been discovered on, wouldn't you know it, Bok?

Needless to say, their shipment of Bromils had grossed far less than she had needed it to.

Captain Eri leaned back in her chair, shifting her weight slightly to put less strain on her wings. *Horse feathers.* What was she going to do?

Captain Eri was Captain of the *Dark Horse*, a mostly legal transport ship. She and her crew, a human named Red, and now a vissy named Wiq, would take most jobs, regardless of the law, if Captain Eri saw fit. They didn't do the nasty stuff, killing, kidnapping, trafficking, etc., but smuggling... they were pretty good at smuggling. They were pretty good at honest jobs too, assuming the bloody market didn't collapse under them.

But here she was, on Bok, with barely enough coin to buy fuel, food and water for the crew. Forget paying them. She cursed under her breath. They had passed up a far more lucrative, albeit illegal, job for this Bromil job. So much for trying to do the right thing, like getting needed medical supplies to a rural planet.

Captain Eri spun in her chair. She sat on the bridge, a small compartment from where she not only piloted the ship but also came to think and go over the numbers. Someone she knew had to be in need of a job on or around Bok. She sat up and flipped on a second monitor, pulling up her contact list. Shady things happened on Bok, and she could make more shady things happen. After all, pelters were all over the planet, like a plague, not that she wanted to get mixed up in that. She had standards, but Bok didn't – a grey area for sure, but one that would ultimately work in her favor.

Idly she clicked through her contacts. She had quite a few from her old life. This whole smuggling/transport ship business was her second career, although the only real difference between what she did now and what she had done before was for whom she worked for and how much she got paid. Well, that and the extent of her illegal activities. When she had been a pilot for the Federation, she had made far more money and done far more illegal things. She allowed herself a small smile. It was funny how many people from her old life had contacted her for her services. Well, not funny exactly but ironic. Such high ranking people should have been straighter than that but then again, here she was.

The screen hummed in front of her. Randmal was on Tirious, two planets away, and no doubt he would have work for her. Then there was Granko on Reo, Hakil on Mannik, and Pavoc on Wast. She could get to all of these planets in a few days, and the likelihood of work was great. Captain Eri sighed. She had worked with all of these men and women while in the military. They had been her superiors and equals, and they had always found the letter of the law too binding. They took 'justice' into their own hands. "The end justifies the means, right Eri?" All she had had to do was nod and do what they asked. Not that it had mattered in the end...

"Cap'n?"

Captain Eri turned. Red stood in her doorway. A tall, well-built human, Red was her muscle, or had been until Wiq joined their crew. Well, that wasn't quite true. Red was imposing. He made a statement when he entered a room. With thick arms, a square jaw, tattoos and always a fare amount of weaponry on him, Red sent a message to those with whom Captain Eri dealt.

"Yeah, Red?"

"So, uh, I was doin' some math, you know, in my mind, and I'm comin' to the conclusion that we didn't get as much as we shoulda from that gig."

Captain Eri sighed.

"That's right, Red," she clicked the screen. "We got here one day late. They discovered a forest of Bromils on Bok. The market's gone... gone by *one* day."

Red squinted at the screen.

"You gotta be kiddin'. One day and we lose out on how much gold?!"

"I know, Red, I know. I've done the math myself. I'm trying to figure out what to do next."

"I know what we do," Red said straightening. "We go back and beat the crap outta our buyers until they give us what we was quoted."

Captain Eri shook her head. "We can't do that, and you know it. This was an honest job. We don't beat people up on honest jobs."

"Well, we could start," Red muttered.

"I've got some contacts, but who knows if they'll answer my messages. In the meantime, I think we should consider staking out the private for hire booth. We won't get much, but it'll be better than nothing."

"This is dog crap."

"I know. I'm going to send some messages, then get to the private for hire booth."

"You want me to come with you?" Red asked. "Those booths can have some rough crowds."

"Thanks, but no. I need to think, and I do that best alone."

Red looked at her, then pulled a knife and a small phazer from his pocket.

"At least go armed," he said.

"Thanks, Red," Captain Eri said, taking the weapons.

Chapter 25

Filion found the private for hire booth, although without Salin's directions he would have guessed it to be a bar. The inside of the booth was poorly lit and smoky. Distant music drifted through the thick air, the wavering song occasionally interrupted by a slurred voice. Filion looked through the gloom and saw several wobbly tables. Rough looking men surrounded them. Most of the men were playing cards and drinking, but some just sat and stared, their eyes burning through the haze. Chairs squeaked and bottles and coins rattled every time someone slapped down a card or thumped a table in victory. The men's auras hummed with violence. Filion took a deep breath and stepped inside. The room fell quiet. Even the music seemed to dim.

"Hello," Filion began. "Um, I'm looking for a pilot to take me to Hifora."

Someone laughed but quickly stifled it. No one moved.

"Uh, perhaps I've come to the wrong place..." Filion said, backing up.

"No, I don't think so."

A large okkar stood. Filion took another step backwards. Okkars made Filion uneasy. Okkars had originally been water dwelling beings. Then their planet was rendered toxic as a result of war. Most okkars eventually died from the effects of that war, but a small percentage of the original population mutated and evolved to live on land. What resulted was a particularly nasty set of facial gills and metallic scaly skin. Okkars stood at over seven feet and used their thick tails to balance. It wasn't the okkar's physical appearance that made Filion uneasy though; it was their demeanor. Filion suspected that it wasn't just the okkar's physical structure that had mutated during their rapid evolution, but their brains as well. He had never met a trustworthy okkar, and the okkar in front of him didn't look like he would be the one to dispel Filion's prejudice.

"What's it worth to ya?" The okkar said, his moist face close to Filion's. With every breath, the okkar's gills moved and gave off a heavy squishing sound.

Filion shuffled backwards. "I... I was quoted 100 silver, unless it was Federation marked, then the trip was to be 75 silver."

The okkar burst out laughing. "75 Fed sil? You crazy? Double that and you still ain't close to getting to Hifora."

Filion frowned. It was said that Dream Searchers were the best negotiators in the universe, but in Filion's opinion, such a statement gave Dream Searchers *way* too much credit. Sure, he was a master negotiator in the *Tierameng*, but live negotiations were another matter entirely. So far all of this Summoning had occurred when he was awake, not asleep. He again wondered why he had been given this particular Summoning. His face-to-face interactions typically went quite poorly, especially when he was intimidated, which was often. What had the Eoans been thinking? What had *he* been thinking?

"Hmmm, well that is what I was quoted by the Terminus. Are you not required to work for the price the Terminus sets?" Filion asked, filling himself with false confidence.

The okkar stared at Filion like a piece of meat. His beady eyes lingered on Filion's exposed fur. This made Filion uncomfortable.

"Grawlix the Terminus. You go for our asking price, or you don't go at all. Take the bus next week. Good luck not gettin' yourself killed on the journey. I hear the bus passengers ain't too keen on foreigners." There was a resounding chortle from the rest of the pilots.

Filion flushed. The money was no longer an issue. He didn't want to be alone with this okkar or anyone else in the booth, but he couldn't wait for the bus. What was he going to do?

"Leave him alone Ulin. You're spewing rocks and you know it."

Filion turned. A small woman stood behind him – a ringer, but something was wrong with her wings. The black feathers were misaligned and crinkled. Her wings looked as if they had been broken and had never healed correctly.

"Ahh, Captain Eri. You finally come to be my first mate?"

There was another booth-wide laugh. Someone from the back said, "First mate?! You ain't no virgin Ulin!"

The laughter continued.

Captain Eri ignored the group. "I'll take you to Hifora for the set price, 100 sil or 75 Fed sil."

Filion looked at her. She was dressed in clean, but well-worn clothes. They fit her form, but he wouldn't say they were particularly fashionable. No, they were functional.

"Ahh, yes. Thank you." Filion said.

"Ok, let's go." She walked out of the booth, the okkar staring at her coldly. There were several more inappropriate comments and more laughs. Filion hurried after her.

Captain Eri moved fast for someone with such short legs. They walked, twisting their way through the crowds, without stopping or slowing. It wasn't a particularly big terminus, but it still took them several minutes to reach the private hangar. Before they entered, Captain Eri turned.

"I'm Captain Eri. I'll be your captain. Payment please," she held out her hand.

Filion started to fish into his pocket and stopped. Salin had warned him not to pay in full up front, but compared to the men in the booth, Captain Eri was an angel. Still, she was a pilot…

"I'll pay half now, half when we land."

Captain Eri looked at him and smiled, "Not as dumb as you present. Deal."

He emptied 38 Federation Silver from his pouch into her hand. She counted it, pulled a scan card from her pocket, scanned it, and then nodded. "This way," she said.

The ships in the hangar were all older models. Many had modifications to their generators, shield systems and guns, at least from what Filion could tell. When he was a kid, he had been into ships, wanting to be a pilot. After he had discovered Dream Searching though, he'd never looked back, but that didn't mean he didn't remember a thing or two. He could tell these were not first class ships. Sure, the modifications spoke to this point, but so did the ships' disrepair. Scratched, patched, and splattered with paint, these ships were not elite. He actually saw a ship with a broken outer window in its airlock!

They stopped in front of a small Nisian Boulder. As with the other ships, Captain Eri, or someone, had modified the Boulder's generators, shield system and weapon systems. Made of dark seam welded metal, the hull of the ship was shaped like a teardrop, excluding the modifications and engines. While nothing too important seemed to be broken, Filion wasn't sure he wanted to take his chances.

"Here she is, the *Dark Horse*. Welcome."

Filion looked at the aging ship and took a deep breath. Captain Eri opened the cargo hatch and stepped inside. Filion followed.

Chapter 26

The inside of the ship was as modified as the outside. Normal Boulders were used to transport large amounts of heavy cargo between close planets. This meant that Boulders had a sublight drive but no hyperdrive, yet this Boulder had hyperspace straps throughout the cargo bay. It appeared someone had modified the ship to make the hyperspace jump, but Filion didn't think that was possible. When he had dreamed of becoming a pilot, such a change hadn't been deemed feasible, at least not for a reasonable cost. It would have been cheaper to buy a new ship with hyperspace capacity than to modify the Boulder's engines. He wondered what Captain Eri had done, and what she used this ship for.

In addition to the hyperspace straps, the open area where cargo was usually secured was crisscrossed with ramps and platforms. These were also addendums. There was still plenty of storage space in the ship, but the added partitions created more space for the crew. Filion did not doubt that Captain Eri and her crew lived on this ship.

"Our trip should only take 10 hours or so. I'll show you the common areas. I'll expect you to stay in them while you're on board unless you're told differently and accompanied by a member of our crew." Captain Eri said as she stepped onto one of the added ramps.

They ascended the ramp and entered one of the ship's original rooms – the kitchen. Attached to the kitchen was what appeared to be some type of lounge. Squat squish chairs (older models based on their cracked casings and rusty legs) and a few card tables filled the small space. A coin-sized music box sat on a shelf. No one was in the room.

"Do not eat any of our food. A single bite will cost you a Fed sil." She looked at him, "This is our food not yours."

Filion nodded. In space, food was guarded more closely than silver and water more closely than gold.

"I won't drink anything either."

She looked at him, a wry smile on her face. "I would like to see you try. I don't have the money to upgrade our locker security, but in order to access the ship's water supply you need a DNA scan and a pass code. Feel free to attempt to hack the system. Theoretically, it's unhackable. It might keep you busy though. If you get past the security, you can have some water, and I might give you a job too."

She turned and began for the door. The light caught her damaged wings. In the dim ship terminus, her wings had looked as if they had been broken and set incorrectly. Now Filion wondered if something else had happened, something worse. Withered and disfigured with patches of featherless skin, her wings almost looked as if someone had poured acid on them. Unnerved, Filion jerked his eyes away.

Captain Eri stopped, and Filion ran into her. He hadn't realized he had been following her.

"You stay here, remember? I have to run some preflight sims. I'll let you know when we're going to take off," she said, turning to face him.

Filion froze. Despite his four and a half foot height advantage, he felt small under her gaze. With dark purple eyes and flawless deep brown skin, she wasn't just pretty. She was beautiful, and strong. Her shirt and pants highlighted her lean muscles. It was as if her wings did not exist.

"Oh, right, sorry. I'll just settle in…" Filion said, turning quickly towards the lounge.

A small smile creased Captain Eri's face. She turned and disappeared down the hallway. Filion walked to one of the squish chairs and sat. *Wow*, he was embarrassed. He had acted like he had never seen a woman before. He buried his face in his hands. This was why he didn't leave his room. He couldn't talk to people, especially beautiful women.

Nearly a full minute passed before the chair even began to conform to his body. By the time it finished shaping to his back and butt, his embarrassment had faded enough for him to be productive again. He pulled out Didrik.

A loud crash came from the kitchen.

"Grawlix!"

Filion sat up. People had quite the language set here on Bok. He slid Didrik back into his pocket and slowly stood. He took a step towards the kitchen.

Once he got close enough, Filion could see the top of a human male's back. The man was bent over, rooting around in one of the kitchen's bottom lockers. Pots and cartons flew from the locker as the man spit obscenities. Filion took another step.

The man whipped to a standing position. His left arm pointed at Filion, a Talik phazer in his hand.

"Who in the gods' good names are you?" The human growled. Despite the fact that the man was several feet shorter and significantly lighter than Filion, his aura itched for a fight. With unkempt hair, an impressive five o'clock shadow and biceps which, while small for a lossal, were bigger than Filion would ever have, the man seemed to study Filion. Filion shifted uncomfortably under his gaze. His eyes drifted to the man's ammo belt, which was draped over his chest like a sash, then to the long knives and energy guns strapped to each of his legs, and then back to the Talik in the man's hand. It occurred to Filion that the man had a lot of noticeable weapons on him, but no doubt there were more. After all, none of the visible guns required ammo…

"Uh," Filion said, slowly putting up his arms. "I'm Filion. I've paid for passage to Hifora."

The man squinted at him. "Hifora? Now why would any self respecting lossal want to go to Hifora?" The man stepped closer, the Talik still trained on Filion.

"Uh, want is kind of the wrong word…" Filion started.

His story sounded worse the second time. He wished he were in the Tierameng.

The man didn't say anything. After a few moments he lowered the Talik.

"Women, always gittin' themselves in over their heads." He shook his head and walked over to the squish chair next to Filion's.

Plopping down he said, "I'm Red." His head bobbed back and forth. "Well, that's what people call me. My real name is Reddrick Canner. Just call me Red."

Red stuck out a hand. Filion grasped it and shook. While Filion was easily stronger than Red, he knew Red was a practiced fighter, which Filion was most certainly not. Red's aura had changed. While it was no longer violent, it radiated with unpredictability.

Red shook his head again. "Women. I mean, I know what you're thinkin'. I work for a woman right? Well, I know, it's strange. She's pretty all right though. *For a woman*," he added. "And she can fly. She's a pretty good captain, not that I wouldn't be better, but I do this until I can move on, you know? I mean, in the military I woulda had a future, I coulda been a general or somethin' great like that. I can command, move people, you know what I'm sayin'? But when I came down to thinkin' about it, I just plain don't like the Federation or any other governmental structure. I'm too much of a free spirit to be put into a box and be made to fight like cannon fodder. No. Me, I'm an independent man. I got places to go. This is merely a stop on my way to becoming something great." He leaned closer to Filion, his voice dropping, but not quieting. "Ideally, and I don't tell everyone this, I would like to command my own ship, a smuggling ship, you know? Run an interstellar piracy ring," his voice returned to its normal tone, "but we all gotta start somewheres, and here is as good a place as any." He hit Filion on the shoulder.

Filion looked at the man, Red. Filion didn't trust him, but there was somewhat of an illogical loyalty about him.

"Uhh," Filion said.

Captain Eri appeared. "Ahh," she said. "I see you've met Red."

The color drained from Red's face. He got up too quickly.

"Ahh, Captain Eri. Hi, uh, I was just meetin' our traveler here. Nice lossal, seriously, nice. But, ahh, I gotta go do… stuff… preflight stuff. Yes, so uh, it was nice talking to you Fil!" He tried to slither around her. Despite the fact he was easily a foot and a half taller than Captain Eri, he seemed small next to her.

"Why don't you clean up this mess?" Captain Eri said, gesturing to the kitchen. "I don't know what happened here, but if I catch whoever trashed my kitchen I'll arrange for their new quarters to be in the airlock."

Filion noticed the food packets and pots Red had scattered across the kitchen floor.

"Yes, Sir!" Red said, snapping to an undisciplined salute. "I don't know who would have trashed your kitchen so, but I'll right it!"

"Thank you, Red." She moved past Red as he dashed into the kitchen. He gave Filion a devious smile.

"I'm sorry, I don't think I caught your name." Captain Eri said, taking Red's chair. The chair shook a little as it began to shape to Captain Eri's small frame.

"I'm Filion." He stuck out his hand.

"Nice to meet you," Captain Eri said. She squeezed his hand. Filion jerked back. She *was* strong. Captain Eri didn't immediately let go though. When she did, Filion realized she had grabbed his hand so hard she had pulled out some of his fur. He took his hand back and clasped it with his other. Her aura was dark and confident. He didn't like it. "Now, if you don't mind me asking," Captain Eri continued. "Why are you en route to Hifora? One doesn't see many lossals in these parts."

He repeated his tale about the abusive brother-in-law. Captain Eri's face remained unreadable throughout his story, and she didn't speak until he finished talking.

"Well," she said. "When I said there weren't many lossals in these parts I guess I should have said there aren't *any* lossals in these parts. Hifora is a mining town. I've transported mining supplies there on several occasions, and there aren't any miners with a lossal wife. That would be the talk of the town, and the talk isn't about lossal wives, it's about when the next shipment of grog arrives. What are you really doing in Hifora?"

Filion looked at her, doing his best to show no emotion. He racked his brain. He couldn't tell her what he was really doing, which meant he stuck to his obviously flawed story or invented another lie. He said, "My sister is no lossal. I grew up in a foster family. She's human. Unfortunately, she has always ended up with the wrong guy. While she may not be related to me by blood, she's still my sister and I will do everything I can to protect her."

Captain Eri looked at him, her face still blank.

"Very noble. She's lucky to have you as a brother. Now, if you'll excuse me, I need to go see to more preflight checks." She stood and gave him a small nod.

Filion exhaled. Captain Eri left the kitchen. Red popped his head up from behind the counter.

"Whew! That was close. Thanks for not ratting me out! I owe you one!"

"Sure thing," Filion nodded.

Red finished his version of cleaning – cramming the pots and foodstuffs back into the locker without any discernable order – and started for the door.

"Later!" Red said as he disappeared into the hallway.

Filion gave Red a nod, and he was, once again, alone.

Chapter 27

Filion paced the kitchen and the common area for several minutes. Finally, he returned to his squish chair and pulled out Didrik.

What do we do now? Filion wrote.

We need to make contact with her.

With who? The Portal Keeper?

No.

Filion waited. The book seemed to sigh again and then wrote,

The Chozen.

How do I do that?

Didrik didn't respond. Filion was getting annoyed. Sure, it may seem obvious to a Living Document with all of the knowledge of the Eoans, but Filion was new at this. He was about to say so when Didrik responded.

Really? You don't have any idea?

Filion had had it.

You don't need to be snarky. This isn't my typical Summoning. I mean, I rarely even leave my bedroom when I'm working! All this traveling and dealing with awake people – homicidal okkars, disfigured ringers, and Red... I'm tired. I'm slightly stressed. You could at least be a little empathetic.

Filion stopped writing. *Oh.* He thought.

Didrik flipped shut. Taking a deep breath, Filion reopened Didrik.

The Tierameng...

You think? Didrik responded.

Didrik didn't flip shut again, but he didn't say anything else. Filion set him on the table. He decided to leave Didrik there, afraid that putting him in his pocket might anger him more.

When Filion prepared to enter the Tierameng, he usually went through a series of meditations and stretches. Looking at the dirty floor Filion decided he would skip the stretches. He could still do his breathing exercises though. He took a deep breath and closed his eyes.

*****

Those who know of the Tierameng, but who are not Dream Searchers or Summoners, often perceive the Tierameng to be a special type of dream. This is not true. The Tierameng is a real place. In fact, the Tierameng is another dimension all together. What confuses people is that the only way for a Searcher or Summoner to reach the Tierameng is for that Searcher or Summoner to be asleep. Once asleep, through focused meditation, Filion can reach the Tierameng, then link to the dreams of anyone whose physical body is in the same dimension as his own. At least, that was what Graftin had taught him, and he had had no reason to doubt his lessons. That is, until the Eoans had summoned him.

The Eoans aside though, the other rules of the Tierameng hadn't changed. The Tierameng allows a Searcher autonomy of his or her actions. Most people report an inability to do what they want while dreaming. A person might say that they drowned in a dream. They swam and swam for shore, but never reached it. Such things do not occur to Searchers linked to dreams from the Tierameng. If, while linked to a dream, Filion wants to swim to shore, he can. His link to the Tierameng grants him control.

While Filion may have control of his actions when linked to another's dream, that dream also has a will of its own. A dreamer cannot control his or her dream's will. The Searcher, on the other hand, can influence that dream's will, which is the primary reason behind Searching. Once a Searcher has linked to another's dream, the Searcher has *tenuous* control. If a Searcher were to try and take complete control of the dream, the Searcher could be killed. If a Searcher were to take too little control, the Searcher could lose themself. The Searcher has to strike a balance between too much and too little, which is why most Searchers work to subtly persuade the dreamer to consider an idea. Filion will suggest something at just the right time, and hopefully the dreamer will consider his counsel when he or she wakes.

Persuasion is the art to Searching. The obvious way for a Searcher to convince a dreamer of his or her intentions is to have a conversation with the dreamer, but Filion is more creative than acting by just conversations alone. He will trigger key memories in the dreamer at the optimal moment, or he will induce physical cues at the perfect instant. Maybe a door blows open, or a child laughs, or a photo falls from its frame just in time to convince the dreamer of whatever idea Filion wishes them to believe. If Filion succeeds in his persuasion, the dreamer will then act on his suggestion when awake.

Even if Filion strikes that perfect balance of control, the Tierameng is still a dangerous place. From what researchers are discovering, access to our universe's dreams is only a small part of what goes on in the Tierameng. Not only that, but nothing is ever the same in the Tierameng. It is an unpredictable dimension. Filion can enter it in the exact same way over and over again, and it will be different every time. Sometimes, when he opens his eyes after a successful link, the Tierameng is just infinite space – grey or black – stretching on forever. Then sometimes it isn't. He will open his eyes to find himself in a house, or a field, or a restaurant. Sometimes he knows these places. Maybe he enters the Tierameng through his childhood backyard, or his dorm room at Graftin, but then there are other times he opens his eyes to a place he doesn't know, like a crowded ship platform on a foreign planet or the kitchen of someone he has never met. He rarely enters the Tierameng to where he wants to be – his energy cloud. He always has to search for that Orku, and every time he has to take a different path to reach it.

Then there are the knotters.

Very little is known about knotters, as Tierameng researchers have only recently discovered their presence. They look to be a cross between a medium sized boulder and some sort of animal, a rabbit maybe. Knotters change colors randomly and have silky fur which is usually long and curly. With large ears, a squat round body, and no legs, knotters never seem to touch the ground. Rather they appear to hover, and they can disappear from sight in an instant. They do not speak, at least there are no reports of any speaking, but Filion knows they are highly intelligent. They also don't seem to have a social structure. Research suggests they are not asexual, but there have never been any reports of more than one knotter in the same place at the same time. Regardless of these facts, their population seems to be growing. Perhaps even more worrisome than their population growth, knotters can link into the dreams of people outside of their own dimension. Filion had seen this first hand.

He had been linked to a dream when a knotter appeared. The knotter had been disguised – its disguise so well crafted it rivaled Filion's (initially) – but the knotter's intentions hadn't been so amicable. Not only that, but the knotter had an aura – a strange aura.

Filion had been summoned to help a Queen restore the balance of power in a neighboring kingdom. To fulfill the Summoning, he had disguised himself as the Queen's best friend. One evening, he and the Queen had been having dinner when the Queen gave off the briefest aura of sickness. It was so strong and unexpected, that Filion was quite shaken and temporarily unable to continue the charade of being her best friend. Rather than lose the entire evening, Filion excused himself to use the bathroom.

For no reason in particular, Filion cut through the kitchen to access the bathroom. As he navigated the rows of stoves and ovens, he collided with a cook. The cook, who had been carrying a heavily laden tray, dropped the tray at Filion's feet. The food hit the floor and disappeared. Startled, Filion looked at the cook. The cook, a pale male human, began to back up, his face twisting in fear. Filion took a step towards him. The man's face appeared to melt but the terrified look did not. His arms, his body, his clothes, everything disappeared. In the cook's place hovered a red and black knotter. The knotter gave off the smallest aura of familiarity and then winked from the dream. Filion thought about following it but did not, putting his Summoning first. He looked at the spot where the food had fallen. A smoking hole now blackened the white tile.

When Filion had reported the events to the Board of Summonings, his Summoning had been temporarily suspended until a full investigation had been conducted. Nothing conclusive was ever found, but Filion was still troubled. Sure the knotter had attempted to poison the Queen and him, but what bothered him was the aura. It was as if he somehow knew the knotter. It was impossible. He didn't know the knotter, but still...

The Board hadn't been concerned with Filion's 'feeling' (which is how he explained it, a feeling) that he knew the knotter. What concerned them was the fact that he and the Queen had almost been killed. What happens in the Tierameng does not stay in the Tierameng. While a dream allows the dreamer to die without consequence, the Tierameng is not so forgiving. Once Filion enters the Tierameng, there is no guarantee he will wake. What amplifies this danger even more is that when Filion enters another's dream from the Tierameng there is no guarantee that the dreamer will wake up either. When a dream is linked to the Tierameng, it becomes real. If the Searcher makes a mistake or the dream is too unstable to enter, the Searcher puts themself *and* the dreamer at risk.

No one knows what happens when someone dies while linked to the Tierameng. To those unfamiliar with Dream Searching, it is simply thought that the person died in their sleep. While this is true, the real question is, what happened to their consciousness? This is a hot topic of debate among researchers. Some theories speculate that the deceased's consciousness never leaves the Tierameng. Others argue that dying in the Tierameng is no different than dying in our dimension, but no one knows.

If the knotters and the act of dream searching itself are not dangerous enough, there is evidence that beings from other dimensions also visit the Tierameng. Some argue that such findings are only evidence of unknown knotter behavior, but others argue that the findings suggest something else. Whatever the truth, Filion did not doubt that the people from his universe only knew the beginning of what went on in the Tierameng.

Chapter 28

Wiq watched the lossal from the hall. She loved lossals, although she had never met one personally. They reminded her of big dogs. BIG dogs. This one was short though. He couldn't have been more than ten feet tall, but his body was covered in that wonderful lossal fur. That was what did it for her. She wanted to run up to him and give him a hug. That clean, silver fur looked so inviting, so comfortable. It was no wonder they were hunted on some planets for their, she hated to think it, *pelt*. She wondered why he was traveling, and especially why he was alone. The universe could be a dangerous place for a lossal. Bok was a dangerous place for a lossal. *Hifora* was a dangerous place for a lossal.

The lossal finished his walk around the kitchen and common room and sat down. He pulled a book out of his pocket and began to write in it, stopping often. At one point his large ears went back, and his mouth twisted into a scowl. She could see his rows of teeth. They were white and well cared for. He came from a good upbringing. Why was he here?

Suddenly his face relaxed. He looked almost embarrassed. He set the book carefully on the table and then switched the squish chair to recline horizontally. The chair shook, it was so old, but it completed the task. The lossal shut his eyes, and within moments seemed to be asleep.

Wiq waited several minutes before entering the kitchen. She wanted to know what was in that book. He had been so upset. She wanted to make it better. Not only that, but that book was special. It was different. She could tell.

She crept, completely silently, until she stood next to him. Even if he opened his eyes, he wouldn't see her. Wiq was a vissy, part human, part nanotechnology. Vissys were originally bred as a form of stealth super soldier. She and other vissys could move without being heard. Perhaps even more impressive, they could cloak their movements. 'Cloaking' was the earliest form of invisibility technology. If Wiq stood completely still, she couldn't be seen. When she moved, only the slightest disruptions appeared in the air around her. The visual effect was comparable to that of a gas cloud moving through the room.

As technology advanced, however, vissys became obsolete. Their cloaking technology gave them away. Enemy soldiers quickly learned to recognize 'moving gas clouds', and vissys went from being an elite stealth super soldier to cheap cannon fodder. Wiq herself had been born in a breeding camp on Ralich, a desolate border planet. She had been auctioned to the Tiori warlord, Tofic, on the planet Repack where she had served as a foot soldier for Tofic until he had been accidentally killed in a ship crash. After

Tofic's death she was sold to a war research group, Canki, where she was experimented on. Several months after her sale to Canki, Unifree, an intergalactic personitarian and environmental group, succeeded in making it illegal to keep and sell nanotechnology based beings against their will. With her newfound freedom, she found work as a mechanic in a semi-legal chop shop on Bok. Even though she *technically* had 'rights', they weren't very well recognized throughout the universe, and honest work was hard to find.

When Captain Eri had visited the shop in search of a modified capacitor, Wiq had installed it for her, making a few extra modifications that would allow Captain Eri's Boulder to integrate advanced sublight technology into the existing systems. Captain Eri came back a few days later, asking for Wiq. Wiq was afraid she had done something wrong and so was her boss. Her boss promised Captain Eri to punish Wiq for her mistakes, but Captain Eri said she only wished to speak with Wiq.

"Where did you learn to do that?" Captain Eri asked.

Wiq looked at her. "Do what?"

"Modify a ship like that? You're a vissy right? That's what the marks on your face mean?"

Self-consciously Wiq covered the right side of her face. Every captive born vissy had been branded with a barcode. They were branded on their face to prevent them from passing as human. Other than the barcode, she could have passed. 5' 10'' and pale, Wiq had black hair that matched the color of her barcode. She was strong and deadly but unconfident. That was what spending her whole life in captivity had done to her. She could kill a person without blinking an eye but talk to them like an equal or look them in the eye? Impossible.

Wiq nodded, eyes on the floor.

"Well, where did you learn to do that?"

Wiq shrugged, still looking down.

"You don't know?"

"It is like I have always known. Like it is in my blood."

Captain Eri nodded. "Maybe it is," she paused. "I want to offer you a job. An honest… well, mostly honest, job. No more chop shops. I want you to be my mechanic. You've seen my ship, she isn't grand, but with the right modifications, she can be. We live, eat, and sleep on the ship. We travel every day, and the hours are terrible. The pay isn't much better, but I'll pay you what I can. That, and I won't discriminate against you because of your make up. With your talents, you deserve better than this chop shop. What do you say?"

Wiq looked at her. She had worked with many ringers, and some of them she had trusted. She didn't know if she could trust this one, but compared to her okkar boss, this ringer was an angel.

"Are you speaking the truth? You want to pay me to fix your ship and travel the universe?"

Captain Eri nodded.

"Well, yes, I would like to go," Wiq said. "But I cannot. Yerii, my boss, said I owe him three years of work because he gave me, a *vissy*, a job. He will not permit me to leave."

"Don't worry about that," Captain Eri said. She stuck out her hand. "I'm Captain Eri. Welcome to my crew."

"Wiq," Wiq said, taking Captain Eri's hand half-heartedly. This was too good to be true. Yerii would never allow her to go.

Captain Eri stood up. "Master Yerii! I demand your presence!"

Yerii skittered around the corner and burst into the room. He looked at Captain Eri, who seemed mad enough to do some serious damage, and then at the vissy, who wouldn't meet his eyes. He knew taking on a vissy had been a bad idea, despite her skills. Private pilots were his only legitimate form of business. If this vissy had damaged his reputation, she would pay.

"Yes?" he asked, as courteously as he could.

"You promised to punish this vissy for her mistakes?"

Yerii's eyes shone. He smiled. "Yes. She will pay for whatever damage she has done to your ship."

"Good. I request that she pay by working it off on my ship."

His eyes widened. The vissy was a good worker. Despite her race, he wasn't ready to lose her. She was the next best thing to having a slave. Near free labor didn't come around every day.

"Well, I don't know about that. She has a three-year requirement with me. She isn't even a year into it yet! I can't just let her go!" His gills smacked loudly.

"I do not know what she did to my ship, but I know that only she can sort it out, and she will sort it out under my purview. I need to leave tonight, and I can't do that without her. She may have another few years on her contract with you, but I have contacts on all the planets in the system. I will not hesitate to broadcast the fact that your shop is an untrustworthy stop for any private pilot." She paused and looked straight into the okkar's eyes. "I know you don't want that."

The okkar swallowed. This pilot wasn't as dumb as he had assumed. If she did have contacts on every planet in the system, which could be a bluff, though he guessed it wasn't far from the truth, then his honest money would disappear. An audit from the Federation Revenue Service would be in his future. An audit would not prove good for business nor for his freedom.

He frowned. "You can have her but for a cost. She has some outstanding debt to me. I require 100 Fed gold before I can release her from my service."

The ringer didn't say anything. Finally she said, "Any pilot knows that you always half the quoted price from a chop shop. I'll pay you fifty, nothing more."

Yerii grimaced but nodded. Pocketing 50 Fed gold from this mess wasn't a total loss.

That had been four months ago. In her time on the *Dark Horse*, Wiq had modified the ship to achieve long distance hyperspeed travel. According to Captain Eri, such a modification had never been done before. Wiq didn't know anything about that, but the first test had proved successful and Captain Eri had been happy. That made Wiq happy. She had never met someone like Captain Eri before. Captain Eri didn't seem to care that she was a vissy. She talked to Wiq like an equal. Wiq liked it but always feared that one day Captain Eri would realize what she was doing and treat her like the rest of the universe did. This made her sad.

She smiled though. Here she was, standing only a few feet from a real live lossal. Such an opportunity would make anyone, even a vissy, smile.

Chapter 29

Filion opened his eyes. He was in the Tierameng. Today the Tierameng was a deep shade of gray with purple at the corners of his vision. Amazingly, he had entered into a space that he could use, a place he called the Dansa. While the Dansa wasn't his Orku, it was the next best thing. Bright spots littered the Dansa, like stars on a clear night, the twinkling energy signatures were exactly what Filion was looking for – dreams. Every person in the universe emitted a particular energy signature. When a person slept, their energy resonated in the Tierameng, and that signature was how a Searcher located a particular dreamer. Filion moved through the Dansa, gliding without effort. He stopped at a bright orange signature. The signature was long and narrow, dancing in the nothingness like an incandescent length of string.

Looking into a signature was like looking down a straw. At the other end of it he could see the being's dream and identify whose it was. He peered into the orange energy. A young girl played in a snow bank. This wasn't her.

Filion drifted away from the signature. He hoped she was asleep. If she wasn't, this would be a huge waste of time. He took a deep breath and opened his mind.

The Eoans had warned him that her signature would be difficult to find. Most dreamers emitted constant energy while they slept. People who didn't want their energy signature found, or Searched, altered their energy, causing slight irregularities. These alterations were known as traps, mimics, and duplicates.

Out of the three alterations, traps were the most likely to get a Searcher hurt. Filion had known a Searcher who had been caught in a trap and had died. Most dreamers didn't know how to set such elaborate traps though. Usually after attempting to link with a trapped dream, the caught Searcher would just end up awake in their bed with a splitting headache.

Mimicked signatures were the most benign of the alterations. When a Searcher attempted to access a mimicked signature, everyone woke up, but no one was harmed. The Searcher, the person whose signature had been stolen, and the mimicker would simultaneously wake, but only two would know why. Filion had never heard of anyone getting seriously hurt from entering a mimicked signature.

While linking with a trapped signature would most likely hurt a Searcher, linking with a duplicated signature would most definitely kill a Searcher. The nice thing about duplicated signatures was that they were obvious. If a Searcher saw two identical signatures, they knew not to link with either.

Filion was one of the best Searchers in the universe, and while he had spotted plenty of altered signatures, he knew that this Summoning was different. The stakes were as high as they could be. He couldn't make a mistake, yet he knew that the signature for which he looked was probably mimicked, trapped or duplicated. Not only that, but the person for whom he searched was far more powerful than he. He had to be careful.

He searched for what seemed like hours before he found anything close to what he was looking for. Just as he was beginning to think she wasn't asleep, he came across a clump of pale yellow, snaking signatures. They didn't match normal dream behavior. In fact, all of the signatures in the bunch appeared to be identical. He watched them closely. They wavered and blinked at the exact same time. This was unusual. Energy signatures were like DNA; they were unique. Two identical signatures might exist, assuming one came across a duplicated signature, but an entire group of identical signatures? That shouldn't exist.

There were twelve signatures in total. He watched them a moment longer, not daring to enter any of them. This had to be her. It just had to be. If it wasn't, he didn't want to face whoever it was.

He studied the signatures again. He knew he had no chance of peering into this person's dream. If this person could duplicate their own signature 11 times, they could prevent him from seeing into their dream. He had two choices – walk away, or pick one and link. If he picked the wrong signature, he would be killed. His consciousness would become a topic of debate among his colleagues, and his body, well, who knows what would become of his body, since it was on the *Dark Horse* over Bok. He could not choose a duplicated signature.

It was impossible, for most Searchers, to determine an empty duplicate signature from a true signature, which is why those who were able to duplicate their own signature were pretty much assured their dreams would not be Searched. Research had not offered any conclusive ways to tell the difference 100% of the time, and Searching wasn't worth dying for, except in this case. If this was the Chozen, then he had to contact her. The entire fate of the universe was riding on his shoulders. He couldn't just walk away.

Filion took another breath, and then circled the flickering mass of energy. There were no discernable differences between any of the strands. *Grawlix.* What was he supposed to do? Then it hit him. These signatures were a resonation of the Chozen's energy, so logically the Chozen's energy should give off an aura, even in the Tierameng. How had he forgotten this? Well, in all fairness to him, he instinctively turned off his ability to sense auras when he entered the Tierameng, and he had been doing it for years. It was now habit.

He opened his mind to the signature's auras, and immediately a dull grey haze obscured eleven of the signatures. Those were empty. There was no life in that grey. One signature, however, remained clear, emitting seemingly nothing, then a whiff of fear. The fear was so slight that Filion doubted he would have been able to sense it if he were awake, but it was there. That was the real one. That was the real dream. He took a breath and prepared to initiate the link. He prayed it was she.

Chapter 30

Captain Eri did not trust the lossal. She didn't sense that he was evil or even bad, per se, but her gut told her that he was not telling the truth. She had learned to trust her gut, thanks to her Federation military service (or disservice as she often thought of it), which is why she wasn't running preflight sims as she had told the lossal she was.

She turned the corner to her quarters, her right hand clutched tightly. Some of the Federation's more clandestine procedures had rubbed off on her, which was evident by her current life style choices. Not illegal exactly but not honest either. Not that the Federation cared one lick about honesty. She smiled. Come to think of it, neither did she, well, almost.

She reached her door and slid it open. As soon as she was inside she shut the door, and moved to the room's far wall. Above her bed was a panel. She banged it with her left fist. The panel groaned and then popped open.

Inside the hidden space were a series of objects, many valuable, illegal, or both. One item was an I-DNA machine. She hit the power button and waited for it to boot up. Its screen came to life and asked her what she wished to do. She hit the analyze button. The machine beeped once and a tray ejected from its base. Captain Eri opened her hand and let the lossal's fur spill onto the tray. She hit another button and the tray closed. The machine made a whirring sound and a rotating circle appeared on the screen.

Captain Eri slid onto her bed. It could take the machine anywhere between a few seconds and an hour to get an ID. She didn't have an hour to just wait around, but she had a few minutes before she actually needed to start the preflight sequences. If she didn't get an ID on the lossal in the next few minutes though, it didn't matter. They could take off before she got it. Hifora was 10 hours away, and that was more than enough time to get a hit.

Captain Eri had a decision to make. She either brought the lossal to Hifora, where he would certainly be killed, or refuse to take him there, no doubt saving his life but breaking their deal. Pelters were active in Hifora, and they would know he was there within moments of him leaving the *Dark Horse*. Bringing an innocent lossal to his death for 75 sil did not sit well with Captain Eri. If he wasn't so innocent though, then maybe she wouldn't feel so bad. She just needed an ID before she made any decisions.

She grabbed a stuffed ball from one of her shelves and began to toss it in the air. If he really had a sister in Hifora, he would have known about the pelters. Captain Eri did not doubt that the lossal had money, it was as apparent as Wiq's facial barcode. The lossal could have easily paid someone to come and extract his sister, or if he was up to something less noble, he could have paid someone else to deal with it. Something did not add up.

The machine beeped and Captain Eri sprang from the bed, the ball falling onto the floor. The small screen blinked with a red and black seal – the Federation seal. She clicked past it and saw the elite Thog University seal, and then she saw something she had never seen before.

She took a deep breath. Her gut had been right. There was more to the lossal, a lot more, than she had thought, and they weren't going anywhere until she got to the bottom of it.

Chapter 31

Closing his eyes, Filion took a deep breath. He was nervous, and he couldn't link in this state. Several times he had almost linked, only to pull himself back at the last moment. Linking required a Searcher to completely surrender themself. This could be very unpleasant, especially depending on whose or what kind of dream a Searcher linked into. Not only that, but he had never linked to the dream of a Chozen before. He didn't know what to expect, and a large part of him was afraid he was going to die. He took another deep breath and surrendered before he could second guess himself.

The link sucked him in, submerging him in an icy blast. He shivered and opened his eyes. Colors surrounded him, washing over him like rolling clouds. Suddenly, he was warm and he could smell something sweet, then acrid. Then there was the energy. The link pushed in on him, strongly, and then pulled away from him with equal force. Every time the link pulsed he could hear what sounded like a heartbeat. Da-da, da-da, da-da. He felt himself sliding downwards, away from the Tierameng and into the dream. He wasn't necessarily going fast, but he knew there was no way he could stop himself. He watched the colors slide by – green, red, blue, orange – and he felt the beat of the link in his bones – then he felt his feet come into contact with something, something hard and stable. The colors, smells and noise disappeared, and he found himself in a thick jungle.

It was night, and the temperature was pleasant. He looked up. Through the dense canopy he could see stars. A clear night meant a stable dream. He smiled. *Thank the gods for that,* he thought. *And it's nice to be out of the rain.* Birds squabbled in the distance, and the smell of a fire found his nostrils. He moved towards the smell, stopping when he saw it. A small woman sat next to the fire. She seemed to be concentrating on something he could not see. She did not see him.

Suddenly, there was a flash of energy. Filion felt it resonate through his body. The flash had been small, so small in fact he doubted he could have felt it if he had been only a few feet further from her, but the energy was strong, very strong.

The woman now held something dark in her hand. She smiled and put it in her mouth, chewing slowly. Filion stepped towards the fire.

His foot hadn't completed the step when he was hit. The force was powerful, so powerful it paralyzed him. Panic washed over him. He wanted to fight, but he couldn't. Unseen bonds held him in place. His right foot hovered above the ground, suspended in a step he could not finish.

Ryo looked at the creature, her eyes calm and inquisitive. It was tall, really tall, and covered in immaculate silver fur. The animal stood on two legs, its long arms and big hands frozen in mid air. With wide green eyes and flaring nostrils, the creature's face was full of fear. Its snout and mouth were twisted at an awkward angle, and its muscles were tense, but Ryo did not sense that this being intended to hurt her.

No, she thought. *It was afraid of her.* She stood silently and moved closer to the thing. Despite its fur, the creature wore brown pants and a red vest. The clothes looked well worn and comfortable. She touched its fur. The animal's eyes rolled wildly, but she ignored it. The thing's fur was soft; softer than anything she had ever felt. Part of her wanted to hug it, but instead she quickly stepped back.

Once again, she hadn't realized what she had done until after she had done it. She had sensed something and out shot her hand. There had been no slow bubbling. No, this time, it was instant. She had sensed it, her hand had shot out, and here it was frozen mid step, in her camp.

Filion was afraid, very afraid. As a Searcher *he* was supposed to have control of her dream, not *her*. Yet here she was holding him captive, without so much of a trace of effort. He tried every trick he knew to break the bonds that held him but nothing worked. She stared at him curiously, her small dark face symmetrical and smooth. She tilted her head to the side causing her short black hair to shine in the firelight. What struck him though were her deep blue eyes. They stood out from her face like sapphires in the dirt. It was as if they contained a light of their own. They didn't quite glow, but they held him transfixed, and Filion knew that even if he had been able to move, he would have been paralyzed.

The creature watched her. She was confident that it had not come to kill her or take her to this Yalki, but she knew he was here for a reason. She loosened the bonds that held his voice.

"Who are you?" she asked, her voice low and melliferous.

He took a deep breath but didn't say anything. At first Ryo thought she hadn't released the right bonds. Mentally, she began to break down the bond's thought structure, but before she got anywhere with it he said, "My name is Filion Ker III. I am a Dream Searcher. I was sent to protect you."

Ryo looked at him. She had no idea what he was talking about. She searched her memories.

"A Dream Searcher..." she said with familiarity. "I'm asleep right now? You contacted me through the, Tiera-meng?"

"Yes."

She had a thousand questions but started with just one.

"What's going on?"

"It's a long story, may I sit down? I am not here to hurt you."

Ryo looked at him again. She didn't think he had any weapons on him.

More importantly, she believed she could trust him. She released the bonds.

Filion fell, his outstretched foot failing to catch him. The girl did not move to help him but instead sat on a stump by the fire. She turned her head away from him, and her wonderful blue eyes were suddenly far away.

Filion gathered himself, brushed the dirt from his knees, and sat next to the fire.

"I think it's best if we start at the beginning."

She nodded, but continued to stare into the trees.

He opened his mouth. He would tell her just as Didrik had told him. He knew it backwards and forwards, but still he wasn't prepared. She was their last hope, yet she was so small...

He didn't say anything for several seconds. Finally, he took a deep breath. He had been sent to protect her. He had better get to it.

"The universe, as we know it, was created as a result of an exercise of thought. In another dimension, far away from here..."

Chapter 32

Captain Eri strode towards the kitchen, a communicator with the lossal's ID clenched in her hand. According to his file, he was a Dream Searcher, a real live Dream Searcher. She had heard of Searchers before, in films and the like, but she had always assumed they were creatures of myth. After all, no one could, how did they say it, link into another's dream? Yet, here this lossal was, with a Fed stamp in his ID papers, and a Dream Searcher seal. Something was not right.

She turned and climbed onto the ramp that led to the kitchen. What did she do now? Even before she knew he was a Dream Searcher, she hadn't really considered tossing him to the Hifora pelters (well if he had been some kind of escaped murderer, maybe), but now it seemed even more important that she didn't. From what she was able to research, most Dream Searchers did all their work from their rooms. In fact, they could do all of their work while sleeping in their beds. There had to be a reason, an important reason, for him to be so far away from his post on Thog. Captain Eri was going to find out what that reason was.

She turned into the kitchen and stopped. The lossal was asleep in one of the squish chairs. A small book hovered over his head. Wiq was there. Captain Eri shook her head. If her nanites had been a little more advanced, anything she picked up would have turned invisible as well, but they weren't, and Wiq was made.

"Wiq!" Captain Eri hissed.

The book jumped and the air surrounding it shimmered.

"Get over here!" Captain Eri whispered. "And bring that!"

The book floated towards Captain Eri, the air swimming around it. Captain Eri stepped into the hall and so did Wiq, her body slowly reappearing.

"What are you doing?!" Captain Eri growled, grabbing the book from Wiq.

"Sorry. I just, I just wanted to get close to him. He was writing in this, and he looked so sad. I just wanted to see what upset him." Wiq wouldn't meet her eyes.

Captain Eri didn't say anything. She opened the book. The pages were empty. She opened the back cover. Those pages were empty too. All of the pages were blank. She stared at Wiq.

"You said he was writing in this?"

Wiq nodded.

"There's nothing in it."

"I know. I do not understand either. I saw him writing. I swear."

Captain Eri frowned.

"Get Red. Tell him to guard him until he wakes up. We're going to take off. Come get me the moment he's awake, you understand?"

Wiq nodded. "Is he in trouble?"

"I don't know. He might be but not by me."

Captain Eri pocketed the book and the communicator and walked towards the bridge.

Wiq watched the Captain go. With a final glance at the lossal, she started off to find Red.

Chapter 33

Filion finished reciting the message. The girl hadn't moved. She still stared into the trees. Finally she said, "You're Filion Ker III. You're dad was Filion too?"

Filion looked at her. Had she not been listening? Had the metamorphosis warped her brain already?

"Ah no," Filion started. "His name was Granij. The III means I am a level III professor. It's an honorary title."

"Hmmm. I'm Ryo." She turned, looked straight into his eyes and extended her hand. He skipped a breath.

"Oh. I'm so sorry, I never asked. Nice to meet you." Filion fumbled. He stuck his hand out clumsily. He couldn't believe he hadn't asked her name.

They shook hands, their eyes locked. Filion felt as if he were melting. Her eyes seemed to warm him from the inside out. It was such a pleasant feeling...

"So, I'm a Chozen, huh? My destiny is to save the universe," she said, turning back to the trees.

"Yes," Filion said. He wanted her to turn and look at him again. He needed to look into those eyes.

"The universe that was created by aliens from a different dimension. Who," she added, "are our gods."

"Yes."

She looked at him sharply. His heart fluttered.

"What are you?"

"Me? Uh, I'm a lossal."

"A lossal. Do all lossals look like you, tall and covered in fur?"

Filion's cheeks burned but thankfully his fur covered that. He dropped his eyes. "Well, I'm considered short for a lossal, but thank you for thinking of me as tall."

"Taller? Still with the fur though?"

Filion nodded.

"You have nice fur. Do you shampoo it?"

"No, this is just how it is. We are renowned for our fur. So much so," he sniffed. "That lossals used to be hunted for our... *pelts,*" He spit the word out as if it was cursed. He, and all other lossals, hated thinking of their skin and fur as a pelt. "There weren't many of us left for a while. Luckily Unifree stepped in and made... *pelting*... illegal. Our numbers have started to come back up."

"You were almost hunted to extinction?"

He nodded, wanting to change the subject.

"Huh. I can see why. You're pelt is very fine."

Filion stiffened. "Please, do not refer to my skin and fur as a *pelt*. To do so is a great insult."

"I'm sorry," Ryo said, her eyes back on Filion's. "I didn't know."

Her apology calmed him. His muscles relaxed, his shoulders sagged. She hadn't meant to offend him...

"It's okay. Don't worry about it," he said.

"I'm sorry!" Ryo said, jumping up.

"What's the matter?" Filion asked, the calm feeling gone.

"I just do it, without realizing I'm doing it. I don't even know what I'm doing. I'm sorry. I didn't mean to. I'm sorry about calling your fur a pelt, but I didn't mean to do that." She paced back and forth.

"What are you talking about?" Filion said.

"Whatever I did to you. I'm sorry. Are you alright?"

What had she done to him? "Yes, yes. I'm fine. Don't worry."

Ryo paced once more and then sat back down.

"I just don't know what's happening to me, you know? I mean I wake up, running from some guy, in a body I don't recognize, with a mind that's mine but not mine. Suddenly, I'm shooting fireballs from my hands, healing myself, reliving memories that I have no memory of, getting trapped in my own mind, and now here you are. A Dream Searcher, I don't even know what a Dream Searcher is, but I do! I feel like people are watching me, but I can never find anyone. I can start fires with my mind. MY MIND! I feel like I'm going crazy." She gave him a pained look, and then buried her face in her hands.

"Well, you... you kind of are." Filion said, regretting it immediately.

"What?"

"Well, when a Chozen metamorphosizes, their mind, your mind, becomes extremely stressed. You are, simply put, going crazy."

She looked at him.

What was the matter with him? He had more tact than that!

"So, so this is how it's going to be?" she said softly. "I'm just going to lose it?"

Filion struggled. Her eyes pleaded for the truth. He couldn't lie to her...

"Well, that's why I'm here. I'm here to help you. To protect you."

"From myself?"

"And the Tioris."

Her eyes burned into his, and the words began to tumble from his mouth.

"You see," Filion started. "When the Eoans created you, something went wrong. All Chozen were designed to wake up and realize their potential in their first life. The Eoans knew that your metamorphosis would be difficult, so they created one Living Document per Chozen. These Living Documents are like Chozen instruction manuals. They contain all the knowledge of the Eoans. The Living Documents were made to guide you during your transformation. They were supposed to keep you safe, to keep you alive, and to keep you sane. Without a Living Document, a metamorphosing Chozen is extremely vulnerable."

"Something happened though, and no Chozen woke up in their first life. There was no plan for keeping Living Documents with their Chozen beyond that first life, so when Chozens finally started metamorphosing, they didn't have the guidance they needed because their Living Documents had long ago been lost."

"Not only that, but when a Chozen starts their transformation, they release a great amount of energy, and that energy attracts Tioris like a flame attracts moths. As a result, Tioris have been able to kill, well, permanently Erase, most of the Chozens' consciousnesses – their Eoan memories. The few who weren't killed went mad as a result of having no Living Document. You are one of the, if not *the* last, living *and* sane Chozen."

Ryo looked sick.

Damn it! What was wrong with him?

"So, I'm the universe's last hope, but the odds are stacked against me," she smiled a crooked, wrong smile. "I could go mad, or some Aforitiori could kill me long before I save this place."

"Yes." Again, he was talking without thinking. "You see, right now, you're giving off an energy signature. During your metamorphosis this signature is very strong, and the Tioris are looking for it. They kill Chozen by waiting until they begin to metamorphosize, because that's when you are most vulnerable, and then they strike. They know you're here. They're looking for you."

"To Erase me," Ryo said distantly. "What does Erasing entail?"

"Ahh, well," he stopped himself. He had to be tactful here. "Apparently the process is very painful. The Tioris will separate your Eoan consciousness from your body. After they do this, you will know that the Tioris have taken something from you, something very important, but you won't know what. From then on, you'll be their slave, and what they have done to you will haunt you until you die. Once you do die, you'll be reborn over and over again. You, Ryo, will be reborn, but you'll never know it."

"They know I'm here? I don't even know where here is." She turned back to him, her eyes intense. "How am I supposed to fight them? You say I have powers, but," she looked at her hands. "I don't understand them."

She lifted her hands. The fire grew in size and the air seemed to wobble. Everything went quiet. Then suddenly, there was a burst of noise. Birds called, animals squealed, and the forest seemed to dance. Flowers popped out of the ground and the trees seemed to grow even taller. Then Ryo dropped her hands and the fire dwindled, the animals and birds quieted, the trees seemed to slouch back to their former height, and the flowers fell over, their stems no longer connected to the ground.

Filion stared at her, his mouth open.

"You see?" she said. "Powers, sure. But control? Understanding? I had no idea that would happen when I lifted my hands. It just did. All I know is that I am afraid, but I know I can't show it. When I use these powers," she raised her hands again, but nothing happened. "I am even more afraid, but I know it is even more important that I don't show it. I'm supposed to save you? And the universe? I don't even know if I can save myself." She put her hands down and began to laugh, a low, uneven laugh.

"Uh," Filion gasped. "Uh, you're on a planet called Handu. We're trying to get to you before they do."

"We..."

"Uh..." Filion picked up one of the dying flowers. Round and a shimmering yellow, he unconsciously pinched it in his hands. "Yes, we," he recovered. "There is one Living Document left, a rather snarky document known as Didrik. He and I are attempting to make it to Handu to find you. We're on another planet right now, Bok, traveling to a town called Hifora. From Hifora we hope to be able to reach Handu."

"A Living Document? You have a Living Document? It could help me?" she said, her eyes shining.

"Yes, he told me most everything I told you. Didrik knows what's happening. He can help you."

"He can explain how to control this, this, power?" She looked at her hands as if she had never seen them before.

"Yes, but we need you to hold on! You have to fight. Don't give in to the madness. Don't let them catch you. Do whatever it takes to stay alive, physically and mentally, until we reach you. We're coming as fast as we can."

She nodded. After several minutes she asked, "Would you like some chocolate?"

"What?" Filion said.

Ryo extended her hand. Suddenly a dark square appeared in her palm.

"How did you do that?"

She shrugged and took a bite of the chocolate.

"Want some?"

"Uh, no thanks. I have to go. Can I meet you again?"

Ryo nodded.

"Okay, I'll meet you in another twenty hours. Until then, stay alive."

Ryo nodded, a sad look on her face.

"Are you okay?"

"Yeah, it was just nice having you here, you know? I didn't feel so lost or so crazy."

Her eyes held him. He didn't have to go…

Finally Filion breathed, "I'll be back. Be asleep in twenty hours. That's when we'll meet."

"Okay."

He stood up and opened his mouth to say something more but stopped.

She was staring into the forest again, that far away look on her face. She was so powerful, yet so fragile... They had to reach her and soon. He took one last look at her then severed the link.

It sling shot him back to the Tierameng. Colors slid past him until he was back in the grey and the twelve energy signatures wavered beside him. She probably had no idea that she had masked her dreams – she had just done it. Then it hit him. To link with her dream he had turned on his ability to see auras, but he had never shut it off, not even when he was in her dream, yet he never sensed an aura the entire time he was with her.

Chapter 34

When he opened his eyes, he was back in the *Dark Horse's* common room. The first thing he did was reach into his vest pocket and take out his pocket watch. He clicked the timer, twenty hours. He needed to meet her in twenty hours. Putting the watch back in his pocket, he grabbed for Didrik. His hand touched nothing. Looking up he saw the table was empty. Didrik was gone. His stomach dropped. He jumped from the chair and peered under the table. Maybe Didrik had fallen onto the floor?

"Stop. I don't know what you're doin' but just stop."

Filion looked up. Red stood in the kitchen, the Talik retrained on Filion's chest.

"Uh, have you seen my, uh, journal? It was right here when I went to sleep and now it isn't. I... I need to get it back, as soon as possible."

"Take a deep breath and sit down. Captain Eri will be here in a moment. You can ask her."

Filion sat down unwillingly, still scanning the floor for Didrik. Moments later, he heard feet banging the metal ramps outside of the kitchen. Captain Eri, and another woman Filion had not seen before, entered the kitchen.

"So he is," Captain Eri said. Without hesitating she moved into the common room. Captain Eri did not sit but instead took a place against the wall nearest Filion. She leaned back and looked at him with curiosity.

"So, Filion Ker III, graduate of Graftin, Senior Dream Searcher of Thog University *and* the Federation, what are you really doing here?"

"Where is the book? Do you have the book?"

Captain Eri arched her eyebrows, "This book?" she asked, pulling Didrik from her pocket.

"Yes! Let me see him. Did you hurt him?"

Captain Eri squinted Filion and slipped Didrik back into her pocket. "Him? I think you have some explaining to do, lossal. Tell me what I want to know."

"No! I need the book first. I won't say anything until I know he's okay."

Captain Eri looked at Red and the woman. Red wore a sick smile on his face, the Talik still held ready. The woman looked at the floor. She seemed uncomfortable.

Captain Eri took Didrik from her pocket again. Filion eyed him. Didrik's aura said he was scared, but Filion couldn't determine if he was hurt.

"I'll make you a deal, lossal. I'll give you the book, and you tell me what I want to know. You lie and I'll have Red blow a hole in your pretty chest. I'll then take the book back and rip it apart, page by page. Got it?"

Filion nodded. He believed her. She held the book out. Filion took one step and grabbed Didrik from her hands. He opened Didrik and flipped through him. He saw no damage.

Returning to his chair, Filion took a pencil from his pocket. Before he could write anything Didrik said,

Filion?

It's me. I'm so sorry. I left you out because I didn't think you liked my pocket! I won't do it again, Filion wrote.

Didrik seemed to sigh.

It's okay. Don't worry, they didn't hurt me. Did you make contact with her?

Yes. She's okay, for now, but she's in rough shape. The Tioris haven't found her, but, well, sometimes she seems a little crazy.

That's to be expected.

Captain Eri stared at Filion, her mouth slightly open and her anger bubbling.

"Excuse me, remember our deal?"

Filion looked up. Captain Eri's aura was dark. He looked away.

"Uh, yeah, just one more moment, please," he said.

What do we do? Filion penciled.

Tell them.

Tell them what?

The truth. We don't have much of a choice. After all, you're a terrible liar. Plus, I think we're going to need their help.

Their help? Are you sure?

Yes, that, and like I said, I don't think we have much of a choice.

Filion put the pencil down. He set Didrik on his lap.

"Okay, what do you want to know?"

Chapter 35

Captain Eri smiled. She motioned for Red to lower his gun. He didn't put it away, but it was a change in the right direction.

Captain Eri moved towards Filion and sat in the squish chair across from him. The woman in the kitchen looked up. Filion saw a large barcode tattooed on the right side of her power white face. She was a vissy. What was she doing here?

"Let's start at the beginning. Why are you really going to Hifora, Senior Dream Searcher?"

"I'm looking for a woman, Amalia."

"She is not your sister."

"No."

"Who is she?"

"She's the Portal Keeper."

"Why do you want to see the Portal Keeper?"

"Because I need to get to Handu."

Red snorted.

"Handu! Have you not heard? Tioris have taken the planet! It's Black! It's suicide to go there, especially as a lossal," Red said smiling. "I'll bet them Tioris would really like a lossal coat though."

Captain Eri shot him a look, and he stopped talking.

"He's right. Handu is suicide. But that's not your most immediate problem. You won't make it out of Hifora alive," Captain Eri said, her voice steady.

"Why?" Filion asked.

"Hifora is a pelter hideout. You walk in there, and you'll become someone's coat before you know you're dead."

Filion sat back in his chair. He glanced at Didrik.

I didn't know.

"Why is it so important you get to Handu?"

"A very important person is on Handu. We need to get her off of that planet."

"We?"

"Yes, Didrik and I."

"Who's Didrik?" Captain Eri asked.

Filion picked Didrik out of his lap and set him on the table.

"This is Didrik."

Hello. Didrik wrote.

Captain Eri looked at the book and gasped.

"What is that?" she said.

"A Living Document," Filion answered.

"A Living Document? I thought those were a myth."

"I thought pelters were wiped out. I guess we were both wrong," Filion said.

Captain Eri continued to stare at Didrik. Red's and the vissy's eyes were also glued to him.

"It can't like, read our thoughts, can it?" Red asked. He was now crouched low behind the kitchen counter.

Captain Eri looked at him. "Stand up!"

Red did so but hesitantly.

"No, he can't read thoughts," Filion said.

Not that he has any to read anyway, Didrik added.

"He's kinda sassy isn't he?" Captain Eri said.

"Why what'd it say?" Red asked, now half crouched.

"First a Dream Searcher and now a Living Document. Until a few hours ago I thought both were creatures of stories. Why are you here?" Captain Eri asked, ignoring Red.

"I told you, we need to get to Handu, and this is the fastest way."

"Start at the beginning." Captain Eri commanded.

Filion sighed, and then said, "The universe, as we know it, was created as a result of an exercise of thought. In another dimension, far away from here..."

Chapter 36

They were all sitting now, Captain Eri in the same place, the vissy in the chair next to her, and Red on the kitchen counter, still concerned about Didrik, and now Filion as well, since finding out what a Dream Searcher was.

"And that's it. In a nutshell, this girl, Ryo, is our last chance at beating the Tioris and stopping the enslavement of our entire universe," Filion finished.

He sat back and exhaled. First his visit to the Tierameng, and now this, he needed to sleep, but he knew that they would have questions.

But no one said anything for some time. Finally Captain Eri said, "Are you telling the truth?"

Filion nodded.

"How do we know you aren't some crazy, just trying to talk your way out of being thrown off this ship?!" Red asked, his eyes frantic.

"I don't even know how to begin to answer that," Filion said, his eyes closed.

Captain Eri didn't say anything for some time. Red looked hurt but tried not to show it. The vissy continued to sit, her eyes on the floor.

"You are asking me, *us*, to believe that aliens from another dimension, aliens that created us, are trying to enslave our universe?" Captain Eri said.

"I'm not asking you to believe anything. I'm telling you. What you choose to believe is up to you." Filion said, his head back and his eyes still closed.

"You know what I think?" Captain Eri said.

"No," Filion replied.

"I think you're crazy."

"Okay," Filion said.

"Okay?! Okay?! You don't care?"

"Not at this point. I told you, I'm not trying to make you believe anything. I just need to get to Hifora."

Captain Eri sneered. "I'll get you to Hifora. You and your fancy toy there, but don't think for one moment that I believe that thing is a *real* Living Document. I'll let you two off, but you won't live long enough to get out of the ship terminus. Once you step off this ship the pelters will be on you like black on space. You'll be done for. But you paid me to get you there, so get you there I will."

Filion nodded, uncaring. He was so tired.

Captain Eri stood up. "You've got four hours to live. Enjoy them."

She stormed out, followed by Red. The vissy didn't move.

Filion looked at Didrik.

"I guess their help is out of the question."

Didrik didn't say anything.

"Do not be so sure."

Filion looked up. The vissy stared at him, her golden eyes unblinking.

"Why do you say that?"

"Because I know you speak the truth," she said, her eyes dropping back to the table.

"How?" Filion asked, straightening.

"Because I know Tioris are not of this universe. Until you spoke I did not know so specifically, but now that I hear you, I know."

"What? How do you know?" Filion asked.

"Their life signature is different. They have a foreign element to them."

"What do you mean?"

"Vissys were built for stealth, but we were also built to kill. My programming allows me to detect the life signatures of all living things. Your life signature tells me you are a lossal. Captain Eri's tells me she is a ringer. Tioris' signatures try to tell me that they are human, or ringer, or whatever, but their signatures are always," she paused. "Wrong. It is like their signatures have been forged."

"You're trying to tell me that you can detect the ' life signatures' of all living things in the universe?"

The vissy nodded.

"What does that even mean, life signature?"

"A life signature is a pattern of energy. My nanites allow me to see not only you but your energy as well," she paused again. "The best way to describe it is like seeing people through a heat seeking lens. My nanites allow me to see the 'heat', so to speak, of every individual. I can see their energy. Without nanites, people like you can only see a person's body not their energy. Each being's energy is different, but everyone has underlying patterns. While your life signature may be unique, it has fundamental properties that all lossals share, so my programming allows me to recognize you as lossal."

Filion thought about this for a moment. What she was describing sounded like a binary version of his ability to see auras. Auras, after all, were just another form of energy a person emitted. While he interpreted that energy in terms of colors and abstract feelings, this vissy saw energy in terms of species type.

"How do you know that your programming contains the signatures of everything in the universe?" Filion said. "What if your programmers missed something? We are only just beginning to leave our galaxy. What about the life forms that your creators never encountered? How could they program you to recognize them?"

The vissy nodded, her eyes still on the table. "I anticipated your question. It is not that I am coded to recognize all life forms in the universe. There are life forms that I am not programmed to recognize," she looked at Didrik and then back to the table. "But I know when I am looking at something unnatural. Even life forms that I have not encountered will give off a certain *truthfulness* to their signatures. The Tioris signatures are false. They are a cover. I know because maybe they say they are human, but their signature is broken. I have met all sorts of beings. The only ones whose signatures do not match what they should be are Tioris."

Filion looked at her.

"How many Tioris have you come into contact with?"

"Enough to detect a pattern. I used to be a foot soldier. A Tiori owned me. I was often taken to protect him when he met other Tioris."

"You seem to smart to be a foot soldier. Why were you never promoted?"

The vissy laughed, savagely. "Vissys do not get promoted."

Filion didn't say anything.

"Take the Living Document," she continued "I have never encountered such a being before, but I can tell that its signature is real. Your Living Document is what it claims to be."

Filion looked at her. When she had first walked in, he had sensed something broken about her aura. That damage was still there, but there was a spark about her, a hopeful spark.

"I know you will need our help if you are to reach Handu alive. I also know that you will need our help if you are to leave Handu alive. Captain Eri might not like or believe your story, but Captain Eri, just like all of us, has her price. If you offer her the right thing, she might take you on as a client." The vissy spoke slowly, picking her words carefully.

"What do you mean, client? She's a private for hire pilot. How can I be of any assistance?"

"Captain Eri is a pilot but that is not all. She needs to make ends meet just like anyone else. She takes jobs. Sometimes those jobs are not as simple as acting as a private charter." The vissy looked up. "I need to go check on the engines."

She stood.

"Wait," Filion said.

The vissy froze.

"I'm Filion," he extended his hand.

Wiq looked at the hand. Slowly she reached out and grabbed it. It felt wonderful. "I am Wiq."

"Thank you, Wiq."

Wiq nodded and walked out.

Filion watched her go. She moved with such grace and power, but there was something sinister about her movements... No, that wasn't the right word, or was it? His eyelids were so heavy... He pushed the recline button on the squish chair. He was asleep before it went horizontal.

Wiq stood cloaked in the hallway. She watched the now sleeping lossal. He had shaken her hand. He had said thank you. She wanted to cry.

Chapter 37

Yalki sat in Harick's tent. The day was over by several hours, yet they were no closer to locating the Chozen than they had been that morning. Harick had mobilized his troops, but there had been no more energy surges since the third burst. Without even a direction in which to send his men, Harick had them standing by, ready and waiting. All day they had hoped for another signature, weaker than the third but strong enough. None had come though, and now it was too dark to send anyone into the forest. Harick wasn't really concerned for his troops' safety, but their numbers mattered to him. Every pawn mattered. Their lives had to be spent wisely.

"We have to do something," Yalki complained. "We can't just sit here. We need to find it first. We can't let it have the advantage."

"I agree," Harick said, without taking his eyes from the map he was studying. "Tomorrow I will send out the troops. I have divided the forest into grids. We will search one grid at a time. Once we clear a grid, we'll surround it with an Invisifence. We'll track its movements that way."

"This is so stupid. If we had the Coalition behind us we could find it in a moment. Physically searching is so far beneath us."

Harick nodded. He agreed, but due to Yalki's rash decision to take the planet by storm, and the fact that Etulosbas were something that Afortiori never spoke of, they did not have the technology to scan the planet. They also did not have the manpower to send his troops to their deaths needlessly. If he or Yalki had been more powerful Afortiori, maybe they would have had a ship capable of scanning the planet. Maybe they would have had lives to waste. They were middle ranking Afortiori though, so here they were.

Yalki sighed dramatically. She stood up and went to the tent's door. She could hear the soldiers in the dark. They were out there and so was it. It was hers for the taking, if she could find it. She and Harick would be heroes if they killed an Etulosba, but she would get the most credit, after all, she started this. She would have the best ships, the best planets, and the best slaves. No more rural, cultureless rocks. Only the best palaces and food would do. No more slop like here on Handu. If she caught this Etulosba, she would become the most powerful being in the universe…

Chapter 38

Captain Eri sat in the captain's chair on the bridge. She stared through the glass windows without seeing. *Chozens, Eoans, Tioris, Searchers, Living Documents, universal slavery...*

She spun the chair. It rotated slowly as she unconsciously kicked the floor to keep it spinning. As much as she didn't want to believe the lossal's story, deep down, she did. She had been in the military long enough to hear things she shouldn't have, things like what she had just heard, and such things were the reasons for her current situation.

She took a deep breath. The Federation knew if a planet was under attack from Tioris, and they knew before it was too late. The Federation always knew, because word always got out. No matter how subtle and conniving Tioris were, there were always spies, and with the ability to broadcast information halfway across the galaxy in a matter of seconds, there was no way a Tiori could keep their movements secret until the last moment. The Federation didn't do anything to stop the Tioris because the Federation was afraid. It was easier to declare a planet Black than to risk everything to fight for it.

*****

Seventeen and a fresh foot soldier for the Federation, Soldier Eri Everfar had been given the task of delivering a message from her platoon captain to the Warrik airbase commander. It was early, maybe three or four in the morning, when she was given this task, and she set about completing it with full enthusiasm. It was exciting to have been given such a job, it meant her platoon captain had noticed her, and now so would the airbase commander.

She walked with efficiency through the metal base halls, turning with military precision at every corner. The base commander was in the communications room, so she had to take a set of stairs up one level to reach him. The metal stairs flexed and popped under her feet and she did her best to limit the noise of her footsteps to but a whisper.

As she stepped from the stairwell, her ascent nearly silent, she heard the crackle of a radio. If she had been a more experienced soldier, she would have known how unusual it was to have heard the radio from the stairwell. Usually the communications room was kept sealed, but perhaps due to the early hour, or the fact that the deputy commander had only planned on dropping something off to the base commander, the door had been left open. She paused, hoping to hear something she shouldn't, and she did.

"This is Rethia 5," a woman's voice sounded. The woman was probably the same age as Eri, but her voice was brave, much braver than Eri's had ever been.

"Rethia 5 is under attack from Tioris. I repeat. Rethia 5 is under attack from Tioris. We request reinforcements. Please, send reinforcements. Do you copy?"

The words hit Soldier Everfar like a ton of rocks. *Tioris attacking.* This is what they trained for. This meant war. She was going to have to fight the Tioris.

Fighting the Tioris meant certain death.

Then the location of the attack registered, *Rethia 5*. Her mother's family was from Rethia 5.

Memories and images bombarded her. Her aunt smiling, her uncle holding her cousin, her niece waving on a cloudless day…

It was all she could do to not vomit on the freshly mopped floor. She stood as the world spun, her right foot still in the stairwell, concentrating on not throwing up, when she heard the base commander say, "Encode it and scrub it. No response warranted."

It was at that point something broke inside of Soldier Everfar, something small but vital. Something she would spend the next several years hiding and pretending didn't exist – but it did. That something would grow into a ragged, bloody wound, and that wound would nearly kill her, but she would survive, if only so she could later risk her life trying to redeem herself. She would survive.

*****

It wasn't until much later that Captain Eri found out the true reason for the lack of response to Rethia 5. It wasn't what she had been told – the Tioris weapons were too advanced for even the Federation to fight (although that was partially true) – but rather that the Federation didn't want to risk it. If they declared war on the Tioris, especially for some backwater planet, the Tioris might turn on the Federation. The Tioris might attack the capital with everything they had, and the Federation leaders would, surely as night catches day, suffer the same fate as those on Rethia 5, and all of the other Black planets.

This much Captain Eri knew. She suspected more. She suspected there was a reason that Tioris typically attacked backwater planets and not federally important ones. She suspected that the Federation had machines capable of fighting the Tioris. She suspected there were Tioris in the Federation. She suspected that there was a deal between the Tioris and the Federation. She even suspected that there was some sort of pact between the Federation and Tioris that dictated which planets would be attacked, which people would be enslaved, and which people would be spared.

Her friends dismissed her theories as conspiracies.

"The Federation exists to govern and protect its people, not sell them out to the Tioris," they would tell her.

Captain Eri didn't believe that for a second, which is why she and her crew were going to help the lossal.

She knew it was a bad business decision – money was tight, jobs were scarce, and taking on clients for free didn't pay the bills – but it was what had to be done.

Or was it? She stopped spinning. There was no reason why she couldn't help the lossal and make some gold at the same time.

She stood up and headed towards the armory.

Chapter 39

"Red?"

Red looked up from the phazer he was tuning. "Yeah? In here."

Captain Eri popped her head into the armory. She was calm now, more resolved. Red hoped she had decided to dump the lossal in Hifora. Better yet, they could sell him to the pelters themselves. He would fetch a good price, despite his height.

"Whadda ya think's wrong with him? The lossal, I mean?" Red asked.

Captain Eri didn't respond. Her eyes scanned the armory.

"I mean, you think he's got the Bout? I hear that does nasty stuff to the brain. Could make a lossal wander into a pelter's den. Could also make a person think they were the last hope of the universe," Red chuckled. "Ha. What'd he say, Chozens? Some lady Chozen is waiting for him to save her on Handu? He must be desperate if he's willin' to risk gettin' caught by pelters AND Tioris. I mean you can't risk everything just because some woman, lady Chozen or not, wants your junk. A man has to have limits, ya know?"

Captain Eri gave him a flat stare.

"No, I don't know, Red, and I know you don't either."

"Ah, well, anyway..."

"We aren't going to dump him."

Excitement welled in Red.

"You mean we're going to sell him to the pelters? That's great. I know, I know, we could save money by pelting him ourself, but that's a messy process. You know, sometimes it's better to employ a middleman." He nodded, knowing he was right.

"We aren't selling him to the pelters."

"Ahh, okay. I know that you and the vissy will make me skin him though, so I demand more of a cut then. I mean I'm the one getting my hands dirty. It's only fair."

"We are not skinning him."

Red's face fell. "Well, what are we going to do with him?"

"We're going to help him. We're going to help him get to Handu, then we're going to help him get off of Handu."

Red blinked. "Eri, Captain, Sir. I don't think I understand what you're sayin'. It sounds like you wanna help him get to Handu. He's crazy. Not only is there no lady Chozen waiting for him, I mean really, you know no ladies're after him, look at him, but also he wants to go to HANDU! Tioris are there. It's BLACK! No matter if they're evil aliens from another universe, or anti-Federation rebels, they still enslave an' kill people! I AM TOO YOUNG TO BE ANYONE'S SLAVE!"

"It's what we're doing. You can either do as I say or find other work."

Red looked at her but didn't say anything.

"You've got until Hifora to decide. I hear working in the mines is nice this time of year." She smiled and left.

Chapter 40

Red stared after her. They were really going to help that crazy lossal? He had seemed like a nice enough guy in the beginning, going to save his sister and all, but then he started talking about lady Chozens and other universes. How could Captain Eri believe anything he said? His story about his sister was more plausible than the story about the Tioris. But then again, he had that book. That book could talk, well kinda, but still. Red had never seen something like that. He supposed it could be some fancy technology, but he knew, deep down, it wasn't. Which meant logically, and he was a very logical man, that the rest of the lossal's story was true as well.

He thought about that for a moment. If the book was real, then the lossal was telling the truth. If the lossal was telling the truth, then everyone in the universe was in danger of being enslaved. More importantly though, there was a *real* lady Chozen in need of assistance. If this lady Chozen was just waking up, or whatever he had said, the chances of her being involved with anyone was slim to none. If he helped the lossal find and protect her, she might fall for him. That meant he had a chance at least and a much better chance than the lossal. Sure, the lossal had nice fur, and his fur was *technically* cleaner than Red's hair, but Red could wash his hair. No woman liked too much fur. That was a universal fact.

He had a chance.

"Cap'n!" He yelled, standing and dropping the phazer. "Cap'n!" He ran into the hall. Captain Eri stood, watching him.

"Yes?"

"I'll do it. I'll help you but under one condition." Captain Eri looked at him, her eyebrows arching. "If this lady Chozen's all that the lossal says she is, she'll need to be guarded 'round the clock. I'm the most skilled combat fighter here, so I'll guard her. She can sleep in my bunk if need be."

"You're volunteering yourself as her personal guard because you are the most skilled combat fighter on the ship?"

Red nodded, knowing she knew he was right.

"Well Red, I agree with you that she will need to be guarded, and giving her the best personal guard we have seems proper."

Red smiled.

"But unfortunately, you aren't our most skilled warrior. Wiq is. She's fought in dozens of wars as a foot soldier, dirty hand-to-hand combat, and she's equipped with cloaking technology. She will be the Chozen's personal guard. I'm glad you brought this to my attention."

"Wait, but…" *GRAWLIX!* He'd forgotten about the damn vissy.

"You can be deputy guard though. You're our next most skilled fighter, much more so than the lossal, so if something happens to Wiq, you're up."

"Yeah," Red said nodding. He was way more skilled than the lossal. "Okay, well as long as we keep her safe. I mean, she's the key to our freedom, an' whatever, so only the best'll do. If Wiq is busy or something, you can count on me!"

Captain Eri smiled and gave Red a slight nod. "Thank you Red. I knew I could."

Red nodded and then turned back to the armory. If he was going to be the deputy guard, he had better get outfitted. There was no telling when he would need to jump in and save that vissy's ass.

Chapter 41

Filion opened his eyes. He was on the floor of the lounge. The ship hit another bump, and he bounced into the table leg. This was some turbulence to have ejected him from the squish chair. He pushed himself from the floor and sighed. His nap had been too short, but it had done what he needed it to. Since he was now awake and a little less tired, he may as well do something productive.

Filion struggled to his chair. He sat and pulled Didrik from his pocket.

What should we offer her? Filion wrote, his pencil skipping over the page in tune with the turbulence.

We could start with money, Didrik suggested.

Yeah, but how much?

Does it matter? That bag of yours will last you until the end of time, as long as you don't lose it.

Filion pulled the bag from his pocket, and opened it. The coins were platinum Federation stamped.

Wow. This is going to be expensive isn't it?

Probably. I think she will want something more than just money though.

What do you mean?

She might demand use of your skills.

Filion paused as the ship shook. When the ship quieted he asked,

What skills?

You are a Searcher…

It's illegal to Search without a Summoning.

Just as it is illegal to fail to report a Summoning.

But that was different. I mean the fate of the universe was at stake.

And it still is.

Filion sighed. He was no law-breaker, yet Didrik was right. He had failed to report his Eoan Summoning to the Board of Summonings. He was in direct violation of the Searcher's Code of Conduct. He risked court martial. Not a good fate, but he knew that what he was doing was more important than himself which is why he was here now. But to use his 'skills' to help Captain Eri, that was asking too much. Or was it?

Captain Eri walked into the common room. They had finally passed through the up and downdrafts of a particularly large thunder cell. Now she could stop focusing on flying and start focusing on her newest set of problems – the lossal – and what she was about to do for him. She had not told Wiq of her decision. She knew that Wiq would remain in her service, no matter what she decided, but Captain Eri had promised to treat her as an equal crewmember… it didn't matter. Wiq was the least of her problems right now.

"Lossal," Captain Eri said.

Filion flinched, accidentally shutting Didrik. He looked up. There she was, the woman who stood between him and her. He knew what he had to do. Ryo was more important than the Searcher's Code, but still…

"Hi…" Filion started. He reopened Didrik and placed him on the table.

"Hello. I have considered your story."

"Ah," Filion said, twisting uncomfortably in his chair.

"I believe you."

"You… wait, what?"

"I know, deep down, that what you have said is true. It bothers me. It more than bothers me. It terrifies me, which is why I know you speak the truth. The fear I feel is real."

Filion didn't say anything.

"I realize I implied I would leave you to the mercy, or the lack of mercy, of the pelters. I cannot do this. I also realize that you are attempting to reach Handu via the portal because you cannot reach it by ship without being captured. I know that the portal on Handu will most likely be guarded. I also know that you have never touched a weapon before, let alone used one against another person."

"Well," Filion started. "I used to whittle as a kid."

"Yes, my point exactly. Even if you were to make it out of Hifora alive, you won't make it to Handu alive, and you certainly won't make it back alive. You need us. You can't save this Chozen alone."

"Yes, I know…"

"I will aid you, me, my crew, and my ship, but I need something from you in return."

"I know," Filion said, his head hung.

"Then you agree?"

Filion paused.

"Yes. I will do what it takes to protect her."

"Good."

Chapter 42

He had agreed to the terms without argument. Captain Eri almost felt bad. He had seemed so beaten when he imprinted the contract. For as long as the lossal stayed on the *Dark Horse*, Captain Eri could use his Searcher skills to locate potential jobs, and she was guaranteed at least three jobs. Captain Eri sensed that what she asked him to do was illegal, but surreptitiously entering a planet overtaken by Tioris for a person who might not exist was quite a risk. She wanted it to be worth it.

"Okay," Captain Eri said, shoving the contract into her pocket. "In order to get you to the portal, we'll need to disguise you. We'll also need to disguise ourselves."

Filion nodded.

"You're going to have to go in chains."

"Chains? Why?"

"There's no way you can walk freely through Hifora. If you don't start in chains, you'll end in chains, or worse. You need to already be captured."

Filion shook his head. "No chains."

"Then no deal. Trust me. This is the only way."

Filion sighed. Was this really happening?

"We'll be there in one hour. We need to get ready."

*****

Groy watched the Boulder circle before setting down. It was a weird looking Boulder with lots of patchy modifications. Something had been done to the capacitors. A strange thing to modify on a Boulder, but Groy wasn't paid to contemplate the repercussions of ship modifications. He was paid to see that the ships docked correctly. He pushed the pad lights and guided the Boulder into the docking port.

Once the ship set down, Groy lumbered up to its cargo door. No doubt the Boulder was carrying mining supplies. He had seen this ship before, a mostly attractive ringer, if you overlooked her wings, owned it. He couldn't remember her name though. Not that it mattered. She had never shown any interest.

The door opened with the normal steam release, and Groy strained to see the ringer, the next best thing to talking to her. His view was temporarily obscured, but when the steam cleared, Groy's jaw dropped.

There she was, the little ringer, holding a thick chain. The chain floated upwards and connected to a collar, which wrapped around a lossal's thick neck. The lossal appeared broken, a sad, resigned look on its face. Its hands were cuffed together, and it looked as if it had put up a fight. Next to the lossal stood a human male and a, *a vissy*, both holding Electroprods. The prods were turned towards the lossal.

The group stepped from the Boulder. The ringer, the human and the vissy were all heavily armed and all wore heavy looking synthetic backpacks. The human also carried a large synthetic duffle over his shoulder. All three of the captors wore tactical clothes, and all three looked ready to fight.

"Groy. So nice to see you again," the ringer said.

Groy blushed, and nodded in response. If only he was better with names. "Ahh, you have a lossal," he said stupidly.

If only he were better with women.

"So we do," the ringer said, jerking the chain. "We found him outside the beta site. Didn't know what hit him. What a lucky coincidence for us that we currently know someone who is in need of a lossal coat. Thought we would hand deliver it ourselves."

Groy nodded. His uncle was a pelter, so Groy knew a little about pelting. This lossal had an exceptional coat, but it was rather small.

"I hope your client is short," Groy said.

The lossal glared at him.

"Don't worry. This is exactly what they're looking for."

Groy nodded. "Where are you taking it?"

"To our client who wishes to remain anonymous. Sorry Groy, no disclosures today."

Groy frowned. All lossal transactions went through Qin, the Master Pelter. If they were doing anything behind his back, that was against pelter code.

"Does Master Qin know?" Groy asked.

"Of course he does," the ringer said, glaring at him. "You think we want to fight him and his pelters? There is only so much anonymity when buying a pelt."

The ringer smiled and strode past Groy, her odd looking convoy following.

"Yeah, well, as long as Master Qin knows" Groy said.

He watched them go, frozen in place. Then, as if he had been kicked, he dug his communicator from his pocket and called his uncle.

*****

"How much time you think we have?" Red said, eyeing the people in the waiting bay of the docking station. People looked at them, that was for sure, but no one approached them.

"Not much. No doubt Groy has already alerted the pelters. These people are probably calling everyone they know." Captain Eri said, steering Filion through the door.

"What happens if they find out we lied to them?" Filion asked.

"You mean *when* they find out I lied to them? You don't want to know. Just keep up and try not to look too suspicious," Captain Eri said.

They stepped outside. It was raining.

Big surprise, Filion thought.

Red threw a poncho over Filion's shoulders and they hurried into the dark

110

streets. Filion waited for his eyes to adjust to the deep purple light, but they didn't. In fact, the purple gloom only seemed to grow worse.

From what Filion could see, Hifora was a dying city. The unkempt stone buildings appeared to crumble in the rain. Ragged shutters hung lifelessly from dark windows. Trash and mud, ankle deep, filled the streets, and the air, despite the cleansing rain, reeked of methane, no doubt a byproduct of the mines. Filion took a step and heard a soft crunch. He looked down and saw he had stepped on a discarded headless doll. He shivered.

Inky figures dotted the streets. What they were, human or otherwise, was impossible to tell. Occasionally, a figure would pass under a dim streetlight, but all Filion would catch was a wet cloak and, at best, an off-putting aura. While such people were a concern, they didn't worry Filion nearly as much as the people he couldn't see. Unkind auras spilled from seemingly empty alleys and corners. No matter where he looked, something terrifying seemed to be waiting.

"Where are we going?" Filion asked after several minutes of hurried walking.

"To where we need to go," Captain Eri answered. She still held the chain attached to the collar, but she held it loosely, allowing him freedom of movement.

"We're being tailed," Red said.

"I know. It was to be expected," Captain Eri said without looking back. "Here."

They stopped in front of a decrepit building, identical, at least to Filion, to all of the others they had passed. Made of ruined stone, the building seemed to sag under the oppressive purple haze. Its edges were inconsistent, and its boarded windows bulged from the walls. In places the stone had massed together, causing swollen lumps in the building's face. Black mold crisscrossed the edifice's exterior, and some sort of aquatic flies seemed to be feasting on it. Despite the rain which drummed on Filion's hood, he could hear the building shifting. Cracks and groans emanated from its inside. Captain Eri stepped up to a rotting, engorged door that hung from cracked hinges. A rat pushed its way through the mildewed door boards causing Filion jumped backwards. No one else reacted.

Captain Eri pushed the door open and stepped inside. Filion hesitated, searching for more rats. Captain Eri jerked the chain.

"Hey!" Filion said.

"Standing around gets you killed. Let's go."

Filion stepped inside. Whatever lighting they had been privileged to in the street was gone now. Filion stood, in complete darkness, listening to what he assumed to be rats scurrying over the filthy floor. He took a deep breath.

"Bend down!" Captain Eri hissed.

"Me?" Filion asked.

"And shut up!" she added.

Captain Eri pulled on the chain, and Filion crouched. Someone removed his soaking poncho and put their hands on his face. Suddenly, he could see. Captain Eri and Red wore niteglasses, as he now did. Both Red and Wiq had sheathed their Electroprods, and all three held Talik 5 phazers. Captain Eri grabbed his hands and unlocked the cuffs, stuffing them into Red's backpack.

Filion adjusted the glasses on his face. They didn't really fit, but they would do. Everything was still the dark purple of the outside, but anything was better than the darkness.

"Wiq, don't you need a pair?" Filion asked, pointing to his glasses.

Wiq shook her head and Captain Eri made an annoyed 'SHHHHHH!' sound.

"Follow me."

Captain Eri led the way, still holding onto the chain. Filion wanted to ask if he could hold it, but he knew if he asked she would hold it longer just to spite him. He also knew better than to ask for a phazer.

They wound their way into the basement of the dilapidated building. It appeared that the building they entered had been the access point for a large network of underground tunnels. The tunnels, made of slick, stinking stone, caused Filion's fur stand on end. He did not trust them.

They twisted and turned through the catacombs. They entered areas where the ceilings had collapsed, passed rooms where he knew unspeakable things had occurred, and once, a part of a wall failed in front of them, spraying them with bits of rock and sending Filion into an internal panic.

When he was calm enough to focus on something other than himself, Filion searched for signs of life. Other than the rats that regularly ran across his feet, he found none. He saw no souls, nor auras, but he could not shake the feeling of being watched.

They continued, now no doubt several stories underground, in silence for what seemed like hours, when suddenly Captain Eri stopped. Filion nearly ran her over but caught himself. Red and Wiq went completely still as well. Filion looked around. They were in a small square room. With walls made of the same cold stone as the rest of the tunnels, the room did not stand out to Filion. He could still feel the thick wet air clinging to his fur, and his breath still fogged up his niteglasses. The only thing that really stood out to him were the piles of trash. Each room's trash heaps were different. Here the mounds seemed to be made primarily of bits of corroded plastic and some sort of black slimy stuff.

Filion turned his attention back to Captain Eri. She and the others had their heads tilted, as if they were listening to something. The only noise Filion could hear was his own breathing and the blood in his ears. He worked to calm himself, doing first year meditation and breathing exercises. Slowly the blood stopped pounding, and his breathing grew quiet. He was able to listen to the silence, or at least, what should have been silence.

From down the hallway to their left, came a steady *skitch, skitch, skitch*. At first Filion passed it off as a rat, but the longer he listened, the more convinced he became that the sound emanated from a mechanical source. The noises occurred at regular intervals, and they seemed, much to Filion's horror, to be growing in volume.

No one moved. Filion looked at Captain Eri's back. Her aura implied she was terrified, but her body did not shake. She looked as if she were carved from rock. Red stood to Filion's right. Like Captain Eri, he was totally still. His aura also spoke of fear, but there was something else. *Red was praying*. Sensing that was like being struck by lightning. Filion knew Red wasn't religious. Something very bad was in the hallway.

Filion, without moving, dragged his eyes from Red and looked left. Wiq was gone, but her aura was still there. She was cloaked. Her soft pink aura said Wiq was concerned, but her concern was mild. It was nothing like what Captain Eri and Red were experiencing.

The sound moved closer. Filion's eyes snapped to where he thought it should be, but he saw nothing. He strained to see something, anything, but all he saw were purple shadows. *Skitch, skitch, skitch*. Finally, he saw it.

Low to the ground and small, the object making the noise did not look menacing. With four legs and a long thin tale, the thing looked like a rat. The legs were the source of the *skitch, skitch, skitch* noise. It wasn't a rat though. It had no aura. It rounded the corner and moved mechanically towards them. Captain Eri's aura stayed the same, but Red's flashed without order. He was panicking.

The thing was in the room now, headed directly for Captain Eri. It reached her and stopped. Captain Eri's aura seemed to skip, its colors exploding and then disappearing all in the same second. The creature lifted its pointed head and sniffed the air. Filion watched, terrified, but unable to turn his eyes away.

The creature walked onto Captain Eri's foot, and her aura seemed to deflate. A resigned defeat washed over her. Filion held his breath. Captain Eri did not move as the creature stood up, its front legs on her shin. Filion sensed Red was about to implode. His aura blinked in and out of existence, the colors fluctuating and the shape morphing into unreadable orders.

There was a sharp intake of air. Captain Eri had taken an unintended breath. The creature froze, its front legs still on Captain Eri's leg. Filion could have sworn it smiled.

Then, time seemed to slow.

Red lunged towards Captain Eri, his feet inching into the air as his arms stretched before him. Some sort of cry escaped his lips. Wiq's violent aura crept towards Captain Eri, stopping when it stood directly in front of her. Captain Eri took a heavy step backwards, her arms sluggishly wind milling. The rat reared and then sagged, its body slowly collapsing, and suddenly, time was back to normal.

Red slammed into Captain Eri. She crumpled to the ground with a low *Uof!*

"Get it away from me! Get it off of me!" Captain Eri thrashed on the ground, struggling to throw Red from her. Red scrambled, pawing in the gross floor.

"Where is it?! Did it get you?! I can't see it!"

"Both of you calm down," Wiq said. "I got it. I got it before you almost killed us, *Red.*" She held the rat, now limp in her hand.

Both Red and Captain Eri stopped moving. Red jumped from Captain Eri and grabbed the rat.

"You sure it's dead?" Red said, eyeing it suspiciously.

Wiq nodded.

"It didn't have a chance to call the others?" Captain Eri said, frantically examining her leg.

"I cannot be sure, but they are not here yet," Wiq said.

Captain Eri grunted in return and stood, the color gone from her face.

"What's going on?" Filion asked, finally daring to speak.

"It's dead for sure now," Red said.

He had a knife to the back of the creature's head. With a flick of his wrist he cut into the creature. Something popped from its body and landed on the floor. He crushed the object with his boot heel.

Captain Eri took a deep breath.

"Salinders," Wiq said.

"What?" Filion asked.

"That was a Salinder," Captain Eri said, sitting back down.

Red shot her a disgusted look. "You're sittin' back down?"

Captain Eri ignored him. "Tioris… they're used by Tioris," she breathed, her head in her hands. "To hunt and capture non-enslaved beings. Once a Salinder finds you, it bites you and injects you with T. Tryx – the virus the Tioris use to capture planets."

"How can that be?" Filion asked. "The virus only works if a person's mind is primed to accept it. Wouldn't injecting it into an unwilling person just kill them?"

Captain Eri nodded, shaking bits of grime from her hair. "Yes, in most cases, but not all. Some people can survive a T. Tryx injection."

"Yeah," Red said. "Evil people."

No one said anything. Finally, Captain Eri said, "Supposedly the more corrupt one's soul, the longer one can survive after being bitten. The virus causes that person to get sick, really sick, but they don't die, not immediately at least. First they get boils, or their skin turns sickly shades, maybe their eyes film over, sometimes their limbs fall off…"

"Infecteds," Red breathed, his face ashen.

Captain Eri nodded, her filthy face grim. "They essentially become a walking chemical bomb. They ooze T. Tryx. They sneeze it, they cough it, and they bleed it. Anything they come in contact with gets it."

"How do you kill them?" Filion asked.

"Infecteds are easy to kill," Wiq said. "Physically, they are extremely compromised. One shot will do. The problem is the spray. You cannot come into contact with anything from the Infected's body. We used to snipe them with fire ammo. The shot would kill them, and then the round would ignite. Fire ammo isn't strong enough to cause an explosion, but it burns hot, very hot. One bullet can burn a 300 pound soldier in under a minute."

"I thought you used to work for a Tiori?" Filion asked.

"I did. Infecteds are only loyal to the Tiori who programmed the initial Salinder. We were ordered to exterminate any that had not been programmed by Tofic himself."

"What happens if you come into contact with an Infected?" Filion asked.

"You either die, as you would if a Salinder bit you, a terrible, painful death wherein you ultimately explode, contaminating all those around you, or you turn into an Infected yourself. Depending on your soul's condition, you might not show signs of infection for several hours. You can still infect during those hours though. The period before the virus visually manifests the body is the most dangerous time for everyone else. You may think the guy next to you only has a cold. What if he sneezes on you? It could be the end. A simple sneeze, and you're done," Captain Eri said.

"No, that can't be..." Filion breathed. How many sick people had he been in contact with today? Two planets, two terminuses, two ships... that man, the man with the brown aura! On Thog! Had he sneezed on Filion? Coughed on him? It seemed like so long ago.

"Don't worry. You would know if you had been around someone who had been infected. People would be exploding all around you. It takes a very evil person to not die from T. Tryx. No one you came into contact with today had it," Captain Eri said.

Filion let out a long breath. Wiq moved to Captain Eri and tried to help her up, but Captain Eri waved her away. Wiq wasn't pleased, but she took a step back and looked around anxiously.

"Besides," Captain Eri continued. "Tioris would rather not enslave people via Salinders. Most don't survive, and those who do have a shelf life. Tioris tend to use them on the outskirts of their territories. They use them in places like these, borderlands, places where the Federation could be amassing armies to fight the Tiori. A single Salinder can destroy an entire army."

"Okay, so why didn't we just kill it as soon as we heard it? What was with the standing around and waiting?" Filion asked.

"Speaking of standing around," Wiq said. "We should get moving."

"They hunt by sight and sound. If you don't move or make noise, they can pass you by," Red said, ignoring Wiq. The color hadn't yet fully returned to his face.

"I still don't get why you didn't just take it out as soon as you knew it was there. It was the size of a rat," Filion said.

"No Tiori programs a single Salinder," Captain Eri answered. "The Tiori that programmed this Salinder probably has thousands of them. They're all linked to each other, on a network. If one sees something it thinks is noteworthy, like a free being, it sends a message to all of the Salinders it's linked with. If we had killed it out right, we could have had thousands of Salinders on us in seconds. You can fight one rat, but thousands, you're as good as dead." Captain Eri seemed to be shaking.

"This is not good," Wiq said, looking around.

"No kidding," Red said.

Filion moved next to Captain Eri and helped her from the floor. He did his best to touch as little of her as possible since she was covered in refuse.

"There is either a Tiori on Bok, or the Salinders have come through the portal. If the Portal Keeper is an Infected, we will not be able to get to Handu," Wiq said. "That, and we have been here too long already."

"We have to get to Handu!" Filion said. "Ours and everyone's fates depend on it!"

"Let's not jump to conclusions. We've been making a lot of noise, and nothing's attacked us yet. Let's assume that this Salinder is rogue. Maybe it came through the portal accidentally, and it couldn't get back to Handu. Either way, we're almost there. Let's just take it one step at a time," Captain Eri said, doing her best to brush the muck from her body.

Wiq nodded, but Red looked unconvinced.

"We could just go back and leave this forsaken place," Red suggested.

"Not an option," Captain Eri said. "Let's go, it's just around this turn."

They crept forward, stopping often. The claim that wherever they were going was 'just around this turn,' obviously wasn't true. Right as Filion was about to say so, Captain Eri stopped. Glancing around at the tunnel – a featureless stone esker– Filion caught himself before he branded the tunnel the same as all of the others. Obviously it wasn't, or Captain Eri wouldn't have stopped. Through his niteglasses, Filion watched Captain Eri reach out and touch the wall. She pushed a block and a door appeared.

"A hidden door," Filion breathed.

"A cheap hologram will go far," Captain Eri said.

A small puzzle lock secured the door. Without stopping to even consider the type of puzzle, Captain Eri began to move its pieces. Moments later the lock popped, and Captain Eri pushed open the door.

Chapter 43

Blinding light spilled into the tunnel. Filion blinked, unable to see or move.

"Lossal! Let's move!" Captain Eri said, yanking the chain.

Filion stumbled forward, still blind, until he bumped into someone who he could only assume to be Captain Eri. He ripped the niteglasses from his head, and his surroundings slowly came into focus.

He stood in the middle of a wood paneled room. The door to the tunnel had closed, another hologram no doubt shielding its existence. Wooden shelves lined the room's walls. Books, figurines, plants, and many other objects Filion could not identify covered the shelves. Bits of odd furniture speckled the room. A low purple end table filled one corner, several bust statues covering its surface. In another corner stood a tall, water filled, glass case. Inside the case were aquatic plants and strangely shaped creatures. The creatures swam and danced between the plant's long leaves, and the water seemed to shimmer around them. Filion looked at the next corner, where a swarm of multicolored butterflies appeared to be roosting, when he realized that the room was not square. No, in fact it seemed to have an infinite amount of corners. One corner was filled with teapots, another with carved ivory lamps, and one corner was completely dark except for a single shining constellation. The constellation rotated, as if it was a projection, but Filion couldn't determine from where it was projected. Then the constellation disappeared, and a new one sparkled in its place.

Behind Filion, Red dropped into a red velvet armchair, and Wiq stood attentively with her back to a book filled corner.

Captain Eri pushed Filion away from her. "Watch where you're going."

"Sorry," Filion said, taking a step back, his eyes still sweeping the room.

Captain Eri dropped the chain and moved toward one of the shelves. Filion watched her and then realized that the room appeared to have no doors. Was this whole room a holographic trick?

"We should be careful," Wiq started, her phazer still at ready.

"No kidding," Red said, surreptitiously straightening in the chair.

"She might be an Infected," Wiq continued, ignoring Red.

"I know," Captain Eri said, rooting around on one of the shelves. "But we'll never reach the portal if we don't find her."

Wiq nodded but said nothing.

Captain Eri turned. A small clay figurine of a fat brown woman holding a basket sat in her hand. She carried it to a low cluttered table, and placed the figurine on a coaster made from a circuit board.

The coaster clicked to life, electricity running through its incomplete circuits. A hologram flashed above the figurine.

Captain Eri and Wiq dropped to one knee. Red, slightly delayed, jumped from the chair, muttered, and took a knee as well. Filion followed suit.

"Keeper Amalia, we ask to use the portal," Captain Eri said.

Filion looked at the hologram. A beautiful ringer hovered above the clay figurine. Her white hair and white dress drifted backwards, as if propelled by a distant breeze. White sparkles flecked her pitch-black skin, and her white feathery wings worked effortlessly to keep her in the air.

"Captain Eri," the ringer said, her resonating voice powerful and distant. "It seems that not all is as it seems. I had some unusual visitors not moments ago. Salinders. I do not know if I can trust you."

"Ah, Mother, we too were visited by a Salinder, just one, but enough for us to think the same about you."

"Then it seems we are at an impasse," the Keeper said, her eyes drifting around the room. "What strange company you keep, Captain. While you and the human aren't so odd, the vissy is an interesting touch, and the lossal? Very strange indeed," the Keeper observed. "Where do you wish to go?"

"Handu."

"Handu is a Black planet. Why would you want to go there?"

"A woman is there," Captain Eri said, her head still bowed. "We have no choice but to attempt to rescue her."

"Hmmmm. A woman? Surely one life is not worth the price of four."

"In this case, one life is worth much more than four."

"It seems that the pelters are in a frenzy to find you Captain Eri. They want your furry friend…"

"So they do, but they are the least of our worries."

"You must have a lot of worries to not be concerned by several thousand armed and violent men."

"We do."

"This woman you speak of, what is her name?"

Captain Eri faltered.

"Ryo," Filion said, his head bowed.

"So he speaks."

The Portal Keeper said nothing for a few moments.

"I've studied the myths. I know of whom you search. I know of what she is, but I cannot let you through for fear you are not what you say. She has a better chance on her own than in the hands of four Infecteds."

"We are not Infecteds!" Captain Eri said. "Let us prove it to you!"

"Proof is difficult to come by."

"I will do it," Wiq said.

"You will provide the proof I seek?" the Keeper asked.

Wiq nodded then said, "But you must also provide us with proof."

The Portal Keeper hesitated.

"You cannot provide the proof I seek. It must be one of the others," the Keeper said turning away from Wiq.

"I'll do it. I should be the one regardless of Wiq's race. I'm the Captain."
The Portal Keeper looked at Captain Eri then nodded.
"It will be much less painful for me, you know," the Keeper said.
"I know," Captain Eri answered, her head still bowed.

Chapter 44

Filion watched silently as Red and Wiq tied Captain Eri to a wooden rocking chair. Captain Eri's eyes were unfocused and far away. She didn't complain as Red and Wiq tightened the straps around her wrists, the straps stretching her skin to the point of tearing.

"Ahh, this's dung. We've got enough firepower to override an army. We can take the Portal Keeper," Red muttered, triplicating his knot.

"None of us know how to use the portal. Killing her is not the answer," Wiq said.

"Then I should be the one in this chair. I mean, I'm the man here. Captain Eri shouldn't be doing this. It just isn't right," Red said, tying her right leg to the chair.

"I do not think Captain Eri's gender has anything to do with what is right. She is the captain, it is her burden, not ours."

"You volunteered," Red snarled.

"I know, but I could not change the outcome," Wiq said.

"Still isn't right…"

"Are you ready?" the Portal Keeper asked. She did not look concerned, her image floating as gently as ever, and her voice as airy as when she first spoke.

Red glanced at Captain Eri. Her wrists and ankles were strapped to the chair, as well as her thighs, upper arms, chest, waist and head. Red gave each strap a final tug then said, "Yeah, we're ready, but I wan' you to know, if you pull any funny stuff I'll kill you myself. Don't think I care that you're the only one who knows how to work the portal. I don' even wanna go through the portal anyway. This is my captain and if anything happens to her…"

"Mr. Canner, I won't be pulling any 'funny stuff'. Now if you please, lossal, open the wooden box next to the book marked *Tomorrow's Lunar Cycles.*"

Filion jumped. He hadn't really been listening. He had been staring at Captain Eri. Since volunteering for whatever was about to happen she had seemed to slip into another dimension. Her aura was a pale pink. She was trying desperately to be somewhere else.

"Uh, right…" Filion said.

He scanned the room. There were thousands of books.

"Um, do you know where the box or the book might be?" Filion asked.

"Bottom shelf, next to the red chair."

Bottom shelf! Because of his height, Filion couldn't even see the bottom shelf. He walked to the red chair and crouched down.

Regimes of the Middle Ages, The Etulosba Myths, Ganik Warlords and the Heroines who Smote them, Quilting by Thought, The Essentials of Space Travel, Tomorrow's Lunar Cycles.

There it was. Filion reached out and grabbed the dark wooden box. He stood and turned.

"These them?" Red asked, grabbing the box from Filion.

"Yes," the Keeper said.

Red grunted and pried open the box. He pulled out what appeared to be two small mechanical beetles. He handed the box back to Filion.

"I had a feeling you would be coming, so I prepared them. My DNA is there. All I need is the Captain's imprint."

Red grunted again.

"Please put the box back where you found it," she added.

Filion nodded and returned the box to its shelf.

"You know how to activate one of these?" Red asked Wiq, squinting at the bugs.

She let out a long breath and took them from Red.

"Captain, we need your DNA and imprint," Wiq said.

Blank faced, Captain Eri stuck out her thumb, and Wiq touched it to the stomach of one of the mechanical bugs. Captain Eri's thumb dwarfed the bug, but that didn't make Filion feel any better about what was going to happen. There was a whirring noise and a sharp click. Suddenly, the bug started to move. It's tiny legs spun in the air, and its wings clicked sharply. Wiq handed the imprinted bug to Red who took it gingerly. She repeated the process with the other bug.

After the second bug was imprinted, Wiq opened its wings. She studied it for a few seconds, and then handed it to Red. He took it and handed her back the first bug. She examined it. Finally she said,

"They are both ready. Both contain the Keeper's and the Captain's DNA."

"You can send me whichever you like via the totem," the Keeper said.

Wiq looked at the Keeper and nodded. She walked to the hologram and stuck her hand into the image. Opening her fingers, the bug tumbled from Wiq's hand and disappeared.

"This is stupid..." Red started.

"This is all we have," Wiq said.

"Ready when you are," the Keeper said, the bug now in her hand.

"Captain, we are ready to begin. Are you ready?" Wiq asked.

Captain Eri nodded distantly.

Wiq looked at Red and said. "Please open your mouth."

Captain Eri opened her mouth, and Red grabbed her cheeks, forcing her mouth even wider. Captain Eri did not struggle, and Wiq dropped the insect in. Quickly, Red forced her mouth closed, clasping one hand over her lips and the other under her jaw.

At first nothing happened, then her eyes widened and swiveled violently.

She began to twitch – her fingers, her eyelashes, her feet – then Captain Eri's entire body began to buck. The straps cut into her exposed flesh, and blood welled beneath her restraints. She gave off a low moan. It grew in volume. Her head thrashed. Sweat formed on Red's forehead. His muscles tensed as he struggled to keep his hands on Captain Eri's face. She jerked her arms and legs, the moan rising higher and higher. Her chest heaved. She was panting.

"I don't think she can breathe! Let her open her mouth!" Filion cried.

"NO! This is what happens. If she's lucky she'll pass out soon!" Red yelled back.

Filion looked at Wiq. Wiq wasn't watching Captain Eri. Instead she stared at the hologram.

The Keeper was no longer floating. She was on her back, her body twitching mildly. Her eyes were closed, and she made no noise. She looked as if she were dreaming, twitching while dreaming, but dreaming nonetheless.

"What's happening?!" Filion cried.

"This is what happens. It is ugly," Wiq said, watching the Keeper like a hawk.

Filion turned back to Captain Eri. The moan was now a stifled scream. Captain Eri's body convulsed regularly, her back arching and falling like a wave. Blood pooled below her wrists and ankles. Blood also roiled from the strap on her forehead. It mixed with the tears running down her cheeks and ran in red rivulets over Red's hands. He ignored the mess, his face grim but determined.

"She's strong. Anyone else would be gone by now," Red breathed.

Wiq nodded without taking her eyes from the Keeper.

Suddenly there was a click, and Captain Eri's body went limp. Her chest heaved in heavy breaths, but she no longer struggled. Wiq looked at her.

"You can let go now," Wiq said, nodding at Red.

Gently, Red took his hands from Captain Eri's face. Her eyes were closed and her face was purple where his hands had been. The handprints would bruise.

"Open her mouth," Wiq instructed.

Red did so, tenderly pushing her lips apart. A green light shone from inside Captain Eri's mouth. Red let out a long breath. Wiq seemed to visibly relax as well.

"Hand it to me."

Red reached into Captain Eri's mouth and pulled out the bug. It was responsible for the light. Bright green shone from its shell.

Wiq took the bug and turned. The Keeper had stopped twitching. For several seconds she lay unresponsive, then she slowly sat up. She opened her mouth. A green light shone from within.

"Thank the bloody gods," Red whispered, collapsing into a squat. Wiq took a deep breath.

"What's going on?" Filion asked.

"Both tests are negative," Red said, his head in his hands. He looked up, a grotesque smile on his face. "Looks like we're goin' to Handu."

Chapter 45

The Keeper and Wiq exchanged bugs. Wiq took her time examining the Keeper's bug while Filion and Red untied Captain Eri. She was still unresponsive.

"What just happened?" Filion asked.

"Captain Eri just took one for the team," Red said.

"I get that, but..."

"If you do survive a bite from a Salinder," Red said, cutting him off. "The virus goes straight to the base of your brain. To the, ahh, I don' know what it's called – you know – the brain base. That's where it takes ahold of the body, you get me? Those bugs," he shuttered." "Biopsers they're called, they go in through a person's mouth and make their way to the brain base. Once they get there they take a bite. Then they come back out the body by the mouth. Once they leave the body they're either red or green. Red is dead. Green is clean." Red turned back to Captain Eri.

"She's strong. Real strong. I've watched people be Biopsed before. She took it like a champ, like it was just another walk in the park." Red smiled and touched Captain Eri's darkening cheek. He brushed a bloody strand of hair behind her ear. "I've never seen anything like it," he whispered.

Filion looked at him. "That thing took a bite of her brain?"

Red nodded.

Wiq looked up from the Biopser.

"Red misleads you," she said, shooting a stern glance at Red. He responded with a lip curl. "Yes, Biopsers take a bite of a person's brain, but that bite is the size of a medical biopsy. That is what they were originally designed for, early illness detection. They were intended to replace the need for a skilled surgeon in the event of a biopsy. They were never widely used though, due to the pain they put the subject through. It was determined that in order to use a Biopser, a skilled anesthesiologist would still be needed, and if an anesthesiologist was required, then why not use a surgeon?"

"Why didn't the Keeper react like Captain Eri? She almost looked like she was sleeping." Filion said, ignoring the history lesson.

"Because the Keeper is somewhat magical," Wiq replied, tossing the bug to Red. He caught it but unwillingly.

"It is clean, un-doctored. She is not Infected," Wiq said to Red.

"What do you mean 'somewhat magical?'" Filion asked.

"The Keeper has some magical abilities. Such abilities allowed her to block most of the pain, but not all of it," Wiq grimaced. "She is not that good. Captain Eri possesses no magical abilities. She felt everything."

Everyone looked at Captain Eri. She didn't move.

"I see you spoke the truth," the Keeper said. She was floating again, but her voice waivered.

"As did you," Wiq said.

"You may pass. I'll see what I can do for her," the Keeper said. "Go to the wall with the Gumbo plant. Touch the man on the pot. The door will open. Oh, and put the totem back on a shelf. Wherever is fine." The Keeper disappeared and the hologram shut off.

Wiq took the clay figurine from the motherboard coaster and placed it on a shelf next to a green geode.

"Loss... Filion," Red said. "Can you carry her?"

Filion nodded. "Of course." He bent down, scooped up Captain Eri, and carefully laid her over his shoulder.

Red shot a quick glance at Wiq, saw she wasn't looking and tossed the Biopser towards a shelf full of liquid filled jars. It landed with a soft splash, and began to sink. When the Biopser touched the bottom of the jar, the butterflies in the next corner launched into the air. They swarmed towards Red, and the psychedelic cloud engulfed him. For a moment all Filion could see was a vortex of rainbow colored wings. Then, as suddenly as it had taken flight, the cloud landed. The butterflies now occupied the space where the glass jars had been, and the jars now sat where the butterflies had been. Red gave Filion an uncomfortable look and was about to say something when Wiq said,

"Here."

She stood, her bag on her back, in a corner full of Gumbo plants. If Wiq had seen what had just happened, she gave no indication of it. She pointed to a green clay pot. Scratched into the pot was a stick figure. She pressed it with two fingers.

Immediately, one of the walls disappeared. Beyond it stood a dark tunnel. Red gave Filion a final confused look and then grabbed his gear. He and Wiq stepped into the hallway. Filion followed them, Captain Eri's body draped over his shoulder.

Chapter 46

She was so light. In person she seemed strong, solid, fierce. Yet, now, hung over his shoulder, Filion would have sworn she was made of nothing. His only indication that she even existed were her dangling arms, wrists still dripping blood, that lightly brushed his torso as he walked. That and the fact that he was holding her over his shoulder, but still…

Wiq stopped. Red bumped into her and Filion bumped into him.

"What's up?" Red hissed.

"We have reached a junction," Wiq said.

Filion looked right and then left. Both hallways were identical.

"Which way do we go?" Red asked.

Wiq took a step to the right. The hallway disappeared. Nothing took its place.

"The Nothing…" Red breathed.

"We go left," Wiq said, leading them to the left.

Red couldn't believe this. First the grawlix Bromils, then the lossal, then his crazy story, then Captain Eri decided to help him, then the pelters, the Salinder, the Portal Keeper, the Biopser, and now the *NOTHING*?! He took a deep breath. He could die doing this stuff. Normally such a thought didn't bother him, rather it kind of excited him. He always imagined he would go down in a cloud of gunfire and glory, his body shredded by enemy rounds as he defended something worth defending. Maybe he died for gold, a woman, or both, but his death never involved dying in a dark stinking tunnel for a *lossal*. A male lossal at that!

Red glanced over his shoulder. The lossal stared dumbly in the darkness, the grawlix niteglasses sitting stupidly on his face. Then there was the Captain. Red could see her lifeless arms swinging in the cold air. Red winced. Then realized he was mad, very mad. He should have taken the Biopser, not Captain Eri. He glanced back again. She was so small, so delicate, and he… Red looked at his own arms, thick with muscle and anger. This was not right…

The group walked in silence for several minutes when suddenly, Red stopped.

"This is a bunch of dung. I don't know why we're doin' this. This is a harebrained idea, and everyone here knows it. I mean we almost get bitten by Salinders, Cap'n Eri might be dead, we're trying to go to a Black planet, we almost get swallowed by the Nothing, and OH RIGHT, we've got pelters on our asses. This is dumber than my cousins when drunk," Red said. He turned and squared off to Filion. Red dropped his bags, and his right hand instinctively closed on his phazer.

"We're goin' back to the ship. Now! Cap'n Eri is incapacitated and that makes me second in command," he raised his phazer. "You, lossal, hand 'er over. Wiq, grab his chain and get out your Electroprods. We're gettin' offa this forsaken planet and we're gonna sell his pelt to do it."

Filion stiffened.

"You are making a mistake, Red," Wiq said.

"No, no I'm not. Cap'n Eri made the mistake. We shouldn't have come here. Now I gotta clean up, just like I always do. So, lossal, hand her over." Red pointed the phazer at Filion's head.

"Uh..." Filion glanced at Wiq but she was gone.

A sharp crack sounded. Filion turned back to Red in time to see him sink to the floor. Wiq moved quickly, taking his phazer and slinging it over her shoulder.

"Can you carry him too?" she asked.

"Did you..."

"He will not wake up for at least a few hours. No one ever does."

"What did you do to him?"

"I just asked the correct pressure points to do the right thing," Wiq said, hoisting Red's gear onto her back.

"You sure he won't wake up?"

Wiq turned and stared at him, her golden eyes serious.

"Yes, I am."

"Okay," Filion said. He bent down and tossed Red over his other shoulder. No need to be too careful with Red. He was a tough guy.

Chapter 47

Filion and Wiq continued in silence. While Filion wasn't exactly struggling under Red and Captain Eri's weight, he couldn't believe that Wiq wasn't even breathing hard with all of the gear she carried. Each time they stopped Filion would readjust his load while Wiq acted like she had a sweater thrown over her shoulder. They stopped at junctions where Wiq would take a step in each direction and one of the hallways would disappear into the Nothing. This made Filion uneasy.

The Nothing was a scientific anomaly. No one could explain what it was, or what it wasn't. When you looked at the Nothing it almost looked like fog. You couldn't see beyond a foot or two. The Nothing was usually a shade of grey, but it didn't have to be. It wasn't the Nothing's visual appearance that unnerved Filion, it was its feeling. The Nothing gave off the same feeling as the Tierameng. To specify, being around the Nothing was like being around a knotter. Both knotters and the Nothing emanated the energy of two dimensions bleeding together – two dimensions that should have been separate. No one knew what happened if you were sucked into the Nothing. All anyone knew, was once you entered the Nothing, you never came back.

Filion tried not to think about it.

They rounded a corner into a dead end.

"Uhh…" Filion said, shifting Red's weight.

Wiq didn't respond. She stepped forward and touched the wall. It flickered and then disappeared. Beyond the wall was another hallway. Wiq stepped through and Filion followed.

Upon entering the new corridor, Filion had to stop. With Captain Eri and Red balanced over his shoulders, he removed his niteglasses. He stuffed them into a pocket, blinked and looked around. This new hallway was different. First of all, he could see. The lighting, originating from seemingly everywhere, was warm. In fact, the walls around him appeared to glow. Made of thin white paper screens and polished wood, this corridor was the most inviting place he had been since landing on Bok. Filion took a deep breath. The fear from the dark tunnels was gone. Slow music drifted from somewhere, and Filion felt lighter, almost relaxed here. Green and blue vines covered the screen's wooden frames, and the air was fresh. He took a step. The wooden floor was clean and smooth under his feet.

This place is… safe, Filion thought.

They walked through the hallway until they came to a double sliding door, made of the same wood and white paper as the walls. Wiq pushed the doors open. Inside sat the Keeper, her legs crossed, eyes closed, and hands on her knees.

Wiq took a silent step inside. Filion followed, but failed to realize how low the doorframe was. He hit it with his head, tearing the paper and cracking the wood. The Portal Keeper opened her eyes.

"So you have made it," she said.

"Uh, I'm so sorry," Filion started as he untangled himself from the doorframe.

The Keeper waved dismissively at him.

"Uh," Filion said as he ducked into the room. "I can fix it…"

He turned back to where he had hit the wall and saw that there was no damage. *This can't be,* Filion thought. He had seen the wood splinter, and he had felt the paper rip, yet the wood and paper were fine.

"Uh…" he said, looking at the Keeper.

"There is nothing for you to fix," she said.

Filion stood awkwardly for a moment then dropped Red. Red hit the floor with a crash. Filion stepped over him and then gently laid Captain Eri on some white floor pillows. The Portal Keeper stood up and walked to Filion.

"What ails him?" she asked, nodding her head in Red's direction.

"Nothing," Wiq said. "We had a minor disagreement. He will wake in a few hours time."

"I see," the Keeper said, ignoring Red and crouching over Captain Eri.

"This might take some time. Healing is not my specialty."

Wiq nodded and sat down on some pillows. Filion followed suit. He looked at his watch.

"This can't be!" Filion said.

Wiq looked at him.

"My watch says that nearly twelve hours have passed since we landed. How is that possible? Does your watch say the same thing?"

"Time moves differently in the tunnels," the Keeper said, her eyes still on Captain Eri.

Wiq closed her eyes and re-opened them.

"You are correct. Twelve hours since we landed," she said.

Twelve hours in the tunnels, plus the four he had spent on the ship after their last meeting. He had only four hours until they met again.

Chapter 48

Her patience was waning. They had been searching since first light and not only had they found nothing, but their progress had been pitiful. Harick had divided the forest into 157 grids. So far his men had searched 2. They had excuses – the forest was abnormally thick, 'proper' searching was slow searching, the terrain was rough – nothing but excuses. At this rate it would take over 75 days to find the Chozen. They didn't have that long... *she* didn't have that long.

Yalki began to pace the length of Harick's war tent. Through the open flap she could see stars shining in the dying twilight, but they didn't mean anything. Her mind was elsewhere. This had to go faster. There had to be another way.

Salinders. She could always use Salinders, but she didn't like the idea. Salinders would destroy any potential slaves on the unconquered parts of the planet. If she were going to face and fight this potential Etulosba, she would need every last slave she had. Setting Salinders across the planet would kill most, if not all, of her untapped army. Plus, she had no way of knowing if a Salinder would be able to take down an Etulosba... most likely not. Besides, she was running low on Salinders. Several had not recalled successfully after their last mission. She had used them to protect the boarders of Timum during her initial attack (not normal protocol, but desperate times called for desperate measures), and now she was missing substantial number. Normally, she would have pursued the matter, but she hadn't the resources or the time.

Still it was weird... she should have had at least some indication of their location, but it was like they had just vanished.

Ahhh, what could she do? She paced harder. The fastest way to find the Chozen would be to pinpoint its energy signal, but only she and Harick could feel the signal, so that was useless, unless...

Chapter 49

He should have been sleeping. He had hardly gotten any sleep since leaving Thog, but something bothered him. It was on the tip of his tongue, but he couldn't quite process it.

Frustrated, Filion fiddled with the collar around his neck. There was a button on there somewhere...

Click!

There it was. The collar popped open and he wrenched it from his body. That felt better. If only he could fix his other worries so easily...

Filion took a deep breath and stretched his neck. To his right the Keeper knelt over Captain Eri. The Keeper had been bent over her for some time now, and while the Keeper looked much more haggard than when she had started, Captain Eri still hadn't woken or moved. Filion turned his head to the left. Red remained out cold, and Wiq seemed to be sleeping or something. Filion sighed. None of them would be any help to him right now. He relaxed against the wall, gently, and pulled out Didrik.

We made it, Filion wrote.

You've found her? We're on Handu?

We found the Portal Keeper, but we're not on Handu, not yet. The Keeper's trying to heal Captain Eri. We had a run in with some Salinders. I haven't even seen the portal yet.

Salinders? Didrik asked.

Yes. Something's bothering me about them. Something I can't quite figure out...

Where did the Salinders come from?

I don't know. Captain Eri guessed they came through the portal but that would mean... Oh gods. That would mean the Keeper let them through.

Filion's heart hiccupped. He looked at the Keeper and scrambled to his feet.

"Stop! Stop whatever you're doing! Right now! Get away from her!" Filion cried, shaking Didrik at the Keeper.

Wiq was on her feet in an instant.

"What is the matter?" Wiq said.

"She let them through. She's the Portal Keeper. How could the Salinders have gotten through if she hadn't let them? She knew they were here, she brought them here!" Filion said.

Wiq looked at the Keeper. The Keeper backed away from Captain Eri, refusing to meet either of their eyes.

"He is right you know," Wiq said, approaching the Keeper. "You are the Keeper. Such a title suggests you control who, or what, accesses the portal.

You know who or what, has left through it, and who or what, has come through it."

The Keeper shuffled backwards, still not meeting their eyes.

"Where is your serenity, Keeper? Your grace? Your dignity? You do not speak. Is your silence an admission of guilt?" Wiq stepped closer.

The Keeper tried to shuffle backwards again but tripped on her dress. She fell, and Wiq disappeared. Suddenly the Keeper was on her stomach, her arms twisted behind her back, the air swimming above her.

For an instant the Keeper looked terrified, and then the calm returned. There was a loud *Crack!* and the Keeper was off of her stomach. Wiq appeared across the room, her body crashing through one of the paper walls.

The Keeper stood and faced Filion. He backed up, unsure of what to do, but no sooner had he taken a step than the Keeper's head snapped sideways a loud *Snap!* reverberating through the room.

The Keeper stumbled, and was on her back in an instant. Fuzzy air distorted Filion's view of her. The Keeper's head jerked back and forth, her eyes rolling in her skull. Then, suddenly there was another *Crack!* and once again Wiq appeared on the other side of the room, her back blowing through yet another wall.

The Keeper struggled to her feet, and Filion tripped backwards, stuffing Didrik into his pocket. She took one step towards Filion and stopped. Her eyes were out of focus, and her legs wobbled.

"It was an accident..." she whispered as Wiq hit her from the side, sending the Keeper skittering across the polished floor.

"STOP!" Filion yelled. "Wiq! Stop! Let her explain!"

Wiq reappeared, straddling the Keeper's limp body.

"Good gods, Wiq, everyone you touch seems to go unconscious! Stop hitting her! She said it was an accident! Let her explain!" Filion rushed to the Keeper.

Wiq stood up silently. She took a step back but looked ready to pounce. Filion ignored her and rolled the Keeper onto her back, grabbing a pillow and stuffing it under her head.

"Keeper! Keeper Amalia!" Filion patted the Keeper on the cheek. Her head rolled away from his hand and then back.

"It... was... an... accident. You have to believe me," she breathed.

Wiq stiffened.

"What was an accident?"

"The... Salinders..."

Chapter 50

It was brilliant. Why hadn't she thought of it before? Why hadn't anyone thought of it before? This would cut their search time in half, if not reduce it by even more than that. And then there was the glory. If she could pull this off, she would be revered. Where was Harick?

Yalki stood in the war tent. The thing was grand. She scoffed. He always commented on her expensive tastes, but who was he to talk? Harick had Grathian rugs in here! Just one alone was worth more than most houses on Handu. Then there was the furniture. Yalki began to pace, her fingers brushing a finely carved bone end table. Next to it stood a technicolored bookcase that was made from one continuous piece of yellow and red wood. Then there was a brain tanned leather recliner, made without the use of modern technology, a feat that must have taken at least a year's worth of continuous work. She stopped at his map table, a sturdy mass of shiny fluxim stone, a very rare stone indeed. Then there were the accoutrements. Goblets of precious metals, antique tapestries, and leather bound books made by some of the first sentient beings in the universe. What a hypocrite.

She pushed Harick's hypocrisy from her mind and concentrated. If she were able to make this work, both she and Harick would be rich enough to make this tent look like a hovel. His energy signal was nearing her. He was coming to the tent. She waited patiently, refining her plan. She just needed to convince him. She was going to need some test subjects.

Harick appeared looking tired and annoyed. His clothes were rumpled and sweat stained. He glanced at her as he entered the tent but didn't speak. He moved to his leather chair and collapsed into it, thinking his boots off. Yalki wrinkled her nose at the smell but didn't say anything. A second later a goblet floated through the air towards the glass pitcher of apple wine. The pitcher tipped, filled the goblet, and then the goblet floated into Harick's open hand.

"I have an idea," she started.

He didn't respond or even look at her. He took a long sip of the wine, tilted his head back and placed the cup against his forehead.

"Did you hear me? I have an idea," she repeated.

"I heard you, but I'm taking a minute, a personal minute. You see, Goddess Yalki, I spent all day in the hot sun, thrashing through the overgrown jungle, rubbing elbows with slaves, filth, and who knows what else, while you spent your day taking baths and drinking cool drinks."

He opened his eyes and gave her a once over.

"Yes, you did bathe today."

Her face reddened. So what if she had spent the morning taking a bath and getting a massage? It was his job to control the troops and her job to make the plans. This was how it worked. He had no business ridiculing her so.

He put his head back, closed his eyes again, and smiled.

The bastard.

"I have an idea that will make your life much easier," she said, burying her anger.

"Oh?" he said, not moving.

"I will need a few slaves to experiment on though."

He looked up.

"What do you mean, experiment? I have limited resources here. I lost two today. One fell off a cliff, and the other was mauled by something. What, I have no idea, but it wasn't pretty. I spent an entire hour reprogramming those who found him to forget it ever happened. I don't have enough slaves for you to waste them needlessly."

"They won't be needlessly wasted. I think I can program them to recognize its signal."

"You won't needlessly waste them… Wait. What did you say?"

"I've been thinking about this most of the day," she said, glaring. "If we can reprogram the slaves to recognize the Chozen's energy signal, we increase our chances of finding it. It seems that it has found some way to keep the major energy bursts to a minimum. That doesn't mean that we wouldn't feel it if we were close to it, just like we can feel each other. If we can program the slaves to recognize the signal, then they can find it. We won't have to canvas the entire planet grid by grid. They'll just need to be near it to find it – they won't need to see or hear it – just sense it. We can program them to alert us when they find it. Once we get a signal, we can use the slave's knowledge of the area to Jump to it and from there…" she smiled.

Harick sat up, his wine no longer at his head.

"I take back my insults. You have been busy. This just might work."

She smiled.

"Do you have any suitable test subjects?"

Chapter 51

Stay alive. Stay sane. They're coming for you... They. Which they? The good guys or the bad guys? Because technically, they were all coming for her.

She had two more hours. Two more hours before she was to go to sleep and meet the lossal again. Oh gods. She prayed he was on Handu. If he *was* on Handu, maybe she could leave. She had to leave. She had to stay alive. She had to stay sane. She had to survive.

She had spent the day moving. She didn't know where she was going, but she knew that staying still could get her killed. She knew a lot of things, but she needed to know more.

She hadn't felt the fear all day. Every now and then it pushed on the walls of its prison, but she pushed it back – burying it in another memory.

She was stopped now. It was night, and she was uneasy. Something was different. She could feel something she hadn't been able to before – two signals. They were distant, and she wanted them to remain so.

The signals were people. She knew this. How she knew, she didn't know, but they *were* people, and they were bad people. They were the people who wanted to find her and kill her. They were the Afortiori. If they found her, they would Erase her. She could not let them find her.

They couldn't sense her from their position. Their signals indicated they were still looking for her, and they were frustrated they hadn't found her. Frustrated was a nice way to put it. They were livid. They were murderous.

She had two hours.

Chapter 52

"It was an accident. I swear."

The Keeper said as she sat propped against some pillows. Dried white blood stained her now lumpy face. Wiq had made her some hot tea. The Keeper sipped it slowly and painfully. Wiq almost looked sorry – almost.

"Speak," Wiq said.

The Keeper gave Wiq a sidelong glance and shifted. She took a breath and then said, "I monitor all incoming and outgoing portal calls. When someone calls the Bok portal, I know. Once I'm alerted of potential travelers, I initiate contact with them. The portal is programmed to allow sound waves or physical matter to pass and in certain cases both. Initially, I speak with the wishful traveler through the sound wave setting. In the case that concerns you, two days ago I spoke to the Portal Keeper on Handu."

"He said the planet was under attack and that he and his village needed to escape."

"Why did they call Bok?" Wiq asked.

"I don't know," the Keeper said, shaking her head tiredly. "They just did."

"I scanned them. Since the discovery of T. Tryx all portals have been retrofitted with a T. Tryx scanner. I scan every party that wishes to pass. The scanner is not as effective as a Biopser, but it's the best we have. The results are sent via sound through the portal. One tone means green, the other red."

"I scanned the first party and got a green tone. I let them pass." She sat back. Her face was turning a strange yellow white. "I spent most of the day scanning parties and letting them pass."

"Where did they go once they got here?" Wiq asked.

The Keeper shrugged. "People who come through the portal have to leave through the tunnels. Most of the tunnels lead back to Hifora, but some don't lead to anywhere. Others, I don't know where they go. I don't understand why they came to Bok. This isn't an entirely accepting or advanced planet," she looked at Filion. "If I were a refugee I certainly wouldn't want to come to Hifora. The city is dying and violent, plus it rains all of the time. Not the best place to start anew. But they seemed to know where they were going. A woman led them, a human. She was one of the first through. She led the first group out and left one man behind. Once the second group came through, the man from the first group led them out and left another man behind. The process repeated itself until the last group."

"What happened with the last group?" Wiq asked.

The Keeper shook her head. "It was terrible…"

"They weren't supposed to be the last group. From my communications with the Handu Portal Keeper there were many more groups behind them.

The group came through, and just as I was about to sever the portal connection, I got a signal that something else was still in the link." She dropped her eyes. "I should have cut the link. I should have followed protocol, but I didn't. I got emotional. It could have been a kid chasing after his mom, or a family, or who knows what..." the Keeper said, her eyes far away.

"But it was not a kid, or a family," Wiq prompted.

"No, it was a pack of Salinders," the Keeper said, her eyes refocused on Filion. "My scanners didn't alert me. Like I said, they aren't entirely effective. They came through and... and it was over in seconds."

She shuttered.

"How did you escape?" Wiq said.

"I'm never in the portal room while it is active – protocol, just in case something goes wrong..."

"I'm above the room, behind a protective barrier. The control room is on another grid entirely. Air, energy, even water – all of it is separate from the portal. If something were to happen to the portal, the control room would be intact and vice versa."

"I watched it happen. Mothers, children... the Salinders came through... they bit a young boy first, he exploded almost instantly. I watched the rest die. It was... it was the worst thing I have ever seen. It took me several seconds to hit the kill switch to sever the link. I think at least 10 made it through, but I can't be certain. According to the computers some of them were still in the link when I killed it."

"So they were vaporized," Wiq said. "How did the Salinders get out of the portal room?"

"I say they all died, but that's not entirely correct, one survived. The woman left behind to guide the group. She was bitten, but she didn't explode. She just stood there, stiff as a board. Finally, she seemed to wake up. She looked at me. She had dead eyes," the Keeper shut her eyes and put her head back. "The woman coughed once, smiled at me, then opened the door and walked out. The Salinders followed her."

The Keeper opened her eyes. "We have protocol for breaches. I went through them, but obviously I didn't get them all."

"What are your protocols?" Wiq asked.

"First I confuse the tunnels," she said.

"What does that mean?" Wiq said.

The Keeper hesitated. "When you confuse the tunnels, it scrambles their programming, temporarily," she looked at Wiq. "When the tunnels are confused, they all lead to the Nothing. It is supposed to be a fail safe. Anything in the tunnels should disappear."

"Wait," Filion said. "So all of those people, all of those innocent people were sucked into the Nothing?"

The Keeper shrugged but didn't meet his eyes. "Anyone who was in the

137

tunnels should have been sucked into the Nothing. Obviously, not everything was. You found a Salinder. Maybe some of those innocent people survived, or maybe they weren't in the tunnels at all when I confused them. Maybe they had an early out." She met Filion's gaze, her eyes defiant. "But maybe they didn't. Just because you're innocent doesn't mean you can't die."

"What did you do next?" Wiq pressed.

"I firebombed the portal room, then vacuum sealed it. I left the room like that for a day then let the air back in and firebombed it again. I haven't been in since. It should be clean now."

"Should be?" Wiq said.

"In theory."

Chapter 53

"My Gods, how can I serve you?"

Yalki circled the man. He was fit, young, and willing to die for them. He was perfect, especially because in all likelihood he would die. Nothing worked perfectly on the first try, and he would be their first try.

Harick stood in front of the slave. "We need you to become something no one has ever become," Harick said to him. "You are to be the first of a long line of elite super soldiers. You are to be the best of the best. We chose you because you are worthy and you deserve it. Your dedication has proved valuable, and we see it fit to reward you."

Yalki rolled her eyes at Harick's compliments. She knew it was necessary to occasionally feign some semblance of appreciation for the slaves, but she hated doing it.

The slave on the other hand allowed himself a small smile. He stood at attention, his strong arms straining in excitement. Yalki studied his arms, then his chest, then his legs... what a pity, he might have been better fit for other purposes...

"I thank you my Gods!"

"Yes, I'm sure you do. Now I want you to lie down," Harick said gesturing to his map table. The table was clear of its usual maps, adorned only by several thick leather straps. The man climbed onto the table. He lay down and was a mirror image of himself standing at attention.

"Good my son," Harick said. The straps sprung to life. Yalki watched them secure the man to the table. Harick did a good job. The man wouldn't be going anywhere.

"Now, I want you to think happy thoughts. Think about your family, your wife, do you have a wife?" Harick asked.

The man tried to shake his head.

"That's okay. Think of the perfect woman then, without the ties of marriage." He laughed. He was disgusting.

"Now close your eyes..."

The man did.

"You're up," Harick said.

Yalki walked to Harick's chair and sat. She had never attempted anything like this before. This was close to the kind of thing that J-10 was capable of, not that she was anywhere as gifted as it, but she supposed everyone had to start somewhere.

She closed her eyes.

The mind was complicated, no Eoan or Afortiori could deny that, but it wasn't as complicated as this universe made it seem. Yalki knew what part of her brain housed her energy sensor inputs. She took a deep breath and imagined the same area in his.

When she opened her eyes, she was in his brain. She allowed herself a small smile. She had made it, and she was about to venture into uncharted territory. She was going to break the rules so that she could rebuild them to her standards. She *was* a God.

One of the great things about the brain was how organized it was. Yalki could imagine any form of organization, and that's how the man's brain appeared to her. First, she imagined a long hallway with many doors, each door leading to a different area of information. Next she thought of cabinets. With a *Whoosh!* The doors were gone and in their place, thousands of cabinets. After that she thought of bookshelves, then color-coded sets of drawers, after that...

It was amusing, her ability to control his brain, but she had work to do. While she could control how his brain's information was displayed, she couldn't control how the information was ordered. Sure, she had come to the area where his sensory inputs should have been, if he possessed any, but it was a general area. Now she had to wade through everything in front of her until she found the inputs, and she had no idea how long that would take.

Chapter 54

"Look, you can question me, or you can let me help her. She isn't going to wake up any time soon without my help, and I know you have places to be," the Keeper added.

"She's right," Filion said.

Wiq nodded and stepped back. With Wiq no longer looming over her, the Keeper let out a long breath.

"First," she said. "I'll need to heal myself. It'll look like I'm napping but I'm not. Don't wake me."

She settled onto her back and closed her eyes. Her breathing became deeper and her body relaxed.

"Well," Filion said. "I guess we wait."

Wiq nodded and moved back to her wall. She sat down, her back to the paper, and closed her eyes.

Filion looked at his watch. He had one more hour. He might as well sleep until then.

An hour later Filion found himself back in the Tierameng. Her signal would be easy to locate now that he knew what to look for. He found it quickly and this time there were fifteen strands, not twelve. She was learning. He found the legitimate signature and linked.

When he opened his eyes, he was back in the forest. It was night again, but something was different. He stood still. This time there was no fire and nothing moved. He looked around. It was hard to see, the darkness was so oppressive. The multicolored trees stood like shadows, their bright hues black. The air was still, and he listened – silence. The only thing he could hear was his own breathing, and each breath he took seemed to shatter the quiet, as would a scream. He waited for his eyes to fully adjust. Once they did, he still didn't see her.

"Ryo" he whispered.

As soon as the word left his mouth he was hit with a burst of energy. Against his will his body froze, his lips still forming the O in Ryo's name.

A soft crunching sounded from his back. He strained to see but couldn't.

What if it had been the wrong signature?

"Oh. Filion, it's you. Sorry." The energy disappeared, and Filion collapsed to the ground. Ryo stepped into his view.

"Sorry," she said, sitting on a stump. "I'm just trying to survive."

"No, no, you're doing a great job." Filion said pulling himself into a sitting position. "That's weird though."

141

"What's weird?"

"I'm used to having control of dreams. Not having control is… unnerving."

"You don't have control?" she asked.

"Well, I guess I have some, it's just… you have more. Usually, a dreamer doesn't have control of their dream. As a Searcher, I should be in control of your dream, not you. If another dreamer tried to paralyze me, it wouldn't work. I could get out of it. You're different though. You're strong."

"Different. I'm different…"

"Yes. Yes you are."

"Are you here yet? On Handu?" She spoke with new intensity, her blue eyes catching his.

Filion paused. "Ahh, actually, we're almost here."

"What do you mean almost?! I've done what you've said. I've survived, both mentally and physically, but I don't have much more time."

"What do you mean?"

"I can feel them. I can feel their energy. They're searching for me. They're getting closer."

"Do they know where you are?"

Ryo shook her head. "Not yet, but it is only a matter of time. I can feel them, like a distant storm growing closer. They know something I don't. They'll find me."

"Okay, okay," Filion said. "We've found the Portal Keeper, but we're temporarily stalled."

"We? You and the Living Document?" Ryo asked.

"Ahh, yes, and no," Filion said. "Since we last talked I made a deal with a ship captain, Captain Eri. She and her other two crewmembers are with Didrik and me. They agreed to help get you off of Handu. The problem is Captain Eri is badly hurt. The Keeper is the only one who can help her, but Wiq, the ship's mechanic, ahhh, well, she messed the Keeper up pretty badly, so now we have to wait for the Keeper to heal herself before she can help Captain Eri. That and Wiq also knocked out Red, the other member of Captain Eri's crew, so right now only half of your rescue team is conscious."

"I see," Ryo said, looking confused. "Why would this Wiq do this?"

"Well, she had the best intentions. She knocked Red out because he threatened to sell me to the, *pelters*. If it wasn't for her, we wouldn't have found the Keeper."

"Keepers," Ryo said distantly. "Keepers of the Portals. We are those who pledge our lives to the continuation of magical travel. Our job is not one of glory, nor is it one of thanks, but necessary it is more than most. We protect the ways of a time in danger of extinction. We live underground, beneath seas, overhead and in your hearts. We will not die without a fight."

"I think I was a Keeper once," Ryo concluded.

"The Keeper's creed," Filion breathed. "Yes, they believe in magic before technology, but I think it's a bit of a hypocrisy," Filion said. *Who knows what she once was,* he thought. *She could have been a Searcher for all anyone knows.*

"Yes, I know," Ryo said. "Magic before technology, but the system is not as pure as it once was – too many outside dangers. No matter how strong *you* are; *they* are always stronger. Technology evens the field," she paused then laughed. "That, and magic doesn't really exist."

Filion looked at her.

"What do you mean?" he asked.

Ryo held out her hand. A small yellow bird appeared. It chirped once, then erupted into a ball of orange fire.

Filion gasped and the fire went out.

"Anyone who is 'magic', is only magic to those who don't understand how 'the universe' works." Suddenly, yellow letters appeared in the air next to Ryo. They scrambled to form words. "You see, it's just about knowing how to think and ordering your questions correctly."

The words became sentences and the sentences became questions. *Why do I want a fire? What would it mean to have a fire now? How would the fire affect the surrounding area? What temperature does the air need to be to make a fire? How much friction will be needed to make a fire?*

Filion couldn't read the questions fast enough. They swirled through the air, disappearing and scrambling into new questions. Then they ignited into flames. Filion shrank backwards, the heat searing his face. Then as suddenly as it appeared, the fire vanished and in its place floated the yellow bird. In its mouth hung another shimmering flower. Ryo held out her hand, and the bird dropped the flower.

Ryo smiled and the bird disappeared. She turned back to Filion and tucked the flower into his vest pocket.

"You see? *Magic*," she laughed. "Or not. Anyway," Ryo said sharply. "Keepers are renowned for having little to practically no 'magical' ability. You become a Keeper when you can't become anything else. Mostly, Keepers are the black sheep of high standing magical families. Being a Keeper is an acceptable way to continue on in the family's name but not do anything spectacular."

She stopped. "How do I know that?"

"Know what?" Filion asked, staring at the flower.

"Know this stuff about Keepers?"

"You're a Chozen. Who knows how many lives you've lived, and what you learned in those lives. How are you feeling, mentally?" Filion asked, tearing his eyes from the flower.

Ryo waved her hand at him. "I'm dealing with it. I ignore most of what I think. I try and stay in the moment. When I let my mind wander, things like that happen. I start thinking about one of my many pasts. Images, thoughts, sayings, all sorts of things come into my head. It's distracting. I try not to let it happen."

"Some of those thoughts could help you," Filion said.

"And some of them could get me killed. I try and concentrate only on staying alive. The thoughts I need come to me. The thoughts I don't, don't," her voice had a hard edge. "But you do bring up a good point," Ryo continued, the edge gone. "You'll be traveling via portal. I'll see if I can find it and meet you there."

"That's good but be careful. The Tioris might have it guarded."

Ryo tipped her head back and laughed, a long, uneven laugh.

"I'm counting on it."

Chapter 55

Filion awoke with a start. She had seemed so sane, so with it, until the end. That laugh... he shuddered. They had agreed to meet in another twenty hours, unless of course they had found each other by then. Filion hoped they had. He didn't want to meet her via the Tierameng again. Not being in control of her dream disturbed him. They had to find her.

Filion pushed himself from the floor, when it caught his eye. The flower. It was still in his vest pocket. He sat back down, his legs unsteady. It was impossible for physical things to travel from a dream into reality, yet there it was, petite and yellow, just like the bird and real as day.

He reached towards it, his fingers shaking. This couldn't be happening. His fingers brushed the flower, and it disappeared with a small pop. Filion let out a long breath and slumped against the wall.

What was happening?

It took Filion several minutes of breathing exercises before he felt comfortable getting up again. He checked his pocket once more for the flower, which was truly gone, and finally stood.

He looked around the room. The Keeper was no longer on her back. She was, once again, hunched over Captain Eri. The Keeper's face hadn't fully healed, ugly yellow spots crowded her cheeks, like constellations in the night sky, but she didn't seem to notice them.

Wiq was nowhere to be seen, and Red still lay in a heap where Filion had dropped him.

Filion took Didrik from his pocket and began to pace.

I saw her again, Filion scribbled.

Wait, Didrik said. *Fill me in. What has happened since we left the ship?*

*****

And now it looks like we're just waiting for Captain Eri and Red to come around. And for Wiq to come back, I guess. Once everyone is here and awake hopefully we can get to Handu.

You said that she seemed all right until the end?

Yes, Filion wrote.

We need to find her.

I know. I'm doing my best, but I can't do anything but wait right now.

Didrik didn't respond.

Chapter 56

She found them – the inputs for the energy signatures. It had taken her long enough. Slave's brains were more demented than she had thought. No doubt the virus didn't help. Actually, it seemed that the virus was working against her. She hadn't anticipated its pervasiveness throughout his brain. She had assumed his brain to be like hers, less complex of course, but still viable. His was damaged though, most certainly in part to hers and Harick's doing, but that couldn't have been helped. The virus was necessary, yet it might be the reason why she couldn't reprogram him as she wanted.

Reprogramming was not new, but reprogramming a slave to recognize energy signatures was. She had assumed that once she found the inputs she would just have to modify them to match hers. Unfortunately, they were already in use.

It appeared that the virus used the inputs to help control the slave's brain. The inputs appeared very influential in keeping the slave brainwashed. If she rerouted them, the virus might stop working. It might stop working permanently, and if that happened, he would have to die.

She thought about asking Harick's opinion but decided against it. If she appeared beaten so easily, Harick would respect her even less than he already did. She couldn't lose the one edge she had. She had to try.

She took a deep breath and began to meddle.

Chapter 57

Red rolled to his side.

Bloody grawlix... my head... feels like it's in a vice.

He looked around. His eyes refused to focus, but he could see he was no longer in the tunnels. Wherever he was was too light and too clean to be those rotting tunnels. He could smell plants and water maybe, and the air was un-oppressive, welcoming even. Did he hear music? Part of him wanted to be afraid, but this new place gave off such a calming feeling. He felt safe, well, almost.

He blinked. The room sharpened. He recognized the brown as wood and the white as – was that paper? He blinked again. Suddenly a large figure loomed over him. Panic gripped him. He tried to reach for his phazer, but his arms felt so heavy and his hands were like clubs.

"Red! Red! It's me, Filion!"

Filion stood over Red. He had been watching Red like a hawk ever since the Keeper and Wiq had taken Captain Eri to another room. The entire time Wiq had been gone Filion had been in a panic. What if Red awoke, and only Filion was there to face him? Filion had replayed that scenario over and over again in his mind, until he heard the paper door slide open. The moment Wiq had stepped back into the room, Filion had felt as if a huge weight had been lifted from his shoulders. Now with Wiq back, Filion felt a little braver, and hence was able to stand closer to Red.

Red said something unintelligible.

"What?" Filion asked.

Red squirmed back and forth.

"What's wrong with him?" Filion said.

Wiq walked to Filion's side. She liked Filion. She knew she had upset him when she had attacked the Keeper, but Filion did not understand. He knew nothing about combat, which was fine, he was a Searcher, not a mercenary, but it didn't make her feel any better. She felt like she had betrayed him when all she had really done was protect him. She did not know how to tell him though, and then there was Red.

Wiq was pretty sure that Filion was not upset at her for putting Red down. Red had threatened to sell Filion to the pelters. She had just been trying to protect him, and she had. Did he see it that way?

"He is waking. Not all of the body's systems come back on board at the same time. Right now he can probably see a little and process a little. We are most likely making him nervous, standing over him. We should step back."

Filion nodded and backed up. Wiq didn't. Instead, she moved forward.

"What are you doing?" Filion asked. "You said to step back!"

"Yes, but this must be done for our safety."

"Don't you knock him out again!"

"I will not," Wiq said softly.

She felt bad, but pushed it from her mind and concentrated on the task at hand. She should have done this earlier, this was a rookie mistake, but she had not. No excuses.

She frisked him and removed his phazer, two handguns, three grenades, seven knives, and a garrote. He probably had more, but she didn't have time to find them. He was beginning to thrash. She took a length of cord from her vest and tied his wrists together. He continued to struggle but was too groggy to put up a real fight.

She stepped back and dumped the pile onto the floor.

"He had all that on him?" Filion asked.

Wiq nodded. "He has more, but finding all of his weapons could take hours. He is disoriented. Red is the kind of person who is dangerous when disoriented. His fight or flight reflex is telling him to fight, but he does not have the muscle coordination to do it... yet. That is why I tied his hands. We do not want him to attack us while he is in this state."

"What about when he gets oriented?"

"At that point, he should have enough processing power to know that we are not his enemy."

"He didn't seem to have that 'processing power' when we were in the tunnels," Filion said.

"Yes, but the situation is different now. Captain Eri is being helped. That was what he ultimately wanted."

"I don't know," Filion said.

"Well, we know how his last attempt to start a fight turned out," she said.

Filion looked at her. She was so small, yet Filion was more willing to fight Red than her, and Red had threatened to sell him to the *pelters*. She was methodical, logical, and strong. He had noticed her arms when she had tied Red. Her muscles had flexed with purpose in a no nonsense way. Filion had been both frightened and captivated by her. There was something about Wiq though, something almost innocent, that conflicted with her murderous attitude. She reminded him of a child in some ways, if a nanotechnology based mercenary could remind one of a child.

"How do you know all this?" Filion asked.

"Know all of what?"

"These things, like how to incapacitate a man twice your size, or kill Salinders, or even tie someone up like that?"

She looked at him, and then quickly dropped her eyes. "I was born with the knowledge – programmed with it. Then I trained, and then I fought for years. This is all that I have ever been, and while I have a new purpose in life, now that I am free, I cannot undo what has been done to me. I cannot forget my past."

"You don't like how you are?"

Wiq sighed. "I know seven different ways to kill you from where I stand with just my hands," she held up her hands. "*Just my hands*. I used to not question such knowledge. I used to yearn to learn more of it, but things are different now. My life is not about killing anymore. It is about something else, something better, but I do not fully understand what yet. I do know that I do not like what I was, what I was made to be. It is one thing to know how to fight, to know how to defend yourself, but to always be on the offensive. To always be prepared to kill anyone – even a friend–," *not that I have any,* she thought, "is something I would do anything to change. I am violent by nature, and it pains me."

Filion paused. "You don't seem all that violent to me."

She smiled. "Yet you say everyone I touch goes unconscious. You are just being nice, which… which I like. Thank you," she looked at him.

"Well, you may be prone to knocking people out, but I can tell you mean well."

"You can?"

"Yes. I know that you're honest in what you say, and that you aren't as confident as you wish everyone to believe."

Wiq took a step back. Her aura, which had been indigo, flashed to red.

"Don't worry!" Filion said taking a step towards her. "I won't tell anyone. I just can tell these things about people. You aren't as bad as you make yourself out to be. Cold-blooded killers aren't unconfident. They certainly don't care what people think of them, and they would never wish to be less violent. You care. I like that. *People* like that. You may be programmed for violence, but that's not all you are."

Wiq stared at him.

"Whaaat… whyyyy… whyy am I… whooo… YOU!"

Wiq turned away from Filion and looked at Red.

Red's eyes were fully open now. He stared at Wiq, his mouth twitching.

"Red," Wiq said. "Do not worry. You will be able to move and talk soon enough. No permanent damage has been done. You became too hostile towards Filion, and we needed your cooperation. We got it," she hesitated. "So, thank you."

Red's mouth twitched more. "Leett me OUT!"

"In time. Right now I do not trust you."

"YOU. I'll git YOU!"

"No, you will not. If you try, I will put you back down. This is not up for discussion."

Red snarled and tried to spit. His lips didn't seem to be fully working though, and he ended up coughing.

"Bit –" he wheezed.

The door on the other side of the room slid open. The Keeper wafted through. Despite her injuries, she seemed to have regained her poise.

"Captain Eri is awake. She asks for you."

"Me?" Wiq said.

"Both of you."

Wiq nodded and turned back to Red. "We are going to go see Captain Eri. You should regain full use of your motor functions by the time we return. We will ask Captain Eri what she wants to do with you."

Red glared, but didn't say anything.

Filion and Wiq followed the Keeper into the hallway and onto a wooden boardwalk. The air was different on the boardwalk. It was cooler, as if they were outside. Filion also noticed that the distant music was gone. In its place was a muffled silence, like that of a snow-covered forest. Filion looked up, all he saw was black, like a starless night. Maybe they *were* outside, but Filion doubted it.

They walked along the boardwalk, following the wooden and paper walls. The only sound the click of their feet on the wooden planks. They turned a corner, and the walls on their right disappeared, a pool of water in their place. The pool appeared to be for swimming, its bottom made of thick wooden slats. Benches lined its edges. Steam drifted from the water, rising to where it met, was that snow?

"Is it snowing?" Filion asked, watching the fat, white flecks dance through the air until they melted on the steam.

"Something like that," the Keeper said.

They continued on, following more wooden and paper walls until once again, the walls dropped away, this time to their left. Instead of a pool was an organized mass of thick plants. The plants swayed as if moved by a breeze, although there was no breeze. In fact the air was completely still.

"Your garden?" Filion said.

"Someone's garden."

Finally, they came to a stop in front of another set of wooden and paper doors, identical to the doors of the room they had just left. The Keeper pushed them open.

Captain Eri was on her back on a high wooden bed. The blankets, pillows and sheets were white, just like the floor pillows, but the room's walls were a dark blue.

Filion paused.

"The blue aids with sleep," the Keeper said.

Captain Eri lifted her head. Filion immediately noticed she had been bathed. Bits of trash and ooze no longer clung to her hair, and her skin had been scrubbed clean.

"Filion? Wiq? Is that you? Where's Red?"

Her voice was soft.

Wiq moved to her side.

"Red became obtuse. I had to put him down. He is recovering now. He will be fine."

"Ahh, Red," Captain Eri put her head back on the pillow. "What did he do?"

"He threatened to sell Filion to the pelters to get you, and I assume me, off of Bok."

Captain Eri chuckled. Filion couldn't believe it.

"Sounds like him. The Keeper says I should be ready to go in a few hours. Will you be ready to leave by then?"

"We will be ready whenever you are."

Captain Eri nodded.

"Ok, time to go. She needs her sleep. Besides, if you plan on using the portal, I'll need to reboot the system." The Keeper looked at Wiq. "I could use your expertise."

Wiq nodded.

"Lossal, can you find your way back?" the Keeper asked.

"Uh, sure. Don't worry about me," Filion said.

The Keeper nodded and left the room. Wiq followed her.

Filion stared after them then turned back to Captain Eri. She was asleep. Her aura matched the walls. Filion sighed, stepped into the hall and closed the thin door.

Chapter 58

No one, NO ONE, tied him up and got away with it. No one especially knocked him unconscious, took his weapons (although not all of them) and then left him in some alien palace. He was going to escape, find the vissy and that stupid lossal, teach her a lesson, kill him, skin him, and then rescue Captain Eri, sell the pelt, get the ship, and then leave Bok, NEVER to come back again. Captain Eri would be grateful. How would she ever make it up to him? He had a few ways in mind...

Red struggled against the cord. That vissy knew what she was doing, but she hadn't covered his fingers. That, and she had left his hands on his front rather than behind his back. Not that it would have really mattered, he would free his hands regardless, whether they were behind or in front of him, but in front was almost too easy.

He kept a small blade hidden in the seam of his right pocket. All he had to do was get it...

Filion walked slowly down the boardwalk. He felt so useless. Captain Eri had undergone a Biopser for him, Wiq had taken out Red, gotten the truth from the Keeper, and now was in the process of preparing the portal, and Red... well, Red was good to have along because at least he could handle himself, most of the time. What could Filion do? Dream? A lot of good that was going to do when it came time to face the Tioris. They were all so brave, and so tough. He wasn't. Even Didrik, despite the fact he couldn't walk or speak, was more courageous than he. Didrik had all of the knowledge of the Eoans stored away in his pages, and he wasn't afraid of it. Filion was.

Filion reached the pool and sat down on the boardwalk, his feet dangling over the water. He held out a hand and caught a few flakes of snow. They felt like snow – cold and wet – and they melted quickly upon contact with his hand. He looked up. The black sky, or ceiling, the grey steam and the white snow were beautiful. He wanted to smile but didn't.

He felt alone. Everyone but Red and him had a task, but Filion didn't really want to hang out with Red. The man hated him, and he had reason. After all, they were in this mess because of Filion.

Filion reached for Didrik. He held the Living Document over the water. Did he actually want to talk to Didrik? He liked him and all, but the book had a way of being snarky and making Filion feel bad. He sighed. No, he did not want to talk to Didrik. Filion moved to put him back in his pocket, when he heard a small noise.

Filion turned just in time to see the butt of a phazer coming straight at his face. The phazer hit him, knocking him sideways and into the water. Didrik bounced from his hand.

The water was warm, hot even. Under different circumstances it would have been pleasant. Filion kicked to the surface.

Red jumped from the boardwalk.

"A bath'll be good for you! The cleaner your *pelt*, the better price it'll fetch!"

He landed on Filion's shoulders, knocking him back under the water.

Red was heavy and strong. He kicked at Filion, attempting to wrap his legs around Filion's neck. Filion pushed off of the wooden bottom and resurfaced. The pool's bottom was at an incline, and they were in the deep end. Luckily, Filion could stand and still breathe.

"Get off of me!" Filion screamed, now standing with his head and part of his shoulders above the water. He pushed at Red.

Red slipped from Filion's shoulders. He clawed at him, attempting to climb back up.

"This is your fault! This is a harebrained plan! I'm not goin' to no Black planet for a girl, no matter how hot! There's plenty of girls in the universe. This one isn't worth it!" Red threw a punch. It hit Filion in the nose.

Filion stumbled backwards. He slipped and fell underwater, effectively separating Red from his shoulders. Red kicked, trying to swim to Filion, but his heavy boots and combat gear weighed him down. Filion stood back up. He had been knocked towards the shallow end. Now all of his shoulders stood above the water.

"I think you broke my nose!" Filion said, cupping his face. Blood streamed down his snout – first the phazer and now Red's fist. He wasn't built for fighting. He wasn't tough enough.

"First, I'm gonna kill you, then I'm gonna tie up that damn vissy, then I'm going to rescue Captain Eri, then I'm gonna skin you, then…" Red thrashed towards Filion.

This couldn't be happening. They were so close and now this guy, Red, was going to end it? It couldn't end this way. Filion had to live. He had to save her.

"NO!" Filion roared. *Take the offensive!* Wiq was always on the offensive, he could learn from her. He could be tough like her, or he could die, here, now.

Filion ran towards Red. Well, he waded quickly towards him. Suddenly, Red was in arm's length. What should he do? He should hit him, right? He was stronger than Red. He could do it. He balled his fist, brought his arm back, and then swung it forward.

Filion's hand made contact with Red's face. Red stopped swimming. He stared at Filion with confused eyes.

"You hit me… maybe you've got… more balls than I thought…"

Then Red sank.

Filion stood, soaking wet, blood streaming from his nose, and in shock. He had just hit another person. He had hit him so hard he might be unconscious. Filion stared at his fist. It hurt. Hitting someone hurt. He moved his eyes towards Red. Red lay on the bottom of the pool, a dissipating stream of bubbles rising from his nose and mouth.

If Filion left him there, he would die. Then again if he saved him, Red might try to kill him, again. Filion hesitated.

What are you doing?! You don't kill people!

Filion sprang into action. He reached into the water, caught Red's vest, and pulled. The man was heavy! Not so heavy Filion couldn't handle him but still, was he made out of bricks?

Filion dragged Red to the surface then tossed him onto the boardwalk. Red landed on his chest and coughed.

He's alive. Filion let out a long breath. He didn't kill people. He was no killer.

He pushed Red's legs onto the boardwalk, and then began to hoist himself from the water.

Didrik!

Filion dropped back into the water. Didrik wasn't in his pocket, where was he? He scanned the pool. It moved in waves, like a lake during a storm. The steam made it hard to see the entire pool. Filion rushed to where Didrik had first fallen.

Had he sunk? What happened when a Living Document got wet? Did his pages fall out? Could he re-grow them? He had to find him.

Something in the corner of the pool caught his eye. *Didrik!* Filion lunged towards him and grabbed him. The book was soft and limp. Filion loosened his grip and set Didrik on the boardwalk. Red was didn't move.

Filion pulled himself onto the walkway. It was cold out of the water. Snow had begun to accumulate on Red's wet clothes and hair. Red shivered. He would have to wait.

"Didrik!" Filion yelled, gently peeling the book open. The Living Document's pages stuck together, and in some places they seemed little more than mush.

Letters and ink swirled, but he got no response.

"Didrik! Can you hear me?!"

Fil... ion. Wh... at happ... ened?

Didrik's words appeared jumbled and broken. Occasionally, an extraneous letter floated across the page.

"Red attacked us. We both fell into a pool. Are you alright?"

I n... eed to dr... y. Y..ou n... eed to dr... y me.

"Okay!"

Filion stood, Didrik balanced carefully in his hands. Across from the pool stood a wooden door. Filion pulled it open. A wave of heat hit him.

A heat room!

Perfect! Filion thought.

Made entirely of wood, this room had no paper walls. Wooden benches lined the wooden walls, and in the middle of the room stood a firebox. A smoke stack ran from the box to the roof, and on top of the box sat a canister of stones. Next to the box was a large stone pitcher. This room's humidity could be adjusted. Right now it was a dry heat, and Filion wanted to keep it that way.

Filion opened Didrik and placed him on one of the benches. Hopefully Didrik would sweat out the water, and the air would dry him. This could work.

"How's this?" Filion asked.

Better.

"Okay. I'll be right back."

Where... are you going?

"Just to get Red. It'll only be a second."

Don't get him! He almost... killed us! Let... him die... out there!

"I am NO killer!"

Filion didn't wait for a response. He opened the door and stepped outside.

Red still lay sprawled on the walkway. His lips were blue, and he was shivering, but barely. Filion grabbed his wrists and dragged him into the heat room.

Filion left Red on his side on the floor and sat on the bench next to Didrik. It hit him how cold he was. Shivering, Filion pulled the bag of gold, ID cards, and orb out of his pockets. He then slumped against the wall.

They sat like that for several minutes. Filion occasionally opened Didrik to a different page, or touched his swelling nose, but other than that, no one moved.

Red stirred.

"You hit me... you actually hit me." Red rolled onto his back, and sat up. He coughed once, then turned from Filion and vomited.

Filion stiffened. Red looked around the room, clearly not understanding where he was.

"Where am I?" he said.

"A heat room," Filion replied, balling his hand.

"You hit me, lossal," Red said, rubbing his jaw.

"You almost killed me and Didrik."

"So I did. I didn' think you had the stones. Good for you."

"I saved your life."

"Only after you put it in danger."

"You're the one who attacked us!"

"Yeah, but I wouldna attacked you if you hadn' gotten us into this mess in the first place. We're even."

Filion stared incredulously. Could he be serious? They were even?

"I guess I should say thanks for not leavin' me on the bottom of that pool to die," Red said, pulling himself onto one of the benches.

He took off one of his boots and tipped it upside down. Water cascaded onto the floor.

"No wonder I sunk, huh?

Filion didn't respond.

Red took off his other boot, and then began to undo his vest.

"What are you doing?" Filion asked.

"Don' get the wrong idea now, lossal," Red said pulling his vest off. "I jus' want my clothes to dry. I ain't interested in you, no more than you in me." He pulled off his undershirt and stripped down to his skivvies.

"Well, lossal, this is the moment of truth, huh? Do I show off my birthday suit, or do I walk around with wet britches the rest the day?"

Filion turned his head, saying nothing.

"Well, I guess that settles it."

There was a shuffling, and then Filion heard Red sit on one of the benches. He didn't look at Red. Instead, Filion repositioned Didrik.

"Hey! Look at this!" Red said.

Filion turned his head reflexively. Red stood, butt naked, pointing at something on the ceiling.

"Ahhh, what?" Filion asked, whipping his head the other way.

"There's dryin' lines up here. I can hang my clothes, dry 'em out faster."

"Yes, that sounds like a very good idea," Filion said.

"You know, lossal, I hear Handu's a cold place. It's pretty far from the system's sun. If you don' dry your clothes you might freeze. Little good you'll do your lady Chozen if you're froze to death."

"Why are you trying to get me to declothe?"

"Declothe? Seriously, lossal? What does that even mean?"

"You know."

Red shrugged. "I'm not tryin' to get you to do nothin'. I'm just givin' you some friendly advice, that's all."

Friendly advice from Red? Maybe the near drowning had damaged his brain. Filion clenched his jaw but didn't say anything.

Suddenly, Red was on Filion's bench. Filion tried to scoot away, but Red threw an arm over his shoulder.

"Filion, we're just bits and pieces. It ain't no big deal."

Filion looked at Red. The man had to be damaged. He just had to be. Red winked at him, got up, and began to hang his clothes.

Filion didn't move. When Red finished he sat on a bench, separate from Filion's.

Neither said anything for a long time.

"Are your clothes drying?" Filion asked.

"Yup. I know who won't have wet britches, and it ain't you."

Filion huffed. He certainly didn't like the idea of freezing on Handu.

156

"FINE! But I don't want to hear a word from you! You got it! Not one word, and this doesn't get out. No one knows that we were in here, *naked*, together!"

"Filion, outta the two of us I wouldn't have picked you to be the homophobic one."

Filion ripped off his vest. "I'm not homophobic... I'm... I'm just a private person. That's all."

"You're a prude. I get it."

Filion glared at him. With a huff, he turned away from Red and slid his pants and underpants off. He gathered his clothes without facing Red and walked to the other side of the room where there was another set of drying lines. After he hung his clothes, he walked backwards to his bench where he sat and put his hands on his lap. He glanced at Red. Red was reclined on a bench with his head against the wall and his eyes closed. Filion let out a sigh.

It took him several minutes to relax. He took a breath. Despite his discomfort from being wet, cold, naked with Red, and possibly having a broken nose, he couldn't deny that he was drying faster without his clothes. Still, he didn't know how long it would take him to dry completely. He hoped Red was wrong and that it wasn't too cold on Handu.

Neither he nor Red said anything for at least another half of an hour. Red never moved, and Filion only moved to aid Didrik in drying. He was pleased at how fast Didrik was dehydrating. He was also pleased at how fast his own fur was drying. Maybe Red had been right, although it was strange to not only think that he could have been right, but that he had also voluntarily tried to help Filion. Maybe they *were* even.

Suddenly, the heat room's door banged open. Filion jumped up, his hands leaving his lap. There stood Wiq. Her eyes fell on Filion. They moved from his head to his toes and back again. He scrambled to cover himself, but it was too late. Wiq met his eyes, a curious look on her face then turned to Red.

Red stood, one leg on the bench, a crooked smile on his face, unembarrassed and proud.

"Wiq, honey," he said. "How nice to see you. Properly see you, now that my pressure points have recovered."

"Why are neither of you wearing any clothes?" she asked, her eyes on Red.

"Well, buttercup, Filion here slipped into the pool out there and, wouldn't you guess it, he doesn't know how to swim." He slapped his knee, the crooked smile growing even wider. "I went after him, naturally, and saved him. We had to come in here to warm up, and the fastest way to do that is to strip down."

"You're, you're a terrible person, Red," Filion said.

Both Red and Wiq turned towards Filion. Red stifled a laugh, and Filion felt his cheeks burning. He didn't need Wiq to see him this way.

"He lies," Filion said. "He attacked me. Me and Didrik. He said he was

157

going to kill me, and tie you up, Wiq. We all fell into the pool. I hit him." His arm tensed. "I knocked him out and then pulled him from the bottom of the pool. I dragged him in here so he wouldn't freeze."

Red's face didn't change. Wiq looked at Filion, and then at Red.

"Captain Eri is going to be very disappointed when she hears of this."

Red gave Filion a satisfied smile.

Wiq took a step towards Red. "But," she said softly. "She will be even more disappointed if she hears I had to kill you because of your own foolishness. I did not survive ten tours before I was fifteen because I was easy to tie up. You may think you have skills, Mr. Canner, but they pale in comparison to mine. You have trained to become a killer. I was born one. Remember that, it may save your life."

The mirth disappeared from Red's body. He put his leg down and stood, awkwardly, the hollow smile still staining his face.

"Also," Wiq said, her voice at a normal volume again. "I like the lossal. You kill him and you will learn what pain means, one fingernail at a time."

Red swallowed.

"Both of you, put your clothes back on. Captain Eri has recovered, and the Keeper and I have re-booted the portal. I have all of our stuff. We are ready to go."

Neither Filion nor Red moved.

"I will wait outside."

It took both Filion and Red a few seconds to react after Wiq closed the door. They stood, staring at the door, until Red let out a long, "Bloooody lossssaal…"

Filion faced him, no longer embarrassed if Red saw his 'bits and pieces'.

"What do you mean 'bloody lossal'?"

"You're the worst thing to stumble into my life since Salkin, and she only left me on a barren planet to die!"

"I've never left you to die! I saved you from the pool!"

"That's old news, lossal, but you know what isn't?"

Filion didn't respond. Red approached him, stopping only a few inches from his face.

"Handu isn't cold," he whispered. "But Wiq's seen you naked. Now we're even."

Chapter 59

Grawlix! Yalki sat back on her heels. She had been at this for hours, attempting to re-route the slave's brain. She had made so much progress, and now, well, now she was pretty sure he was dead. Apparently crossing those two signals hadn't been a good idea. She apathetically uncrossed the wires. Nothing happened. He was dead. She had known it was going to take more than one slave, she had known that this one would die, but she had hoped he would die after she had learned more. At this rate she might burn through an entire battalion, not that Harick would let it get that far.

She took a deep breath and closed her eyes. When she opened them again she was back in Harick's war tent. She looked at the slave, his eyes had begun to glaze over and dried blood dotted the corners of his lips.

"He died horribly."

She turned. Harick sat in his chair, his feet up, boots off, and a smug look on his face.

"I don't know what you did to the poor guy, but he didn't like it. Since he's dead, I can only assume that you failed."

He casually reached for a goblet of wine.

"I made progress. You and I both knew that he wouldn't survive. The first ones never do. It's part of the process."

He arched his eyebrows, the wine glass at his mouth. Finishing his drink he said, "First *ones*? And just how many, Goddess Yalki, are *ones*?"

She pursed her lips.

"You knew as well as I that he wouldn't survive."

"Oh, I know, but how many more of my slaves will you kill? I don't have that many to spare, especially if this doesn't work and we have to go back to doing things my way."

She narrowed her eyes and growled,

"Bring in another."

Chapter 60

Filion waited for Red to leave the heat room. Red took his time, slowly pulling on his pants, tying and re-tying his boots, rearranging his grenades, and buttoning and unbuttoning the top of his shirt.

"Whadda think, lossal? Unbuttoned or buttoned? I mean, my chest is manly but is it too over the top to flaunt it so?" He turned and faced Filion, who sat on the bench, his hands over his lap, staring straight ahead.

"Oh, don't be a sore loser. It's not the end of the world if a lady sees your pieces. I mean it *is* kinda a travesty that you didn't get anything from it, but maybe next time!" He slapped Filion on the back. "Yes, maybe next time. In the meantime I think I'll leave the top button undone. I mean, yeah, Wiq's already seen the entire package, but I'll bet with a little encouragement," he pointed at his undone button. "I'll bet she wants a taste."

Red smiled, gave Filion a little wave, and opened the door.

"Don't keep us waiting," he said, slamming the door behind him.

Filion exhaled. How could anyone be that abrasive?

"Can you believe that guy?" Filion said.

He turned and looked at Didrik, who was now mostly dry.

Unbelievable. If beings like him solely populated the universe, I would be on the Tiori's side.

"I can't say that you'd be wrong."

After several minutes, Filion was calm enough to dress. He pulled on his vest and pants, and then put Didrik, the orb, his purse and the ID cards back in his pockets. With a final look around the heat room, he walked to the door. His under garments were dry. As much as he hated to admit it, Red had been right. That almost chafed as much as wet underpants.

He made his way to Captain Eri's room. The door was open. He poked his head inside. The room was lighter now. The blue walls had paled, like the sky turning from day to night.

Captain Eri sat on the bed, her head in her hands.

"Captain Eri?" Filion said.

"Filion. Hi." Captain Eri looked up. Her face was haggard, but she smiled anyway. "I'm just getting my land legs back. That Biopser took it out of me."

"Of course... I'll just, go...."

"Do you know where to go?"

"Ahhh, no actually."

Captain Eri smiled. "Just wait a minute. I'll walk with you. You can't believe the headache I have. The Keeper helped me, but wow."

Filion stepped into the room.

"Just take your time."

"Do we have time?" Captain Eri asked.

"Ahh…"

"That's what I thought." She smiled again and squinted in the gentle light.

"So," she said. "What'd I miss?"

"Ahhh, well, a lot."

Captain Eri waited expectantly. Finally she said, "A lot? That's it?"

Filion shuffled his feet. "Uhhh, you know, the usual. Red got upset, Wiq put him in his place, Wiq coaxed the truth from the Keeper, Red tried to kill me for a second time, you know, the usual."

"Huh. That explains the nose I guess. Everything else okay?"

"Everything but my pride."

"Well, pride is a fickle beast, but she heals."

Filion let out a huff.

"You want to talk about it?" Captain Eri said.

"No, I'd rather not relive it, other than the part where I knocked Red out cold."

"Ahh, getting your space legs are we?"

"What?"

"Well, you aren't really part of the crew until you hit someone." She stuck out her hand. "Welcome to the crew, Filion Ker III."

"What?"

"We're crew. We're kin. We watch each other's back. You can count on me. I can count on you. Plus, I already heard everything from Wiq, you did good."

Filion didn't take her hand. "Red wants me dead."

She shook her head. "Red is a petulant child with advanced combat skills. He won't be a problem; you two are kin now. That bond goes deeper than love and hate. Actually, it is love and hate, in one body. You can't escape it. You hate him, but you love him. He's your kin. We're all your kin and you're ours. Welcome aboard." Her hand hovered in the air.

Filion didn't know what she was talking about but took her hand anyway.

Chapter 61

Yalki sat back. *Uhgg.* Sweat, dirt, and brain bits covered her face and arms. She wouldn't have imagined reprogramming to be this disgusting. Normally it wasn't, but then again *normally* she knew exactly what she was doing because someone else had done it before. Breaking new ground required her to actually get into the slave's brain and physically manipulate it. This wasn't as sanitary as she had thought it would be. She brushed a strand of hair from her eye, smearing black across her cheek. *Repulsive.*

She took a breath and pushed her revulsion away. She was making progress. This was her third slave. The second had died rather quickly due to overconfident (and hence incorrect) programming, but she had slowed for this one. She had been in here for at least three hours, and she was so close. She had figured out how to reroute most of the virus through his emotional capacitors. As a result, the slave would be as emotional as a board, but what did slaves need emotions for? Maybe this would be a two-fold improvement.

All she had to do was finalize the energy input updates. She had modeled them off of her own, but this brain was far less advanced than hers. She had to make sure she didn't overload the system.

Taking another breath she extended her arm and pushed it deep into the wall of brain before her. The mass was soft, squishy and alive. It pulsed angrily as she plowed into its depths. All she had to do was find the right fold. She would know when she hit it... and there it was. She pushed her body against the wall, it spasmed, kicking against her, but she was so close. She snapped the fold backwards. The wall quit kicking.

She withdrew her arm. It, and the entire front of her body, dripped with brain ooze. She shook her head. There was only one way to tell if it had worked. She closed her eyes and took a deep breath.

She opened her eyes. Harick sat slouched in his chair, his mouth open and drooling. He was asleep, that lazy cur. Asleep while she wallowed around in primitive brain matter! *Disgusting.* She flicked her arms in attempt to rid them of the brain mess when she realized she wasn't covered in anything. She looked at her arms and at her dress, and she felt her face and hair. She was clean, just as clean as she had been that morning after her bath.

She didn't wake Harick. With him asleep it would be easier to get another slave without his notice, which she would need assuming her latest programming hadn't worked and she had accidentally killed this one.

She faced slave. Her success or failure would be immediately apparent as soon as he woke. Her failsafe was the slave's signature. If he emitted an energy signal, he could receive them too. If he had no signature, she still had work to do. Knocked out though, his signal, if he had one, would be too small to conclusively detect.

She walked to the slave. He lay strapped to the map table. His eyes were closed, and his chest moved in even increments. At least he wasn't dead. She placed her hand on his head and smiled. No doubt the first Afortiori who discovered how to wake an unconscious person had spent hours slogging through their brain. Now all she had to do was think.

The man sprung awake, his eyes bulging, and his body straining against the straps. His eyes spun wildly until he realized who stood over him.

"Goddess Yalki," he said. "How may I serve you?"

Yalki smiled. A beautiful, albeit empty, signature rose from the table.

"You just did."

Chapter 62

Filion and Captain Eri walked in silence down the boardwalk. They moved slowly at first, Captain Eri walking as if she had just stepped off of a boat for the first time in months. Filion was alert as they moved, his hands ready in case she stumbled. But she didn't, and after a few minutes, she seemed to have recovered significant strength.

The boardwalk began to change. It went from wooden slats, to brown tile, and eventually to white tile. The brown wooden frames turned white, and soon Filion could see that the walls were no longer paper but cement and finally metal. They rounded a final corner, and the corridor dead-ended at two large metal doors.

"These seem so out of place," Filion said.

Captain Eri nodded. "Well, no matter what a Keeper tells you, they rely on technology at least as much as they do magic, if not more."

"So I've heard," Filion said.

Captain Eri gave him a sidelong glance. "I thought this Keeper business was new to you."

"I've been studying while you were out."

Captain Eri nodded. "We should ask the Keeper to take a look at your nose."

Filion agreed. His nose was swollen and thick with pain, but he hadn't wanted to bring it up, after all, Captain Eri's injuries were far worse than his own.

She knocked on the door. It echoed hollowly, and Filion heard a soft *thock – thock – thock,* and then the door rolled open. The Keeper stood on the other side.

"Come."

Captain Eri and Filion obeyed by stepping through the giant door. The Keeper pushed it closed and secured it with a long metal latch.

They stood in an empty white room. Its walls were smooth and continuous, free of any blemishes, save for the door they had just come through.

"You wish me to attend to your nose?" the Keeper said.

"Uh, yes, please," Filion said.

"Oh, don't look so shocked," the Keeper said. "I don't have to be magical to know it hurts."

She moved towards him and placed her hands over his nose. He felt a tingling and the pain peaked.

"Ahhh!" he cried.

Then the pain was gone.

"There, that is the best I can do with so little time."

Filion reached up and touched his nose. It was still tender, but that was all. The throbbing pain and swelling had disappeared.

"Thanks," Filion said, still touching his nose.

The Keeper nodded, walked to one of the walls and touched it. It flickered and disappeared. Beyond the wall was nothing but black.

"Through there."

Captain Eri and Filion entered the blackness, and the wall closed behind them. They waited, but nothing happened.

"Is this some sort of trick?" Filion asked, his voice heavier in the dark. He could just barely make out Captain Eri's outline.

"No, I don't think so," Captain Eri said. She reached out. Her hand came into contact with one of the walls. Slowly she began to move to her right.

"This is probably some sort of test," Captain Eri said.

"What do you..."

Suddenly, there was a flash of light, and Captain Eri vanished. The room went dark again and a loud whirring noise sounded. Filion clamped his hands over his ears, but it didn't help. The noise grew, and his head began to pound. He crouched down, but the noise and pain only intensified. He felt the pain spreading from his ears to the rest of his body, and he could feel the noise in his bones. He opened his mouth to scream, but nothing came out.

The pain was wild. It seemed to be ripping him apart. He collapsed, his body folding into the fetal position. His fur stood on end, and it felt as if it were being torn from his skin. He struggled to breathe.

A test. Captain Eri said this might be some sort of test, he labored.

What kind of test, he didn't know, but if he was going to figure it out, he needed to be able to think clearly. His eyes were already closed, so he took a deep breath. *Start with a first year exercise. Clear your mind.*

He started his breathing exercises. Inhale, exhale, inhale, exhale. *Get a regular rhythm.* He repeated the Searcher's Code and then pictured peace.

Picturing peace was a basic exercise. One let their subconscious create a peaceful place without any effort from the conscious mind. Peace varied from person to person, and it was usually different every time Filion conjured it. Now, peace came to him in the form of a wide-open field of green grass. He lay in the field, his back to the grass and his face to the sun. He took a deep breath. A breeze blew. He could smell cherrymelon flowers. A flock of rakins purred in the distance. A brook burbled somewhere to his left. The sounds were calming and pleasant. The grass shifted with a soft *swish* beneath him. He let out the breath.

When he opened his eyes, he found himself in a large metal room. The room was several stories high and other than a window with panes of tinted glass in its upper right hand corner, the room appeared empty. Was this the portal room?

"A test all right. Whoa."

Filion looked to his left. Captain Eri was again at his side.

"That was a molecular trap," Captain Eri said. "It threatens to pull you apart, molecule by molecule, unless you are centered and sure of who you are. No doubt a version of what we can experience from the portal."

She was wobbly in Filion's grasp.

"Are you going to be okay?" Filion asked. "I felt like I was going to die in there and I wasn't even Biopsed."

"Yeah, I'll be fine. Just don't let go for a second."

Filion didn't reply but stood and held Captain Eri. She was small, like Wiq, and like Wiq she was strong. He could feel the muscles in her shoulders beneath her shirt, and they shook, as did her entire body. Her aura was a loud yellow. She was in pain, intense pain, and she wasn't making a sound. He stood silently and watched as her aura faded to a calm green, and her body quit shaking.

"Thanks," she said.

"No problem," Filion said softly.

He let her go, and she moved towards the center of the room.

"This is it, the portal room," she said.

"How can you be sure? And where are Wiq and Red?" Filion asked.

As if on cue, they appeared next to Captain Eri.

"Hey," Wiq said, seemingly startled. "Did you just get here?"

Captain Eri nodded.

"We've been here a while. You get a kick outta the molecular trap, lossal?" Red said.

"You just appeared," Filion said.

"So it may seem, lossal, but nothin's what it seems around here, now is it?"

Filion frowned. Red and Wiq were going through the bags of gear they had brought, sorting and repacking things, but Filion was confused.

"I don't get it, where's the portal?" Filion asked.

Wiq looked up.

"It is wherever the Keeper decides it is. You will see."

Filion let out a huff.

"What?!"

Filion turned towards Red's voice. He and Captain Eri had moved away from the bags of gear, and Red didn't look happy.

"You heard me. He's crew now."

Red shifted his gaze from Captain Eri to Filion.

"The lossal? He's done nothing but put us in danger! How could you wanna keep him around? You made him crew?"

"You know what this means. I can't have infighting, and I won't tolerate it."

Red looked at Captain Eri and then at Filion. "This is a bad idea. He won'

166

bring nothing but trouble. Us keepin' him around, and treatin' him like crew, only increases our chances we run into that trouble."

"He's crew. I don't want to hear anything more about it."

Captain Eri moved back to the pile of bags. Red didn't move. He stared at Filion. Filion swallowed and wished he had something to do, but it was obvious that he didn't. He stared awkwardly back at Red.

Red moved, and in a flash was at Filion's side.

"I don't know how you hoodwinked her, lossal, but you did. I guess I ought to give you credit, but... Well, we're crew now. I'll do my best to not kill you and keep others from killin' you too."

Red spat on his hand and extended it to Filion.

"Uhh, me too?" Filion said.

"Yeah, whatever. I'm not worried about you tryin' to kill me, and I doubt you stop a threat before I do. You're like a baby sister, worthless and annoying."

"Did your baby sister not become the youngest chief Digth has ever seen?" Wiq said. "I hear she is a planetary hero."

Red dropped his hand and rounded on Wiq. She appeared not to notice him, intent on disassembling some sort of gun.

"Listen here, you leave my overachievin' baby sister outta this."

"I do not think I was the one who brought her into this," Wiq said, removing the gun's barrel. "And did Filion not almost kill you just a little while ago?"

Red took a sharp breath, opened his mouth, shut it and smiled.

"I believe I got him back for that one."

Filion colored and turned from Wiq.

"Give me your hand," Red said.

"What?" Filion said.

Red grabbed his hand and shook it. "We be crew now."

By the time Filion realized what Red had done, Red had let go of his hand and was back at the bags. Filion stared after him for a moment then wiped his palm on his pants.

"We gonna give the lossal a gun? Or will he shoot himself?" Red asked.

"He gets a weapon," Captain Eri said. She seemed to have fully recovered, and if it weren't for the slightest indication in her aura, Filion wouldn't have known she was in pain.

She handed Filion a phazer.

"You ever use one of these before?"

"Ahh, not while awake, no. Although I understand how one works, and in theory, I can operate one."

"Great. Don't point this end at yourself or any of us," Captain Eri pointed at the muzzle. "Squeeze this to shoot. One quick squeeze will issue a three second pulse. If you hold it down, you'll get a continuous stream." She pointed to the trigger. "The weapon has a fully charged battery, so you

167

should be good for several days."

"Got it," Filion said, turning the weapon in his hands.

Red shook his head.

"That's your bag." Captain Eri pointed at the duffle. "There are straps on the back so you can wear it as a backpack."

Filion picked it up. It was heavy, but nothing he couldn't manage. He smiled. He *had* managed Red.

"Also, we're suiting up. The biggest suit we had is in your bag. Try it on."

Filion nodded and pulled the suit from the bag. It was a haz suit. Used around the galaxy for the most disgusting of tasks, haz suits were designed to protect the wearer from most hazardous materials. Synthetic and air tight, this haz suit might have fit a young lossal, but it wasn't going to fit Filion.

"Uh, Captain? I don't think this is going to work."

Captain Eri turned, now in a suit herself, minus her hood and gloves.

"Try the hood. Does that fit?"

Filion pulled the hood over his head. It smashed his ears and snout, but technically it fit.

"That's good. Lie down," Captain Eri commanded.

Filion lied on the floor. Captain Eri grabbed his suit and laid it on top of him.

"Huh, you need another two feet, at least."

She reached into her bag and withdrew a long knife.

"What are you doing?" Filion asked, his voice echoing in the small hood.

"Just making some modifications," she bent down and cut the suit at the knees and elbows. "Wiq, you have that patching material?"

"Here," Wiq said, tossing Captain Eri a roll of synthetic patching.

"Take the hood off. Put the suit on," Captain Eri said.

Filion obeyed, happy to take off the hood. He unzipped the suit and stepped in. The suit should have covered his whole body but did not. The cut legs barely reached his knees, and the cut sleeves only reached his elbows.

"Okay," Captain Eri said. She wrapped the patching material around one of the legs of Filion's suit and then down to his foot. Once she reached his foot she wrapped that too.

"Alright..." She said.

The material molded to his leg and foot and then set, bonding to the suit without any issue.

She finished his other leg then moved to his arms. She wrapped the material around his arms and stopped at his hands.

"You're going to have clawed mittens."

She wrapped the material around his thumb and index finger individually, and then wrapped the rest of his fingers together. She repeated the process on his other side.

"Done!" she stepped back, admiring her handy work.

"He looks like a multicolored boogie man," Red said.

Filion looked at his suit. The original suit was white with florescent yellow stripes down the arms and legs. The patch material was a greenish blue. He did look ridiculous.

"And this multicolored boogie man won't be an Infected anytime soon," Captain Eri said. "Can you manipulate the trigger of your phazer?"

Filion picked up his phazer and stuck his finger over the trigger.

"Lossal!" Red yelled, knocking the phazer from his hands. "Remember what the Captain said, muzzle control! Don't point that thing at us!"

"Oh, sorry," Filion said, realizing he had had the phazer pointed at Captain Eri's chest.

"His finger fits fine," Red said.

Captain Eri nodded.

"I'm ready when you are," a voice boomed. It was the Keeper.

Filion looked up towards the glass. He couldn't see her, but he knew she was there.

Red, Wiq and Captain Eri shouldered their bags. All three now wore haz suits. They put on their gloves and sealed their hoods. Filion followed their lead, fumbling with his clawed mittens.

Captain Eri gave a thumbs up to the glass.

"Wiq will assist you in returning through the portal, if you return."

Captain Eri glared at the dark glass.

"Are you all ready? And here we go..."

Chapter 63

Yalki collapsed into Harick's chair. She had been at this all night. The sun was just beginning to peak over the hills, and she was tired. Harick had never been as gifted as she, and after he permanently maimed three slaves, it was concluded that she would be the one to reprogram *all* of them. While the reprogramming had become easier with each slave, it was still not a simple process. Having just finished reprogramming her eleventh slave, she was exhausted. She had to sleep before she did any more.

"I must rest," she said.

Harick looked at her. He had become considerably more agreeable since her discovery and even more so since the discovery that he couldn't duplicate her work.

"Send these eleven into the field. Have the rest of your slaves continue searching manually. When I am rested, I will resume the reprogramming."

"That sounds great. Do you want to rest here?"

Yalki shook her head. "No, I want to go back to my estate."

"Are you well enough to Jump?"

The question pricked at her, but he had a point.

"I don't think so."

"I'll do the Jump then."

He moved towards her and took her hand. In an instant they were outside of her palace's gates.

"Thank you," she said. "I'll see you in a few hours."

She turned and opened the gates, shuffling through them and up the dirt path.

Harick watched her go. It smarted that she had been able to figure it out, and it smarted even more that he couldn't replicate her work. He shook his head and made the Jump back to his tent. If he located the Chozen while she was sleeping, he had a chance of regaining what little edge he had once had on Yalki. She had become increasingly more condescending since his failure, and if he didn't have a victory soon, she would become unmanageable. What scared him most though was that he wasn't sure he could stop her if she exerted her full power, and as soon as she knew he was the weaker of the two…

He had to have a victory.

Chapter 64

The group stood in the middle of the portal room, their backs to each other and their phazers at ready. With a loud bang, the whirring noise returned, and it was all Filion could do to keep from clamping his hands to his ears.

"What's happening?" Filion yelled.

"Just wait!" Captain Eri yelled back.

Filion watched as the air began to shimmer and shake. Suddenly the air flashed.

"That's it!" Captain Eri cried.

Filion shielded his eyes. For a moment all he could see was white, then the portal room came back into focus. A dark ragged line now cut through the room. With a loud crack, the line snapped into a spiky circle. The circle's edge, dark as pitch, wavered and danced. From the inside of the circle shown two colors, black and a faded teal. The teal formed a thick ring between the portal's jagged edge and the portal's inner darkness. Filion stared into the foggy black center of the aperture and shivered. He knew that's where they were going.

"We ready?" Captain Eri called.

"Affirm," Wiq answered.

"Affirm," Red echoed.

"Uh, me too, affirm," Filion said.

"Right," Captain Eri yelled. "I'll go first, then Red, then Filion, then Wiq."

Red and Wiq nodded, and Filion felt sick. Captain Eri gave a final nod then stepped through the portal. Red followed, hot on her heels.

It was Filion's turn. Panic welled inside of him, but he forced himself forward. He wasn't prepared for this, but it didn't matter. Ready or not, he had no choice.

She needed him.

The universe needed him.

He closed his eyes and stepped into the void.

Chapter 65

Ryo was concerned, distantly. She could now feel thirteen, rather than two, energy signatures. The eleven new signatures were different, vacant almost, but still dangerous. While they had to be closer than the original two to find her, she now had over six times the number of signatures to keep track of. She let them bounce around in the back of her mind while she concentrated on locating memories involving portals.

She needed to find the portal. She had no memories of Handu, although there was a chance she had been here when it was called something else, but even if she had, it probably wouldn't have helped her. That left two options – finding the portal by chance or finding it using her 'powers'. While unlocking some secret portal finding power would have been the most effective way to locate the portal, Ryo wasn't convinced she possessed such a skill. Spending time trying and uncover something that may or may not exist in her subconscious sounded like a waste of time. Then again, wandering around blindly also felt like a waste of time.

In the end, she decided to bet both on chance and power. She wandered and thought, always keeping a small section of her mind dedicated to monitoring the signals. She used the rest of her mind to conjure up what she knew about portals.

Her memories of being a Portal Keeper were patchy, which she guessed meant she was one a long time ago. This also meant that things had probably changed in the portal world since she had been apart of it. Her information was most likely outdated. She knew that what she was looking for was made using 'magic', meaning that someone with power, someone like herself, or maybe even an Eoan or Afortiori, had built it. There was a chance, however, that due to advances in technology, this portal now used more technology than 'magic'. Science certainly could have advanced enough to explain certain aspects of portal travel. Even so, she should be able to sense the portal before she could see it. Just because technology could explain portals didn't mean they didn't emit energy.

It would most likely be hidden from plain view, maybe underground or in a secret room. It could even be in the middle of the forest, obscured by 'magic'. None of this really helped.

Wait, she knew that she would be able to sense it before she saw it. In her memories she could always feel the portal once she was within a certain distance of it. What did it feel like? Did all portals feel the same? Had she ever been around a portal different than the one she had kept?

She had, and they had emitted different signals, but there had been underlying similarities. Portals were like humans or ringers. All humans were different, but all were identifiable as human. She knew what a portal should feel like. She opened her mind.

Where are you?

Chapter 66

Pain ripped through his body. Filion felt as if he were being torn apart limb by limb and turned inside out, all at the same time. He wanted to scream, but opening his mouth might have caused him to pass out. The high-pitched hum that had filled the portal room was louder now, so loud that he feared his eardrums might burst. He was glad he had had the foresight to close his eyes before he stepped into the portal. Not only did he not want to see what was happening to him, but he also wasn't sure he could have closed his eyes had they been open.

Whack! The world quit moving and so did he. He had hit something hard, like a wall. The abject pain was suddenly gone and in its place, a dull throbbing. Filion tried to take a deep breath but was quickly reminded of the suffocating hood. He inhaled again, his eyes still clenched tight.

"LOSSAL! GET YOUR ASS UP!" Red hissed.

Filion's eyes flew open. At first he couldn't see anything, but he quickly realized he was lying face first on what he could only assume to be the ground. Wherever he was was dark, and while he couldn't see the others, he could hear them moving nearby. He raised himself to his knees, pushing off of the floor with his hands. His hands sunk into something soft. *What?*

He sprang to his feet. Bits of goop dripped from his hands and hood. Slimy, red and white pieces of... He swallowed hard... Person. He had been kneeling in a person, or rather, pieces of a person.

Filion tried to back away from the mess, but it was futile. Bits of skin, fur, bone, and blood covered the room. Everywhere he stepped and looked, he encountered a piece of someone – a part of their face, a bit of jewelry still on a hand, a piece of clothing, or some other indefinable mass of dead flesh. Spots floated in front of Filion's eyes. This was sickening, terrifying, he might pass out...

"We could be underground," Red said.

Red, Wiq, and Captain Eri all had their phazers drawn and were quietly scanning the room.

"No windows, dirt floor, solid walls, low ceiling – wherever we are is secret, or was," Red said, glancing at the organic fragments.

Filion lifted his hands. Through the small hood he could see the sticky mess dripping from his fingers. He felt his body begin to spasm. Something stirred in his gut. It welled through him and he yelled, "Ahhhhhh! GET IT OFF OF ME!"

Someone grabbed his arm.

"Shut up!" Wiq hissed.

Filion closed his mouth. He was covered in blood. What if there was a hole in his suit? What if Captain Eri's patching hadn't been airtight? How long until he exploded? Wasn't it supposed to be instant? WAS HE EVIL?

"Whatever happened here happened a while ago," Captain Eri said.

"I am not picking up any life signs or mechanical signs," Wiq said.

"This place gives me the creeps," Red said. "Let's get out of here."

"Red, mark it," Captain Eri said.

Red pulled a mapping unit from his pack. He poked a few buttons then stuck it back in his bag.

"Got it."

"Good, let's move."

There was one door in the room, a crude wooden thing. Wiq and Red positioned themselves on each side of it. Wiq threw the door open and Red scanned the opening. They moved diagonally into the room, Wiq moving to the left and Red moving to the right. Captain Eri followed, leaving Filion by himself.

Panicking, Filion raced after them, plowing into the next dark room.

"Guys?" he said.

"I'll kill you myself if you don't shut up," Red hissed.

"Found it," Wiq said.

There was a scraping noise and then a shaft of light split the room. Wiq and Captain Eri were the first to enter the new room followed by Red and then Filion.

It took Filion's eyes a few moments to adjust to the light. They stood in what had once been a nice parlor. With high painted ceilings and thick carpet, the room spoke of ruined affluence. The walls, which had been a crisp ivory, now dripped with blood, and hair and bone littered the decimated blue velvet furniture. Strips of curtains hung from blood streaked windows, and broken polished wood lay scattered across the room. Filion took a deep breath. The hood sucked to his snout. He wanted to rip the thing from his face, but he fought the urge.

"Clever," Red mumbled.

Filion turned. They had entered the room through what appeared to be a false bookcase, its books, now soaked in fluids, sagged on the bowing shelves.

"Why was the door closed? How'd these poor suckers explode if the door was closed?" Red asked.

"Obviously, someone let them in," Captain Eri said, stepping over part of an arm. "Let's go."

"Who? Who let who in?" Filion said.

No one answered him.

They left the parlor, following the trail of blood into a once beautiful, marbled hallway. High columns lined the corridor. Between the columns were large windows, their thick curtains drawn and tattered. To Filion, this hall wasn't as upsetting as the parlor or portal room. While blood and

175

remains smeared the floors and walls, the mess was more spread out, maybe due to the expansiveness of the hall, or maybe because fewer people had died out here. Unlike in the portal room, Filion could see other things mixed into the drying blood. Pieces of wooden and stone statues littered the floor. Swaths of well-made tapestries and bits of what appeared to be precious metals and stones lay scattered in the gore. This place had been trashed.

Their footfalls echoed on the stone floor. Filion shivered, as he looked around. Who knew what was lurking in the shadows.

"Is this a castle?" Filion asked. "Where are we?"

"We're in Rincoy," Captain Eri whispered. "It's a town on the border of Handu's north and east quadrants. It's a vacation spot for the wealthy. We're in a hotel."

"Ahh grawlix," Red said. "A rich man's vacation town? It's probably crawling with Infecteds – everyone knows that you can't git rich without selling your soul."

"Enough talking," Wiq said.

Red shut his mouth.

"ARGH!"

Filion spun. A man, covered in boils and dragging his right foot, hobbled towards them. He foamed at the mouth, and black fluid dripped from his eyes and nose.

"SHOOT HIM!" Red yelled, running to Filion's side.

Red and Wiq fired their phazers, hitting the Infected in the chest. The man staggered backwards then collapsed.

"Son of a god! What were you thinking?" Red said, flinging his arm at Filion. "Shoot them! Always shoot the Infecteds!"

"Right," Filion said nodding. "Right."

He stared at the man for a moment. He was dead now, but when he had been up and walking, he had had no aura. Filion shivered.

They continued walking, winding their way through the devastated corridor until they came to a glass door. Despite the glass's bloody coating, Filion could see sunlight on its other side. Red and Wiq positioned themselves on each side of the door. They paused for a moment then kicked the door open and charged into the outside.

Filion stood, blinded by the sun. He didn't move until he heard a hiss from Red wherein Filion stepped outside. Handu's two suns were warm and scintillating, and they felt good, even if Filion had to experience them through a haz suit. He closed his eyes and tilted his face upwards. He shook his shoulders as if trying to separate his body from the death inside the building.

"What the grawlix are you doing, lossal?" Red growled, pushing Filion away from the door.

Filion opened his eyes. They were in a courtyard which Filion could see

176

was surrounded on three sides by the building's tall walls. The open end of the courtyard led to a thick forest. Wiq stood with her back to one of the corners and seemed to be studying the sky. Red was in the other corner and appeared to have fervent interest in the edge of the courtyard. Captain Eri had positioned herself next to the door, and she held her phazer at ready, pointing it into the building.

Filion felt out of place. He pushed his back to the nearest wall and decided he had better study something too. Holding his phazer awkwardly, he looked around the courtyard. Adorned with colorful plants and flowers, the courtyard was grand. A marble fountain flowed peacefully in its center, and white benches adorned its edges. Fruit trees shaded each bench and freshly painted tables poked out from bright patches of blossoms. If it wasn't for the Infecteds and Tioris, this would have been a very nice place. Filion glanced back at the door, its glass smeared with blood. Yes, peaceful, if not for the Infecteds...

"Before we go any further, we need a plan," Captain Eri said. "Do you have any idea how to find her?"

"Ahhh," Filion said. "Well... OW!"

The orb!

Filion began to dance, his left hip leading the way. He dropped his phazer, letting its sling catch it, and hopped away from the wall.

"What..." Captain Eri started.

"I need to get into my pocket. I have a locating device, I think. It gets hot when it wants me to follow it. It's burning me! I need to get it out of my pocket!"

Filion tried to move his body away from the heat, but in the suit, there was no room to escape.

"Are you sure you want to take off your suit?" Wiq asked.

"No! Yes! No! I have to if we're going to find her."

"Fine. Spray him," Captain Eri said, her body still facing the door.

Red threw down his bag and ripped open the zipper. He dug for a few moments, and then pulled out a small spray bottle.

"What's that?" Filion said.

"This," Red said, "Is Agent X 2.0. This here liquid will kill any and all organic life it comes in contact with. That includes you, as well as T. Tryx. Hold still."

"I thought only fire killed T. Tryx," Filion said, hopping away from Red.

"Fire and this stuff. Fire is cheaper but more destructive. Agent X 2.0 is worth more than your life, although you are a lossal. You die we might be able to sell your pelt for a bigger bottle, although you are kinda short..."

"You sure it won't kill me?"

"Filion! This isn't our first space walk. Your suit is designed for this. Hold still!" Captain Eri said.

Filion stopped moving. Red walked to him and squeezed the bottle's trigger. A large, orange cloud engulfed Filion, and immediately Filion heard what sounded like sizzling.

"What's happening?" Filion said.

"Give it a minute. It's still orange. When the cloud turns blue, you're good," Captain Eri said.

Filion watched from the confines of his hood. The cloud wasn't turning blue.

"Why isn't it turning blue?" Filion asked.

"Give it a minute," Red said.

Filion waited, his panic increasing with every passing second, then the cloud began to darken.

"Okay, you're good."

"You sure that stuff won't burn me when I take off the suit?"

"No," Captain Eri said.

Filion hesitated, and then pulled at his hood, unlocking the seal. Nothing happened. He wasn't burning, or exploding. He was fine. The stuff had worked.

He tossed the hood to the ground and unzipped his suit to the waist. A burning smell wafted from his suit, and he realized the orb had begun to burn a hole in his pocket. He snatched the bright orange orb from his pants and dropped it onto the ground.

"What is that?" Captain Eri said, her voice muffled inside of her hood.

"I don't know, but I think it can lead us to her."

"Huh," Captain Eri mused. "Well, it's better than anything else we have. Put your suit back on and we'll go. Wiq, you come with me. We'll clear to the end of the courtyard while Filion puts himself back together. Red, you stay here and cover him."

Wiq nodded, and she and Captain Eri moved down the courtyard.

Red grunted and tossed the Agent X 2.0 back into his pack. He re-shouldered the bag and moved to the side of the door, his phazer at the ready.

Filion did as he was told and re-zipped his suit. He stuffed his hood over his ears and looked at Red.

"You ready?" Filion asked.

Red glared at him.

"Of course I'm ready, lossal. That's a stupid question. A smart question would be, are *you* ready?"

Filion picked up the orb. It rolled to the tips of his fingers.

"As ready as I'll ever be."

Chapter 67

Her nap hadn't been long, but it was all she could afford. She could feel it. Everything was converging. Today was an important day. She couldn't sleep through it.

The suns indicated it was midmorning. She couldn't have slept more than three hours, but it was enough. The ex-mayor entered her room, a tray of food and tea in her hands.

"Goddess Yalki," the woman said.

Yalki ignored her and made the Jump, opening her eyes outside of Harick's war tent. The grounds were quiet. Yalki smiled. Harick had his troops out searching. *Good.* She entered the tent. Everything was as she had left it save for a single piece of paper on the fluxim table. She picked it up.

Out searching. Left one unit behind. Staged behind tent. When done, send word. Will send more.
– H

Yalki left the tent in search of the unit. She found them quickly. They were, as Harick had said, behind the tent, training. Their swords clanged in the early morning air. She watched them silently for a moment. They were fine specimens, their body's well developed and their techniques well executed. She liked how they trained in nothing but short pants. It was intoxicating, their determination, their sweat, their skin. Ahhh, the pleasures of a physical world. The Eoans were stupid. There was no other way to say it. In time, that stupidity would to lose them this war, and she would be there to see it. Now though... She watched the men move in the sunlight... She could see their muscles ripple as they swung their blades. They worked hard, as did she...

"You. What is your name?"

The men jumped at her voice. They turned and kneeled instantly. She pointed to a tall dark man. She liked tall dark men.

"Jat," he said.

"Jat, you come with me. The rest of you, keep training. I will be with you shortly."

Jat stood and walked to Yalki, sheathing his sword. She smiled. She had earned one quick indulgence...

Chapter 68

Filion walked to the end of the courtyard, the orb balanced on his hand. Red followed him, walking backwards, his eyes on the glass door.

They reached Captain Eri and Wiq. The women stood at the corners of the courtyard, their phazers pointed into the forest.

"You know how to use that thing?" Captain Eri said. "I've never seen a locating device like that."

"Uhh, well, last time this thing got hot it led me to the ticket counter where I bought the ticket for Bok. I think we should follow it."

Captain Eri frowned. "How does it work?"

"Perhaps we can discuss this later?" Wiq said, her focus on the woods.

"She's right," Captain Eri said. "Wiq and I will lead the way. Then you come, Filion. Red, you bring up the rear."

Wiq nodded and then disappeared.

"Let's kill some Infecteds!" Red said, charging his phazer unnecessarily.

Captain Eri looked at Red. "You've seen too many films Red."

Red looked slightly abashed.

Filion turned away from Red and looked out at the technicolored woods, which he suddenly realized were farther away than he had originally thought. The courtyard and the building were not at the edge of the forest. Rather, it appeared that the forest had been cleared away to make room for the hotel, and as a result, several hundred yards of open space stood between the buildings and the trees. This was the space that they were about to cross, and while Filion knew that they had to reach the forest to find Ryo, every molecule in his body told him that cutting through that field was a bad idea.

Captain Eri turned to Filion. "Ready?" she said. "We run on three. One... two... three!"

Captain Eri took off. Filion watched her go, his legs seemingly rooted to where he stood.

"Lossal! Move!" Red growled, shoving Filion into the field.

Filion stumbled, his hand closing around the orb, and then he ran, his feet taking over for his mind. He passed Captain Eri, and probably Wiq too, although he couldn't be sure since she was cloaked. He reached the trees well before the rest of the group. He stopped running, his hands on his knees, as he panted in relief. Then it hit him. He was by himself in a forest haunted by Infecteds. He had to defend himself until Captain Eri and the others caught up to him! He fumbled with his phazer, trying to bring it to a ready position while still holding onto the orb. He could feel its warmth through his suit, but he ignored it.

Jerkily, Filion scanned the forest with his phazer. He did his best to imitate Wiq and Red and Captain Eri, but his heart was pounding so hard, and his hands were shaking so much. He was too afraid. The phazer bounced in his hands, and he couldn't see through the sight. Not that it really mattered, he wasn't entirely sure if he had the safety off. Beginning to panic, Filion shut his eyes and took a deep breath.

"You're fast when you want to be," Captain Eri breathed.

Filion opened his eyes. Captain Eri stood next to him, bent over and panting. With each breath the hood sucked to her face.

"Lossal, you're supposed to stay behind Captain Eri and Wiq, not leave them behind. What kind of brother are you?" Red huffed, as he reached the forest.

"What?" Filion said.

"You never leave your team members behind," Red growled, shoving his hooded face into Filion's space.

"Okay, he gets it. We can talk about this later," Wiq's voice sounded. The shimmered air between Filion and Red.

"Yeah, if we all make it to later," Red mumbled.

"Let's move," Captain Eri said, now seemingly recovered.

They walked without speaking, occasionally weaving when the orb shifted directions. Other than their footfalls, minus Wiq's of course, the forest was silent. The silence was so loud that when a shuffling noise emanated from behind them, it was as if a bomb had exploded. Filion jumped. Captain Eri spun and Red looked frantically from left to right.

"GHAA!"

A woman without arms sprung from the bushes. Black wounds covered her exposed stomach. She moved quickly for someone as damaged as she, but three phazer blasts put her down before she was within what would have been, arms length.

Filion took a deep breath, another, and no aura. This was not a good place.

"Let's move," Captain Eri said.

They continued on, following the now red orb. Filion wondered how long this would take, and how long they would last.

Chapter 69

She wasn't far now. The portal's signal was growing stronger but so were the new signals. They were tracking her. No doubt about it, they were on her trail. She tried not to focus on them, but it was difficult. With effort, she pushed them to the back of her mind and pressed on.

She ducked beneath a red vine. The forest was different here. Still the trees were wild colors, blues and purples, but it was silent. No birds called, nothing rustled in the bushes, it was almost as if this part of the forest was dead.

Shhh, shhh, shhh.

Ryo turned. Almost.

A memory surged… invisibility. With the right thought sequence, she could become invisible and hide. Hide from what? The memory was hazy, not all of the sequence was there. She strained to remember the right thoughts when, "GYAH!"

A youth appeared from behind a large indigo tree. His face dripped from his skull, and his arms and legs appeared similarly melted. An eye dangled from its socket while its partner was completely gone.

Ryo jumped back, the thoughts of invisibility instantly pushed aside. From her forearms came the familiar bubbling. But wait, was she really going to blast a kid? The boy couldn't have been more than fourteen or fifteen. What had happened to him?

He staggered forward, a low gurgling coming from his throat. She took another step backwards. Something was wrong here. Images of similarly destroyed people flashed in her head. Infecteds. Infecteds were bad, they were contagious, but usually they were older. She couldn't remember why though…

The Infected continued to shuffle towards her. She took another step back. Then it was done. Her arm came up, the energy shot forward, and the boy flew backwards. A melon sized hole sizzled in his chest.

He wobbled for a moment and then collapsed. A slick crunching noise accompanied his fall.

Ryo stood motionless. She had just killed a person, a boy, but something told her that he was a boy no longer. Something also told her not to go near him. He was contagious, whatever that meant.

She made a large arc around the body and continued towards the portal. She had to get out of here.

Chapter 70

"I think we're getting close," Filion whispered.

"It's about damn time," Red growled.

"How do you know?" Captain Eri asked.

There was a scraping from their left. Another Infected appeared, this one's lower jaw was missing, as well as its ears and it's right leg. Wiq shot it before it took its first hop towards them.

"The orb is getting hot, very hot."

"And that means we're close?" Red said.

"I don't know. I can only assume."

"Great," Red snarled. "It's the blind leading the blind. How do you know that thing isn't leading us to the Tioris? Where'd you get it?"

"Quiet!" Wiq said.

Red fell silent. Filion did breathing exercises to try and dull the burning.

There was another rustling noise, this time from in front of them. The group stopped, Captain Eri and Red's phazers up and ready.

"I'm gettin' sick of this. We should shoot first and ask questions later..."

Red stumbled backwards, clawing at his mouth. The air wafted around him.

"I said be quiet," Wiq hissed.

Wiq flashed for an instant, and Filion could see she had clamped her hand over Red's mouth. She waited a moment then released him and was instantly cloaked again.

Red rubbed his mouth and glared in her direction.

"This is penguin piss," he said, and shot into the bush.

Chapter 71

Ryo walked, her mind concentrating on too many things. The signals were growing alarmingly close. There were Infecteds about – and it was very wrong that a boy that young was an Infected – but she couldn't pinpoint why. Then there was the portal and Filion. Filion was supposed to be at the portal. Would he make it? Was he even real, or was she really crazy?

"I'm gettin' sick of this. We should shoot first and ask questions later..."

She stopped. Voices. Someone was there, near her. The bubbling came back. Who was it? That wasn't what Filion had sounded like in her dreams. She felt her energy surge.

Grawlix! What had she done? She looked at her hands. She was invisible! She had done it, without even thinking about it! She was invisible! But the bubbling wasn't gone. Her energy spiked again, and suddenly everything slowed.

"This... is... penguin... piss."

Ryo stepped to her right and watched as three phazer rounds floated past her left side. They bit unhurriedly through the air, burning it as they moved. She watched them extinguish themselves on a large tree, behind where she had been standing only moments ago. No more rounds came, so she took three heavy steps forward. She cleared a large Yuc bush and saw them.

In front of her stood three figures, well three figures that she could see, all in haz suits. There was a fourth figure as well, also suited, but it was cloaked. While she couldn't see the cloaked figure, she could feel it. She watched as they moved, time still slowed.

The cloaked figure spun, it's arm extending gradually, but forcefully, into the figure with the smoking phazer. The shooter arched backwards as the invisible punch caught it under the hood. The shooter began to fall. Its arms stretched lazily through the air as its phazer drifted to the ground. The aggressor moved over the shooter, cocking its arm backwards in preparation for another punch.

The tallest figure, whose suit was a strange mix of colors, stood with its hand outstretched and flat, a glowing marble on its palm. Initially, the figure didn't move, its body tense, then it began to curl forward, as if it had been hit in the gut. Its hand tilted and the orb floated downwards. The multicolored figure crumpled to the ground, a muffled wail escaping from its hood.

The other figure stood, phazer ready, lethargically turning its head from right to left, scanning the forest.

Wiq hit him again.

"You never fire until you are sure of your target!" she spat.

Red groped for his phazer but abandoned the effort and put his hands up to stop the blows.

"If this lady Chozen is everything he says she is, she'll be fine!" he managed between the punches.

Filion hit the ground. Had the orb just shocked him? Was that even possible? His insides felt like they were on fire. He wanted to vomit but couldn't even open his mouth to do so.

Captain Eri continued to scan the forest. She turned to their six. Red was on the ground, his hands up, and his body reeling from unseen blows. He was becoming more and more unpredictable. She let Wiq beat him. This mission was bigger than his ego.

Swish.

What was that? Captain Eri turned back towards the noise. She gasped.

A woman in a flowing white, blood stained dress stood before her. The dress swirled around the woman, an unfelt wind twisting it and her tar black hair. Her skin was dark and flawless, offset beautifully by the dress, but all of it was insignificant compared to her eyes. Bluer than the clearest of seas, Captain Eri had never seen eyes so intoxicating. She lowered her weapon and stared, suddenly unconcerned for her safety.

Ryo watched the standing hooded figure turn backwards and then forwards. A rush of wind hit Ryo, and the figure froze. Ryo could feel it studying her. Her hair and dress danced around her, but she ignored them. She stared straight at the little window in the figure's hood. The figure dropped its phazer. Ryo let out a small breath, and time reoriented itself.

Filion stopped writhing. The pain was suddenly gone. He opened his eyes and looked up. Captain Eri stood motionless, her phazer dangling from its sling.

"Captain Eri!" He said, pushing himself to his knees. "Captain Eri!"

He looked past Captain Eri, and there she was. Beautiful and alive, Ryo had found them.

"Ryo!" Filion said, grabbing the orb and staggering to his feet.

Ryo looked at the figure. Could it be? Was that Filion?

Filion rushed towards her but was abruptly stopped, his body trapped in a crouched run. Ryo approached him.

She moved with such grace, and Filion momentarily forgot she had, once again, ensnared him. He watched as she drifted towards him, her blue eyes trained on his hood. He looked into her eyes and felt as if he was falling. Down he went, but she was there. She would catch him.

She reached him, unlocked his hood, and pulled it from his suit.

The panic lasted only as long as the hood obscured his view of her. Once he could see, clearly see, those blue eyes, he was calm again.

Suddenly, he collapsed. Ryo had let him go.

"It is you," she said, smiling.

"I told you we were coming for you," he said, grabbing the orb again and standing. He unzipped his haz suit and dropped the orb into his vest pocket. He couldn't believe she was really here!

Filion looked expectantly at the others, but they were all frozen in place. Captain Eri still stared at the spot where Ryo had first appeared. Red was on his back with his hands over his grimacing face. His jaw stuck out at an unnatural angle, and through the hood, Filion could see blood on his cheeks.

"You said you would, but part of me didn't believe," Ryo said, dropping Filion's hood.

"These are my friends. They helped me find you," Filion said, gesturing at his newfound crew.

"You shot at me," she said.

"Ahh, no, Red shot at you." Filion pointed to Red.

"Huh," Ryo said, walking to Red. "You have a vissy with you."

Suddenly, Wiq appeared, frozen on top of Red, her right fist in contact with his jaw.

"Yes," Filion said, staring at Red and Wiq.

"Huh," Ryo said again. She reached out and pulled off Wiq's hood.

Wiq sprung to life. She completed her punch and straightened for another, but stopped when she saw Ryo. Red didn't move.

Wiq was on her feet in an instant, panic flashing in her eyes as she realized she was no longer hooded or cloaked.

"Hi," Ryo said. "I'm Ryo."

Wiq stared at her but didn't move.

"You are she? The Chozen?"

Ryo smiled and turned, a sudden aura of girlishness surrounding her.

"That's what they say," she shrugged.

Filion took a step back. She hadn't had an aura a second earlier or even when they had first heard her in the bushes.

Wiq looked at her, her face unreadable. Finally, she broke into a smile.

"I am Wiq," she said and extended her hand.

Ryo smiled and took it.

"I think we will be friends Wiq." They stood holding hands for several seconds, until finally Ryo dropped Wiq's hand and moved to Captain Eri.

Wiq stared after her.

Ryo stood before Captain Eri, studying her.

"She is dedicated, and dangerous. The damage has made her so..." Ryo mused.

Filion didn't say anything. What did that mean? Suddenly Captain Eri's weight sagged. She spun, and her hood flew off. Her eyes widened.

"Captain Eri, this is Ryo," Filion said.

Captain Eri didn't say anything, but she watched Ryo like a hawk. Ryo stared at her, a distant look in her eyes.

"You've been made to be strong," Ryo said.

"You… you're the Chozen?" Captain Eri asked.

Ryo nodded, the girlishness gone.

Captain Eri extended her hand. "I'm Captain Eri, Captain of the *Dark Horse*, Captain of this crew."

Ryo took her hand and nodded. "I know. Thanks for coming."

Chapter 72

Kiliank followed the signal. He would find it soon, but... He was doing what he should. He would find the signal, as Goddess Yalki and God Harick had commanded. He would do well. They would be proud. He would please his gods... His gods? His mission was all that mattered. He would be loyal to them until he died, preferably serving them. Died? He didn't want to die. They weren't what they said. NO! They were his gods! He was to do as they said, always and until the end... but there was a time when they weren't his gods... when he had had a family – a wife. They had been happy. And now... He had no wife! His sole purpose was to do as Goddess Yalki and God Harick commanded. He knew no other life. The signal was so close.

Chapter 73

Ryo let go of Captain Eri's hand and took a few steps back, suddenly detached from the conversation. Captain Eri watched her go and then moved to Red.

"This is unacceptable. He's becoming too much of a wild card. I can't have this. He almost killed her." Captain Eri said, squatting next to Red.

Wiq nodded but didn't say anything. She appeared unfocused, something Filion had never seen.

"He didn't almost kill me, but he needs to be dealt with," Ryo said, her back to them.

Captain Eri glanced at her.

"Can he hear us?"

Ryo turned and moved to Captain Eri's side.

"He can if I choose. May I?"

Captain Eri hesitated a moment then said, "Ahh, of course." She stood and took a step away from Red.

Ryo squatted, and Red's eyes began to spin, but no other part of him moved.

"Mr. Canner," Ryo said. "My name is Ryo. I'm the one you and your crew are looking for. I am also the one you just shot at."

Red's eyes widened.

"It sounds like you're becoming a mite unpredictable," she continued. "A wild card, you might say. Your captain can't have that and perhaps, more importantly, *I* can't have that. You see," Ryo said, standing. "I aim to get off of this planet, and I intend to live. Apparently I have a lot of work to do, and I can't have the likes of you interfering with that. So, you have two options."

"The first option is I leave you here, suitless," Red's haz suit flew from his body. "And weaponless." Red's phazer, and an array of other weapons, including a side arm, a few grenades, and several knives, rose from Red's body and flew into the woods. "For an Infected or an Afortiori to find."

Sweat ran down Red's face.

"Or, I can give you another chance. I have a feeling, Mr. Canner, that you could be very useful to my cause, assuming you can behave yourself. Frankly, I need all of the allies I can get but don't think that makes me desperate. I will cut you down in an instant if I find you working against me."

She leaned into Red's face. "In an instant, Mr. Canner. Your brain won't even have the time to process that you've died."

She straightened. "So, whadda ya say?"

No one said anything. It was as if the air had left the forest.

"Oh!" Ryo said. "Silly me. He still can't talk."

Red coughed, his breathing suddenly loud and audible.

"Mr. Canner, I don't have all day. I need your decision," Ryo said, idly picking at her fingernail.

"Give me another chance. I won' let you down. I'm sorry for my actions. I'll do better. I promise. Please don' leave me here to die," Red breathed.

Ryo looked up. "Mr. Canner, I will give you another chance, but know, if you renege on our deal, you'll wish I had left you here to die."

Red's arms and legs fell to the ground. He lay there, panting.

"I'm sorry. I'm sorry."

No one moved.

Filion watched Ryo, the distant look back in her eyes. She sat down heavily and looked at her hands as if she had never seen them before.

"Alright," Captain Eri said. "Let's get out of here huh?"

"It's too late…" Ryo whispered. "They've found me."

Chapter 74

Kiliank dropped to his knees. The pain was blinding, *crippling,* and he knew he had found it. It was there, just on the other side of those trees. He clutched his head with his hands. All he had to do was let her know, let his Gods know, but... but something told him not to. But why would that be? It must be the pain. The pain was warping his mind. His mission was all that mattered. Complete the mission. He was in the fetal position now, struggling to breathe.

He had to please his Gods, yet... yet something tugged at him, a face, small and smiling. He felt like she was important to him, but he didn't know who she was, or did he? NO! He bared his teeth, a low groan escaping his lips. His only family was his brothers in arms. He and his brothers served Goddess Yalki and God Harick. He had no family – no wife, no daughter. He needed to complete his mission. He needed to alert his Gods.

Chapter 75

Yalki stood over Jat and smiled. He was her best result yet. She was pleased she had enjoyed him before she removed his emotions, but she was even more pleased with how smoothly the process had gone. She had been able to reprogram him in a little over an hour – her best time yet. That, and the process had been much more polished and efficient. She hadn't spent the hour up to her neck in brains.

Jat sat up.

"My Goddess Yalki. How may I serve you?"

Did he not remember what they had just done? No matter. He had a new task now.

"You are to find the Chozen. Once you locate it, you are to alert me and God Harick."

The pain knocked her to her knees. Jat fell from the table, crashing to the ground beside her. She rolled onto her back, her hands clenching the sides of her head.

One of her creations had found it, near the border of the northern and eastern quadrant. She had the location, but she couldn't go anywhere until the signal died.

"Ahhhhhh!" Jat shrieked beside her, writhing back and forth.

So, they hadn't been perfect. The signal was raw and uncontained. Her creations could recognize and send the signal, but they couldn't handle it. They broadcast it at full strength to anyone who could sense. *FILTER!* How could she have forgot to program a filter?

They were first generation. She couldn't beat herself up. She took a sharp breath. Good thing she had reprogrammed the slaves with a kill switch. She took a deep breath and imagined the switch. Moments later the pain died. She pushed herself to her feet and stepped over the now still Jat. Once she centered herself, she would make the Jump. That idiot Harick had better meet her there.

Chapter 76

"What?" Filion said. "What do you mean they've found you?"

Wiq raised her phazer and disappeared. Captain Eri pulled Red to his feet.

"Your phazer's over there," she said, pointing to the woods. Red stood, momentarily dazed, and then darted towards the phazer.

"They know where I am…" She looked at Filion, a fire in her eyes. "We need to move."

Ryo stood and took off into the woods. Filion hesitated for a moment, locking eyes with Captain Eri, and then they both sprinted after Ryo.

"Wait… please!" Red called after them.

Filion didn't stop. He focused on keeping the disappearing white dress in his vision. She was small but fast. Filion didn't know how long he could keep up this pace.

The dress disappeared from his vision. NO! He couldn't lose her now. He pushed himself to run faster. His breathing became ragged. Spots swam in front of his eyes. He couldn't lose her… one foot in front of the other…

His toe caught on something. His weight shifted forward. He was falling…

He came down hard on his hands and knees. The pain reverberated through his body. He rolled onto his back, clutching his knees.

What the… since when was the forest floor this hard?

He looked at the ground. It wasn't dirt, but instead, moldy broken cobblestones. He took a breath and rolled into a sitting position.

Were his knees broken?

Captain Eri caught up to him.

"Wow… those long legs… they make… you speedy," she breathed.

"I think I might have hurt myself," Filion said.

"What? Is that why you're sitting?" she asked, hands on her knees.

He nodded and flexed his legs. They seemed to work okay. He staggered to his feet, with Captain Eri's help. She held his arm as he steadied himself. Looking around he saw the forest wasn't as thick here, and there were grey stones everywhere. The ground was stone, and stones were stacked on top of those stones. Moss covered and cracking, Filion had tripped over the ruins of a city.

He took a step forward. Pain shot up his leg. He shifted his weight, causing pain to shoot up the other.

"AHHH!" he cried, falling.

He toppled and brought Captain Eri down with him.

Out of nowhere, Ryo appeared at their sides.

"Filion! Captain Eri! We need to take cover!"

"I can't walk. I think I broke my knees!"

Ryo looked at him and then moved her hands over his knees. Filion felt a searing heat and then the pain was gone.

"Let's go!" she said.

He stood. Had she just healed him? He tested his legs. They felt fine. That was amazing! How had she done that? Captain Eri sat, sprawled on the ground, a mystified look on her face.

"Let's go!" Ryo repeated, running into the city.

Filion pushed the matter from his mind, pulled Captain Eri up, and ran after Ryo.

Chapter 77

Yalki was ready. She had assembled the unit Harick had left behind and was prepared to Jump. Unfortunately, the kill switch had killed all of the reprogrammed slaves, including Jat. She would have to work on that filter. They might have lost twelve slaves, but at least they had a location.

She closed her eyes and made the Jump. When she opened them, the entire unit was behind her, staring dumbly at the change of surroundings. They stood in a cramped pocket of bushes next to a small clearing. A dead slave lay at her feet. She stepped over the slave and into the clearing.

"Fan out!" she ordered. "Anything that moves, shoot it!"

They stared vacantly at her.

Grawlix! This planet was so backwards they still used swords. Why hadn't Harick fixed that? She had talked to him about it when they first took Handu, but he had just smiled and said he knew what he was doing. *Right,* she cursed.

"Anything that moves, stab it! Fan out! NOW!"

Understanding flashed in their eyes. Their heads swiveled back and forth and they adjusted their grips on their swords. Within seconds they had taken formation.

Where was Harick?

Yalki surveyed her surroundings. Something had happened here, leaves and bushes were matted down, and there was a haz suit hood…

Something else caught her eye. She moved to a Yuc bush. A grenade, unarmed, sat in the bushes, and a four-inch stealth knife lay not two feet away.

She picked them up. This was strange. Was someone else here?

With a surge of energy Harick appeared. With him came hundreds of sweating, stinking men. They surrounded Yalki and her unit.

"I came as fast as I could. What happened?" Harick asked.

"It was here."

"And the slaves?"

"I had to kill them. They weren't prepared to deal with an energy signal of that level."

She thought he smiled, if only for an instant, and her blood boiled. "We wouldn't be this close without them. They did their job."

"I know they did," he said, his voice unusually gracious.

"I've issued a kill order for anything that moves. Can you feel it?"

Harick shook his head. "Not that it matters. I'm an expert tracker. Just give me a moment."

Chapter 78

Ryo fought to keep the fear imprisoned. It was getting stronger. They were getting closer. It was coming, the moment of truth. Would they make it? Would she make it?

She ducked behind a crumbling rock structure. Glancing around, she saw dilapidated buildings, broken rocks, shattered pains of glass, rotting multicolored doorframes... A ruined city... This was better than fighting in the trees, but a bottleneck... She wanted a bottleneck. Maybe she could find one. She just needed a minute though, just to push that fear down. She leaned against a decaying wall and took a deep breath.

It was hotter in the city than in the forest. The suns were reaching their zeniths, and without a breeze this place would be boiling within minutes... Ryo took another breath and tried to weigh the pros and cons of fighting in such heat, when Filion skittered to her side, followed by Captain Eri.

"We need a tactical advantage." Wiq said, appearing next to Ryo.

"Yes..." Ryo said.

"Up here," Wiq said.

"Wait," Captain Eri said. "Where's Red?"

"I will find him after we reach safety. He is not a priority at this time," Wiq replied.

Captain Eri frowned, but she didn't argue.

"This way," Wiq said.

Ryo followed the vissy through the city. The further they progressed into the ancient metropolis, the more intact the ruins became. The buildings at the city's center weren't made of the same grey cracking stone as the structures at its edges. These buildings and streets were made of white, green, and pink stones. The buildings had been expertly designed with carved statues and stone animal heads adorning their crumbling frames. Large overgrown tracts of dirt lined the streets, no doubt once gardens. Some buildings even had glass in their windows. As they ran, Ryo spotted discarded cups, a wooden doll, tattered bits of cloth, pieces of tarnished metal, and other signs of a rich civilization lost. This had been, at one point, an advanced city.

They ran past a white statue of a female ringer. It stood in a cracked basin filled with murky water. Wiq made a left and entered a narrow alley. The ground was uneven. Broken cobbles stuck out at all angles. Wiq picked her way through the street, the others following her, until it opened onto a plaza.

"Here," she said.

Shaped like a deflated tire, the plaza was round with one flat side. Lining the plaza's curved edges were tall crumbling buildings, none of which had any windows. In the plaza's center was another statue, this one carved into the shape of a female human. The plaza's flat side intersected with a cliff which was several stories high. Holes dotted the cliff. Ryo squinted, not holes but windows. The cliff was a building, a fortress of some kind.

"I think we can reach the top of the cliff from inside this building. We make our stand there, on the top floor," Wiq said pointing. "There are only three streets that lead to this plaza, the one we just came down, another major road and then another alley. I can only guess that this was built as some kind of fortress. Nothing else explains the lack of windows in the rest of these buildings. We rig the streets with explosives and take out the first wave with them. The rest we snipe from the building."

"How did you know this was here?" Ryo asked distantly.

"I am a vissy. I come equipped with scanning technology."

"Okay," Captain Eri said. "We need to hurry, and we need to find Red."

"I will locate him," Wiq said.

"And I'll come with you," Captain Eri said.

Wiq shook her head. "Filion and Ryo are not familiar with our explosives. You are of better use here."

Captain Eri opened her mouth and then shut it. She was captain, not Wiq, but Wiq had a point.

"Fine," Captain Eri said. "We'll rig the street we just came down last."

Wiq nodded and left.

"Okay," Captain Eri said. "Do either of you know how to rig explosives?"

Filion shook his head. Ryo stepped forward and unzipped Filion's bag, which was still on his back. The contents crashed from the bag onto the stone ground.

"Careful!" Captain Eri said.

Ryo ignored her and picked up a charge. She grabbed a knife from the ground and cut it open.

"What are you doing?" Captain Eri said.

Ryo didn't respond but instead started to cut wires.

"STOP!" Captain Eri lunged at Ryo.

Captain Eri never reached her though. Ryo trapped her before Captain Eri's leading foot even hit the ground.

"I'm almost done," Ryo said.

She just had to remember the sequence. She could half the amount of explosive they put in this bomb, if only she could remember which wires to reroute. The bomb would have twice the range when she was done. Oh, that's right. She crossed the purple and white wires, twisted them together and, yes. That was right.

She released Captain Eri.

Enough. This insubordination was no longer tolerable. First, Wiq telling her where to go, and what to do, then the Chozen using some sort of freezing magic on her. This was unacceptable. She was Captain of this crew and ship, of the crew and ship that had risked themselves to rescue *this* Chozen. Captain Eri would be treated with the respect she deserved.

"If you…" Captain Eri started.

"Here. This will use half the explosive and have twice the range. We can set two times the charges now," Ryo said, handing the bomb to Captain Eri. "Sorry I froze you. I just needed to think."

Captain Eri closed her mouth and took the bomb. She examined it.

"Will this work?" she asked finally.

Ryo was already at work on another.

"Yes," she said without looking up.

"Right, Filion, start securing our cover."

Filion didn't move.

"GO!"

"Uh, I don't understand."

She rounded on him. "Go to the top of the building and start barricading the windows. Use tables, refrigerators, whatever you think will do the best job at stopping phazer rounds, bullets, and grenades. Make our hiding place safe so we don't die. Here," she shoved her backpack at him. "I'll take yours. You had most of the explosives anyway. Now GO!"

He dropped the bag from his back, threw her bag over his shoulder, turned and ran.

"It's about time someone obeyed my orders," she muttered.

"Do you have any more wire?" Ryo asked.

Chapter 79

Wiq had a location on a human. One was stopped at the edge of town. She would be on it in a few seconds. She slowed, knowing her cloak would be more effective the slower she moved.

She came to what appeared to have been some sort of warehouse. With its roof missing, and most of its exterior collapsed, the building had seen better days. Inside, rotting shelves listed in various states of decay. Sealed cans of some sort lay in uneven piles throughout the derelict structure, their paper labels bleached and disintegrating in the hot suns. She stopped behind one of the more intact walls and scanned the location where the human should have been, and there it was.

Red stood, behind a cracked mass of stone, haz suit over his shoulder, phazer in one hand, and several knives and a string of grenades in the other, breathing hard.

"Grawlix," he said. "This isn' good."

He threw down the pack and unzipped it then stuffed the suit, knives and grenades inside. He stood up, checked his phazer and then scanned the area.

"Red," Wiq whispered.

His eyes widened, and he brought up the phazer.

"Red, it's me, Wiq."

"Show yourself," he said.

Wiq hesitated. She didn't want him attempting to take retribution for earlier.

"Put down the phazer," she said.

"Grawlix! I don't have time for this." He plucked a grenade from his vest and threaded a thumb through the pin. "Fine," he said. "But if you shoot me, we both die." He dropped the phazer and let it dangle from its sling. He raised his arms, the grenade smiling from his palm.

"Satisfied? Now get me outta here. I think they're after us!"

Wiq disengaged her cloak.

"Over here."

Red's eyes widened as she appeared, but his surprise melted into a smile. He put the grenade back, shouldered his bag, and ran to her.

"I never thought I'd say this," he said. "But I'm glad to see you."

Chapter 80

They certainly hadn't been subtle. The tracks implied a rushed exit and in a northerly direction. Harick stood. *They*. These tracks implied more than one person, maybe even up to five, but he couldn't be sure. Not only that, but some of the tracks were large and unshoed, suggesting a lossal or a yeyer maybe, but that made no sense. Why would a lossal be here?

"They've gone north," Harick said.

Yalki paced behind him.

"They?"

"It appears there might be up to five of them, and one of them might be a lossal or a yeyer."

"What? Why?"

"I'm wondering that myself. You don't think there are multiple Chozens, do you? And that's why the signal's so strong?"

Yalki shook her head. No, she had dealt with two Chozen at once, a long time ago. This wasn't the same.

"No, it got help, but how and from whom, I don't know," Yalki said.

Harick circled his hand in the air.

"North!"

The troops started to march. He had spread them out, shoulder to shoulder in a line, hundreds of them stretching across the forest. Their instructions were to walk and kill anything in their path. If they were dealing with an Etulosba, the slaves would die, but that was to be expected. If enough of them could injure it though…

Harick and Yalki followed the line. They were getting close…

Chapter 81

It appeared that the building had been some type of hospital. It also appeared that the building had, at one point, contained a working elevator but no more. Filion trudged up the building's stone steps, one at a time, the temperature rising with every foot of elevation he gained. He stopped and wiped his brow. His breathing was shallow and tattered; how much further? He reached another landing. The door was labeled in a language Filion had never seen. He kicked the door open and poked his head into the hall. More cots, defunct medical appliances, and plastic curtains, but the stairs still kept going. He gave a huff and continued on.

After what seemed like an eternity, he reached what he believed to be the final floor. In front of him stood a door, and to his left was another. He opened the door in front of him first– more stairs.

Grawlix! He thought, pushing himself forward.

At the top of the stairs was yet another door. He kicked it open.

The roof. He had reached the roof.

He stepped outside and stood in the sunlight. The air was still and hot, but not stale. Inside, the air hadn't been circulated in years, and it was stifling. He took a deep breath.

Wiq had been right. The roof of the hospital was the top of the cliff. Below him to the south was the plaza. To his north stood more forestland. The forest had been cleared back from the cliff in a radius of at least several hundred yards. The top of the cliff had also been painted, although the paint was fading now, with landing areas for incoming medical ships. Filion walked to the edge of the cliff.

The drop was significant. Filion took a reflexive step backwards and dropped his weight. He could see Captain Eri and Ryo at the mouth of the main road. They weren't looking in his direction. He looked beyond them. He could see the entire city. It sprawled out before him until it finally faded into the forest.

This hadn't been a big city, but it was well constructed, especially towards its centre. Most of the buildings, while in disrepair, hadn't yet collapsed. Their green and pink stones shown in the afternoon light, and he could almost imagine what this place looked like before it had been abandoned. It had to have been a clean city. Despite its dilapidation, some of the buildings still shone in the suns and some of the cobbles in the streets gleamed, as if they had been cleaned recently. He thought about Hifora, if that place were abandoned it would never look like this. Then there was the architecture. Designed by someone with a discerning eye, the lines and curves of the buildings were exact and striking, even in their current state.

He didn't doubt this was a good place to have lived. What had happened?

He took another step back and walked towards the door. It didn't make any sense. This had been an advanced society. He opened the door and noticed it was labeled in the same language as the others. That was strange. It wasn't Fedlang, and Handu was a Federation planet. It should have at least had a Fedlang translation.

He re-entered the stairwell and returned to the top floor. He opened the second door and stepped inside. He found himself in a reception area. Beyond the desk were two double doors. He pushed through them into a long hallway. The doors clicked shut behind him. This floor was different than the others. There were no plastic blue curtains here. Instead, thick doors lined the hallway. In each door was a little window, its glass crisscrossed with wire.

He peered into one of the rooms. Inside was a cot and nothing else. He looked through the next door and the next. Each room was the same, empty, other than a cot. What interested him about the rooms, though, was the fact that each had a small exterior window. He turned one of the door's handles. Nothing happened. He tried the next one and the next. They were all locked. He frowned. This was no good.

He set the backpack down. His sweat had caused his haz suit and the backpack straps to rub his shoulders. He was hot and uncomfortable. He shifted the phazer sling...

Oh.

He looked at the phazer, dangling uselessly. Carefully, he switched off the safety then backed up from the door. He moved to its left, hoping that if there were some sort of ricochet the obtuse angle would protect him. He readied the phazer and shifted his weight. Maybe it would be better if he had most of his weight on his left foot, maybe his right? Should he cover his eyes?

Just do it!

He closed his eyes and shot, hoping he was still aiming at the door.

He opened his eyes only after the noise had stopped. Black smoking holes streaked the right side of the hallway. An acrid, slightly toxic smell found his nostrils. He coughed and took a step towards the door.

The door handle was still intact, although next to it he had blasted a fist-sized hole.

He closed his eyes and fired again. When he opened them, the door handle lay on the floor, charred and deformed. He waited for the door to stop smoking then pulled it open.

The room was even more desolate on the inside than it had seemed from the outside. Its air was heavy and stale. Sterile white paint peeled from the stone walls and floor. The rotting cot sagged in a dirty corner, and a layer of grime covered everything.

Filion stepped inside and immediately stumbled backwards. He took a sharp breath. This room had an aura! Thick grey waves of despair washed over him. He backed out of the room, struggling to breathe. He made it into the hallway where he slumped against the wall. This was not right. Auras did not behave like this. He had never heard of an aura existing without a living being. He shut his eyes. There was nothing alive in that room. He knew that, yet the suffocating aura of anguish was there. This was not right.

He sat against the hallway wall with his eyes closed for several moments, struggling to decide what to do. He did not want to go in there, but he knew he must. He gripped his phazer tightly and took a deep breath. Shivering, he stood and stepped into the room. He opened his eyes. The aura was gone! Confused, Filion looked around. The room felt cold, but the despair was gone. The grey cloud had seemingly vanished. He stood for a moment longer, dumbfounded, and then crossed the room to the window.

He had to hunch over to see through the window, but the view was worth it. While he could no longer see Captain Eri and Ryo, he could make out the entire plaza, including the three roads leading into it. He thought this could work. Now all he had to do was get the rest of the doors open, which would be the easy part if there were more disembodied auras lurking about...

Chapter 82

Red followed the vissy. She was fast, much faster than he, and as much as it pained him to admit that, it pained him even more that he was breathing so hard he couldn't focus on her rear. It was a crying shame to run behind a woman, even if she was part machine, and not get to admire her backside. A real shame, considering Wiq had some sculpted cheeks.

"Can... we... take a... break?" Red said, doubling over.

"We are almost there. We do not have much time. They are coming."

"I know they're comin'. I could hear 'em behind me, but they ain't running. We got time for a tiny break."

Wiq stopped and pursed her lips but didn't say anything.

Red smiled. He'd won this round. He took a couple more exaggerated breaths and then straightened.

"Let's go," he said.

He followed Wiq through a narrow alley. The alley ended in a large plaza.

"Ahh, there you are," Captain Eri said, stepping from the shadows.

Ryo appeared as well, seemingly from nowhere. That unnerved Wiq. It was as if Ryo had been cloaked, but Wiq had not been able to sense her.

"He was at the edge of town," Wiq said, not taking her eyes from Ryo.

"Glad to have you back Red," Captain Eri said.

"Yeah, well, it's good to be back. What's the plan?"

"You two head up to the top of the building and find Filion. He's supposed to be barricading the top floor, but he probably needs your help."

"Right," Red said, adjusting his pack.

"I should stay and help with the explosives," Wiq said.

"No. Ryo's doing fine. You're to go with Red."

"Are you sure?" Wiq asked.

"Did I not make my orders clear? You are to go with Red and help Filion. I don't care how gifted of a fighter you are, if you can't listen to your commanding officer, you'll be off this crew. Understand?"

Wiq dropped her eyes and nodded. "Yes, Captain, Sir."

"Good, go then. We'll be right behind you."

Wiq followed Red this time. What was wrong with her? Questioning the Captain's orders? Had she not learned the price for insubordination while a slave? Then again, when she had been a slave she had not had anything to lose. Now she had freedom... freedom to lose. That could not happen. She would die before losing her freedom. She would never be a slave to anybody, ever again.

Chapter 83

"HOLD!" Harick yelled.

He bent down. This stone was not natural. It had been cut. Harick noticed the squared corners. This stone had been placed, as had the matching stones around it. Granted, whoever had put these stones here had done it some time ago, but the stones were person made and person placed. He took two steps forward, more crumbling grey stone. This looked to be some sort of sad road. He stood, peered into the forest, and smiled. Several decades ago, he had learned a neat trick – how to see through solid mass. The trick hadn't helped locate this Chozen so far, but maybe now it would.

He sequenced his thoughts and then selected the trees. That had been his own addition, the ability to differentiate between what you wanted to see through and what you didn't. Right now he only wanted to see through the forest – the trees and bushes. He wanted to know if there was a city beyond this forest, well, that and if there was a Chozen hiding there, but one step at a time.

He closed his eyes and then opened them. Yes. There was a city beyond the trees. He could make out the houses that surrounded the city, the shops that made up the city center, the tall buildings at the city's heart, and then, at the far end of the city... his vision wasn't good enough to see that far, but he had a feeling, a good feeling, that *it* was there, cornered, like a rat.

He took a breath and smiled. This was it. These pathetic cobbles would lead him to either greatness or death. Was he ready?

Chapter 84

Filion blasted the last door. He was getting good at this. Not only did he now keep his eyes open and aimed on what he was shooting, but he had hit four out of nine door handles. He smiled. Make that five out of ten. This wasn't that hard.

He ripped open the door. Again, a heavy wave of despair washed over him, but it quickly disappeared. This was the third room to contain such an aura. The other rooms had been normal. Filion shivered but pushed past the uncomfortable feeling and moved to the window. He had never before encountered auras like these. While he had no formal training in auras (did such training even exist?), he was beginning to suspect that the grey auras did not belong to the rooms. Rather, he surmised, they belonged to the last occupants of these rooms. It seemed that somehow they had gotten trapped until he had opened the doors. Not that it mattered now though. He looked out of the window. This window's view was similar to the others. He hoped this was good. He could see the plaza, the roads, and –

He took a step back, hitting his head on the ceiling. *What was that?*

He ducked down and looked again. A large red cloud had engulfed the outer edges of the city. He squinted. That was no cloud. That was an aura, a violent, bloodthirsty aura. Filion swallowed. No one had that big of an aura, but an army, an army could, and the flavor of the aura certainly fit.

He collapsed onto the cot. It broke under his weight, throwing him to the floor with a crash. He let out a long breath and rearranged himself on the mattress, drawing his legs under him. It hadn't dawned on him, until now, just what he had gotten into. The pelters, the Biopser, even Red and everything Didrik had said, and the Infecteds hadn't truly impressed upon him that he might die. Die. These could be his last moments, here, now, sitting in this abandoned hospital, by himself, on a wrecked threadbare mattress. No one he cared about even knew he was on Handu! He sank against the wall. Would this be his end? In stories these kinds of odds were normal, but this was his life, not a story. He wasn't a fighter. He was a Searcher. He wanted to cry.

He leaned his head against the wall. The haz suit pulled awkwardly against his neck.

That's it! Filion thought. If he was going to die, he wasn't going down in a peacock colored haz suit. If an Infected got him, so be it.

He yanked the zipper and peeled off the suit. He hadn't realized how much he had been sweating until he was clear of the suit. His fur was wet, and he stunk. He kicked the suit's final leg from his foot and stretched out on the ground. The cool stone floor felt good.

He lay motionless for a moment, his eyes closed, when without warning, something bit him on the leg. He jumped, his hands moving to the epicenter of the pain.

Didrik! Filion pulled the book from his pants pocket. While the Living Document wasn't as wet as he had been when he had fallen into the Keeper's pool, he wasn't dry either. Filion grimaced, opened Didrik and put him on the floor.

"Didrik, I'm sorry. We found her, but it looks like she was followed."

What in the god's names were you wearing? Do you have any idea how disgusting I feel?

"Yeah, sorry. I was wearing a haz suit. There are Infecteds about. It's a long story."

Where are we now? Didrik asked, flapping his damp pages.

"We're in some sort of abandoned hospital. It looks like we're going to make our stand here. An army is after us. I can see their aura. They're getting closer."

Where is she?

"She's with Captain Eri. They're rigging some explosives."

You left her!?

"This was the plan. I was to barricade the top floor of the hospital so we could fight."

Can't we outrun them?

"I guess not."

You sound... sad. You don't usually sound sad.

"I just realized I'm going to die."

Didrik didn't respond. Filion didn't care. He glanced out of the window. The aura was getting closer.

We won't die. She'll save us. You must give me to her the moment she reaches you.

"Okay," Filion said without conviction.

"Lossal? Lossal? You up here?" Red's muted voice floated down the hallway.

"Wait here," Filion said. "Red's here."

Chapter 85

"This buildin' has entirely too many stairs," Red said, wiping sweat from his face. "That and it's entirely too hot here. You think that lossal did what he was supposed to do?"

Wiq shrugged.

"Man, what's up your butt? We're about to kill a bunch of people. Doesn't that get you off?"

Wiq did not respond.

"Sheesh," Red said.

The double door opened. Filion stood on the other side, no longer in his haz suit, his fur damp and matted.

"Lossal! Nice to see you. How'd you get in there? It's locked. Whoa," Red took a step back.

"What?" Filion asked.

"Nothing," Red said. "It's just for a minute there I got a really bad feeling." He shook himself and then straightened. "But it's gone!" Filion looked at Red and then at Wiq. He nearly jumped away from her. Her aura was black.

"What's wrong Wiq?" Filion said, ignoring Red.

She looked at him. Filion the lossal. She wanted to hug him, even if his fur was soaked in sweat. It had been so nice, being free. Had she destroyed her one chance?

"Ahh don' mind her. She's got a stick up her butt," Red said, grabbing the door from Filion and stepping inside.

"Wiq," Filion said, dropping his voice. "What's the matter?"

"Nothing," Wiq said, charging her phazer. "What have you got?"

She pushed past him and into the hallway.

"Lossal, you did good. This place might actually work!" Red called.

Chapter 86

"We need to go," Ryo said.

"I know, but just let me finish rigging this last charge…" Captain Eri said.

"No, now!" Ryo said.

"Just…"

Without realizing what she was doing, Ryo thought the charge away from Captain Eri. As it floated, Ryo finished rigging it. She placed it on the wall and grabbed Captain Eri, who stood, mouth open, staring at the charge.

"Now. Run!" Ryo said.

Captain Eri took off across the plaza, and Ryo followed her. The signals would reach the plaza in minutes. They had to move.

Captain Eri hated running, not that she didn't believe in fitness and the like. She tried to keep strong, doing whatever she could manage, whenever she could manage, but as she ran, entering the building and then taking the steps two at a time, she wished that she had taken more time to condition and in particular, to run. This was a tall building, and she wasn't going to be able to keep this pace. She pushed herself though, to the next landing, and a little past it, just a little further, and then to the next landing. She just had to keep going…

"There," Harick said, pointing north. "It's faint, but I can feel it. What about you?"

For a moment, Yalki said nothing. He wondered if she couldn't feel it. Initially that worried him, what if he was just feeling things? But that thought quickly passed, Yalki may be good, but she wasn't the best. Maybe she just didn't have the skill to feel the Chozen. Maybe just he did.

She smiled though, that evil little smirk that she got when things went her way. She didn't fake that smile well. She felt it. *Oh well,* he thought. At least he had felt it first.

"You're right. I can feel it, just through there." She pointed at a narrow alley. "It's faint but there. Ready your slaves."

Harick turned to give the commands. The slaves had dropped their line formation the moment they had entered the city. They were spread out now, crouching behind whatever they could use as cover or concealment. Harick smiled. They actually looked like modern soldiers now, thanks to their reprogramming.

Upon entering the city, he had changed their shorts into body armor and their broad swords into phazers. He always enjoyed doing this to a primitive army. The right moment would come, and he would just think the thought. Like a rolling tide the first slave would change, then the next, and the next, until he had an army of men, not cavemen. Yalki had complained when they had first landed on Handu that he hadn't upgraded the slave's weaponry, but she was no great tactician.

Immediately upgrading an army equated to fewer slaves in the long run. If a planet fought with swords, and an army of futuristic, phazer toting fighters appeared to exclaim the wonderfulness of their new god, the locals weren't going to buy it. Maybe *some* of them would believe Harick was a god, but Harick had learned the hard way that a significant number of them would be skeptical, especially if modern fighters didn't fit into the prophecies of whatever idiotic religion they believed. That meant the virus wouldn't take and a majority of the potential slaves would die. Then again, if an army of village boys from the next town over appeared... Well that was more on the local's level, and it was something they could wrap their minds around, which was exactly what he needed. He needed them to truly believe.

Not that any of that mattered now. At the moment Harick and Yalki weren't in the business of taking slaves, they were in the Chozen killing business, and that required more advanced weaponry.

How did he want to do this? Harick turned back to the signal. He closed his eyes and this time removed the buildings. *The signal.* He wanted to see the signal. When he opened his eyes, the buildings were gone; but the signal was there, several stories above the ground, probably in a building. It was going up on the other side of a plaza. He had a location.

He closed his eyes and turned towards his army. *Enough with the spoken orders.* All of the slaves were networked, he just had to tap into that network...

Harick opened his eyes. He floated, elevated in space above his men. His army stared up at him, their eyes wide and attentive. The city was gone. In its place was nothing but indigo colored space. Harick was in the network.

There is a building at the end of this road, Harick thought in a commanding voice, *a tall building. Our target is headed to its top. We need to eliminate the target. Alpha team, you proceed via this road,* he pointed. The alley that Harick's body stood in front of appeared, bright and vivid out of the indigo cloud. *Bravo and Charlie team, you are to use these roads.* The alley vanished and another road appeared, followed by another. *Go.* Harick closed his eyes.

When he opened his eyes there was a flurry of movement. Within seconds the Alpha team was halfway down the alley, and the Bravo and Charlie teams were gone. Yalki stood silently, that smile still on her face.

"This is it," she said. "We're about to make history. We will rule this universe. We will prove our unsupportive Afortiori brethren wrong. They will repent, but it won't be enough, not after this. We are about to battle an Etulosba, and they did nothing. And that's what they'll get in return. Nothing..."

Yalki's sentence was cut short. A deafening explosion rocked the city.

Chapter 87

Captain Eri struggled up the stairs. *One foot in front of the other. Just keep going...*

The building shook. One of their explosives had gone off. She looked at Ryo. What had the girl done? And how had she done it? The original explosive shouldn't have been able to shake the building from here, especially since the building was built into a cliff.

"We're close," Ryo said, staring at the ceiling.

"So are they," Captain Eri breathed.

They continued upwards, moving as fast as Captain Eri could. Ryo wasn't even winded. What was the matter with her?

Captain Eri stopped.

"What are you doing?" Ryo asked.

"We need to lay one more charge," Captain Eri said, producing their last explosive from her pocket. This explosive was unmodified, which was fine. She didn't want the building collapsing under them.

Ryo nodded. Eri set the explosive on a wire pull.

More explosions rocked the building.

"Are they shooting at us?" Captain Eri yelled. She glanced up in time to see Ryo shake her head.

"What did you do to those explosives?"

"Made them better…"

They reached another landing. Captain Eri put her head between her knees. She worked out, she did…

"Here," Ryo said, opening one of two doors.

They stepped into a reception area. Beyond the desk were two doors, one of which was slightly cracked. Captain Eri could hear Red screaming and phazers firing on the doors' other side. She moved to the door. A haz suit prevented it from closing all of the way.

"This way!" Captain Eri said, shoving the door wider.

"JUST SHOOT, LOSSAL! ANYTHING THAT MOVES! SHOOT IT!"

Filion listened to Red through the stone wall. He could see bodies in the plaza, dead bodies, bodies which had been alive moments ago and were now smoking and charred. They emitted no aura. He turned from the window and slid onto the cot. Red's phazer buzzed from the room to his left, as did Wiq's from the room to his right. Explosions shook the building, and Filion's ears rang. Dust rained from the ceiling and onto his body and into his lungs. He coughed, a small noise compared to the destruction occurring around him. Now was the time to fight or die, or just die. He didn't want to go down without a fight, but he didn't really want to fight...

"LOSSAL! IF YOU DON'T START SHOOTING I'LL COME IN THERE AND SHOOT YOU!"

Filion took a breath and then peered out the window. Men had started to trickle into the plaza, although the charges had slowed them considerably. Many were injured, limping, bleeding, collapsing and crawling, but still, some had the mind enough to shoot at the building. Filion put his phazer to the glass, ducked and pulled the trigger.

Glass rained down on him. The window was gone.

"LOSSAL! DOWN! SHOOT DOWN! THAT'S WHERE THE ENEMY IS! NOT IN THE SKY!"

Filion took another breath and peeked out the window. A man with a phazer shuffled across the square. He passed the fountain statue right as a phazer round hit one of its stone arms. The man flinched as the stone rained down around him. A large chunk hit him in the shoulder, but he kept moving. He was hurt, Filion could tell by his aura, but that didn't mean he wasn't dangerous. Filion took a deep breath, aimed, and fired.

When he opened his eyes, the man was on the ground. Filion sucked in air. He had killed that man. He, Filion Ker III, had just killed another person.

"GETTING BETTER, LOSSAL! THIS TIME HIT 'EM! I DON'T HAVE THE TIME TO CLEAN UP AFTER YOU EACH TIME YOU MISS!"

Filion slid back on to the mattress. He couldn't take this.

Captain Eri ran down the hall. What was this place? It was like a cross between a jail and a hospital. She skittered to a stop when she saw Red. Kneeling on a cot with his phazer aimed out of a small window, Red cackled loudly.

"TAKE THAT YOU SNAIL LICKIN' TIORIS!"

Captain Eri ran to the next room where she found Filion, phazer in hand, sitting on a broken cot facing the hallway, eyes closed and a sick look on his face.

"Filion?"

He opened his eyes. "Captain Eri! Where's Ryo?"

"She's," Captain Eri turned. Ryo wasn't behind her. "Uh, she was right here."

"Here!" Filion said, thrusting his phazer at her. "You shoot. I'll find Ryo."

"Keep it. I've got my own," Captain Eri said, lifting her phazer.

"Right," Filion said, bending down and grabbing Didrik.

Filion ran to the reception area.

"RYO! RYO! WHERE ARE YOU?"

Ryo was in the last room. She sat in the middle of the floor with her knees drawn to her chest. She hugged herself and rocked ever so slightly. She could feel it. His presence was all over the room, his pain, his death. It was all there, written in the fabric of the universe. It was as plain as day to her. Like reading a book she never wished to see, the tears ran in salty rivers down her cheeks.

She wasn't there. Filion turned and ran back down the hall, stopping to check each room. He reached the tenth room, and there she was, sitting in the middle of the floor, crying.

"Ryo?" Filion said, taking a step into the room. He walked to her and squatted. He could feel Didrik quivering.

"Ryo, are you alright?"

She didn't say anything, nor did she acknowledge his presence.

"Ryo?"

"HE DIED HERE!" Ryo yelled, turning suddenly, her sapphire eyes catching Filion's. He stopped.

"He died here. He was like me. I know. I can feel it. And now he's gone and I'm alone. All alone."

Didrik flapped in Filion's hands.

"Uh, you're not alone," Filion said, recovering. I have someone I want you to meet. I told you about him, remember? This is Didrik." Filion extended his hands to Ryo.

She looked up at him, her hair blurring her face.

"Didrik?" she said.

"Yes, Didrik. He wants to talk to you. He *needs* to talk to you. You aren't alone. Here."

She reached out and took Didrik.

"What do I do?" she asked. She held Didrik flat on both of her palms. She moved as if the slightest disturbance would cause Didrik to break.

"Talk to him. He can hear. He'll write back."

Ryo stared at Filion. Her eyes asked a million questions, but all Filion could do was nod at Didrik.

Ryo looked at Didrik, and carefully moved him closer to her mouth.

"Hello?" she said, looking at Didrik.

She smiled.

"You've been waiting to meet me?" she asked.

"LOSSAL!" Red cried.

Grawlix! Filion thought but got up anyway. He took one last look at Ryo then bolted down the hall towards Red.

Chapter 88

Harick cursed under his breath. He hadn't planned for explosives, although he should have. How many men had he lost? This could have been avoided, but he hadn't been thinking. Not thinking would kill *all* of them.

He turned to Yalki. Her face was considerably paled, but she was still with him. He wasn't sure how many battles she had been apart of. Yalki was the type of Afortiori who slowly took over a planet, generation by generation. She was also the type who was easily bored. Once she conquered one planet, she left for something bigger and better. He, on the other hand, enjoyed a good fight. He was the Afortiori you called when the original plan derailed. It was true that the Afortiori preferred to take a planet subtly, without force, but nothing was ever that easy. There was a place for Afortiori like him and right now that place was Handu.

"Should we go in now?" Yalki asked.

"No, we wait until the fighting really gets going. We want them distracted."

Yalki nodded.

"LOSSAL! START SHOOTING!"

Filion ran into an empty room. He blasted the glass without thinking. Outside, more men streamed into the plaza, not just men, Infecteds too, or were they just victims of the bombs? Whatever they were, they were making their way to the building. Panic welled in Filion. He stuck his phazer out of the window and started firing. He watched the phazer rounds strike one man, then a second, and a third. He was *killing* people. That was better than being killed though, or was it? He didn't stop to think. He just kept firing.

"It's time," Harick said.

"We need to take it alive or recover its body. We can't Erase it if we don't have its body," Yalki said.

Harick nodded. "It isn't dead yet."

"I know," Yalki said.

They proceeded down the desecrated alley. Yalki hovered over the still smoking rubble, while Harick scrambled through it. They reached the end of the alley. In front of them expanded the plaza. On the plaza's far side was a large cliff. Yalki immediately detected the signal near its top.

"Up there," she said, pointing.

Harick nodded. "We need to get up there."

"Should we Jump?" Yalki asked.

Harick studied the building. Phazer shots were coming from what

214

appeared to be the top floor. Jumping wasn't the answer. Jumping required you to have knowledge of your landing area. The only reason he and Yalki had been able to Jump to this quadrant was because they had tapped into the slave's brain who had alerted them. They would be Jumping blind. There was no way they would survive.

"No, you know we can't do that."

"Well, what's your plan then?" Yalki asked.

"Let's walk up the stairs."

She nodded. Harick issued a command, and three Alpha team members appeared at his side. He instructed them to cut a path for Yalki and him. They were going into the building. They fanned out, and Harick built a shield around the five of them. Then they started moving.

Wiq fired at the five figures crossing the plaza. Her shots seemed to die before they reached them. She fired again, and again. Nothing.

Grawlix! Two of those figures were Tioris. They were coming.

"Captain!" Wiq called.

"What?"

"Two Tioris, three o'clock!"

"Damn it! I see them. They're shielded! Red, toss a grenade at those five!"

"GOT IT!"

Wiq watched a grenade fall to the plaza, landing not three feet in front of the procession. It exploded. For a moment the smoke obscured Wiq's view, and then the five figures reappeared, all of them fully functional and in one piece.

"Turkey nuts!" Red yelled. "Where's that lady Chozen? We could really use her help right about now!"

"Filion!" Captain Eri called. "Get Ryo. Tell her we need her help, or we're all going to die, including her!"

Filion took a final shot at a crouching soldier. He went down like a pile of bricks. Filion felt sickeningly satisfied. "Going!" he yelled.

Filion ran down the hall, reaching the final room but braking too late. He slid on the stone floor and crashed into the wall.

"Ryo!" he said, pushing himself from the wall. "Ryo! The Tioris, they're coming! They're shielded! We need your help! We can't fight them alone!"

"I can't, not now. I need time." Ryo said, waving at him dismissively.

"What? Did you not hear me? The Tioris, they're on their way! We can't hold them off. We need you!" Filion stood dumbfounded in the hall.

Ryo wasn't looking at him. She smiled at Didrik.

Filion stood for a moment then charged into the room. He grabbed Didrik from Ryo.

"Didrik. Tell her we need her help. Two Tioris are on their way. Our weapons are useless."

I'm working as fast as I can.

"Well work faster. We have limited time." Filion glanced at Ryo. She looked at him like she might a fly under a microscope, but she didn't move to take back the book.

Give me back to her. She is more complicated than expected. This will take time.

"What do you mean more complicated? We don't have time."

Shhhhh. No need to concern her. She doesn't know, but she's different. She is no ordinary Chozen. She's special.

Filion frowned and moved to the window. The Tioris had reached the building.

"They're inside. We have until they reach this floor to live, unless you get her to fight," Filion said.

"Then you had better give him back to me," Ryo laughed.

We might want to think about running.

"Get her to fight!" Filion growled, thrusting Didrik into Ryo's hands.

He took off down the hall.

Filion slid into Captain Eri's room.

"Captain!" Filion yelled.

She stopped firing and turned.

"Did you get her?"

Filion shook his head. "She's refusing to fight until she's had more time with Didrik. We might want to run."

"Grawlix. They're in the building now."

"We can escape through the roof. Make a run for it, into the forest."

Captain Eri nodded. "I rigged a charge on the stairs. When that blows, we run. Maybe she'll come around before then. Tell the others." She turned back to the window.

Red tossed another grenade out of the window. *That turnip-stuffing lady Chozen picked a fine time to go crazy,* he thought. He watched the grenade hit the ground and blow five men and an Infected into pieces. If she didn't fight soon, they'd all die. He knew this was a stupid plan. If he were Captain, this wouldn't have happened. He would have sold the lossal to the pelters, made a few extra bucks and been on his way. He chucked another grenade. It sailed through the air, bouncing off the torn plaza floor once before exploding. He watched two arms whiz through the air. They had better start thinking about running soon. Those Tioris had entered the building.

"Red!"

Red turned. The lossal, the start of all of this, stood in the door.

"You're supposed to be shooting, not chatting," Red said, turning back to the window.

"Captain Eri rigged a charge in the stairwell. When it blows, we go to the roof and make a run for it."

"Why wait?" Red said, blasting the phazer.

"Captain Eri wants to give Ryo all the time she can to come around."

"Bad plan but whatever. It's only my life and yours."

When Red turned back to the door, the lossal was gone.

Filion told Wiq, who only nodded in response. Her aura was still black. He wasn't sure what to do, so he turned to leave when the entire building shook.

Yalki gave an exasperated sigh. They could be moving so much faster, but they weren't, and it was because of the slaves.

"Why are they here again?" she asked.

"They're our decoys. We let them go first, and they soak up any nasty surprises waiting for us." Harick said.

The slaves were fit, but there were a lot of stairs. *Slaves,* Yalki thought. *Everyone has their place.* She glanced at Harick. Even he seemed to be breathing hard, although nothing like the slaves, but still, he should have been better than that. Then again, he couldn't hover. Not everyone could, but she could, which is why she could have been there and had the Chozen by now, if it weren't for the incompetent idiots surrounding her.

They turned another corner. Yalki watched the slaves, their heads swiveling and their phazers ready, crouch up the stairs. She took a breath and...

BOOM!

Yalki was thrown backwards. She tumbled, head over heels down the stairs until she slammed into a wall.

Dust swirled around her. She couldn't see. Someone above her wailed, a high-pitched, unnatural noise. She blinked, but the dust still blinded her.

"Harick!" she yelled, pushing herself up. "Harick! What happened?"

But she couldn't get up. What was wrong with her? A piece of the ceiling crashed down next to her. The thick stone slab sent cracks radiating through the stone floor. She tried to get up again, but something was wrong. She looked at her leg. It bent out from under her at an unnatural angle. Then the pain hit her.

"HARICK!"

Harick coughed. He lay on his back, his head downhill of his feet with something heavy on top of him. He squirmed, but it did no good. The stairwell was thick with dust, and he couldn't see what pinned him. Someone above him screamed, no doubt one of the slaves. He tested his arms. They still worked. He reached towards his middle. A rock, large rock, lay on top of him. He guessed it to have come from the ceiling. He tried to push it off, but it did no good. He closed his eyes, not that he could see anything anyway, and concentrated. He had to lift the rock off of him. He had to do it soon. His head was filling with blood. It was getting harder to think with each passing second.

"HARICK!"

Grawlix that woman! He had no time for her. He closed his eyes again, but she kept screaming.

"Shut up!" he yelled.

"I'm hurt! I can't stand! I think my leg is broken!"

"Well I'm stuck under a rock! Shut up so I can think my way out of this! You should try doing the same thing!"

No response. He smiled, despite the pain, and closed his eyes.

Moments later the slab of stone shifted to his right, and he rolled to his left. It crashed down the stairs. He scrambled into a sitting position and took a deep breath. He looked at his chest, it was crushed, blood leaked from his uniform and it hurt like slow death, but he could fix it. That was one of the first things he had learned upon choosing to be a general – battlefield medicine. He closed his eyes and concentrated. His chest began to mend, his vessels reconnected, his ribs fused, his heart healed, and the blood drained from his head. When he felt whole again, he opened his eyes.

The dust was thinning, but it still obscured his vision. He decided he had better check on Yalki before the slaves. They were probably dead anyway. No matter, they had served their purpose. He crept down the steps, picking his way through the broken stone. He turned the corner and continued down. He could hear her clearly now. Her breathing was ragged and panicked.

"Yalki?" he said.

No response. He continued towards the breathing. Once he reached the next landing, he could see Yalki on the ground, her mangled leg crumpled in the dust. She had her hands over her leg, but she didn't know how to heal.

"Stop," Harick said, kneeling beside her.

She opened her eyes and dropped her hands. She was crippled, and helpless. He smiled. Did he help her, or leave her here?

He knew the answer. He couldn't defeat the Chozen alone, but she needed to remember this.

"Can you not heal yourself?" he asked, feigning ignorance.

She didn't say anything. Instead, she leaned against the wall and shook her head.

Harick couldn't believe it. He had never seen her so beaten. So, she didn't respond so graciously to pain did she?

"Let me see. I might be able to help you."

He put his hands over her leg and closed his eyes. He could heal her, his injuries had been much more grave, but he didn't want her to ever forget this. He would make her whole, structurally but not aesthetically. She would have scars and bumps. She would be ugly.

"There, I couldn't make it any prettier than this," he lied. "Sorry, you'll have scars, but internally you're healed."

He watched her. She looked ready to cry.

"Thanks," she breathed. "What happened?"

"One of the slaves must have triggered a charge. The bomb had to have been inside the shield when it went off, so we weren't protected. In fact, the shield probably made the explosion worse, for us at least."

Yalki nodded.

"We should go," Harick said. "This charge was probably laid as a last warning of our approach. They're most likely fleeing to the roof now."

"I'll be up there in a minute. I just need to center myself," Yalki said, her voice pinched.

"Of course," he said, smiling.

He got up and picked his way through the broken steps. The first slave he came to was really only part of a slave. A torso lay against the wall. He continued up the stairs, stepping over an arm and a leg, until he reached the second slave, this one more intact but certainly dead. Half of his face was missing.

He kept walking upwards. The screaming had stopped now, replaced by the sound of labored breathing. He followed the noise to a pile of rubble. Beneath it was the third slave, alive, but barely. Blood dripped from his mouth, and his eyes were foggy. Struck by an uncharacteristic streak of mercy, Harick killed him.

He felt a surge of energy from below him. Yalki. A few moments later she appeared.

"Thanks for the help," she said confidently. "I was able to fix the rest myself."

She pulled up her dress to reveal perfect legs.

Damn it, he thought, but smiled anyway.

"Ahh, well done. Shall we continue?"

"Why don't we?" She said, smiling.

"It's time!" Captain Eri yelled.

Filion turned and ran down the hall to the last room. Ryo sat on the cot still staring intently at Didrik.

"Let's go!" Filion said, stepping inside and grabbing Ryo's hand.

She looked startled but followed Filion without complaint.

"We need to go! Don't lose Didrik!"

"No. I won't lose him," she snorted.

Filion didn't respond but pulled her down the hall. Wiq and Captain Eri stood by the double doors, bags on their backs, and phazers up. Filion let go of Ryo and ducked into the room with his bag. He stuffed the haz suit inside and shouldered the pack. When he re-entered the hall, Red was there, phazer still smoking.

"Let's move! Red you take point! Wiq bring up the rear. Filion you're in charge of Ryo!" Captain Eri said.

Red led the way down the hall, kicking his way through the double doors at its end. He scanned the reception area and then kicked his way through the rest of the doors. They followed him silently. Finally, they stood in the roof stairwell, paused before the final door.

"Has anyone been up there?" Captain Eri asked.

"I have," Filion said.

"What's it like?"

"We'll pop out on the top of the cliff. We'll be far enough from the edge where no one in the plaza should be able to hit us. To the north are the woods, but they've been cleared back from the cliff. We'll be exposed for at least several hundred yards."

"Right," Captain Eri said. "Once you leave the door, run. Everyone run to the woods, as fast as you can."

Filion nodded. "You understand, Ryo?" he asked.

She smiled crookedly. "Of course I understand. We run. Run like the wind."

Red looked at her. "Is she crazy already?"

"RED! GO!" Captain Eri yelled.

Red kicked the door open and was gone. Filion and Ryo were next. He held Ryo's small hand in his. He tightened his grip and stepped through the door.

The suns' light hit him, and he squinted. He paused and then took a step forward. The chaos from the plaza hit his ears. He could hear phazers firing, rocks crumbling and men groaning. He took another step, then another, and soon he was running, Ryo's hand still in his. He looked back at her. She followed him easily, her steps light and seemingly effortless. She looked around with the mild curiosity of being in a new place but not being impressed. She actually yawned!

He turned from her and looked at the trees. They were almost there. Thirty more feet... twenty... ten... He slid into the trees and Ryo plowed into him.

"Are you okay?" he said, attempting to pull her from his stomach.

"Yes," she laughed. Her voice muffled by his fur. "I'm fine." She pushed away from him and re-opened Didrik, a broad smile on her face.

Filion stared at her. Did she not understand how much danger they were in? With a crash Captain Eri appeared next to Filion. A loud snarl came from their backs. Filion jumped and turned, coming face to face with a growling Red.

"These vines are sharp!" He said, attempting to untangle himself from an orange and purple plant.

"We all here?" Captain Eri said. "The Living Document too?"

"Ryo and Didrik are here," Filion said, glancing at the two of them. Ryo's smile had faded, and she stared raptly at Didrik.

Good, Filion thought. *Maybe Didrik is getting through to her.*

"Red, Wiq, where's Wiq?" Captain Eri asked, turning back to the cliff.

Wiq was nowhere to be seen because she had cloaked herself the moment she had stepped onto the roof. There were two motivating factors behind this, one of which was tactical. Obviously, cloaking herself reduced her chance of injury.

Avoiding injury though, was not Wiq's primary motivation. She wanted to disappear. If she disappeared, Captain Eri could not confront Wiq about her insubordination. If Captain Eri could not confront Wiq, she could not punish Wiq. If Captain Eri could not punish Wiq, she could not take away Wiq's freedom.

While Wiq had only been free for a short time, she did not doubt the price for insubordination. Insubordination was one of the most heinous sins a vissy could commit. When she had been a slave, such insubordination would have resulted in months of torture. Now that she was free, she realized there was a worse punishment than torture. Captain Eri could take her freedom. Running from her punishment was dishonorable, but Wiq did not care. She had tasted freedom, and she was never going to give it up.

"Wiq! Wiq!" Captain Eri called.

Wiq watched Captain Eri. All Wiq had to do was turn and run. She could be free...

Wiq appeared several yards from the trees.

"Wiq! What are you doing? Get over here!" Captain Eri said. Then Captain Eri noticed the look on Wiq's face. "What's the matter Wiq? Are you hurt? Have you been hit?!"

"I am sorry," Wiq said.

"Sorry for what? Get behind some cover! Get over here!" Captain Eri said.

"No, I am sorry."

"Is every female here going crazy?" Red asked, finally freeing himself from the vine.

Captain Eri shot Red a glare. He hunched his shoulders and turned away from her.

"Sorry for what?" Captain Eri asked. "It doesn't matter. I forgive you! Just get behind some cover! What's the matter with you?"

"The insubordination! I should not have questioned you. I should not have ordered you around." Wiq stopped, her voice stuck in her throat. She looked as if she were on the verge of tears. "I accept whatever punishment you decide."

"She is crazy. Captain, you're next," Red said.

"Wiq, I order you to get behind some cover."

Wiq bowed her head and disappeared.

Captain Eri rounded on Red, who seemed to shrink under her gaze.

"Red, can we reach the portal from here?"

He fumbled with his bag, and pulled out the mapping unit.

"Let's see, yeah, it's doable, but it'll take some time."

"Then we should get moving," Captain Eri said, adjusting her pack.

"What about Wiq?" Red said.

"I assume she's here."

"Uhhh, okay," he said.

"No."

"What?" Captain Eri said.

"No," Ryo said, facing the cliff. "This ends here."

"Fine time for her to tune back in!" Red said. "You want us to fight from here? What was wrong with the building?"

"Not us, me," Ryo whispered, her eyes on the door.

She turned to face them, and Filion's arms snapped to his sides, so did Captain Eri's and Red's. Filion's feet left the ground, and he flew backwards. He tried to yell but couldn't. He closed his eyes and tried to ignore the foliage that snapped behind his back. He sped up. Branches and vines cracked as he flew through the forest. He opened his eyes. Bursts of red leaves and black twigs exploded around him. Suddenly, his body snapped to the left and then back right again. Then he was on the ground. Three thumps sounded next to him. He looked to his right. Red, Captain Eri and Wiq were all beside him.

"Hey," he said. *Hey!* His voice worked, and he had looked to his right! He moved his arms and legs. They worked too!

"What…" Filion started.

"That turd brained lady Chozen is about to get herself killed, that's what," Red said, flexing his arms.

"RYO!" Captain Eri yelled.

"RYO! RYO! Ryo! Ryo! ryo! ryo!" Captain Eri's voice echoed back at them.

"What the…" Red started.

Filion stood. They were in a depression behind a small rock formation. He moved towards the rocks. He could see Ryo in the distance. She stood at the edge of the forest talking to Didrik.

"There she is!" Filion said, reaching for the rocks, but he couldn't grab them. His hand hit something smooth. He reached again, but it was like his hand had hit a curved pane of glass.

"She trapped us. There is some sort of shield around us. Grawlix! She'll get herself killed," Filion said, sinking into the dirt.

"What the grawlix was that?" Captain Eri said, pushing Wiq.

"What? Wait, are you two gonna fight?" Red asked, smiling.

Wiq didn't respond.

Captain Eri was on her feet.

"What in the universe is the matter with you?" She yelled, her voice reverberating under the shield. "ANSWER ME!"

Wiq got to her feet but didn't say anything.

Captain Eri took a step closer.

"I am not going back."

"Going back where?" Captain Eri said.

"To Yerii or to anyone who wants to keep me. I am free. I will do whatever you require to maintain my freedom."

"What the grawlix are you talking about?"

"I was insubordinate. I can see how you would take my freedom away for such an action, but I will not go. I will do anything to stay free, or I will die free."

"What? No one is selling you to anyone. You're a person not an object," Captain Eri said.

Wiq hesitated.

"Sell you?" Captain Eri continued, her voice softening. "You think I'm going to sell you because you were insubordinate?"

Wiq looked confused. "Is that not the punishment for insubordination?"

Red began to cackle. "Oh, you're funny, vissy. Fun-ny. I woulda been sold ten times over if it was. Sold for insubordination. HA!"

Wiq looked sick.

"Ah, no. That isn't the punishment for insubordination," Captain Eri said.

"What is?" Wiq asked.

"Uh, I don't know. I guess whatever I decide. But it certainly isn't that I sell you back into slavery."

There was an awkward silence. Filion watched Wiq's aura change from black to blue. She was embarrassed.

"It's okay though," Filion said. Everyone looked at him. "It's okay that you would make that mistake. I mean you're new to this whole freedom thing. Mistakes are to be expected, you know?"

Captain Eri hesitated, seemingly stunned that Filion had spoken, then said, "He's right, it was an honest mistake, you just didn't know. You've never been free before. No matter what you do, I won't sell you, ever. That is not an option."

"You are speaking the truth?"

"Yeah. We're people. We're moral. We don't sell people into slavery, no matter what they did. Everyone is entitled to be free."

"Which is why we're here," Red said. "Hey look, someone's out there."

Wiq was at the edge of the shield in an instant. Filion looked towards Ryo. She stood, still talking to Didrik, seemingly unaware that two figures had emerged from the door.

"RYO!" Filion yelled. "Ryo! They're here! Ryo!"

His voice bounced back at him.

Ryo couldn't hear him, and she didn't look at the Tioris.

Chapter 89

"There!" Yalki said, stopping.

They stood on the top of the cliff. To the north was the forest, and at the very edge of the forest stood a girl, but it was no ordinary girl. It was a Chozen, an Etulosba, and her energy was blinding.

"Yes…" Harick said.

They both stared for a moment, caught up in the impossible. What looked to be an unremarkable girl stood before them, but unremarkable it was not. The Afortiori could see beyond its flesh and bone. They could see the streak of light that it was. Incandescent and powerful beyond reason, the Etulosba radiated with what Afortiori feared most – Free Will. The slash of light wavered, and the world around it bent. With every breath the Etulosba drew, the forest quivered, the air shrank, and color flashed and ran into the space around it. These disturbances, while imperceptible to the mere mortal, meant everything to the Afortiori. It was Absolute. It was everything they feared, and more. The question was, what did it know?

"Get her!"

Harick extended his arm and shot.

"Yeah, okay. I think I can do that," Ryo said.

She could feel the two signatures. They were on the top of the cliff. One was powering up. He thought he would catch her off guard. He fired.

Ryo closed Didrik, set him on the ground, and faced the two Afortiori. The shot had left the male's arms. A fluctuating sphere of candesent energy, it traveled slowly. The air bent behind it in a streaking trail. Ryo put up her hands. The bubbling came back, and three quick shots left her arms. They caught him in the chest before his shot was half way across the clearing.

Harick flew backwards, his eyes bulging in surprise. He skittered across the cliff and over the edge.

"Harick!" Yalki yelled.

What in the universe had just happened? Yalki went invisible and ran to the edge of the cliff. Harick had landed on a small ledge. She closed her eyes and lifted him back to stable ground.

"Harick!" she yelled again, kneeling over him.

Harick sputtered, blood spewing from his chest and mouth.

"Harick! What…"

Crash!

Yalki turned towards the noise. Harick's shot had just reached the forest.

"Go," Harick coughed. "I'll take care of myself."

Yalki pushed herself up and ran towards the forest. *Where was that Chozen?*

A burst of energy hit her in the side and knocked her from her feet. She slid across the smooth rock. Another blow hit her, then another.

No.

She threw up a shield and several shots bounced from it. She struggled to sit. The energy blasts hadn't damaged her too badly, but enough hits and she would be done. That, and the Etulosba's shots were sapping her own energy. With every hit she could feel some of her energy stolen and then forced back at her. Her energy was being used to wreck havoc on her own body. She took a deep breath and concentrated.

She just had to locate the Etulosba. *Scan the forest. Find it.* Nothing. Nothing visible at least. She opened her mind to the signal.

Nothing.

How was that possible? There had to be a signal! There just had to be! Then, there it was, on top of her, inside the shield! Yalki clutched her head. It was as if her brain was in a red hot vice. She writhed, her legs kicking and her fingernails digging deeper and deeper into her skull. It was so strong…

Ryo became visible again and looked at the Afortiori spasming at her feet. The woman clutched her head, a strange groan emanating from her lips.

"You tried to kill me and my friends," Ryo said distantly.

The woman didn't respond. She only shook more.

"I cannot die, not yet. I have so much to do. So many people to save, and so many others to kill. Unfortunately for you, you're one of those people I have to kill…"

The signal became stronger then suddenly it died.

Yalki opened her eyes. The Etulosba lay crumpled on the ground, blood pooling around it.

"Ha! All the power in the universe, and a simple phazer shot took her out!" Harick stood in the clearing, his clothes crumpled and stained, a phazer dangling from one hand. He dropped the gun and hobbled towards Yalki and the Etulosba.

"Good thing she incapacitated you. I wouldn't have been able to stop her if your shield was still up."

Yalki forced herself to her feet. Harick had saved her, but only after she had saved him. This wasn't the time to worry about that though.

"Is she dead?" Yalki asked.

Harick bent down and pressed the Chozen's neck.

"No, but she'll die unless I stop the bleeding. Here, help me turn her over."

Yalki grabbed the Etulosba's shoulder.

"We should restrain her before I heal her…" Harick started.

Suddenly, Yalki was in the air, flying backwards towards the forest. She watched helplessly as Harick flew in the opposite direction.

The Etulosba stood.

It stretched slowly. Then Yalki hit a tree and everything went black.

"Make it stop! Make it stop! We have to get out of here!" Filion cried. "WE HAVE TO HELP HER!"

Their shield had collapsed the moment man had shot Ryo, but now that she was back on her feet, the shield was back in place.

"She's hurt! I can tell!" Filion screamed. He could see her aura, a deep flickering red. She needed their help. Filion paced, wringing his hands. His vision blurred and he was only vaguely aware that he had grabbed his right hand so hard it was bleeding.

Red threw his fist at the shield. It wobbled, bent even, but it held.

"We're stuck!" he yelled.

"SHOOT IT! SHOOT IT!" Filion cried, grabbing his phazer.

"NO!" Wiq said wrenching it from him. "You will kill us all. The ricochet will kill us!"

"You need to calm down, Filion!" Captain Eri said, grabbing him tightly on the arm. "We can't do anything, and you're a danger to us all right now! You need to get a grip."

Filion looked at her and then took a breath. She was right. He had almost killed them all. Without a word he sat down, his back to Ryo, and closed his eyes.

Ryo shook. She wasn't sure how much more of this she could take. She'd only been hit once, but that had been enough. She moved her arms again. She wasn't sure if she had fully healed herself, but it was good enough for now.

She had memories of being a fighter and a warrior, but they hadn't included this fear. She tried to push it down and imprison it, but it was becoming increasingly more difficult. She was terrified.

Not that that mattered though. She had a job to do. She had to end them. An energy blast came from the forest. She went invisible but not soon enough. The shot caught her in the shoulder, and threw her onto her back, causing her to slide across the rock. The pain blossomed in her brain. Another shot followed and another.

She threw up a shield, swallowing her pain and fear. The male Afortiori had struggled to his feet. He stood unsteadily as he fired energy blasts in rapid succession from his hands. She was safe, for a moment, she just needed to figure out what to do.

Harick did not feel strong. In fact, he feared that he might collapse at any moment, but he couldn't let it win. He couldn't die like this. Its signature was faint, somewhere near the cliff. He must have hit it because it wasn't moving. If he could force it off of the cliff, he might have a chance...

Ryo scrambled to repair the damage in her shoulder, but she had no idea what she was doing. She ordered questions and thoughts so quickly and haphazardly that she had no idea if she was hurting or helping herself. Her shoulder stung, then bubbled, then went numb.

She needed to slow down and think. She wouldn't walk away from this if she couldn't slow down.

She took two more breaths, and the questions fell into place. The burning in her shoulder subsided, and just as she rotated it to check its function, she noticed a small breeze inside of her shield.

Before she could react, she realized she and her shield were sliding across the rock and towards the edge of the cliff. She scrambled, looking for something to hold on to, but it was futile. The ground was flawless and smooth. The breeze pushed her, growing in intensity and volume. She moved faster and faster, the wind screaming in her ears, and she knew that if she released her shield she would be blown backwards instantly.

Harick smiled. He had it now. He could feel its energy. All he had to do was push it over the edge, and it would fall out of the bottom of its shield. It had made a rookie mistake when it hadn't attached its shield to the ground. Harick couldn't tell if it didn't have the power or the knowledge to do this, but he didn't care. All that mattered was the result. It couldn't fight him without letting go of its shield, and if it let go of its shield... Well, once he pushed it over the cliff the wind would smash it into the ground several hundred feet below. While that might not kill it, the fall would incapacitate it long enough for him to finish it off.

The edge of the cliff grew nearer by the second, and Ryo couldn't contain it any longer. The fear won. She knew that once the wind pushed her from the cliff she would fall, and that fall would most certainly lead to her death. Even if she could propel herself upward, the wind was strong, too strong. She closed her eyes and let the fear in.

Ten feet... eight feet... seven feet... Then Harick was thrown backwards. The Chozen's energy was visible again, and it hit him like a crashing space ship. The wavering light was so bright... He felt as if his skull had been cracked open. His hands went to the side of his head, and the wind died.

Ryo had stopped moving! She didn't question why but instead released the shield and jumped away from the cliff's edge. She ran towards the trees, stifling the fear as she moved.

The signal went dead, and Harick's body went limp. He coughed, struggling to breathe. The pain in his head was now but a whisper, yet his legs shook as he stood. He had lost his advantage. Quickly, he went invisible,

227

but it was too late, a shot hit him in the arm. He didn't let it distract him though. He closed his eyes and summoned them.

Ryo hit him, and it was clear she had caught him off guard. She could sense he was weakening, but she hadn't won yet. His signature flashed and a loud noise erupted from the cliff behind her. She turned and saw the army. Spitting and screaming, thousands of men floated over the cliff. They spilled onto the land, their phazers firing as they ran at her.

Ryo didn't bother with a shield, and before she knew what she was doing, a wave of fire left her hands. It spread outwards from her and towards the cliff. It incinerated everything in its path.

Harick gasped. He didn't know what it had just done. He had never seen anything like that. The Chozen stood, its torn and bloody dress churning around its body, with its arms outstretched towards the cliff. Its black hair blew diagonally across its face and the space around it seemed to bend. Another wave of slaves burst over the edge, and another wave of fire left its hands. The pulse of flames mowed down his army as if they were nothing. Harick stared dumbfounded at the ash that had been his slaves. He turned back towards the Chozen, but it was gone. He struggled to locate it, but he could not. He watched helplessly as fire wave after fire wave hit and destroyed his army.

She went invisible and kept the tides of fire coming. This was her chance. She could sense he had stopped moving. The last shot must have hurt him, or conjuring that army must have weakened him. Whatever the case, she didn't care. With a final push, she sent one more tsunami of fire toward the cliff and then turned to the Afortiori. She took a breath, and the bubbling came back. This time it was different though. This time it burned, and she could feel her control slipping. Her mind screamed, and she struggled to keep her focus. When she could stand no more, she released the energy. It streaked, red and hot through the air, blurring the space around it. Then it hit him, square in the chest. He winked into visibility and the briefest flash of fear crossed his face before he was consumed. The red expanded and collapsed into nothing. His signal went dead.

Red watched the battle as if he were in a theater. What was unfolding before him could not be real. No army could fly over a cliff, but they did, and then that burst of flames hit them, again, and again, and again. He felt sick. He swallowed, leaned onto the shield, and fell forward. It was down! He jumped backwards.

"The shield's down," Captain Eri said.

"We can help her!" Filion said, scrambling to his feet.

Red grabbed Filion's arm.

"Not so fast. I don't think we'd do anything but get ourselves killed. She was right, as crazy as she is. We need to stay here and not move."

"NOOOOO!"

Yalki's eyes shot open. The sound from her throat grew to a ragged pitch. Had her heart just been torn out? Was the world wobbling in front of her eyes? The ground seemed to spin beneath her. Waves of nausea hit her, and she shook. Harick's signature was gone. Ripped from the fabric of the universe he had helped create. Gone! Was this what it felt like when an Afortiori died? When a *God* was murdered? She had never witnessed the murder of an Afortiori. *We aren't supposed to be mortal!* This was all the Eoan's fault. She rolled to her side, her scream subsiding into a whimper. Die. She might die. Right here. Right now.

No!

She wasn't going to die. She thought herself to her feet. The Etulosba's signature was there – faint – but still there. That Etulosba was going to die. Then Yalki would take its body, and wait for it to regenerate, and then she would kill it again, and again, and again, until she finally Erased it. No more stunning shots. This Etulosba would die by her hand.

Ryo stared at the spot where the man had been. Nothing of him remained, other than a sick burning smell. He was gone. She could feel it.

Ryo spun. The other signal was moving. It was running towards her. Ryo went invisible and ran perpendicular to the signal, her arms bubbling. She shot, not the killing shots she'd used on the man but strong shots nonetheless.

Yalki dodged the Chozen's shots easily. They sung past her body with a crackling yellow glow, which under other circumstances would have impressed Yalki greatly. Now they only angered her. She jumped over a low shot and focused. While she may not have been a general like Harick, she had some battle tricks up her sleeve, some very nasty tricks indeed. Yalki lifted her arms and threw them towards the ground. The ground cracked outwards from her position, like a pond rippling from a raindrop. Only this was no raindrop, she had just thrown a meteor.

Ryo stumbled. The ground heaved beneath her, and fissures opened below her feet. She fell to her knees. The ground slid sideways. She was falling...

No!

She closed her eyes and jumped, the jump propelling her from the widening crevasse. She landed on an island of ground. Detecting the signal immediately to her left, she spun and fired.

GRAWLIX! Yalki thought. Even though the Etulosba was invisible, she still should have been able to see it, but she couldn't locate the signal. She had no idea if the Chozen had fallen and died, or if it had just masked its signal – masked it well.

An energy burst hit her from the side, knocking her off her feet and towards a newly formed crack.

Apparently not dead... yet.

This energy burst was stronger than the others, and Yalki couldn't catch her balance. She fell into the crack and slid down, gathering speed as she went. Yalki closed her eyes and concentrated. She stopped moving. With effort she propelled herself upwards and landed on a solid piece of ground.

She had only a second before the next energy blast hit her, this time knocking her onto her back but not into a fissure. Her breath was gone, her body ached, but she managed to throw up a shield before the next blast hit her.

Holding the shield was more difficult than it should have been. The energy blasts were growing stronger, and they were stealing too much of her power. It was taking her longer to recover from them. She had to get on the offensive. She closed her eyes and took a breath. With every last bit of energy she had, she searched for the signal, and found it.

Ryo knew where the Afortiori was. It had shielded itself, but it was weakening. She could have the shield down in a matter of moments. Then, if she could bring herself to issue another kill shot, she could end this.

She kept firing, and her arms began to tingle. Was that because she was over using them? Then the tingling spread, to her chest, to her legs, to her head, and then suddenly, the tingling became, a searing, scorching, terrible burning. Ryo stopped shooting, but the sensation only grew worse. It felt as if her lungs were filling with acid and her skin was being boiled from her body. Her eyes sizzled, and she wanted to tear them from her skull. Then came the noise.

It started as a low moan, but it grew in intensity and volume. Soon it became a wail, an unnatural, primitive shriek that couldn't have come from anything other than something about to die. It couldn't have come from her, but it did. She was on her back, convulsing, the heinous cries coming from *her*. She was going to die.

Yalki smiled.

So, not so strong after all, she thought.

She took her time gathering herself. She couldn't heal what the blasts had done to her, but it didn't matter now. She had it. The Chozen, *the Etulosba*, was in her sights. All she had to do was finish it. And she would, again, and again, and again, each time more terrible than the last. This Chozen would suffer.

Slowly, Yalki picked her way across the broken clearing and towards the writhing Etulosba. She didn't float, her shield was down, and she was visible.

What she was about to do would require the rest of her energy, so she couldn't waste it on superfluous things. Luckily for Yalki, burning the Etulosba from the inside out had required only a great burst of energy to start with, then the pain had built upon itself. *Exponentiality,* she loved it.

Ryo struggled to keep a hold of herself. The pain was too great, greater than anything she had ever experienced, but it couldn't end like this. She was the last hope. The last hope of a universe. She couldn't let this sick Afortiori finish her. She had to fight. She had to win.

Yet her screaming continued. She rolled to her right then to her left. Nothing seemed to help. She struggled to breathe. One breath... two breaths... and another... and another.

Ryo dove into her brain. She had to find her pain sensors. She had to shut them down. She had so little time... There! They were easy to spot, like a fire on a crowded city street, they were all consuming. The pain rose and engulfed everything around it. She would have to enter that burning building, dive into its heat and flames, and pull the plug. It was burn or die, maybe both.

She took another breath and jumped in. Everything went red. The screaming intensified. Louder and stronger than anything she had ever heard, it resonated within her, threatening to shake her apart from the inside out. She shook and coughed. Blood. She coughed blood. She couldn't stay here long.

She took a step, then another, one foot in front of the other. She could feel the sensors. Overheating and incandescent, they had to be stopped. Another step... one more. She reached them. So much pressure... Her head wanted to pop, her eyes bulged. She had to pull the plug...

Filion stood frozen, Red next to him, his hand clamped on Filion's arm. They had to help her. They had to, but what could they do?

Ryo bucked on the ground. Her head hit the dirt and bounced forward as the rest of her body thrashed senselessly. Blood squirted from her mouth, and her hands opened and closed spastically. The sickening noise grew even louder. Then there was the Tiori, slowly marching towards Ryo, a dangerous look in its damaged eyes.

"We need to do something..." Filion breathed.

No one responded. The shield was down, but they were powerless. What could they do to this Tiori that would stop it? Nothing, and they knew it.

Ryo jerked once more, then lay still.

"Oh gods," Captain Eri breathed.

Filion took a step forward. "What if we shoot it?" he said.

"I don't think the shot will make it out of the forest before we die," Red responded.

"But a phazer hit Ryo," Filion pleaded.

"Ryo is an infant compared to these Tioris," Wiq said, without looking at Filion.

She couldn't be dead...

Ryo opened her eyes. The pain was gone. She blinked. The signal came back. It was coming for her. It would be on top of her in moments.

She jumped to her feet, the burning back in her arms, but this time it was on her terms. The Afortiori had only a second to register the change in events and then Ryo shot, the streaking red energy collapsing in on the god.

All that remained was the sickening, burning smell of death, of a death well deserved.

Chapter 90

Filion struggled to scramble out of the hole. It should have been no problem for someone of his size, but it was as if his legs had turned to jelly.

"Ryo!" he yelled. "Ryo!"

She didn't respond.

With a final push he extracted himself from the crater. In seven long strides he was at her side.

"Ryo! Ryo! You did it! You saved us!"

She had sunk to her knees. He gently pulled her up.

"You won! You saved us!"

Captain Eri, Wiq and Red appeared behind him. Wiq held Didrik.

Filion hugged Ryo and then let her go. She fell. He swooped down and caught her.

"Can't she stand?" Red said.

"I don't know," Filion said. "Ryo, are you alright?"

He held her in his arms, so tiny and light, yet look at what she had done.

Ryo's body went limp. Her arms hung lifelessly, tangled in the tatters of her blood drenched dress.

"Didrik!" Filion said. "Where's Didrik?"

Wiq handed Didrik to Filion.

"Didrik! What do we do?"

She needs a doctor. NOW!

"She needs a doctor! We need to get her to a doctor!" Filion cried. He stuffed Didrik in his pocket and stared pleadingly at Captain Eri.

"The Keeper," Captain Eri said. "She healed me."

"The Keeper is better than nothing," Wiq said.

"Fil-ion," Ryo murmured. "Filion."

Filion dropped his head. "Ryo, I'm here."

"The Federation... they did this."

"The Federation did what?" Filion asked.

Filion and the others stared at Ryo.

"What's she talkin' about?" Red said, backing up. "The Federation did what? Is she sayin' those Tioris were part of the Federation?"

"Ryo what are you saying?" Filion shook her gently, but Ryo's head had rolled back and her eyes were closed.

"Red," Captain Eri said. "Get us back to the portal, and quick."

*****

They ran through the forest. Only Red had an intact haz suit, so he, once again, took point. Filion panted. The heat, the combined weight of Ryo and the duffle, as well as the stress of Ryo's medical state, and the fact that there

233

were Infecteds still about, did nothing for Filion's nerves. He was scared. No, he was terrified. *What if she was dead?* His job had been to protect her, and he had failed. He ran as gently as he could, but still he watched drops of red blossom on his feet. She bled – from her mouth, from her arms, from everywhere– her body was broken. He had failed her... unless... unless they could get her to a doctor... They needed a doctor.

Filion didn't hear the rustling in the brush, but Red did, and the moment the Infected appeared, Red put it down with three swift rounds to the chest and head.

"Everyone ok?" Red asked, recharging his phazer.

No one responded.

"Looks like it then. Let's go," Red said.

Filion took a breath and started running again.

They ran for what seemed like hours, but Filion knew he didn't have the strength to run that long. Red occasionally blasted Infecteds, and they kept pushing forward.

"Here," Red said, stopping suddenly.

The group heaved to a stop. Filion leaned over in exhaustion.

"Just beyond these trees is the hotel. The question is, how do we get in there without getting contaminated?"

Through the trees Filion could see the courtyard walls.

"GRAWLIX!" he yelled.

The group looked at him. Filion set the unresponsive Ryo on the ground, ripped off his duffle, and threw it into the woods. "We came all this way, survived all that, and this is what's going to stop us? BLOODY, BLOOD?!"

"Uhhh," Red said, taking a step back. "Uhh, you're kind of scary when you're mad."

Filion paced back and forth, his hands on his head. *They had to get her to a doctor!*

"This IS NOT how it ends. I did not make it through all of this CRAP to be infected by T. Tryx. I WILL NOT EXPLODE!" he bellowed.

He kicked a tree, several pink branches rained down on the group, one coming dangerously close to Ryo.

"Filion! Calm down! We're not out of options yet!" Captain Eri said.

"WELL GRAWLIX! WHAT OPTIONS DO WE HAVE? SHE DOESN'T HAVE THIS KIND OF TIME! SHE NEEDS A DOCTOR! *NOW!*" he yelled.

Captain Eri took a step back. Wiq and Red also shuffled backwards. Filion watched them go.

"WELL?" he screamed. No one responded, then he saw it. They were moving away from him. The look in their eyes, it was, it was fear. He was scaring them. Him. Filion. He wasn't scary. He was fuzzy. Why would they be scared of him?

234

He looked down. His fists were balled, and his stance was wide. He could feel the hackles on the back of his neck – they were up. He was angry. He was looking for a fight.

"Oh gods…" he whispered.

Then all of the air left him and with it went the anger and the fear. All that remained was a feeling of despair. He sunk to the ground, his back sliding down the pink tree. What had he done? He looked at Ryo. A branch sat not a foot away from her delicate blood stained face. He could have killed her. He, Filion, could have killed her.

"Oh gods…" he repeated.

Wiq took a step forward. "Filion," she said. "Filion. We are okay. We are okay. I have seen this before. We will make it."

Filion looked at her. She reached out and took his hand. She smiled.

"I can deal with this. Just stay with us."

Filion nodded. "Sorry."

"Don't be," Captain Eri said. "We all lose hope occasionally. Red, go get Filion's duffle. Wiq, what do you have left in terms of fire power?"

Wiq let go of Filion's hand and pulled off her pack.

"I knew we would need to get back to the portal, so I brought this, just in case."

She pulled a large case from her bag. Opening it, she began to assemble the contents. In a few minutes she had a long squat gun.

"I have three hundred rounds," she said.

"You think that'll be enough?" Captain Eri asked.

"Do we have a choice?" Wiq said.

Captain Eri nodded sadly then looked at Filion. "Filion, when Red gets back, put your suit on."

Red emerged from the trees behind Filion and dropped the duffle at his feet. He tore it open and tossed the multicolored haz suit to Filion. Filion looked at the suit, but didn't move. Instead, he closed his eyes and silently repeated the Searcher's Code, taking deep measured breaths in rhythm to the prose.

Red looked at him, sighed and went back to rooting around in Filion's duffle.

"I've got six more grenades," Red said.

"Good. Give them and your hood to Wiq. She's going in." Captain Eri turned to Wiq. "When you're finished come back and get us. We'll give you fifteen minutes, then one of us will come in after you. Be out by then."

Wiq nodded and slid the hood over her head. She threw the gun's sling over her shoulder and clipped the grenades to it.

"What is that?" Filion asked, his eyes now open. He nodded at the gun Wiq held.

"It's an Eldur Gun. It's specifically designed for fire ammo. Wiq's going to burn the place clean, then we're going in." Captain Eri said.

"Where's the ammo?" Filion asked, picking up his suit.

"Here," Wiq said, pulling a long bullet belt from her pack. She inserted one of its ends into the gun and kept the other end in the pack.

"Take this," Red said, tossing the canister of Agent X 2.0 at her. "Just in case."

She nodded and stuffed it into her pack.

"I am ready," she said.

"Good luck. You've got fifteen minutes," Captain Eri said.

Wiq nodded and disappeared.

"Will this work?" Filion asked.

"Let's hope so," Captain Eri said.

Wiq crept through the courtyard, keeping a look out for any contaminates. She should have enough rounds to clean a path to the portal. If her memory served, there had not been any contamination *in* the courtyard, so she would save bullets there, but she did not need to rely on her memory. Her life sensors would pick up T. Tryx. She scanned the courtyard, her mind focused on the virus. Nothing.

She came to the door. Bloody handprints streaked the inside of the glass. Her mind buzzed. *T. Tryx.* Her sensors were working. She took several steps back and fired. The door exploded into a ball of flames. Wiq waited for the fire to die down, then approached the door.

A jagged hole now replaced the door, and the immediate area was clean of all organic matter. She stepped inside. Blood, and bits of flesh and hair surrounded her. She might not have enough ammo after all. She went back outside and pulled one of the grenades. She took a few more steps back and tossed it through the aperture. The explosion rocked the courtyard. Wiq waited until the smoke cleared and then went inside.

The blood and guts were gone, and the formerly white and red walls were now black. Her scanners indicated that nothing lived in the blast radius. If only she had more grenades.

She continued down the hall. Four bullets did roughly the same amount of cleaning as a grenade. One hundred and fifty bullets later, she was at the doorway to the parlor. She stepped back, shot the door, and stepped inside.

Squish.

She looked down. Several inches of organic matter coated the floor.

Damn, she thought.

She lifted her foot and hopped out of the room. She tossed in a grenade and pulled the Agent X 2.0 from her pack.

It took a minute or so for the spray to turn blue. Once it did, she lowered her foot and stepped. No print, no virus, she was clean.

She poked her head into the parlor. This room would take another grenade. She stepped outside, pulled the pin, and tossed the device into the room. When she stuck her head in for a second time, most of the room was black, and the floor was nothing but splinters. Bits of charred furniture lay scattered throughout piles of broken stone. A gaping rupture now existed where the ceiling should have been and the windows were blown out. The books on the shelves were gone, as were most of the shelves. She doubted the building's current structural integrity, but they'd have to risk it.

She cased the room. Her sensors indicated that the virus was not present. She moved to the former bookcase and fired. What was left of the shelf erupted into flames. Through the door she could sense T. Tryx. She threw in another grenade, two left, and nearly one hundred and fifty bullets. She would be fine.

Scrape.

She turned. An Infected stood at the parlor room door, drooling teeth. She stepped back, aimed and fired.

When the flames died down, she again moved into the hall and scanned it for contamination. Nothing.

With a final glance around the hall, she stepped back into the parlor and moved to the spot where the bookcase had been. It took her another two minutes to clear the anteroom and portal room. Once satisfied, she moved back through the hotel, scanning for the virus. Nothing.

"Do you think something's happened?" Filion asked.

"She's still got time," Captain Eri said.

"Yeah, lossal, give 'er a minute."

Filion shut his mouth and stared harder at the courtyard. Maybe if he squinted she would appear.

And she did. A suited figure came into view in the courtyard. It moved slowly towards them.

"Why is she moving so slowly? Why isn't she cloaked? Is she hurt?" Filion asked.

"She's bein' careful, lossal. She isn't cloaked because she wants us to know she's coming. She's fine! Good gods, give it a rest!"

Filion shut his mouth again.

Wiq disappeared once she reached the open field. A few seconds later, she reappeared next to Filion. "Let us go," she said. "I cut a path for us, but there are still Infecteds in there."

"Got it!" Red said, shouldering his pack and Filion's duffle. "I got this, lossal. You just keep her safe."

Filion nodded and picked up Ryo.

"Red you take our six. Wiq, you take point. Let's move," Captain Eri said.

The group moved through the trees and into the field. Filion did his best to move quickly without disturbing Ryo, but he felt like he was neither moving quickly nor gently. Finally, they reached the courtyard. Filion would have let out a sigh of relief, except he knew they still had a long way to go. Without stopping they continued on to the doorway and into the hall. Filion kept a sharp eye out for Infecteds, but he saw nothing. None of the others seemed to either. They reached the parlor and moved into the dirt rooms. Once they reached the portal, Wiq gave her hood, pack and gun to Red.

"You take guard. I need to work the portal."

Red dropped his bags and stuffed the hood over his head. He took the gun and pack.

Wiq ran to the far side of the portal room.

"Where's the control room?" Filion asked, adjusting Ryo on his shoulder. Even though Wiq had cleaned this room, he remembered what it had been like when they had arrived. He wasn't putting Ryo down.

"There is no control room here," Wiq said. She stood over a small box that Filion hadn't noticed before. "Whoever built the Handu portal didn't have the same attention to detail as whoever built Bok's. This is a poor man's set up."

She threw the top off of the box, revealing a glowing control panel. She punched a few buttons, and a low hum filled the room.

A gurgling noise came from the parlor. Red fired. He waited a moment then stepped into the anteroom, firing as he moved.

"You might want to hurry it up!" Red called. "Looks like we've been found! I told you a rich person's resort would have a lot of Infecteds!" Red fired twice more.

Captain Eri gathered Red's bags.

The hum became higher pitched, and the air in the room started to shimmer. A blinding flash encompassed the room, and then with a loud crash, the dancing jagged line appeared. Filion watched as the line morphed into a large black and teal spot to Wiq's right.

"Who wishes to come to Bok?" Came a disembodied voice.

"You know who we are!" Wiq said. "We need to come through, now!"

"Scanning for T. Tryx."

"Hurry…"

"This is strange. I've never heard of Infecteds grouping together before," Captain Eri said.

Red stood next to her now, firing the Eldur gun into the anteroom.

"How many Infecteds have you been around?" Red asked, without slowing his firing.

"Ahhh, well not that many I guess."

"Scan complete," the Keeper said. "You may pass."

The light on the box turned green.

"Time to go!" Wiq called.

"It's about time!" Red said, firing twice more then running towards the portal.

"Filion! You and Ryo first! Go!" Captain Eri called.

Filion tightened his grip on Ryo and ran towards the portal, closing his eyes before he stepped into the void.

Chapter 91

When he opened his eyes, he was lying on the floor of Bok's bright portal room. The pain had been bad but not like the first time. Maybe he was getting used to it, or maybe he was just tired.

Ryo lay on top of him, her eyes closed, and her chest slowly heaving.

"I need help!" He cried. "She needs help! Help her!"

No response.

Red tripped through the portal, landing next to Filion.

"Grawlix that hurts! An' the added fall at the end isn't particularly nice neither." Red rolled and stood. He stuck out his hand to Filion. Filion reached up and took it.

"You have to help us!" Filion yelled again, bending down and picking up Ryo.

Wiq appeared through the portal, followed by Captain Eri.

"KILL IT!" She yelled.

Red stared at them.

"How'd the women not trip? Why'd we trip, and they didn't?"

Filion looked at him but didn't respond.

The portal died, and instantly the room became unnaturally quiet.

"HELP!" Filion yelled. "PLEASE!"

A door opened where there had been no door, and the Keeper floated through. Her bruises were gone, and once again, an imperceptible wind blew her hair and dress backwards.

"Come with me. I will see what I can do." She turned and floated down the hall.

Filion adjusted Ryo on his shoulder and ran after her.

Chapter 92

Filion paced outside of the room where Ryo was. The Keeper had kicked everyone out, and Filion wasn't happy about it.

How is she? Didrik asked.

"I don't know. For the thousandth time, I don't know. The Keeper won't let me in to see her."

Didrik huffed.

"I don't know how we managed that," Captain Eri said. She, Wiq and Red lounged in the pool. Snow drifted down, melting on the steam. Filion had had enough of the pool and had elected not to join them. "None of us were shot or injured, other than Ryo of course. We just invaded a Black planet. We fought Infecteds, slaves, Ryo fought two Tioris, and we lived to tell about it. Amazing."

Their lack of concern annoyed Filion. "Well, we aren't in the clear yet. We don't know if Ryo's going to make it," he said.

"Does it matter?" Red asked, his head back and eyes closed.

"What?" Filion said.

Red lifted his head. "I'm not looking to fight, lossal, but shouldn't she just, what'd ya call it, regenerate? I mean isn't she immortal?"

Filion flushed, "Well, in theory yes, but it's never been tested. It might not work. She might not be immortal after all. Technically, there should be more Chozens. She shouldn't be the last one!"

Red looked abashed, and Captain Eri said, "Filion, you need to take a breath. We've done everything we can. Getting upset and pacing isn't going to help her. Are you sure you don't want to get in the pool? It's really relaxing."

The door opened.

"She wishes to see you now," the Keeper said to Filion.

Filion hurried into the room without responding to Captain Eri.

"You have five minutes," the Keeper said airily.

"Thank you," Filion said, as the Keeper shut the door behind him.

The room was the same dark color as the room in which Captain Eri had recovered. It was small and warm, and it smelled of life. Filion could hear the babbling of water from its edges. He waited for his eyes to adjust to the darkness. Small circular lights hovered near the ceiling, giving off a star like glow, and Filion could see that Ryo lay on a heavily blanketed bed. She did not move.

"Ryo?" Filion whispered.

The blankets stirred.

"Ryo, are you awake?"

"Filion?"

"I'm here."

He took a step closer, Didrik open in his hands.

"Filion. You came for me. You saved me." The blankets moved, and Filion could see her face. Her eyes were considerably dimmed, and even in the starlight Filion could see how pale she was. She smiled a weak smile.

"I told you we'd come for you," he said. "And you saved us."

She shook her head.

"How are you feeling?" he asked.

"Weak. The Keeper said I would feel this way for some time. She said that I can be moved in a few hours, but first I need to rest," she said, her eyes closing.

"Yes. Rest. Get your strength up," Filion said. Didrik squirmed in his hand.

"I'm going to leave Didrik here, okay?"

Ryo nodded.

"He's right here, on the bedside table."

She nodded again but more slowly.

Filion placed Didrik on the table and quietly opened the door. He stole one last look at her and slid into the hallway.

Chapter 93

"We need to plan how we're going to get out of here," Captain Eri said.

"We have a more important issue than that," Red said.

"Really?" Captain Eri asked, straightening in the water.

"Yes. I'm starving. Did we bring any food with us?" Red asked.

"I brought a couple of MRE's." Captain Eri said.

"MREs? Seriously we invade a Black planet, fight Infecteds, slaves, *and* Tioris,* and all we get for it are some MRE's?"

"Technically, *we* did not battle any Tioris," Wiq said, floating on her back.

"Whatever. There wouldn't have been a battle without us," Red said.

"There probably would have been," Wiq responded. "They were coming after her regardless of our presence."

"Yeah, but we were the rescue party! I mean, she wouldn't have gotten off the planet without us, and she wouldn't have gotten the book without us! Grawlix! It doesn't matter! We just invaded a Black planet. We deserve more than a bloody MRE, even if there's chocolate in 'em!"

Wiq laughed, causing her to sink a little.

"You're right Red," Captain Eri said. "Let's just eat the MRE's now, and then once we get off this rock we can eat at a restaurant. I'm buying."

"A restaurant?" Red asked. "You mean like a place where they serve you fresh fruit and vegetables and stuff?"

"And stuff," Captain Eri said, leaning back.

"Damn right," Red said, nodding. "Fruit and stuff. Exactly what I want. Way better than chocolate."

"So, now that that's settled, does anyone have any plans for getting outta here? The moment we show our faces we'll have a hundred angry hicks on our back, and then there's the fact that our ship has probably been impounded," Captain Eri said.

"I think I can help you," the Keeper said.

Captain Eri opened her eyes and turned.

"Keeper, I didn't know you were there, hi."

"Hello," the Keeper responded. "I can build you disguises and get you to the ship terminus. You're on your own in terms of flying out of here, but I can get you to your ship with as little exposure as possible."

"Really? How can you do that?" Captain Eri asked.

The Keeper moved to the edge of the pool and put her hands on the sides of Captain Eri's face. A second later the Keeper stepped back.

"What the…" Red said, stiffening. "What did you do to her?"

"What did she do to me?" Captain Eri asked.

Captain Eri looked at Red, her grey wrinkled skin folding into a leer. She stared at him with dull glassy eyes. Gone were her sharp purple eyes, and gone was her rich chocolate skin. Creased and cracking, her face was pale and shriveled. Thin wisps of ugly yellowed hair existed where her thick black mane should have been. Her teeth were crooked and missing. Those that remained were stained a dark red. She lifted her hand from the water. Red jerked backwards. Long curled fingernails waved at him from a twisted stick of an arm.

"You, you aren't you. You're someone else. You're white, and old." Red said.

"What?" Captain Eri asked. She waved her arm in front of her face. "I don't look any different to me," she said.

Red grimaced.

"The illusion doesn't work on yourself. It is an outward projection. Something you yourself cannot see," The Keeper said. "I can disguise you as a medical team. No doubt your ship has been grounded. Lucky for you, I happen to know someone with sway in the terminus. I've alerted them that a medical team will be commandeering the ship to evacuate a high ranking pelter's gravely sick daughter."

Captain Eri stood. Red backed away even further.

"Why are you helping us?"

"Because, I know what she is. I may have few magical gifts, but that does not mean I am ignorant. She needs to be saved, so she can save us. It is a matter of time until the Tioris take Bok, and I'll be nobody's slave." The Keeper turned to leave. "I will let you know when she can be moved."

The door opened behind the Keeper and Filion stepped out.

"She's sleep... What the?" His eyes fell on Captain Eri. He took a step back. "Who are you?"

"It seems we have a plan," Captain Eri said.

Chapter 94

"Alright," the Keeper said. "These disguises will last an hour, no longer. I've given Wiq the tunnel lay out. Once you get to the terminus you show them this card," the Keeper handed Captain Eri a travel itinerary. "They should let you through. Once you get on the ship, you're on your own."

Captain Eri nodded and stuffed the card into her pocket.

"Remember," the Keeper said. "She *cannot* sustain any more trauma until she has recovered further. Once you leave, Bok you *need* to find a doctor. My healing skills are poor compared to what she needs." The Keeper looked down at Ryo. Ryo lay on a white gurney, her eyes closed. The Keeper had scrubbed the blood from Ryo's body and covered her with several white blankets. She reached out and brushed a strand of hair from Ryo's face. "I do not know what you did to her, but anyone else would not have survived this kind of damage. She has endured pain beyond any of our comprehension."

"We'll get her help," Captain Eri said.

"See that you do," the Keeper responded. "Are you ready?"

Captain Eri nodded, and the Keeper stepped up to her. The Keeper placed her hands on both sides of the Captain's head. Suddenly, Captain Eri's features began to change. Her dark skin melted into an alabaster white, her jaw became more pronounced, and her nose shrunk. Her clothes morphed from her torn and bloody pilot's garb into a crisp, ivory medical jump suit, a red cross emblazoned between her now white wings.

"Egads, that's weird," Red cringed.

"You're next," Captain Eri smiled. Her white clothes, skin, eyes and teeth made Red recoil even further.

The Keeper changed Red and then Wiq. She moved to Filion last. Placing her hands on each side of Filion's head she said, "You will be my work of art. I'm changing you into a giant. No one will let a lossal out of this town, but giants are like a plague here."

Filion closed his eyes. When he opened them, he saw Red staring at him. Red's mouth hung slightly, open and his unnaturally white face was screwed into a grimace.

"I prefer him the other way," Red gulped.

"Just wait an hour," Wiq said.

"Go. Your time is dwindling."

Filion had wanted to say thank you to the Keeper, but she hadn't given him the chance. After she had disguised them, the Keeper had pointed them towards another set of wooden and paper doors, and then she had left, claiming she had some pressing portal upgrades she needed to complete.

244

Filion suspected she had begun to like them, and he would have smiled at the thought, if he hadn't been so afraid.

Captain Eri opened the doors, and they found themselves back in the crumbling tunnels. Filion sighed and put on his ill-fitting niteglasses. They weren't made for a lossal, or giant, or whatever he was.

"I miss her already," Red said.

"This way," Wiq said. "Let us move."

They hurried through the dark tunnels. Captain Eri covered their six, and Wiq took point. Red followed Wiq, and Filion, pushing Ryo's cot, struggled to keep up with Red. With every step, Filion fought to keep the cot moving in a straight line. They had stacked their bags beneath it, and the extra weight made it difficult to control.

"Can't you move any faster?" Captain Eri growled.

"I'm going as fast as I can, but this gurney is a little unwieldy," Filion hissed.

"We are almost there. Get ready," Wiq said.

They rounded two more corners and then came to a stop. Wiq reached out and touched a nondescript wall. It melted away and in its place stood a locked metal door. Wiq punched in the lock's combination, and the door popped open.

"This is it," she said. "No going back."

"I think that time is well past gone," Red growled, stuffing his phazer beneath the cot. Captain Eri and Wiq followed his lead.

Wiq gave them one more look and pushed the door open. Filion wrenched off his niteglasses. He stood, blinking in the bright light, then recovered and stuffed the glasses into his pocket. He pushed the cot forward, his knuckles gripping it so hard he could feel the light metal bending.

They stood in a small metal room.

"Through here is the main terminus," Wiq whispered. "Once we leave here, we need to cross the terminus and then enter hangar 6. Captain Eri, you lead the way. Try not to attract any unnecessary attention," Wiq said, her eyes catching Filion's and Red's.

"I don't know why you're lookin' at me. I can blend into any situation," Red said.

Wiq gave him a final glance then slid open the door.

The hum of the terminus hit them, instantly shattering the silence of the tunnels. Children cried, disembodied voices boomed, and footsteps echoed from every direction. Captain Eri strode from the door, an official and important air surrounding her. Wiq followed, managing to look, not meek exactly but certainly not in charge. Filion followed Wiq, and Red walked next to the gurney, playing with the medical box which was attached to its side.

They moved across the terminus. Filion did first year breathing exercises.

You are a giant medic on an important mission. You do this all the time. People see medics every day. Giant medics. You are not a lossal. No one is paying any attention to you.

A young ringer ran up to the cot. "Mom! Look! Medics!"

The girl's mother scurried after her. "Yes, now let them do their job."

Red smiled and waved at the girl.

She squealed and waved back, burying her face in her mom's shirt.

The mother smiled at Red.

"Try not to look so terrified," Red muttered.

"I didn't know you were good with kids," Filion breathed.

"I'm not. I'm good with women," Red said, smiling back at the woman.

Filion looked away from Red and focused on his breathing.

After what seemed like an eternity, they reached the door to hangar 6. Captain Eri pushed through it without looking back. Wiq scurried, she *scurried*, and held the door for Filion and Red. Was Filion the only one not in character?

They passed several ships and rounded a corner before Filion finally spotted it, the *Dark Horse.* They were almost there. They might actually make it!

Captain Eri picked up her pace, her shiny white shoes clicking loudly on the hangar floor.

Two more ships... one more ship... and they were there, standing in front of the *Dark Horse.*

"Hurry! We don't have all day! We need to get her loaded and run the preflight sims," Captain Eri said, her voice strangely prim.

Wiq ran to the cargo doors and entered the entry code. With a hiss of steam, the doors creaked open and she slipped inside.

"Excuse me?" a voice sounded behind them.

Filion stopped and gripped the cot even harder.

"What do you think you're doing? This is a booted ship. No one is authorized to fly it."

Filion turned. It was the same attendant that had helped them dock. What was his name? Groy? Grog? Not that it mattered.

"I believe you're mistaken," Captain Eri said, stepping towards the attendant. "We're on a special mercy mission. Our patient is the daughter of a high-ranking Hiforian. We have the clearance to commandeer this ship in order to save her life."

"What high ranking Hiforian?" Groy asked.

"That's private information. It's classified unless you're family," Captain Eri said, stepping up to the man. She looked him from head to toe. "And you certainly aren't family."

"Let's see your paperwork," Groy said.

Captain Eri fished the itinerary card from her front pocket, and turned back towards the ship.

"Hestur! Who told you to stop! We don't have all day! I want this ship out of here in fifteen minutes," Captain Eri said, staring at Filion and tapping her watch.

Filion looked at the clock on the medical box. She was right! Forty-five minutes had gone by already! How had that happened? He jumped into action and started to push the cot again.

"Not so fast," Groy said.

Filion heard the ship's engines start.

"Let's move, lossal," Red growled.

Filion kept pushing the cot up the ramp.

"I SAID STOP!" Groy yelled.

Filion stopped.

"This paperwork isn't in order. My system has no record of any medical transport on this ship," Groy said, tapping his hand held scanner.

"Well, your system is wrong," Captain Eri said. "The paperwork was filed two hours ago. Maybe your system is slow." She turned back to Filion. "I said get her aboard! We don't have much time."

Filion started walking again.

"I told you to stop," Groy said, in a low voice. Filion heard a phazer charge.

He turned slowly. Groy stood with the phazer trained on Filion.

"You're right. Your paperwork checks out, but you don't. I don't forget a face, or a pair of wings, even if they were a different color before," Groy said, turning towards Captain Eri. "You're that ringer. I don't know what you're up to, but you're not going anywhere."

Filion glanced at Red. Red still had his back to Groy, but his hand was now under the cot. Filion's eyes widened, and Red spun, pushing Filion to the side. Two phazer blasts echoed in the hangar.

"You okay?" Red said, pulling Filion up.

Filion felt his chest. No holes. He looked at Groy. Groy lay on his back, a surprised look on his face, and a hole burned in his chest. Filion looked to Groy's left. Captain Eri lie on the ground, face down.

"Captain!" Filion cried.

"I'm fine," she said, pulling herself to her feet. "I just whacked my knee real good." She rubbed it and walked to Groy, wrenching the phazer from his hands.

"Let's go."

"Oh no," Red said.

Filion's heart dropped. *Ryo.*

He spun and reached the cot in one stride. Ryo lay coughing, a bloody hole ripped in her side.

"Ryo," Filion said, suddenly unable to think. "Ryo... no... Ryo."

"Get on board!" Captain Eri yelled, seizing the cot and pushing it the rest of the way up the ramp.

Red grabbed Filion and pushed him towards the ship. Filion could hear men yelling from somewhere in the hangar. He looked back in time to see a horde of armed men rounding the corner, and running towards the *Dark Horse*. Red gave Filion another shove, and Filion stumbled onto the ship. Red followed him and closed the cargo hatch. He hit a button on the wall and yelled, "We're in! Let's go!"

The ship shook and rose with a roar. Filion ran to Ryo. Captain Eri stood, her hands still gripping the cot, looking down at Ryo. Captain Eri looked as if she were about to vomit.

"Ryo! Ryo! Hold on! We'll get you through this! Just stick with us!" Filion cried, putting his hands over Ryo's bleeding side.

Wiq's voice sounded through the speakers.

"Hold on. We are about to experience some slight turbulence... "

The ship's cannon fired, and then the entire ship quaked. A loud scraping noise filled Filion's ears, and then suddenly, it was silent.

"We have cleared the hangar. Captain, where shall I set our coordinates to?"

Captain Eri looked at Ryo one last time then raced up the metal ramp.

"Ryo! Ryo!" Filion cried, his hands fumbling around her wound.

Ryo didn't respond. Her head lay drooped to one side, her skin was an ashen grey, and her chest didn't rise. Red calmly pushed Filion's hands from Ryo, and placed two fingers onto her neck. He stood, still as a statue, his eyes hollow.

"Is she okay? What can I do? What should I do?" Filion wept. "Maybe if we bandage the wound..."

"Stop," Red said. "Just stop. She's gone."

Filion and The Crew Will Return

Acknowledgments

I would like to thank the following people for their patience and grace throughout my creative process. Thank you for taking the time to read my draft (or in cases, drafts), and thank you for the meaningful comments.

Thank you, Lyn Pring, Jim Pring, Daniel Hobbs, Sam Elzay, Jacques Talbot, and Kendall Swett.

I would also like to give a special thanks to Danny McGee for giving me the right amount of encouragement just when I needed it. I would also like to thank Brain Hogan for being the graphic designer and park ranger extraordinaire that he is. Finally, I would like to thank Sarah Luddington for giving me the chance of a lifetime.